The House of Impossible Loves

The House of Impossible Loves

A NOVEL

Cristina López Barrio

Translated from the Spanish by Lisa Carter

HOUGHTON MIFFLIN HARCOURT
BOSTON · NEW YORK
2013

For information about permission to reproduce selections from this book,
write to Permissions, Houghton Mifflin Harcourt Publishing Company,
215 Park Avenue South, New York, New York 10003.

www.hmhbooks.com

Library of Congress Cataloging-in-Publication Data is available.
ISBN 978-0-547-66119-3

Book design by Melissa Lotfy

Printed in the United States of America
DOC 10 9 8 7 6 5 4 3 2 1

*To Carlos and Lucía, who gave me the time to write
and so much more.*

*To my parents and my sister, Pitu,
for everything.*

. . . —I had a homeland where the Duero
flows between gray cliffs
and the ghosts of ancient oaks,
there in Castile, mystic and warlike,
graceful Castile, humble and boastful,
Castile of arrogance and power . . .

—ANTONIO MACHADO, *The Landscape of Castile*,
Translators Mary G. Berg and Dennis Maloney

It is not love that dies,
but we ourselves.

—LUIS CERNUDA, "No es el amor quien muere"
in *Where Oblivion Dwells*

The House of Impossible Loves

I

THE CASTILIAN TOWN smelled of gunpowder, of partridge and rabbit blood, of smoke curling up from the chimneys. Dressed heavily for autumn, the hunters flaunted their catch at dusk, amid the first gusts of wind. Old women in black shawls sat in doorways whispering about each passerby, their voices as dry as the rustling leaves, weathered by a life of chilblains, peasant stews, and Sunday Mass. In contrast, the younger women hid behind lace curtains to watch the hunters unseen, gossiping at a safe distance from all that death.

In twilight, packs of hounds filled the town square after a day skinning their snouts tracking game through the hills. They peed on the stone fountain with its three spouts, on the doors of the church with its steeple so high you could see the Duero valley from inside it, on houses proudly bearing the family coat of arms over the door. Their barking frightened donkeys, children, and the cats that hid among bundles of wood stacked in the courtyards. Indifferent to the commotion, the hunters soaked up the warmth of the tavern, where red wine and roast goat helped them unwind after a day in the woods. Stumbling out later, they awakened their sleeping dogs lying pierced by starlight.

They all came to this town hoping to hunt not only partridge and rabbit but wild boar and deer. It was this that brought a young Andalusian landowner in the fall of 1897. He arrived on the afternoon coach with two servants and a cart of cinnamon-colored Andalusian hounds, hauled through the Despeñaperros gorge to the Castilian plateau. He took three rooms at the best inn and an entire pen for his dogs. But his goal of mounting a rack of stag antlers was erased from his mind early the next morning when he went for a walk and came upon a pair of amber eyes, the eyes of Clara Laguna.

"Your eyes are like gold. What a beauty you are." He took her by the arm.

Clara jerked away, spilling water from the jug resting on her hip. Water snaked between the cobblestones.

"Let me refill that for you at the fountain."

"I can do it myself." Clara strode away toward the town square.

Laughing, the landowner followed her.

As it always did at this time of year, a metal-gray fog blanketed the early morning, and the landowner watched as the young woman's silhouette slowly vanished into it. He stopped. An icy wind buffeted his face and tangled the curls on his neck. The world had suddenly grown impenetrable, blinding him so he could not follow the girl. He wanted to call out to her, but the air was a frozen gag. His mind filled with warm thoughts of his country estate, orange trees bursting into blossom, until the first church bells rang and his memories slipped away with the fog. By the time the ghostly pealing ended, there was Clara Laguna at the fountain, filling her jug.

"You're pale," she said as he approached. "Serves you right for pestering me."

"This Castilian weather takes some getting used to."

"Return to where you came from if you don't like it."

He leaned against the fountain and smiled as the last of dawn's light glinted off his riding boots.

"Such a beautiful girl, and yet so brusque."

"Concern yourself with other things. Like why such heavy fog fills the square before All Souls' Day."

"I'm concerned with having a name to put with those eyes."

"Your comments are bold, but a few minutes ago you were white with fear."

"All right, I admit I was afraid, but not of the fog or the sad chiming of bells. I was afraid when suddenly you were gone. I thought I'd lost you, just like that, so soon after finding you. I was afraid you'd disappeared like that devilish mist. I don't care where it came from or where it went. All I care about is seeing you."

Clara studied the light in his eyes.

"No one should venture into the square at dawn on the last few days of October — not until the bells have tolled. The souls of gentlemen buried in the church come out of their tombs, through the big doors, to create that fog and that wind. They're condemned to fight with their phantom swords and armor until they expiate their sins. Once the bells ring, they return to their graves and the town prays for their souls. Do you understand? Until the bells ring, this town square belongs to the dead. Every hunter is told this — and will pay the price if he refuses to respect tradition."

"What about you? You went into the square and vanished."

"In this town, I prefer the dead. We get along much better."

"You're a clever one, aren't you?"

"Why don't you leave me be and go on your hunt?"

"I came here hoping to bag a trophy stag, but think I've found something much more beautiful."

Clara passed a hand over her hair.

"I am not an animal, señor."

"You're right. Let me carry that jug by way of apology. I don't want that lovely waist of yours to break under the weight."

"This waist carries water from the fountain every day, then bends in the garden tending to my tomatoes. There's no need for concern. Besides, it's best if you stay away from my house. You should know my mother's a witch. She made this amulet to protect me from men like you." Clara held out a feathered rabbit's foot she wore on a string around her neck.

"I'm just a gentleman offering to help."

"The only gentlemen around here are in tombs in the church . . . what's left of them, anyhow."

"But I'm no Castilian. I come from Andalusia."

3

"And where is that?"

"In the south, where the sun toasts the afternoon the color of your eyes."

"My eyes, I'll have you know, are my father's eyes—he came from a place called La Mancha. That's what my mother says."

Clara shifted the jug into the curve of her waist and headed down one of the narrow streets leading away from the square. Wisps of gray clouds were starting to gather. The scent of bacon and fresh bread wafted her way as she walked. Doors opened onto courtyards, piles of wood sparkled with dew, donkeys were loaded with saddlebags already filled with crockery and sheepskins, and guard dogs stood with ears perked. Clara turned her head and saw the young man not far behind.

"Tell me your name."

"Clara. Clara Laguna. And proud of it."

Two middle-aged women in thick wool coats, fur stoles, and morning hats crowned with a pheasant plume appeared at the end of the street. Clara handed the young man her jug. As the women approached, she smoothed her dress over her waist and, for the first time, flashed her companion a smile. At that, one woman took the other's arm, whispering something in her ear. The Andalusian stepped aside to let them pass, and they acknowledged him with a slight nod of their heads.

"You do have a lovely smile, even if it was directed at those ladies and not me."

"Go hunt now and leave me in peace." Clara snatched the jug back and settled it on her hip.

Still, she did not stop the young man from accompanying her home, to the outskirts of town, where cobblestones gave way to mud and poverty distanced one house from another. The roof tiles were discolored by damp and neglect, the façades speckled with moss. Hungry dogs skittered, their tails between their legs, as dry leaves whirled. The house perched on the edge of a dry streambed, where Clara had planted tomatoes. Out behind was a pen holding four chickens and a goat. Farther back was a pine forest crossed by a gravel road leading to the next town. The girl lived with her mother, an old woman who cast spells to ward off or cure evil eye. She made amulets that ensured a good hunt, repaired hymens, and read the future in the treasured bones of a cat she kept in a rigid sack anointed with resin and lily sap.

Clara stopped at the door. The cool autumn perfume of soft pines and mushroom-carpeted earth enveloped her. Her mother's snoring could be heard from inside; she had spent the night reading the fortunes of the apothecary's wife and daughters.

"Tomorrow, at this time, I'll come take you for a ride."

"Do whatever you like."

Clara went inside and closed the door, then hurried to peer out the window. She watched the young man walk away, his hands beneath his cloak.

Maybe he won't come back, she thought as she washed the pots her mother had used for her potions; maybe he won't come back, as she fed the chickens in the pen; maybe he won't come back, she thought as she milked the goat; maybe he won't come back, she thought as she woke her mother and they lunched on crumbs of bread and chorizo; maybe he won't come back, she thought as she harvested tomatoes from the garden; maybe he won't come back, as she gathered the thread and floral anesthesia her mother needed to restore a girl's hymen; maybe he won't come back, she thought as the sun fell behind red treetops; maybe he won't come back, as they dined on garlicky vegetable stew; maybe he won't come back, she thought as she dreamed of his eyes. But the next morning, when she returned from the square with her jug of water, wearing her Sunday shawl, the Andalusian landowner was there, on the back of a dapple-gray horse, waiting for her at the bottom of the streambed.

"I've come for you," he said, dismounting.

"You've wasted your time." Her heart pounding against the earthen jug, Clara slipped into the house and shut the door.

It was a misty morning, the last day of October. The young man walked over to the window, rested his elbow on the dusty sill, and began to sing a song. He loved folk songs as much as hunting.

"Are you trying to rile up the hens?" Clara asked as she opened the door.

Behind her, the landowner saw a woman with a knot of gray hair, her left eye dry and gray with blindness.

"Good morning, señora. I'm sorry if I woke you."

"Good morning," the old woman replied in a raspy voice. "What brings you here so early with a song?"

"Would you kindly tell me whether you are Clara's mother?" The landowner tried not to stare at her blind eye.

"I am. Though it might be hard to believe, I was once as beautiful."

"I would like to ask your permission—or her father's—to take Clara for a ride."

The woman laughed out loud.

"You'd have to go a long way to ask her father! I'm the one to give permission in this house—me and only me, and my mother before that, may she be rotting in peace." The dark pupil of her right eye flickered. "You're a hunter."

"Indeed."

"Then you should buy an amulet from me."

The woman turned back inside, returning with a boar's tusk covered in partridge feathers.

"I assure you, young man, that with this, the animals will come to you. All your shots will find their mark."

The young man handed her a few coins.

"You can take Clara out. My daughter does what she likes, but judging by the dress and shawl she's wearing, I believe she'll accept."

"Don't be ridiculous, Madre. I put these on to go to the square. But since you're here, let's go for a ride."

The landowner mounted his horse and helped Clara on behind.

"There's an oak grove not far from here. I could show it to you if you like."

Following her directions, the Andalusian led the horse into the pine forest, away from the road with its carts and coaches. The wind was cold that morning, and gunshots could be heard far off in the hills.

"Gallop."

"It's too dangerous among the pines."

"Coward," Clara declared, her face damp.

The young man shook the reins, and the horse began to gallop. The animal's hooves pounded against the mossy, fern-covered ground. She held on to the Andalusian's waist, felt his strong back. He had never ridden like he did that day and would remember it always: his arms tense as he steered around trees and over the rocks that rose up between them, eagles soaring in the mist, his horse whinnying whenever it slipped on a bed of needles, his own perspiration. A soft drizzle blanketed them, his thighs firm against the horse's flanks and Clara's against his. When they reached the last few pines scattered at the foot of a hill, a storm erupted.

"The horse needs to rest."

"It's not much farther to the grove."

As the horse climbed the hill, Clara let go of the landowner's waist, her arms aching. From the highest point, they could see the outline of the valley below, the tops of enormous oaks. It was pouring rain. Lightning lit up the ground, now a muddy red. The Andalusian shivered under his cloak, and Clara pressed against his back to warm him.

By the time they reached the grove, the fog had dissipated, the thunder and lightning had ceased, the wind had died down, and the clouds had parted, giving way to a translucent light rain. Before dismounting, Clara Laguna pulled off her amulet and put it in the pocket of her dress.

A river ran through the grove, its waters forming eddies and pools. Clara found shelter under a worn old oak at the river's edge; she leaned against the trunk and waited for the young landowner. He was soon by her side, running his fingers down her neck to the soft depression where the amulet had lain; it was now filling with rain. Clara took his hand; his palms had been cut by the reins.

"You're hurt."

He gave no reply but lifted her chin.

The Andalusian landowner returned to his inn for lunch. A young boy led his exhausted, puffing horse to the stable. One of his servants helped him remove his boots and wet clothing and lit a fire. He sat next to it eating garlic soup and stewed partridge and drinking red wine, then he fell asleep in the armchair until late afternoon. As soon as he woke, he went to check on his hounds. They nuzzled him with their snouts, relieved to finally be out of their pen.

"Soon. We'll head to the woods very soon."

The sky had cleared after the storm, twilight slowly giving way to darkness peppered with a thousand stars. The streets filled with the aroma of stew, and there was no sign of the old women who sat and watched the hunters. The Andalusian headed to the tavern in the square. The burbling fountain with its three spouts reminded him of Clara Laguna. His yearning for her had not abated even during siesta. He had promised to take her for another ride the next morning and could not wait for dawn to come.

The tavern was thick with tobacco smoke. Mounted stag heads hung from the rough whitewashed walls. An enormous rack over the stone fireplace caught the landowner's eye. Before meeting Clara Laguna, he had dreamed of such a trophy. He walked over to the bar to wait for a table. Two locals finishing their wine saw him and called to the barmaid. The woman, a redhead they affectionately called La Colorá, was drying glasses with a rag.

"Dinner, señor?"

"If possible, a nice roast goat."

"The tavern is very full, but if you like, you could sit with those gentlemen from Madrid." She pointed to three young men at a table by the fire. "They're a nice group of hunters."

"As long as they don't mind."

The barmaid was right. The Andalusian spent a pleasant evening; they ate roast goat, drank four bottles of red wine, and swapped hunting stories. As the landowner bade his companions good night, the barmaid, clearing tables, intercepted him.

"Did you have a good time?"

"Excellent. You've been most kind. Thank you."

"Then let me offer a warning, señor, and please don't think me insolent. I'm just a goodhearted woman who sees danger ahead. It seems you've been spotted with the witch's daughter. You know who I mean, the girl with the flaxen eyes."

Desire flooded his heart like poison. She placed a hand on his forearm.

"Clara is cursed, beautiful though she may be. Cursed, and good and cursed, like all of the women in her family. I swear." She kissed her thumb and index finger, an oath promising a secret kept.

"I don't understand," he said.

"Don't they have curses where you're from?"

"We have our superstitions, señora."

"Well, what you call a superstition, here is a curse as big as a pile of dung — especially when it comes to the Lagunas, and to Clara, who is the last of her line. As far back as the town can remember, every single one of the Laguna women has been cursed."

"So the men in the family are not."

"Men!" She slapped her thigh. "What men? The belly of a Laguna has never carried a male. Not one of them has ever married, either. They're doomed to a life of disgrace, to bear only girls who will suffer the same fate."

"And no man — "

"Not one," the barmaid interrupted. "Not one man has dared break the spell. Keep in mind that only misfortune will come to any who tries."

"What sort of misfortune?"

"No one knows for sure. They say that years ago the Laguna witch, as she's called, tried to cast a spell on one but failed, and was left with a blind eye."

. . .

The next morning, the moment he woke, the Andalusian landowner recalled his conversation with a burly man who had walked him back to the inn in his inebriated state.

"Oh, I understand," he said. "Me and every other man in this town. If only the Laguna with the flaxen eyes weren't cursed . . ."

It was the morning of All Souls' Day. After the first church bells rang, the fog dispersed and the townspeople came into the streets in their Sunday best to honor their dead. Flower stalls had been set up on every corner of the town square. Women dressed in mourning attire sold red and white carnations, daisies, even a few roses to the rich. On one side of the church, a cobblestone path led up a hill. Beyond the last of the houses, a dirt track continued on. Shrubs along one side bordered the cemetery. Tucked into a portico on this hill, the Laguna witch was selling lilies sprinkled with a potion to ensure the spirits stayed buried in their graves. Women in whispering skirts and veiled hats, men in corduroy pants and berets passed. Many stopped, avoiding their neighbors' eyes, to buy one of those lilies, sparing them a visit from a relative's soul.

The cemetery was bordered on three sides by cypress trees. Half a dozen family vaults bore the same coat of arms as the noblemen's homes, and the rest was a jumble of graves. As the crowd filed in, magpies greeted them with caws and bright shiny wings. Every headstone was scrubbed clean before prayers and flowers were offered. Women scoured the gold-lettered epitaphs and oval portraits, while men pulled weeds. Those whose dead lay in a vault brought their servants to clean with hands already chafed and red. By noon, the cemetery smelled like a freshly mopped floor.

The Andalusian spent the morning recovering in his room, drinking coffee and recalling the barmaid's warning about the Laguna curse. Meanwhile, Clara sat at home waiting for him to take her for a ride.

After lunch, the landowner set out with the hunters from Madrid. More than once his hounds followed the scent of a stag, but when he had the animal in his sights, crouched in the bush, the rifle would begin to shake in his hands. The flanks of his prey became Clara's mane of chestnut hair, and the stag would disappear into the woods. Nor did he catch any of the rabbits his hounds tracked. The yellow beech leaves so like Clara's eyes made him forget why he was even there. He sat on a bed of ferns, damp seeping into his pants, his rifle silent on his lap. The hunters from Madrid wondered what was wrong; this man had traveled half of Spain to hunt in Castilian lands and now dragged himself around, unable to fire a shot.

The four of them returned to town when the forest swallowed the sun. The Andalusian declined their invitation to dine at the tavern, excused himself, and had his horse saddled. Within minutes he was digging his spurs into its flanks and galloping off.

A ghostly full moon lit the way to Clara Laguna's house. Her mother had gone to town, entering kitchens and sitting rooms through back doors to predict the future of the living and the dead. The landowner found Clara sitting in the dry streambed, next to the pearl-shaped tomatoes. He walked down to the rocky ground muttering, "So what if she's cursed, and so what if I can do nothing to change it."

Clara stood up the moment she saw him, her face stained with tears. The Andalusian sank to his knees and sang a folk song, disturbing the sleeping stray dogs near and far. It was a warm night for All Souls' Day. Clara threw a stone at him, opening a small gash on his forehead. He felt the slow trickle of blood and began to intone a *saeta*. The moonlight shined intensely, and Clara threw no more stones. Instead she looked at the landowner's blue-black hair, his bloody forehead, his olive-black eyes. She kissed him and cleaned his cut with the hem of her dress. He did nothing to stop her. Then he took her by the waist and helped her up onto the back of his dapple-gray horse.

They galloped to the oak grove, dismounted, and kissed. Stepping on the animal-shaped shadows projected by the trees, they came to the river. He took off his cloak, laying it on red soil where his wound dripped blood. Clara removed her wool shawl and the amulet she had put back on that morning. The wind stripped them of thoughts of spells, his cartridge belt, her petticoat, his hunting pants. Their bodies sank into soft earth, and as she listened to the murmuring water, the pain of her first time tasted of river moss.

2

THE ANDALUSIAN STAYED until the first snows of December. He and Clara met in the oak grove, their preferred place for lovemaking. Only when the wind froze their faces did they seek refuge in her house. Clara's mother would leave for town, hauling her sack containing the bones of a cat, and they would frolic among pots used for potions and jars of magic ingredients in that house that had only one room. The lovers went to his room at the inn once, but Clara was uncomfortable in that bed with its starched sheets, warmed by the fire, where crackling logs reminded her of the townspeople's chatter.

Everyone was whispering about Clara Laguna and the young Andalusian: the widows in church, counting their rosary beads, gossiping in their huddles of black shawls; the kitchen servants of noble homes, and their ladies in lace-filled parlors over *café con leche;* the young women at the fountain, jugs perched indignantly on their hips, and at the river, washing clothes; the men in the stables, in the fields with their oxen, at the bar over an anisette.

One evening the landowner went to the tavern after a successful hunt where he downed a stag. His rifle finally held steady and the animal's flanks no longer reminded him of a mane of hair, for he knew Clara Laguna was waiting, and she was a trophy much more beautiful than any rack. After he'd waited awhile at the bar, La Colorá seated him at a table alone. His hunting companions had returned to Madrid.

"How about a nice plate of pig's ears?" she asked.

"And a good bottle of wine. I want to celebrate my catch."

"I hope the hunter is not being hunted. You didn't take my advice."

"You should know a man is sometimes reluctant to give up certain things. Now, bring me those pig's ears. I'm hungry."

The Andalusian savored his meal, the wine, and the look of envy in other men's eyes. That young landowner had achieved what most wanted but never dared attempt, or had been spurned when they did.

The afternoon before leaving town, the Andalusian headed to Clara's. She was waiting at the bottom of the dry ravine. Since their affair began, she had taken him to the most scenic places around: fields of wheat and barley, cobalt mountains where vultures soared overhead, green pastures with winding paths and shepherd huts in the distance. But that last afternoon, Clara wanted to show him a place that appeared fleetingly in her dreams. A few miles from town, along the gravel road that crossed the pine forest, was an abandoned estate. The manor house was two stories high, topped by an attic. Despite the grime and mildew, the exterior was still a vivid red. An enormous yard surrounded it, protected by a stone wall. Out front, vegetation crept up stables, twisted around troughs and corral fences. Weeds filled hard beds of hydrangea and morning glories, surrounded the trunks of peach and pear trees and a chestnut tree that cast its shade over a stone bench. Out back was a garden where tomatoes and squash grew out of sheer habit. Farther back, the foliage grew thicker in a whirl of honeysuckle with a clearing in the middle; beyond that was a lilac grove and a wild rose garden.

The horse stopped before the high iron gate that led into the property. Clara contemplated the drive leading to the front door—big cobblestones, with ribbons of earth snaking between.

"It's a magnificent estate, but there's something that makes me uneasy. There's a sad air about it," the Andalusian said.

"Perhaps because it's abandoned."

"Would you like to live here one day?"

"I think so."

Clara pressed her cheek into the back of his cape. "I want to show you something. Come. I know a way into the garden."

They followed the stone wall and climbed into the rose garden where part of it had crumbled. Several paths wound in a circle, where dry stalks clung to tall posts, creating a skeletal pergola. Rain clouds were scattered across the sky, reaching down, creating an opaline fog that filtered through the dried stems. Wind rustled the remaining petals rotting on top of dry leaves amid patches of snow. Clara showed the Andalusian a yellow rose that was still in bud.

"If it can survive the first snows, then I can survive until you return."

He took Clara in his arms.

"I'll return next fall—before then, at the end of summer, if my lands allow. Wait for me, Clara. Don't love another. Don't even look at another."

"Do you promise you'll return?"

"I do, Clara. I promise I'll return."

When the landowner arrived at the inn, he settled into the armchair in front of the fire to warm bones chilled through by the Castilian cold. He drank a cup of red wine and closed his eyes. He missed the warmth of his estate, rows of orange trees, the sun, black bulls in the fields and horses harnessed with bells, the songs young Gypsies sang picked up by the breeze and carried across his lands. He was anxious to cross the plateau, now covered in snow, hauling the cart with his Andalusian hounds past castles perched high on hilltops.

Suddenly, there was a knock on his door. He opened it to find Clara's mother with her one blind eye, one black pupil, and ashen, windblown hair. The woman held her sack with the cat bones in one hand and, in the other, a magnificent vulture's claw on a string.

"I brought this amulet," she said, holding it out, "to protect you on your trip home."

"I have no doubt it'll do just that. The one I bought for the hunt was very effective—I've got a big rack to take home."

"Among other things." The old witch clucked. "Among other things."

"Let me pay you."

"I'd expect nothing less. A few coins are always welcome to a woman like me, who has to look after her only daughter."

"Take good care of her while I'm gone." The Andalusian handed her the money as she hung the claw around his neck.

"So you plan to come back."

"As soon as my lands allow, I'll come see Clara and hunt again." The Andalusian tried to smile, but this woman unsettled him deep in his gut.

"Think it over. My daughter is already a lost cause; nothing can save her. But you still have time. I suppose you've heard about our curse?" the Laguna witch asked. Her blind eye seemed to glow.

"They told me at the tavern, yes: that the Laguna women are cursed, that you only ever have daughters, that you're doomed to a life of disgrace." He cleared his throat, wishing he could take back that last word.

"They forgot to tell you the real bane of our existence. It's true we only ever have girls who never marry, and they call this a life of disgrace, but we're doomed to something far worse, my friend: we're doomed to be unlucky in love. We're fated to suffer for love, for the one love that steals our soul. It's why no spell can end our suffering or make us forget. Once the soul is gone, no magic can cure it."

"I promised Clara I would return, and I will keep my promise." The landowner felt the heat from the fire on his cheeks.

"My daughter is a fine example of her father's stock." The old woman looked up at the ceiling, her blind eye staring blankly. "She's attractive, proud, and brave. She knows how to take care of herself, but this thing with you was bound to happen sooner or later. The amulet I made her is useless. It was only to protect her from other men until the one who was destined to come came along. But she knew to stay away from the others. Clara fears the curse; it might be the only thing she fears. Now pour me some wine." The old witch pointed to the bottle on the table. "All this talk of curses makes me thirsty."

He poured a glass, and the witch swallowed the wine in a single gulp.

"Now, would you like me to predict your future with the cat bones? When you throw the bones, the position of the tail will tell whether you'll have male heirs."

"I have to get up early to catch the morning coach. Perhaps when I return."

"I understand." The tip of the old woman's tongue, blackened from tasting her potions, protruded between her lips, and the Andalusian could not help but stare. "Why don't you give me a few coins for something more useful, then." She pulled a greenish bottle out of a leather bag that was slung across her shoulder and sat at her hip. She handed it to him. "Drink this when the moon wanes, then wash the area over your heart with thyme and rosemary water. It'll help you forget, and you won't ever have to return."

"But I don't want to forget."

"Keep it. Pay me and I'll be on my way."

The Laguna witch picked up her rigid sack, took the Andalusian's coins, and left. The landowner stood with the little jar in his hands as a soft pulse beat behind the glass. He let go, and it shattered on the floor. A yellowish liquid stinking of rotten figs seeped out as a lizard tail thrashed on the floor.

The young landowner was hardly able to sleep that night; whenever he did, his mouth grew dry and he dreamed of the potion's smell and reptiles. The next morning, he took the first coach home to Andalusia, his eyes shot through with insomnia, his hounds in the cart behind, their barks throbbing in his temples.

Clara Laguna settled in to wait for the Andalusian landowner. She continued to fetch water from the town square at dawn, but now everyone she passed — man or woman, young or old — studied her belly to see if it had grown, to see if it hid another Laguna girl. The months passed as Clara tended her tomatoes, cleaned the pen, fed the chickens and the goat, helped her mother repair hymens and stir potions, as she went to the oak grove and to the estate to contemplate the yellow rose that ignored the tedium of the seasons. But the belly everyone expected to swell remained flat and silent.

Every two or three months Clara received a piece of mail from the Andalusian: pages drenched in olive oil and dried in the sun, orange blossoms and jasmine flowers wrapped in tissue paper rather than words because Clara was illiterate. She replied with dried leaves, bark from an oak tree, yellow rose petals, pine needles, and locks of her hair stuffed into blue envelopes it took all her courage to buy at the general store and fill out, copying her lover's address in a tremulous hand.

By the middle of spring, when daisies and poppies bloomed in the fields, Clara Laguna had grown sick with impatience. She begged her mother to predict when the landowner would return. Dumping the cat bones onto the cot, Clara gathered them up and threw them as she thought only of him.

"He'll be back in rutting season. I see it clearly here, in the shin-bones."

The Laguna witch was right. Just as the September foliage began to turn, the Andalusian arrived on the afternoon coach, accompanied by his two servants but without any trace of his hounds. He could hear stags bellowing in the surrounding woodlands as he settled into the same rooms at the inn. The animals' howling grew more desperate as he dug his spurs into the flanks of a horse and headed to see Clara, where the echo of their first kisses sent rumbles all the way down to the outskirts of town. They set off for the oak grove, where they made love under a full moon.

The Andalusian's skin was darkened by the joy of long summer nights. He also smelled of the sea, a scent unfamiliar to Clara. But he was not the only one in town to carry with him a hint of the ocean. A new priest, the man who would guide the souls of the faithful from the pulpit, arrived on the next morning's coach.

The local priest had died a few months earlier, cursing old age and his liver, and parishioners had been forced to attend Mass in the neighboring town. The moment the new priest heard this, he knew this inhospitable land and its inhabitants had been exposed to the whims of evil. A fervent believer in the devil since his seminary days, he knew it was just a matter of opportunity before Lucifer appeared in the world. His obsession only grew when he volunteered to serve as chaplain with Spanish troops battling the rebels fighting for Cuban independence. For two years he hastily performed last rites over young men felled by bayonets, gunpowder, and fevers, crouched amid mosquitoes, sugar cane, and tobacco plants. Though he had sworn not to return to Spain until victory was won, they brought him home against his will after his battalion was ambushed and he wandered deep in the jungle for over a month, with hunger his only companion. They found him feverish in the hut of a Santeria priestess, who had read in his palm that his life would forever be linked to the devil's, that wherever he went, the devil was sure to follow. The priest was a young man — not yet thirty — but his face was aged by the Caribbean sun and the sight of death.

Resigned to his fate, the young priest acquiesced to his superiors' mandate that he go to this Castilian backwater, where news from the colonies rarely arrived. They hoped a pastoral life of sermons, card games, and anisette in this forgotten town surrounded by mountains and harsh terrain would rid him of this obsession with the devil — and if not, then the frigid air might freeze it out of him.

But on that first Sunday, as the new parish priest stood in the pulpit, his sermon was not about the coming harvest of wheat and rye. Instead, spreading his arms wide, like an eagle soaring over mountain peaks, he regaled the congregation with a sermon on the glory of the Spanish Empire, of witnessing the devil's trickery in a land surrounded by turquoise water that evil hoped to drown. Expectations surrounding this new cleric were high, and the church was filled to capacity. Even the shepherds had come down from their pastures to hear the young priest with a face the color of *café con leche*. By the end of Mass, many parishioners felt their eyes brimming with tears without knowing exactly why—they had not understood a word of the sermon, confusing the devil with mosquitoes. Others left uncertain who the Spanish troops were fighting, or who in fact wanted to steal the empire from them. That feverish sermon was repeated on subsequent Sundays with just as many parishioners in attendance, squeezed into the pews. A censer swung from one side of the church to the other, incense masking the smell of sheep and other odors exuded by the faithful as the sermon grew more heated, with its battles in far-off, crocodile-infested lands where the sun caused faith to boil. If anything was clear to the townspeople after those first few sermons, it was that this dark-eyed young man in the oversized cassock knew how to reach straight into the hearts of his listeners, though they understood not a word. His name was Juan Antonio Escabel de Castro, but they began to call him Padre Imperio, a name he bore proudly for the rest of his life.

All of the commotion surrounding the priest's arrival and his sermons deflected attention from the rekindled affair between Clara Laguna and the Andalusian. Whenever the old women saw him stride by, they gave only a moment's thought to whether he could break the curse by marrying the Laguna girl and making her happy. Their minds immediately returned to Padre Imperio's tropical crocodiles—no doubt the devil incarnate—devouring not only crabs but the fists and legs of Spaniards.

One night when the landowner went to the tavern for dinner, La Colorá offered him only mushrooms sautéed with egg and had no more to say than "I guess we'll see what you're willing to give up for a pretty woman now."

Clara was one of very few women in town that fall of 1898 whose life was not affected by Padre Imperio's sermons. Not exactly welcomed at church by the women in veils and mantillas, she and her mother did not go to Sunday Mass. Besides, the Laguna witch had taught her daughter that a cursed woman sets foot on hallowed ground only when the taste of death is on her lips. Clara, who barely believed in God, cared not at all. If she felt like praying, she would recite the only prayer she knew, wherever she was, to God or the town's patron saint, Saint Pantolomina of the Flowers, a martyr with irises in her blond hair who was put to death by quartering.

Clara's relationship with the Andalusian kept her busy enough. They rode out through forests and flocks in between his hunts, making love wherever they chose. She adored the feeling of his hands, inhaling his persistent salty aroma in the yard surrounding the estate, under the pergola with the last of the roses. Late one afternoon, after their pleasure, he asked her why she never went to church to hear the priest's sermons; though their meaning was somewhat obscure, they were fascinating nevertheless.

"I can go with you this Sunday, if you like," Clara replied, picturing herself walking into church in her Sunday best, her cursed arm entwined in his. She also imagined her dress was white and they were walking to the altar, where two rings and blessings awaited, her family's curse barred at the door, shaking with fury.

The Andalusian, who had pictured the same thing, minus the wedding, knew he had gone too far. It was one thing to be seen walking with Clara in the street or on horseback in the woods and hills, quite another to be seen taking her arm in church.

"I think you should go with your mother."

"Yes, or maybe the best thing to do is not go at all, or go with whoever I want."

Clara walked away from him. A liquid cold surged through her bones as tears pricked like knives and the taste of blood filled her mouth, making her queasy. She recognized the symptoms her mother had described more than once: the symptoms of the curse, the first pain inflicted, announcing the corrosion of more to come.

The next Sunday, as usual, neither Clara nor her mother went to church. However, at midday Padre Imperio himself appeared at their door. Slices of stale bread toasted in the fire along with a piece of tallow, some mandrake root, and a pot brewing toads to ward off evil eye. The priest pulled out a handkerchief and pressed it against his nose and mouth.

"Good Lord above! This house smells of witchcraft!"

"What it smells of is breakfast and a poor home," Clara's mother replied.

The priest, pale in his black cassock, pressed the handkerchief even harder. A tropical sweat broke out on his brow. The smell of that concoction brought him back, and for a moment he thought he was in a ramshackle hut deep in the jungle, the Santeria priestess sucking on goat bones, smearing a yellowish poultice on his throat.

"Sit, Padre. You're as pale as a dead goat," the Laguna witch said, offering a stool. He refused with a wave of his hand.

"What they say seems to be true: you practice witchcraft in this house. Now I must know if you invoke the devil as well." Just then he glanced into a corner of the room and caught Clara Laguna's startling eyes.

"The only devil I know is the one I treat in my customers." The woman's blind eye crossed, and Padre Imperio felt the need to cross himself.

"Come to Mass, señora, and bring your daughter. You may be in mortal sin."

"You should know we're cursed, and a cursed woman only goes to church to die. At least that's what my mother always said."

"I've been told about your family affliction, and I'm here to tell you the only remedy is chastity. You must not bear children."

Clara Laguna's eyes bore into Padre Imperio. He stuffed his handkerchief into his pocket and quickly said goodbye.

Having felt the first symptoms of the curse, Clara believed she could follow the priest's advice and not give herself to the Andalusian. But she was wrong. The more she denied him, the more his desire for her cursed flesh grew. He bought her a bracelet of freshwater pearls and appealed to her heart with verses he sang on one knee under an oak in the moonlight. Clara lost her appetite, the ability to hear or speak until she gave herself to him again in the rose garden on a bed of dried petals and leaves. When she returned home, the Laguna witch said: "You did well. You had no other choice." She opened Clara's mouth and inspected her gums, as if she were a horse, then had the girl urinate in a cauldron, added a handful of roots, and put the cauldron on the fire to boil. When the room filled with the sweet smell of entrails, the old witch half closed her blind eye and said: "You're with child. You conceived in rutting season, over a month ago."

It was the time of the fog of the dead souls. An icy wind swept through the plaza. And yet, when Clara Laguna sat on the edge of the fountain, the wind turned warm as it caressed her face, the spirits' laments mingling with her own. She loved a man she had known for just a year, she told them, and now she was expecting a child. The bells tolled their sad warning, and as the mist began to dissipate, Clara noticed a dark blot outside the church. It was Padre Imperio, splashing holy water. Through what remained of the fog, he saw those amber eyes and crossed himself. No matter how the bell ringer tried to explain the origin of this phenomenon of the fog, Padre Imperio was determined to blame it on Lucifer's breath.

"What are you doing here, inhaling these demonic signs?"

"There's nothing demonic here, Padre. Only a great sorrow. You'll get used to it."

On the morning of All Souls' Day, as the townspeople made their pilgrimage up to the cemetery armed with flowers and scouring pads, Clara went with the Andalusian to the oak grove. The day had dawned to a stormy sky, and just when she told him she was pregnant, thunder and lightning erupted and rain fell. Those still in the cemetery took refuge in family vaults, but all those wide mourning skirts and hats took up space, so a stampede of mourners raced along the ridge to the first porticoes. Meanwhile, Clara and the Andalusian embraced under a magnificent oak tree. As Clara wept, her tears mixed with the rain. He tried to whisper words of comfort, but they were not the ones Clara wanted to hear. He recalled La Colorá's warning that no man had ever dared break the Laguna curse, and that a mysterious misfortune awaited anyone who tried.

The rain stopped when there were no more tears for Clara to cry. Still, the sky threatened more storms until night fell and, with frigid bones, she fell asleep alone in her bed.

The next day the young Andalusian made inquiries in town and then boarded the afternoon coach to the provincial capital, five hours away. He took his two servants but left several trunks of clothing and rifles at the inn. He returned four days later, traces of exhaustion etched on his face, and immediately set out on foot for Clara's, a leather case under his arm. He found her in the streambed garden. She had been waiting and hoping, and the moment she saw him, her chest burned with pride — and hope.

"I thought you'd left for Andalusia without saying goodbye."

"I leave the day after tomorrow. My lands need me. But first I want you to come to the estate with me."

"Why?"

"I'll tell you when we're there."

They walked in silence along the gravel road that crossed the pine forest until they came to the high iron gate. The biting cold flushed their faces.

"This time we'll go in the proper way."

The Andalusian took out a key and unlocked the gate. The hinges creaked as it opened. Clara stepped onto the cobblestone drive that led to the door and knew she had walked it in her dreams as daisies sprouted in her hair.

"You'll earn a living here," the young landowner announced.

"All I want is to be with you."

"I bought you this property. It's for you and the baby."

"Then it will be a girl."

He handed her the case he carried under his arm.

"What's this?"

"The deeds. Everything is in your name. There's a bit of money as well, to help you get started. I went to the city and arranged everything. As I said, I leave the day after tomorrow, but I'll be back when the child is born."

"I dreamed of living here, but only if it were with you."

"I swear I'll be back to see what God has sent us, boy or girl. And I look forward to seeing you as a proud owner here."

"And will you marry me?"

"No, Clara. I will never marry you; that was never my intention. You're a beautiful girl, but I can't love you like a woman of my class and position. Your mother practices witchcraft and divines the future in the bones of a cat. And you, little one, you can't even write your own name. How could I present you in society? I would grow tired of you, and you would come to hate me. You're like that precious yellow rose in what is now your garden: it took time to fade, but in the end it did and now it's gone. Do you understand what I'm trying to say?"

"I understand. I'm not as ignorant as you think. But you promise you'll return?"

"I do."

"Then I will wait for you."

Before the landowner set out on the evening coach with his servants and trunks, he and Clara said goodbye in the oak grove. The last rays of sun were sinking into the river when Clara heard the horse's hooves pounding against the earth as she sat on the moss, waiting. That galloping beat reverberated in her belly, and her bones turned to ice. The Andalusian dismounted, handsome as ever, and carved a heart with their names and an arrow on a hollow trunk as he repeated his promise to return. He kissed her on the lips, climbed back onto his horse, and trotted off slowly, following the riverbank.

The wind carried the sound of church bells announcing seven

o'clock Mass. Cloaked in the shadow of an oak, Clara Laguna knew her love would forever smell of that tree and cursed God. In the distance, she watched her lover's silhouette wind along the river. He would marry a woman other than her, a woman with beauty marks and stiff flounces, a woman who could write not only her first and last names but love letters as well. Clara cried so hard imagining this rival that the moment her eyes dried, her belly, then her vagina, which had known such passion only to have it snatched away, began to weep, too. She spent the night outdoors, lying in frost-filmed oak leaves. She returned home in the morning, woke her mother, and begged her to predict whether the Andalusian would keep his promise to return.

"He won't ever be back," the Laguna witch foretold in a voice still heavy with sleep. "I see it clearly in the ribs."

"Why do you lie to me, Madre? Why?" Clara pounded her fist on the table. A rib bone and the thread for repairing hymens went flying.

"What did you expect, Clara, even more from a rich man? You set your sights too high. I guess I didn't teach you as well as I thought. You are carrying a girl, and your lover has abandoned you. You're cursed."

"I refuse to be cursed! I will not suffer from it! He'll return. He promised, and he has never broken a promise. But when he does return, he will be the one to suffer."

"You can't refuse the cards you're dealt, stubborn girl!"

"Oh, yes, I can. Besides, Madre, you have one blind eye and another almost as bad. I don't trust what you see in that rotten, fly-infested bag of bones. Just listen to this: he gave me the estate and the manor house, for me alone, and money, too!"

"Oh! I knew he was a good young man, and handsome, too. You chose well."

"But you will not set foot on the property that makes you so happy. And you will never get your hands on my money!"

"Clara, I know what it is to suffer. When lovesickness bites, it sinks its teeth in deep. The day your father abandoned me, he left nothing but tears, misery, and a yellow-eyed girl in my belly. At least this Andalusian left you a wealthy estate. What more can a poor, cursed girl like you ask? Once your aching heart calms, you'll understand: if your lover bought you a house, there's no need for him to return."

"You're wrong! I need him to return."

"For what, silly girl? To make you suffer even more?"

"No, Madre. So I can take my revenge."

3

No one ever knew why that spring miracle occurred, but the moment Clara Laguna stepped onto the cobblestone drive that led to the red manor house, daisies like the ones in her dream sprouted in the strips of earth. Unaware, confusing the sound of their birth with the crunch of fallen leaves, Clara walked to the door, obstinate as the foliage smothering the stable, fences, and trough. Seeking refuge from the peasants' sticks, stray dogs had snuck into the yard through the hole in the stone wall. Their barking shattered the calm in the unkept yard.

On the main floor was a clay-tiled entryway, a parlor with a large hearth, a kitchen with a back door leading out to rows of wilted tomatoes and squash, a pantry with whitewashed shelves next to a small bedroom smelling of spices and herbs. A staircase corroded by woodworms and draped in cobwebs led from the entryway to the second floor and attic. As Clara climbed the stairs, she noticed moths trapped in the structures of silk, alive and at the mercy of a spider. A bathroom and four bedrooms ran along the second-floor hallway, each with a balcony overlooking the yard. In a corner of the biggest bedroom was a forgotten blue arabesque washbasin on an iron stand. The other rooms were so empty that Clara could hear the echo of her own breath.

At the end of the hall, the stairway reached farther up into the attic. The stairs were frail and creaked with each of Clara's steps. At the top, a puff of light came in through a small, moon-shaped window. Several beds were draped in sheets that smelled of rotten lavender. A hunting rifle was propped against a dilapidated French-style chest of drawers. The dust of the forgotten filled Clara's lungs, and she went back down the stairs. Having decided to move into the biggest room on the second floor, she lay down on the hardwood and rested her head on her bundled belongings. Though it was only midday, she settled into sleep. She would need all her strength to carry out her revenge. The next morning she would wait for a carriage to take her to the provincial capital. There she would buy everything needed to turn this property into not what her lover hoped it would be, a prosperous estate, but a magnificent brothel.

Clara's first trade was with a scrap merchant: an hour of love beneath the pines for four candelabras, one for each corner of the parlor. He became her first client, and was determined to hold tight, forever, to the kindness she'd shown him as he sat perched in his mule-drawn cart.

Once in the city, Clara Laguna completed her parlor furnishings with two crimson silk-covered sofas, pictures of harem concubines framed in mauve tulle, a carpet depicting the scene of a hunt, and green damask curtains. All this she found in a store that sold the furniture, décor, and props no longer wanted in theater productions because they were old or out of style. The owner, a baritone who had fallen from grace, was entranced by Clara's rustic beauty in her brown wool Sunday dress, patchwork skirt, shawl as coarse as a donkey's fur. At first he assumed she was only there to look, drawn in by his grand window display. Her expression was as dazed as that of any peasant seeing the city for the first time: its square filled with people and taverns, its stately buildings and churches, its streets lined with shops and horse-drawn carriages, all unknown in the countryside. But when Clara, determined to have her revenge, explained what she wanted, the baritone offered excellent advice on how to turn her estate into an opulent brothel, attracting men used to yokes, plows, and scythes, as well as the bourgeois, world travelers, and hunters.

In addition to the parlor furniture and fittings, Clara bought several negligees and Moorish outfits used in a performance of *Il Seraglio*. Their soft, supple shapes captivated her at once. Like flies and worms used to catch trout, they were the perfect bait to reel in the desire of men.

Just when she had spent her budget, Clara became infatuated with a bed used in a production of *Othello*, for that play's final death scene. It was a black iron four-poster with a purple canopy. Far too big to be repeatedly dismantled, it had graced the stage on only a few occasions. So insistent was Clara that she would have it, whatever the cost, the baritone traded it for her country favors. Clara had her second client on top of a trunk in the storeroom, dazzled by a *Rigoletto* aria. Her third was a lawyer the baritone recommended when Clara no longer had the money to pay for her room at the guesthouse, where she wept all night, remembering her Andalusian lover.

The next morning Clara set off for the estate. It was not hard to find her fourth client. The young man who unloaded her purchases was easily persuaded to stay and clear the overgrowth, rake the leaves, in exchange for a few days of love and chickpea stew. The blacksmith became her fifth and final barter. In three feverish days, he made Clara a sign that looked like a funeral wreath, engraved in gold with the words WELCOME TO SCARLET MANOR. It was this local client who advertised her new business.

"The Laguna with the flaxen eyes can be had for a few coins or a sack of rabbits at the estate her lover gave her," the blacksmith told everyone who came to his shop and those he met at the tavern for a drink or game of cards.

As far as Clara was concerned, her business was inaugurated the moment the sign was hung over the iron gate. Though most men could not read it, because they couldn't read anything at all, it was a place for the birds to leave droppings, like the headstones and crosses at graves.

Outfitted in her negligee and Moorish pants, Clara received locals who had always desired her beauty and youth and now flocked to the brothel without fear: there was no risk of a curse, as this was a simple transaction of the flesh. The men, used as they were to receiving such favors in a stable or granary, or up against a mountain pine, were stunned by the exotic aura created by Clara's outfit and the parlor where they were made to wait, with its opera curtains and pictures of concubines. Hunters fell victim to these charms as well. The brothel run by a prostitute with golden eyes, bursting out of tulle and satin, became one more reason beyond wild boar and hares to return to the Castilian town year after year.

The start of Clara's amorous endeavors that early December of 1898 turned the spotlight away from Padre Imperio's sermons. All talk of tropical crocodiles, swamps, and jungles crawling with Cuban rebels ceased among the black shawls. The brothel that Clara had opened on her estate, now known as Scarlet Manor, became the primary topic of conversation.

When Padre Imperio learned of the brothel shortly after it opened, he pictured the Santeria priestess warning him that his destiny was forever linked to the arrival of evil on earth. He put on a cassock sprinkled with holy water and set out for Scarlet Manor. Riding the mule that carried him to the homes of his faithful, scattered throughout the hills, the priest witnessed how the beech trees stood naked to greet travelers, their yellow leaves shed on the earth, their branches swaying in the wind.

The gate was open. Padre Imperio hitched his mule to one of the iron bars and walked down the cobblestone drive to the door at Scarlet Manor, his ecclesiastical boots trampling the clumps of daisies. Crossing himself first, he knocked on the door. It took several knocks before Clara opened it, yawning, wrapped in a wool shawl.

"Come in, Padre."

"I'll stay right here."

"As you like."

The house was damp and dusty inside, and the smell reminded Padre Imperio of sulfur. There was an abandoned look in Clara's eyes, and a shiver ran through him. He had come to find out whether the devil hid in this house of ill repute.

"There's nothing hidden here," Clara replied. "Not even my revenge."

Padre Imperio came with the courage of his stiff priest's collar, prepared to march straight back to the church for his exorcism tools if necessary, prepared to confront the human face of evil if it had set up residence on Clara's estate and filled her heart with wicked ideas.

"I don't need an exorcism, Padre, just a loaf of bread. No one will sell to me, and I haven't had time to bake."

"Despite your cat's eyes, the bad habit they say you have of speaking with the dead and the profession you have chosen, willingly or unwillingly, I am here to save you, whatever the cost, from the devil or yourself," he said with all the sternness he had learned in the tropics.

Padre Imperio walked back down the cobblestone drive, got onto his mule, and left for town.

Clara Laguna did not want her mother to live with her—not, that is, until the weight of her household obligations and loneliness made her change her mind. She couldn't please clients in the big canopy bed and attend to those arriving in the meantime. If she left the front door closed, men piled up in the frosty night; if she left it open, they wandered through the house, coming to stand in the doorway and spy on their neighbors, or into the pantry to eat the few provisions Clara managed to store. Nor did she have time to tend to the lettuce she planted next to the tomatoes and squash; to clean the parlor and her bedroom of the mud tracked in on her clients' boots, their gobs of spit and tufts of mule hair; to prepare meals, buy supplies, and sweep the leaves from the drive being inundated by daisies.

Late one afternoon, as she stood on the second-floor balcony, Clara realized she could never live alone in that brothel and bury her memories. Even the sight of the lonely moths awaiting death was a torment. She missed the odor of her mother's potions, missed helping her butcher small animals and repair hymens. She missed the rattle of cat bones in the rigid sack. She even missed milking the goat each morning. And yet she blamed the Laguna witch for her misfortune, for passing along her cursed inheritance.

That evening, Clara wanted to rid herself of any affection she might feel toward her mother or the child growing inside that would carry on their name. As she watched the moon disappear behind the clouds, she cried for love lost, for orange blossoms and olives, for *saetas,* for a revenge that now tasted of other men. Clara found no solace in the cold mountain air, in the icy stillness that caused her bones to ache. It was only when, instead of stars, she saw a pair of black eyes shining in the night that her pain subsided. Clara took in the air and closed the balcony doors. Those eyes belonged to Padre Imperio.

The next morning she set out for her mother's house. The sky was white, as if it held all of the snow that had yet to fall over the town that autumn. It was mid-December, that month of frozen streams and struggling to keep warm. Clara found her mother in bed. She hadn't seen her since the day she told her she was opening a brothel upon her return from the city. Hearing her daughter arrive, the old woman sat up. Her blind eye was closed, the black one watchful. Clara saw how much thinner and older she looked.

"Did you stop eating?"

"I'll soon have no choice. Just look at your poor mother! Yesterday I had to kill one of the hens. But don't you worry, you just enjoy your mansion."

When her daughter began receiving locals, the witch's own business suffered. The cat bones had not been out of their sack for days. This was how the women in town — who most required her divination — settled the score for their husbands, brothers, and sons letting off steam with Clara in her house done up like a castle. All orders to repair hymens or prepare potions against evil eye ceased. Only the occasional hunter, unaware of their collective revenge, dared buy an amulet. If things continued this way, it was quite possible she would not be able to pay her rent at the end of the month.

"Gather up the remaining animals and come with me."

"It's about time you reconsidered. Your pigheadedness in becoming a whore is ruining my business."

"Then come help me with mine. I suspect it's going to do very well."

"It could do even better if you listen to me. You need more girls. I'll take care of finding them. After all, in a few months, when you start to show, you won't be able to receive them."

They gathered up cooking and stew pots, jars of magic ingredients and kitchenware, the three remaining hens and the goat. They piled it all into a rickety cart and set out for Scarlet Manor.

Not long after the Laguna witch moved into the brothel, news came of Spain's defeat in the war against the Cuban rebels and the United States, and with it the loss of the few remaining lands belonging to the empire. Cuba, the Philippines, and Puerto Rico would now be held by the Americans. Shaken by the misfortune, Padre Imperio climbed into the pulpit that Sunday, spread his arms like an eagle, and sermonized on the evils of sugar, which came primarily from Cuba, forbidding its consumption in coffee and sweets, calling on the faithful to protest in the bitterness of defeat. As Mass ended, the first snow began to fall and autumn became winter at last. The streets, the square, the church and fountain, the cemetery on the hill, the fields all around, the pine forests, the mountains, and the banks of the Duero River were covered in a layer of powdery snow. Padre Imperio recognized the devil's dirty trick, sending a dusting of Cuban sugar to humiliate him. He locked himself in the sacristy, tormented by the sight of white caps softening mountain peaks. The entire town suddenly plunged into the eternity of winter and refused to come out until freezing nights turned the snow hard, and men and animals alike had soiled it with their comings and goings. When the snow was just snow again, Padre Imperio went on walks to free his mind of his memories of dead soldiers piling up in the Caribbean. He wished the townspeople would stop calling him Padre Imperio, but no one ever remembered to call him Juan Antonio, and habit overcame his preference.

News of Spain's defeat and the priest's sugar prohibition distracted the townspeople from the scandal when two more women arrived at Scarlet Manor. At the tavern, men played cards and bet on national politics and what charms these new girls might provide. All whispering in doorways stopped, the old women's tongues silenced by the snow, the bitter desserts and coffee.

Clara's mother had always considered herself a practical woman who could make the best of a lost cause, such as the curse that tormented her family. And so, when she realized her daughter would not renounce her crazy plan for revenge, she decided to take full advantage of it. She recruited two girls from the neighboring town. Their names were Tomasa and Ludovica. They were poor but beautiful, and they were willing to work for a warm bed, three meals a day, and a few coins to spend on Sunday, their one day off a week. Their services were soon prized by the growing clientele, though not as highly as Clara's.

Every day coaches and carriages rumbled along the gravel road connecting nearby towns and the provincial capital. Many a traveler would stop at the brothel by chance or drawn by its increasing fame. There they would rest from their journey, spending a day of passion under the purple canopy or in the beds Clara had rescued from the attic for the new prostitutes.

In the wee hours on the last day of the year, a girl with a deformed nose slipped into the Scarlet Manor's kitchen without anyone noticing, entering through a door that someone had forgotten to bolt. Clara's mother was in the parlor, which had been decorated with streamers for the holidays, serving clients as they waited their turn upstairs. She poured mulled wine and read the fortunes of those who asked, throwing the cat bones to see the fate of their crops or businesses in the coming year. The smell of wood burning in the large hearth took the chill off the wait and the prophecies. Every now and then, a long moan of victory or the creak of an old bed about to collapse came from the second floor.

Cold and hungry, the girl with the deformed nose had taken a tomato from the garden, but its frozen flesh nearly chipped her tooth. She stole into the kitchen without a thought for any consequences beyond her own well-being. The light of two oil lamps flickered. On a table in the middle of the room she found a jug of steaming wine and several glasses. She took several gulps before her throat began to burn and the bits of frost on her eyebrows, whiskers, and chin started to melt.

The girl could hear voices in the parlor but paid no attention; she had just spied two rabbits a client brought as payment. After biting into an onion, two cloves of garlic, and a loaf of bread, she skinned and butchered the animals, licking the blood off her fingers. She lit the iron stove, set a pot on top, and began to prepare a stew. No one noticed her presence until a delicious aroma wafted into the parlor, silencing the noise from the waiting, the wine, and the prophecies.

Clara's mother hurried into the kitchen, followed by a few clients whose appetites had been whetted by the magnificent smell. There they found the girl between the shadows, stirring the pot as if nothing were out of the ordinary. They startled at the sight of her. Apart from her deformed nose, the girl's face was bruised, her eyes mad, her short, dark hair giving way to wide sideburns ending in a modest beard. The Laguna witch did not recognize her from town. She asked the girl who she was and what she was doing in that kitchen. A stream of grunts and half-words spewed from her mouth. All they could decipher was that her name was Bernarda and she was making rabbit stew. In a wretched, velvet dress and boots with holes plugged by ice, she fell to her knees, covering her head with her arms, when Clara's mother approached.

"Who beat you?" one of the clients asked.

Still crouching, the girl gestured with hands enlarged from a life of work and muttered something no one could understand.

"So you ran away because they wallop you, eh?" another client asked.

The girl, who smelled as if she'd been living in a stable, said not a word.

"Well, wherever you're from, it seems you know how to cook. I'll have some of that rabbit when it's done," one of the clients said.

"So will I," another agreed.

"Get up, then, and finish that stew," Clara's mother ordered.

Filled with a joy no one could understand, Bernarda tied a kitchen towel over her eyes and juggled the wooden spoons she'd used to stir the stew. Then she picked up a knife. Everyone watched with bated breath as she minced a clove of garlic, leaving her fingers unscathed. Just as she was about to drop it into the pot, the girl stopped, arched her back as she listened for a moment, then threw the knife at a mouse scurrying toward the pantry, cleaving it square in the belly.

"Who the devil is this girl?" Clara Laguna had followed the smell of stew to the kitchen.

The girl removed her blindfold, and the sight of Clara with her golden eyes in an orange negligee, her hair loose and falling below her waist, her pregnancy-enlarged breasts bursting out of the tulle, pierced Bernarda like an arrow through the belly. She picked up onions off the counter and began to juggle as incomprehensible grunts streamed from her mouth until Clara demanded she stop. Bernarda mumbled, "I'm not leaving," and devoured the onions with a feverish appetite.

That night, Bernarda repeated "I'm not leaving," and she stayed until her death. It took two years as brothel cook before anyone in the brothel could make sense of her grunts and mutterings. They learned her father had sold her to a circus on account of her facial hair. It was then clear where she acquired her skill and love of juggling cutlery, fruit, and vegetables. But Bernarda's skills did not end there: she had an innate sense for food, and her stews became as famous as Clara's pleasures under the purple canopy, drawing clients who savored a good plate of food before or after lovemaking. Bernarda communicated with the world through her stews more than her mumbles and grumbles.

She was also exceptionally good with animals, who calmed at the touch of her giant hands. As a result, she looked after not only the kitchen but the corrals and stables. As the brothel grew, so did the number of animals: chickens, sheep, and goats, even a pair of horses that whinnied with pleasure at the whiff of mare exuded by her skin.

A few years after she arrived, they learned that Bernarda was from Soria and had lost her mother at birth. It was clear she fled the circus because someone had abused her, but it was only then they learned it was the lion tamer who drank and beat her with a stick while tugging on her beard for kicks.

What they did learn within a few days of her arrival was that Bernarda's simple nature was a result not of shyness or trauma but of a dreamy head lost in the clouds.

That night they set her up with a straw mattress on the floor in the room next to the pantry. As she undressed, her odor drifted through the rooms, up the stairs, creeping silently toward Clara Laguna. Clara sensed it in her dreams, and the child in her belly stirred.

4

THE YARD AT SCARLET MANOR was bursting with flowers, bees, and grasshoppers. It was the next winter when they began to whisper in town about its refusal to heed the changing weather and seasons. The first sign of this was the daisies that began to sprout between the cobblestones the day Clara set up house. They continued to grow, even during the chill of winter, their robust faces seeding in the snow and dry leaves, taking over the land and Clara's dreams once again.

When she was six months pregnant, Clara stopped receiving clients and sent her mother to recruit a replacement as she resigned herself to wait for the child's birth. She moved her bed under the window, framing it between the iron bars. There she sat with her swollen belly, staring out at the cobblestone drive. She still dreamed of the Andalusian, striding up the drive, singing a folk song to announce his arrival, followed by a *saeta* to beg her forgiveness. That drive was the first thing Clara saw when she woke, the last thing before she slept, and the vision continued in her dreams. Her hair still smelled of flowers in the morning, just as when she first brought the landowner to see the estate, only the daisies now sprouted in the earth instead of her chestnut strands.

One morning, when she was seven months pregnant, her vision still fogged by her dreams, Clara thought she saw a man walking toward the house. She rubbed her eyes, not wanting sleep to come between her and her desires: he was back in town, earlier than promised.

But this man was not wearing riding breeches and boots; there was no cape or oiled hair. His pants were black and coarse, his heavy boots calf-length, his coat two sizes too big, and peering out above the collar, a snow-white band bearing witness to a dedication to Christ: it was Padre Imperio. Clara burst into tears. He knocked and Clara's mother answered. For a moment, the priest wondered whether the devil hid in the blind eye of that woman still reeking of witchcraft, and he crossed himself in his thoughts.

"What a surprise. Come in."

"I'm fine right here." Padre Imperio did not intend to ever cross that threshold.

"Well then, tell me why you've come."

"I'd like to see Clara."

"She's resting, Father. She's pregnant and needs all the rest she can get."

"So I heard. I can wait. Tell her I have something for her."

"But she's not even awake and might not be up for hours! Pregnant women sleep late."

"I'm up, Madre. Go inside. I'll take care of him." Clara Laguna appeared in the clay-tiled entryway. Her eyes were red from crying, her hair tousled, her pregnant belly bulging under a thin muslin *Il Seraglio* dressing gown.

The Laguna witch went into the kitchen for breakfast.

"Tell me what you want, then leave. I don't want any deals with God until my death."

The priest stared straight down at a violet-covered Bible in his hands.

"I came to bring you this." He handed Clara the Bible. "You shouldn't wait that long."

"Does it look like I can read, Padre? Men and their obsession with educated women! Do you think he'd have abandoned me if I'd been able to read this book?"

"If you can't read it, I'll read it to you. I'll be back this same time tomorrow morning. I'll wait for you in the garden. But this time, be dressed." He replied with the determination that had kept him alive in the jungle for over a month.

Padre Imperio's eyes, those dark eyes in which Clara found solace one winter night, bore into her own. She said nothing but felt spring slipping in through the door with a breeze of tender shoots.

Clara spent the afternoon wandering among the tomatoes, lettuce, and squash in the garden, amid the fruit trees, hydrangea, and morning glories, their flowers intensifying the ache in her heart. It longed for the bare rigidity of winter. But her treasonous baby stirred in a belly nourished by spring. Nature's creaky buzz reached deep inside Clara, the herbage exploding on what not long ago were barren branches rattling in the wind. But the most painful of all, what she could never forgive the fertile ground around Scarlet Manor, was the effervescence of multi-hued buds that filled the rose garden. Clara had not set foot on those paths where she'd once loved, where she had been happy, where a yellow rose — no less treasonous — would fade just like her, where its blue, white, and red companions had grown so big their petals were like tongues mocking her misfortune. She hated the place that had given her hope only to tear it away. Clara forbade her mother, Bernarda, and the other prostitutes from tending to that garden. She ordered that the breach in the stone wall, where the Andalusian had passed, be sealed and built a barricade of wheelbarrows under the arch at the entrance, condemning stray dogs to a fragrant death or a back scraped raw if they dared escape through the path of thorns. That rose garden would die bitter, dry, and abandoned.

That night, Clara vomited pollen, was tormented by nightmares of cologne and salve, used to soothe wounds. Her agitation finally abated under a cloak as black as a cassock, and she fell into a dreamless sleep.

Padre Imperio arrived at Scarlet Manor precisely on time, riding his mule, his priest's collar in crisp contrast to his face lined by wrinkles acquired in the tropics. Clara spied him from her bedroom window as he marched over the daisies. She told her mother to send him away with the excuse that she was unwell. I haven't got time for salvation, Clara thought, only for revenge. She began to brush her hair as she watched the old woman give the priest her message; rather than leave, he sat on the stone bench under the chestnut tree and stroked the violet cover of a book Clara sensed was sacred.

"That man is as stubborn as his mule! He says he's not leaving."

"So I see."

Unable to squeeze her breasts and belly into her own dresses, Clara wore one of her mother's. The birds sang too loudly for her liking, the sky was too blue, the breeze too soft. Padre Imperio stood when he saw her approach.

"You do know you're in the garden of a brothel?"

"I'm in a garden blessed by nature, and therefore blessed by God's generosity." Padre Imperio shivered, as he did whenever he looked into Clara's eyes, wondering whether the fires of hell might burn behind them.

She sat on one end of the bench, he on the other, a stone arm between them preventing any contact.

"I'd like to read you a passage from the Bible that will explain why I'm here and what I want to tell you." The violet cover stuck to his sweaty fingers.

"Someone once told me about your sermons, said I should go hear them. What were they about?"

Padre Imperio set the Bible down. He inhaled the morning air in that garden that seemed to lean back, ready to listen, and began to speak of a far-off island called Cuba, where soldiers went to defend the glory of the empire. Clara looked at the ground, at the wildflowers swirling at her feet, but as the story wore on, she glanced at the priest, then turned her whole body and looked straight at him. She had never noticed his lips before; they were thin, a star-shaped scar in one corner. Dressed in a soldier's uniform, a priest's collar at his grimy throat and nothing but faith in his heart, Padre Imperio had marched with a battalion of men through swamps where rebels hid, where ceiba and palm trees harbored enemies and, in the distance, a beach. The priest's eyes were no longer black but tinged Caribbean blue. There was gunfire and death; the first soldiers fell in the yard at Scarlet Manor, blood splattering the cobblestones and daisies, gunpowder and granules of pollen filling the air, crocodiles crawling out from behind the chestnut tree, holy water splashing from a canteen onto the priest's boots, Clara's feet, and the forehead of a fallen soldier. It was an ambush. Midday beat down on Scarlet Manor. Padre Imperio loosened his collar, and Clara Laguna saw the scar slashing right across his throat.

"I'll come another day to read biblical parables." He picked up the holy book and got to his feet, his mouth dry. His mule, tied to the gate, was getting restless.

"Come as long as they let you."

"Or until you repent and come listen to my sermons where they should be heard, in church."

"You obey God, I my revenge."

"You're still so young, and with child."

"But my soul is gone, Padre, stolen by love and the curse on my family."

"That's not true. Your soul belongs to God."

Padre Imperio wanted to say he would find the soul she thought she lost, but he said nothing. They did not shake hands or touch but said goodbye with their eyes. The priest walked toward his mule, dragging behind him the same solitude that engulfed Clara.

It was a while before Padre Imperio returned to Scarlet Manor. Clara tried to think of him only when the pain of her curse was unbearable, like a balm, a dark-eyed remedy. She looked for other things to keep her busy. She grew to like her trips to town, not to fetch water from the fountain, like she had before, with her jug and her memories of a man who surely belonged to another by now. There was a never-ending well of fresh water just next to the vegetable garden at Scarlet Manor. Instead, Clara liked to parade her pregnancy in the square, up and down the narrow streets where the old women sat forming rows of black shawls. She wanted them to whisper about her, about the cursed line of Laguna women who would not die out but wantonly reproduced girls and disgrace. If the curse had stolen Clara's soul, then she would steal their men.

Sometimes, when Clara passed the church doors, she would forget her name, her background, her misfortune, just for a moment, and wish she could enter that sacred place with its crucified Christ on the altar, the gravestones of Castilian gentlemen set into the floor, the stone coffins of noblemen in somber side chapels. She wished she could sit on a pew and admire Padre Imperio in the pulpit, arms spread in his Sunday robes, his lips savoring his sermons, the yellow of her eyes reflected in his.

But those strolls grew farther apart. By mid-May, Clara's belly was so big she could no longer walk the distance from Scarlet Manor to town. Clara's mother, wishing her daughter would stop parading before her clients, convinced her to help with her potions again. Although the Laguna witch's business was initially affected by the brothel, it slowly picked up, thanks to the men curious about their future as they waited for their turn of carnal pleasure, and the women who missed her prophecies and cures for evil eye cast by rural envy. Since Clara had started to busy herself with the clients waiting in the parlor as well, the Laguna witch would some nights go to town, hauling her sack of cat bones.

Bernarda did not like that half-blind woman in her kitchen, taking up the whole stove to prepare her potions and balms in blackened pots. She grunted that there was no room left to cook, scratched her deformed nose, and tugged angrily on her whiskers.

"Be quiet, girl. You sound like a wounded boar! There's room enough for two in this kitchen."

Bernarda stalked off to lie on her straw mattress, but when Clara started helping her mother, the cook showed a sudden interest in witchcraft, and in the needle and thread for repairing hymens.

"Lady, lady good," Bernarda grunted as she sharpened and polished the knives Clara used to dismember lizards, toads, and rodents.

Bernarda shadowed Clara's every move, watching her cut and store the pieces in a jar or simmer them in a pot. The moment her mistress was distracted, she devoured any little piece of meat or entrails Clara had touched. For Bernarda, love was a matter of the stomach.

"Madre, did you take the lizard tail?" Clara asked.

"Of course not! Be quiet now. Don't distract me. I don't want to mix up the herbs."

"And you, Bernarda?"

With her mouth open, teeth and gums stained with blood, the girl laughed, savoring the touch she loved so much.

"Don't we feed you enough? These are for the potions, you beast!" Clara smacked her across the head.

Still smiling, Bernarda ran to her room with one hand over the exact spot her mistress had struck.

"Come out of your room and stop stinking up the place!" Clara yelled.

But Bernarda hid away to cut off that piece of hair where Clara had slapped, swallowing it eagerly with a piece of fruit from the pantry.

Any other stomach would have cramped in unbearable pain, but Bernarda could digest anything her mistress's love demanded and not feel the slightest prick of indigestion.

"Go on and prepare dinner for the men tonight," Clara ordered when Bernarda returned to the kitchen, her anger subdued. "And stop following me around!"

Bernarda grunted in reply. She plucked a chicken and disemboweled a rabbit, working as close to her mistress as possible, keeping an eye on which ingredients she touched.

The magic smell from the pots Clara's mother stirred rose up over the gypsum counter where Clara worked, over the table in the middle of the room where Bernarda plucked and skinned the meat for lunch and dinner, intermingling with the whiff of blood, snaking among the ropes of garlic and onion hanging from the wall, through the cupboards, and over the dining room table where clients were served.

When Bernarda was alone, she stuck her hand in the pots, scooped out the ingredients her mistress had touched, and saved them jealously to cook later. Sometimes she went through the bother of replacing them with others that looked the same—but did not bear Clara's touch—but most often she indulged in her feast without worry. And so potions to cure evil eye suddenly became remedies for a migraine or young love. The old woman's credibility was being undermined by these alterations, and she could not understand why. Until one day, suspecting the cook's voracity, she hid behind the door and caught her stealing a pair of frog's legs. The Laguna witch whipped Bernarda so hard she never stuck her hand in a pot again, and settled instead for licking clean the utensils Clara had used for tomato sauce or porridge.

Another of Clara's distractions was to oversee the grooming of the three women who now worked for her. The most recent arrival, a shepherd's daughter from a nearby town, had a habit of sticking tufts of wool behind her ears, receiving clients with ears that stuck out and smelling like a flock of sheep. If it weren't for her wet nurse's breasts flapping about in her dressing gown, few would have been willing to lie with her. Before sending her into the parlor, Clara dressed her in negligees and Moorish pants that complemented her skin and hair, and inspected behind her ears. If the girl disobeyed, Clara docked her Sunday pay or cuffed her across the head.

Although the girls were about her own age, Clara rarely spoke to them about anything other than brothel affairs, chores, or tricks of the trade to better satisfy clients. This was her business and her revenge, and there was no room for friendship or chitchat. For that, she met with the dead gentlemen in town once a year. They understood her better than anyone. And yet sometimes she was jealous of the secrets Ludovica and Tomasa shared, wondered what it might be like to have a living friend to share her happiness, dreams, and sorrows.

One day Clara decided to shave Bernarda's circus beard and sideburns. Though the cook did not have to satisfy clients, when they wandered into the kitchen for a taste of her stews, they were startled to see her tugging on her whiskers in the light and shadow thrown by the lamps. Bernarda squirmed and squealed like a pig at slaughter the morning Ludovica and Tomasa led her to a chair on the back porch, the Laguna witch approaching with a razor, a bowl of water, and a bar of soap.

"Quiet! It's not like we're going to slit your throat!" the old woman yelled, rolling her blind eye.

Bernarda calmed the moment Clara appeared, letting her mistress cover her face with a warm cloth, lather it, and shave it as she reveled in the closeness of Clara's breath and touch.

From that day on, Bernarda would run her hands over her face in search of any hair that would draw near the soft, fragrant skin she adored.

"Lady, lady, lady," she said, pointing to the fuzz that would offer another ration of her mistress's time.

"Not yet, Bernarda. When there's more."

"Itchy, itchy," she complained, scratching her cheeks, pouting her lips.

"Then scratch like it's just another of your many fleas."

On one of the days she shaved Bernarda on the porch, Clara was struck by her cook's smell of lonely horse stables. She had smelled it many times before, but that morning it reminded her of her rides with the Andalusian, and she was overcome by nostalgia. The razor trembled in her hands. Without realizing, Clara began to tell Bernarda about that day galloping through the pines, rocks, and beech trees, ending deep in the valley, in the shade of an oak tree, with a wet kiss. The cook shivered at all that talk: Clara wasn't barking orders and scolding, and her voice was rich with confidence and trust. Bernarda did not know how to swallow those delicious sounds she could neither see nor touch. She had never imagined anything inedible could fill her with such a feeling of glory.

This was how Clara Laguna found someone with whom to share her sleepless nights, her memories. Bernarda listened adoringly each time her mistress shaved her, the only time Clara felt comfortable enough to share. The cook never interrupted her mistress, but if Clara cried, Bernarda cried, too; if she laughed, Bernarda laughed, too; and if she was angry, Bernarda was angry, too.

"Not a word to anyone, or it's the whip for you, do you understand?" Clara warned.

"Shhh." The cook brought a finger to her lips and smiled.

Clara Laguna's daughter was born in the canopy bed early that month of June 1899. Bernarda, used to helping birth sheep, pulled the baby from her mistress as she bawled in pain and, between pushing and panting, swore revenge. The newborn sucked her little fingers covered in blood and placenta, demonstrating from birth a primitive appetite that would dominate her for the rest of her life. Clara named her Manuela.

The arrival of another Laguna girl was seen in town as proof of the family's curse. The old women huddled, having exchanged heavy black shawls for lighter ones, delighted over the stigma the girl would carry for having been born in a brothel to a whore, predicting even worse disgrace. The young women wondered aloud whether the father would come back to meet his bastard child, whether they would see him with his curly black hair, rifle slung over his shoulder. The men in the tavern celebrated the news with shots of anisette and cigars; the Laguna with the flaxen eyes had given birth to the girl she deserved and would soon receive them in her ethereal pants and dressing gowns.

Padre Imperio came to Scarlet Manor in the heat of July. If he was to save the mother at all costs, then he must also look out for her daughter, and that began with a Christian baptism. He tied his mule to the gate. From her window, Clara watched him walk his melancholy walk down the cobblestone drive, stomping on the daisies. The high temperatures that baked the region reminded him of the time he spent fighting with his battalion; his faith, the mosquitoes, and the dust reminded him of their defeat and his exile to this town of crude souls. On his last visit to Clara, a few days before she gave birth, he had told her about the Santeria priestess who found him in the jungle and treated him with poultices that he didn't tell her reminded him of the color of her eyes. He took advantage of her good mood that day to read a few parables from the violet-covered Bible and gave her a holy card featuring Saint Pantolomina of the Flowers, which Clara slipped into her bra, next to her heart.

Suffocated by the severity of his cassock, the priest loosened his collar, revealing his scar. The sun was blinding, and the only stirring of the air came from his speech, as he sat on the stone bench under the chestnut tree, the cicadas trilling.

"I'll baptize my daughter when her father returns," Clara said.

Padre Imperio's dark eyes turned fierce.

"And when might that be?"

"This fall, a few months from now."

"What if he doesn't return? What makes you think he will?"

"A promise."

"Men like him don't keep promises, Clara. Your lover is never coming back."

"How dare you say that! Maybe you're the one who shouldn't ever come back, you and your sermons and your parables. The only thing that's going to save me is seeing my revenge in the eyes of the man I still love."

The priest stood from the scalding bench, his scar a red hangman's noose. The cicadas trilled even louder.

"Go! I don't want your salvation to distract me any longer!" Tears and reproach caught in Clara's throat.

Padre Imperio walked down the drive and mounted his mule.

"Bernarda! Bernarda!" Clara yelled.

The cook was plucking a hen when she heard her mistress call. She dropped the bird and ran into the yard.

"Lady! Lady!"

Padre Imperio's silhouette moved away down the gravel road. The sun became a mirage, split by a flock of swallows.

Bernarda wiped her bloody hands on her apron, chewed on her lip, and smiled.

"Time for a shave, Bernarda!"

The girl ran a hand over her face but found not a hair along her jawbone or under her chin.

"I don't care there's nothing there! Bring the soap and razor."

When Bernarda returned, she sat on the bench where the priest had sat. Her mistress stood and shaved her clean face until Padre Imperio vanished into the woods.

"He'll be back," Clara muttered, "just like that other one." Then she soaped Bernarda's face once more and began to tell her about Padre Imperio's scar, as red as an island snake.

Autumn fell, leaving behind a summer of breasts dripping with mother's milk, the scent of shaving foam, and strolls through the yard. Padre Imperio came back to Scarlet Manor one October afternoon, handing the Laguna witch the Bible with the violet cover, now wrapped in brown paper. He did not ask to see Clara or send any message: this Bible, which no one in the house could read, was offered as an apology, a desire for baptism and reconciliation. The one who did not return was the Andalusian landowner. The beech leaves turned color and fell to the ground, slowly burying Clara's heart. The bellowing stags returned, mating in the mountains, the sound of horns colliding. I'll see him any moment, standing on the cobblestone drive, Clara thought. I'll hear his Andalusian accent any minute. But more leaves fell, the stags grew tired of mating, foals gestated, Clara's breasts filled and emptied as she fed her daughter, and the entrance to Scarlet Manor remained empty. The hunters returned with their catch of partridge and rabbit, their gunpowder, and their packs of hounds that peed on the fountain in late afternoon. Clara returned to the grove where she'd first made love, to the red earth of the riverbank, to the smell of rain on stiff leaves, to their names carved in a trunk. She went there so often that her skin began to smell of oak. The smoke in the chimneys returned; the fog of the dead, the biting wind, and sad bell tolls all returned as the leaves continued to fall. Only when the branches were bare, awaiting the first snow, did Clara demand that her mother cast a spell to make him return.

"It won't work," the old woman warned.

"If you want to live in this house, you'll try."

A pot was placed on a stand in the fire, its black belly filled with forget-me-nots, sheep fat, spider legs, a sheaf of the Andalusian's olive-oil-soaked letters, and dried jasmine, among other things. It simmered for an entire day and took hours to cool enough for Clara to drink. She called to him from her bowels, her liver, and her heart, but the potion rotted inside and he did not return.

The first snowfall blanketed the town. Clara Laguna put on her negligees and Moorish pants, and the canopy danced once again to the rhythm of a revenge that only grew more frenzied the longer she waited. But first she took her daughter to the kitchen in search of Bernarda. She wore a satin dressing gown that left her sheer stockings and garters exposed.

"Shave?" the cook grunted.

Clara shook her head, handing her the girl.

"Make sure she's fed," Clara ordered, "and keep her warm. If she dies, I'll kill you. Do you understand?"

Bernarda stood staring at her, not saying a word. Clara's dressing gown revealed a glimpse of one breast, and the cook imagined it in her mouth, smeared with garlic and tomato.

"Answer!" her mistress demanded.

Bernarda looked down at the baby, who had begun to cry and kick her in the ribs. She plugged the child's mouth with a finger coated in chicken blood, and for the first time, Manuela Laguna tasted the sweetness of death.

5

THE FUTURE THE DAISIES foretold came true that winter of 1900. The yard at Scarlet Manor no longer obeyed the weather or the seasons and settled into eternal spring. Not only did the daisies flower, but so did the hydrangea and morning glories near the chestnut tree, the honeysuckle patch, and the rose garden with its multi-hued buds that opened as wide as a man's hand. Even the vegetable garden was continually overgrown with legions of tomatoes, lettuce, and squash. Such prodigious fertility, which only increased over the years, gave them something to talk about in town. The old women on stools and their daughters while sewing or standing over pots suspected the reason was as wet as it was shameful: that yard was fertilized with semen. No one in town wanted to forget that Scarlet Manor had become the most famous, most opulent brothel in the entire province. The baritone at the shop where Clara bought her furniture was partly to thank. He sent customers and acquaintances who were passing through, some as elegant as the diplomat who celebrated his return from far-off lands by making love to the prostitute with the golden eyes. Between clients, Clara stood by the bedroom window and stared out at the cobblestone drive.

Winter turned to spring, but it was all the same to Clara and her gardens. The daisies continued to sprout and the Andalusian failed to return. Next autumn, Clara told herself; of that I'm sure. And if not, then the snows will bring him, but I will see him before I die. It was then that she began to worry about her health. So as not to catch a chill that might become pneumonia, she often received clients wearing a wool chemise under her negligee.

"Your newfound modesty will ruin our business," her mother warned.

"Let me throw the bones to see how long I have to live. I don't want him to come back only to find my grave."

"I told you years ago, I saw in the ribs that he's never coming back. You didn't believe me then; what's different now?"

"This time we're talking about my death."

"But it's the same bones and the same witch's eyesight!"

"Read the bones and tell me if my death is near! Whether or not I believe you is up to me."

Spring light streamed in through the window. Clara sat cross-legged on the bed, opened the sack, and spilled the bones on the sheets as she thought of her Andalusian lover.

"The skull tells me death is not ready for you yet," the old woman predicted.

"When? When will it come?"

"You have many years of life left, but you won't reach old age."

"Then he'll be back before I'm as ugly and wrinkled as you."

The Laguna witch put the bones back into the sack and left the room. Clara brushed her hair as she stared out at the daisies.

Death came instead for the Laguna witch late one night that spring. She had been reading the future and repairing a hymen in one of the noblemen's homes. On her way back to Scarlet Manor, she ventured out of the empty roadside ditch and onto the dark road itself and the sound of chirping crickets surged. Suddenly, a speeding cart ran right over her. A client found her on his way home after an amorous session and a serving of Bernarda's stew. He lifted the old woman into the back of his cart, laying her down with his hoe, scythe, and shovel. The woman's teeth were bloodstained, a trickle of pink spit running down her neck toward her heart. Her good eye was closed; her blind eye shone like a marble. Her crushed hands gripped her treasured sack. The cart was filled with wheat, millet, and flour.

"Let go of the sack," the man said.

The old witch shook her head and sucked her lips. She tried to speak.

"Don't say a word. I'll go get your daughter." The man returned to Scarlet Manor.

"Back for more?" Tomasa asked when he opened the door.

"Tell the owner, tell Clara. Her mother's in my cart, half-dead."

Tomasa found her mistress in the kitchen, eating a meal of potatoes and rabbit, recovering after a long night of revenge.

"I think they've killed your mother," Tomasa said.

Clara ran a hand over her lips, wiping away a bit of gravy.

"A bad weed never dies," she murmured.

Clara met the man in the clay-tiled entryway and followed him out to his cart. She was wearing a long satin dressing gown and a pair of Moorish pants. The wee hours were fresh, with crickets still chirping.

"Madre?"

The old woman's head was resting on a bag of flour.

"Church, church," she croaked.

"But what happened to her?"

"Looks like she was hit by a cart," the man replied.

"Church," the Laguna witch insisted.

"I'll take you."

Clara climbed into the cart and ripped the sack of bones from her mother's hands.

"Up and down these roads with this filthy cat! I knew it would kill you."

"No," the old woman protested.

The cart clattered over the stones that early morning.

"Why does she want to go to the church? Shouldn't we take her to the doctor or the apothecary?" the client asked.

Wiping the spit from her lips with a broken hand, the witch muttered the word *cursed* followed by the word *death*.

"Cursed women only go to church when they're about to die."

Her mother nodded as bloody vomit filled her mouth behind her teeth.

"Hurry!"

The man snapped the reins. Flour inside the man's cart puffed up into a pale cloud. The town's cobblestone streets shined brilliantly with dew, and the sound of hooves echoed against the mildewed stone façades. The town square opened up before them, free of fog. The cart came to a halt in front of the church. Clara climbed out and banged away on the big wooden doors. She cried for Padre Imperio, cold splinters shredding her knuckles.

The priest woke in his spartan room next to the sacristy. He was dreaming about Clara Laguna, salvation in her golden eyes, when he heard the voice in his dream, and banging on the door. Wearing the same gray pajamas he wore in his seminary days, he shuffled along in slippers one of his parishioners had given him, his hair disheveled, his sleep-filled eyes unfocused, his cassock hanging open in place of a robe, and his red scar vivid across his throat, and opened one door. The first rays of light shot in like a lance, followed by Clara in her harem clothes, and the man carrying the Laguna witch's battered body.

"She's dying, Father, she's dying!" Clara clapped her hands on the priest's chest, the first time she had ever touched him. She snatched them back and formed two fists.

Padre Imperio blushed.

"Lay her on a pew, by the altar."

Spring air slipped through cracks in the windows. You could hear the Castilian caballeros rolling over in their graves.

"What happened?"

"I think she was hit by a cart. I found her on the side of the road as I was leaving . . ." The man stared down at the floor. "Forgive me, Father."

"No time for that now. Has she seen the doctor?"

"No. She asked me to bring her here," Clara replied.

Padre Imperio knelt beside the dying woman and ran a hand over her hair. The woman opened her one good eye, murmuring the priest's name. He brought his ear to her bloodstained lips, listened to her soft words. The priest buttoned his cassock, went to the sacristy, and returned a moment later with a stole around his neck and the tray of holy oils. He made the sign of the cross over the old woman's face and gave her last rites. The smell of sorcery she had brought into the room disappeared, giving way to the aroma of blessed oil.

Clara would never forget Padre Imperio's hands tracing a cross in the air, his tenderness in anointing the oil, the faith on his tanned face, the devotion on his lips reciting words in Latin.

"Come. She wants to tell you something."

When Clara's mother saw her daughter's face, she closed her eye. Clara leaned close to her lips and took her by the hand. The old woman whispered a few last words as her soul began to take flight. She squeezed Clara's hand and died.

Beyond the church windows, the sun stretched across the sky in tones of orange and gold.

"She's gone," Clara said, resting a cheek on her mother's chest.

Padre Imperio stared, fascinated by her chestnut hair fanned out over her back, smooth in the sunlight, but he did not touch it.

"Don't be afraid," he said, consoling her. "Your mother went in peace."

"I'm not afraid for her but for me." Clara lifted her head. She was crying.

"But you still have your daughter. Manuela, isn't that right?"

"She's the cause of my misfortune. Her father would have returned if it weren't for her."

"The sun's up now," the client interrupted. "I'd best get to work."

"Please take Clara home."

"Don't ask me to do that, Padre. You must understand, I can't, in broad daylight, and right through town? Look how she's dressed," the man protested, pointing to Clara's Moorish pants visible under her dressing gown.

"Go! I'll walk home," Clara said.

The man hurried out of the church, climbed into his cart with its flour sacks now stained red, and left for his farm.

Morning came to rest on the pew where the corpse lay; it came to rest in Padre Imperio's eyes and in Clara's tears. The priest removed his stole. Clara rose unsteadily to her feet.

"Thank you."

"No need. I'm simply Christ's servant." He smiled.

"I'll be back to sit vigil."

"I'll take care of the paperwork."

"Yes, you know I can't read, not even the Bible you sent. Come read it to me again soon. Goodbye, Padre."

"Wait. You can't go out like that. I'll loan you the charwoman's clothes. They're not very elegant, but at least you won't be out in public in your nightdress."

The priest led Clara to a small broom closet where a rough skirt and white blouse were hanging on a hook.

"Take your time," he said, closing the door.

Clara listened to his footsteps recede.

A short while later she found Padre Imperio kneeling in the side chapel dedicated to Saint Pantolomina of the Flowers. He had covered the old woman's corpse with a blanket and put on his priest's collar.

"I won't bother you any longer. I'll be on my way now."

Padre Imperio turned to look at Clara. The clothes were too big, but her hair was still loose, her eyes the same.

"Wait. Take my mule. I'll come for her another day."

Clara crossed the town square on Padre Imperio's mule and continued down the narrow streets to the gravel road. A few townspeople spied her with her silk dressing gown and harem pants tucked under her arm, her hair loose. Before long the old women in black shawls all heard how that vixen left the church on the priest's mule, wearing his charwoman's clothes, how the Laguna witch lay dead on a pew, run over by a cart. Before long they heard that this was not the priest's first contact with that cursed family: his mule had been seen tied to the gate at Scarlet Manor on more than one occasion. The townspeople, who had adored him from the very first day, began to look at him with suspicion. After all, he was a man under that cassock, a young man just turned thirty. The rumors only intensified when the Laguna witch was buried in the cemetery of cypress trees and magpies one morning. Clara attended with the girls from Scarlet Manor, Padre Imperio officiating in Latin with his holy water. But not one local came, even though the old woman had read their futures in the bones of the cat, repaired their daughters' hymens, and cured their evil eye for years. They wondered why that Laguna—who had never set foot in church until the hour of her death, a witch of all things—should be given a Christian burial. They wondered whether the daughter had asked, and the priest could not refuse. Padre Imperio, however, was simply complying with the deceased's wishes. "Give me my last rites," she had said, "then bury me in hallowed ground so I can rot in peace."

When earth covered the coffin, Padre Imperio offered Clara his sympathies. He took her hand and shook it. She felt her skin grow warm. They both blushed.

"Don't come back to Scarlet Manor, Padre. People talk in this town. I'll have Bernarda bring your mule back tomorrow."

"Close your business. Bring your daughter to be baptized and come to church on Sundays."

"I already told you: I'm committed to my revenge, my abandonment."

"And I told you I will do whatever it takes to save you."

"Save yourself, Padre. You need it more than I. Just leave me be."

Clara Laguna walked down the path past headstones and crosses, in tears, determined to never see Padre Imperio again.

On orders from her mistress, Bernarda carried the blackened pots, the thread for repairing hymens, the sack containing the bones of a cat, and jars of magic ingredients up to the attic. The townspeople and brothel girls forgot all about them as layers of dust grew on top of Clara's mother's possessions. They forgot, too, about the investigation into the death of the Laguna witch after the Civil Guard tried for weeks to find out who was driving the cart that hit her, without any luck. But Clara was never able to forget her mother's things or the night she was killed. From then on, she dedicated herself to the brothel and awaiting her lover's return. She arranged the girls' amorous encounters, looked after distinguished clients waiting in the parlor, offering red wine and games of hearts, and supervised Bernarda's dinners. By now the only clients she allowed into her canopy bed were the elite sent by the baritone — for they demanded the charms of the prostitute with the golden eyes — or any man whose features or smell reminded her of the Andalusian.

Clara tried not to think about Padre Imperio. Whispers about his visits to Scarlet Manor and what happened the day the Laguna witch was killed died down after consecutive Sundays, when the priest recaptured the hearts of his parishioners. The old women in black veils lining the pews still did not understand his sermons, in which pastors set off for hills in search of sheep to be saved from wolves. And yet such verbiage, fired up by faith, always made their eyes brim with tears. The congregation quivered as they followed that flock, eating dry bread and cheese, tormented by lightning, shivering from cold and the tricks beasts played, forging through undergrowth that burned in fiery flames. The censer swung from side to side, Sunday after Sunday, its sweet smell impregnating the old women's veils, the rich women's lace mantillas. After Mass they murmured, "He wouldn't have left his mule in plain sight if he'd been doing anything wrong. Surely he would have hidden it. He was demanding she close the brothel, but she refused — that's how brazen the cursed Laguna is."

Clara bought a dapple-gray horse and cart she used to ride into town. Whenever she and Padre Imperio crossed paths, she would look away, lashing the animal's back with the reins, the Saint Pantolomina of the Flowers card pulsing inside her bra.

One morning in early summer, Clara had Bernarda return the priest's violet-colored Bible. Pigeons were roosting in the bell tower, and old women escaped the heat inside their whitewashed houses. Holding little Manuela on her hip, the cook went into the church through the back door, which opened onto the cemetery hill, and handed the priest his Bible wrapped in brown paper. Padre Imperio asked her to wait on a pew while he went to the sacristy.

"Why?" Bernarda grunted, shrugging her shoulders.

"You'll see. I know why you've brought the child."

Padre Imperio returned wearing his tunic, a jug of holy water in his hand.

"Give me the girl."

Bernarda resisted with a growl.

"I'm not going to hurt her, woman!"

The priest took Manuela in his arms, walked over to the baptismal font, and poured holy water over her head.

When Bernarda arrived back at Scarlet Manor, Clara was waiting in the kitchen.

"Did he pour water on the girl?" Clara asked.

"Water, water," the cook repeated, passing a hand over her dark hair.

"Good. At least he got some of what he wanted," Clara muttered. "No more niceties. It's time for me to get on with my revenge."

Clara pulled the Saint Pantolomina card out of her bra and tossed it behind cans of peaches in the pantry. She looked down at her daughter. Manuela was now a year old, and her eyes had grown even darker.

Manuela Laguna did not have a pampered childhood. Every morning Bernarda repeated the instructions her mistress had given her — "make sure she's fed and keep her warm" — then fattened the girl up as if she were preparing a lamb for slaughter. On cold nights she pulled the child to her body with its smell of stables, putting her to sleep with no more affection than the rhythm of her breath. Whenever Manuela cried, the cook grabbed oranges or tomatoes and juggled. But she did not bother to teach the girl to walk. Manuela took her first steps holding the hand of a regular client who often came into the kitchen to warm his chilblains by the stove with a bowl of stew or plate of roast. Nor did Bernarda teach the girl to speak. The cook had little faith in words and tried to use them as rarely as possible, preferring to communicate through her cooking and the occasional grunt. It took a new prostitute recently arrived from Galicia, a young girl with long, black braids and a eucalyptus heart, before Manuela spoke her first words in a northern accent she never lost.

It was early autumn 1902. Manuela was three years old and — apart from the few babbles and grunts she learned from Bernarda — as mute as the insects that were her friends. For the rest of her life, Manuela Laguna would groom cockroaches and centipedes as pets. She would bathe them in warm water, dry them with a cloth, and any that survived she would fit with a tiny leash requiring an artisan's patience.

When the Galician woman first saw the little girl using a stick to pull cockroaches out from under the cupboard, she thought her mother was the woman with the deformed nose who stood smiling beside her, revealing the blackened teeth of a mule. Manuela was wearing a moth-eaten dress and booties the cook had knit for cold nights.

"What's your name?" the Galician asked.

Manuela stood staring with big eyes, then brandished her stick.

"Aren't you a little terror?" The woman smiled. "Would you like a present?"

In one hand she held the last of summer's blackberries. The little girl dropped her stick, snatched the berries, and stuffed them all into her mouth.

"I'll tell you a story if you tell me your name."

With berry juice dripping down her chin, Manuela grunted and fled to the room where she slept with Bernarda.

As the leaves fell from the beech trees, the Galician woman learned that Manuela — who was always sucking on fruit or a chicken bone under Bernarda's skirt or catching bugs in the garden — could not say a word. At breakfast one morning the spring air surrounding Scarlet Manor drifted in through the kitchen window. Wind lashed the pine forest, blanketing the yard with dry needles. The Galician prostitute sat at the table before a cup of milk and a slice of bread and butter, sweeping crumbs from the table with the end of her braid. Manuela laughed, drew closer, climbed onto the woman's lap, took hold of the braid, and began to sweep.

"Your name is Ma-nue-la." The Galician woman took advantage of this opportunity. "Little Manuela."

First Manuela learned her own name, then Bernarda's, then the names of fruits and vegetables. After that she learned the words for kitchen utensils and the meat used for that night's dinner. Day after day, drenched in the aroma of warm milk and butter, bathed in the golden light of an autumn stretching beyond Scarlet Manor, Manuela learned to imitate the sounds that came out of the Galician woman's mouth. If she did well, she would receive a strange smack of lips on her cheek. She had never felt such a thing; Bernarda only ever licked her as a cow does a calf. It was not long before Manuela learned this was called a kiss.

The cook watched suspiciously the girl's progress with language and her fondness for the Galician woman.

"Lady say food, no cold. No say words." She brought her deformed nose close to the Galician's face, threatening with her quiet eyes, strange odor, and goose-pimpled skin, but she let Manuela continue learning.

"Does the madam tell you how to raise your own child?"

"No me daughter, lady daughter."

This was how the Galician woman learned that Manuela's mother was the woman who always seemed to be waiting for someone to arrive. She spent day and night dressed in diaphanous negligees, dressing gowns, and harem pants, painting her lips red and her eyelids blue, brushing her long hair as her gaze became lost in the cobblestone drive. Whenever she instructed the girls about brothel affairs, she always ended with the same phrase: "Do as you're told. Any day now, his boots will trample those daisies." The Galician had no idea what boots her mistress was referring to but assumed the daisies were those snaking through the front drive. All she cared about was doing her job to earn her keep and teaching that little girl about the world beyond the kitchen and pantry where Bernarda raised her.

When snow covered spring at Scarlet Manor, daisies broke through like chicks from an egg. One day the Galician woman took advantage of a flu that kept the rest of the house's inhabitants, including her madam, bedridden, and took Manuela into the parlor. By the warmth of the fire, she recited the stories of sailors and mermaids she had been told as a child. And so Manuela Laguna learned about a body of water other than the Sunday soup in which chunks of leftover bread and the last of that week's eggs floated. This other was a bluish green and devoured lives on a whim. Manuela would forever repeat its name — sea. She learned, too, about the steep Galician coastline and white-sand beaches where that mass of water splashed or rested, about the faces and smell of the fishermen whose tears were extracted by the sea, tears that now belonged to her, always letting her know the location of the sailors if on a whim she felt the need to kill them, with the violence of her waves.

That sea never changed, nor did the sailors, but Manuela grew and changed in the warmth of those stories, her imagination filled with sea foam and waves, seagulls and cliffs that Castilian hills and oak groves could never understand. Her big eyes grew even larger, her black hair curled like seaweed. By the age of fourteen, Manuela could speak Galician, wring a chicken's neck, pluck and cook it with all of Bernarda's skill. She never suspected that at that age she would learn her mother's lessons as well.

One October morning in 1913, Clara Laguna strode into the kitchen having decided it was time to introduce Manuela to brothel life. Her heart no longer heard the hunters' gunshots in the hills, the bawling stags, the crashing horns, the wind stripping beech trees of leaves, or the ghostly fighting in the fog. Just as the yard at Scarlet Manor had come to a standstill in spring, Clara's heart had come to a stop on the cobblestone drive. All it could hear was the birth and death of the daisies. By now her hair was streaked with gray and the first wrinkles etched around her yellow eyes. She appeared in a purple

negligee and silk dressing gown, her flesh no longer as firm as her revenge. She searched for her daughter's face and found it distracted by
the blood of a chicken she had just finished butchering with Bernarda.

"Shave?" the cook asked, running a hand over her freshly shaven
face.

"No. I didn't come for you but for her." Clara looked at her daughter. "You already know I'm your mother. Come here so I can see you
better."

Manuela trembled in her ragged dress and refused to move. She had
seen this woman flying through the parlor or up the stairs to the second floor, where Manuela was not allowed to go, her body sheathed in
a jumble of transparent fabrics, her brown hair falling to her waist, her
face more beautiful than that of Our Lady of Good Remedy, whose
image the Galician woman slipped under her garter before and after
every amorous assault.

Bernarda pushed the girl with a grunt. Trying not to look directly
at her mistress, the cook anxiously sought a glimpse of white skin she
could remember later, on her own.

"She scares me," Manuela whispered into the cook's chest. "She
looks like a witch."

Not understanding, Bernarda shoved the girl toward her mother.

"Do as you're told!" Clara ordered, a thigh escaping from her
dressing gown.

Manuela walked toward the golden eyes that time and hate had
turned to stone.

"You've got your grandmother's dark eyes and your father's curly
hair. I'll teach you how to oil it." She held her daughter's chin.

Her cold touch made the girl imagine her as a mermaid, instead of
a witch.

"As for the rest, you don't take after anyone. Your skin is too coarse
and hairy for a Laguna." She pinched her daughter's arms. "It'll take
some work to make you the best of all of us."

Clara opened her dressing gown, pulled a roll of bills out of a lace
bag attached to her garter belt, and handed it to the cook.

"You did well. My daughter is no longer your responsibility."

Bernarda grabbed the money. Now she had something for dessert: she would cook the bills in chocolate, savor them as she thought of the delicious thigh that appeared fleetingly a moment ago.

"Come. Hurry up," Clara said as she led her daughter into the parlor. "I've just received garters from the city that will go nicely with your hair. Your father could arrive any minute, so I want you to be prepared."

The first time Manuela Laguna tasted a man, a butter maker from Burgos, she scrubbed her skin raw with a horse brush afterward. Hiding in the stable, she scoured and scoured until her skin no longer smelled of another human. Then she ran to the rose garden, wandering its paths for the rest of the day. Clara searched for Manuela in every room, even the attic with its dusty reminders of her mother. Unable to find her, the prostitutes searched the yard, all to no avail. Manuela dug a hole along one of the back paths. Whenever she heard footsteps on grass crunchy with frost, she slipped into it, covering the opening with branches and leaves. When night fell, the Galician woman feigned it was her time of the month and prayed to Our Lady of Good Remedy that the autumn chill would not kill the girl in a flash. Meanwhile, for the first time in fifteen years, Clara hoped her Andalusian lover would not stride up the daisy-strewn drive.

Late the next morning Clara shook off her sleepless night and headed to the pine forest. She searched for her daughter behind every granite rock rising up between yellowing ferns and beech trees. She called to Manuela, shouting herself hoarse, but still she did not find the girl. She decided to try the oak grove. She had told her daughter about it, how her father carved their love into an ash-gray trunk, how he sang folk songs along the riverbank. All of a sudden, a mule carrying bulging striped saddlebags came down the hill, and Clara distinguished the shape of a black cassock on top. Padre Imperio was on his way to give last rites to a parishioner in the hills. They had not spoken since her mother's funeral. Clara had often seen him over the years but always managed to avoid him. That autumn morning, however, the landscape was vast and deserted.

"Good morning, Padre."

The lines etched by the Caribbean sun on his face in youth were now joined by wrinkles acquired in his Castilian maturity.

"Good morning," Clara repeated.

A saddlebag brushed against her dress.

"Good morning," Padre Imperio replied.

"Is someone sick?"

"A shepherd."

The mule carried on, the bottles of holy oil clinking in the saddlebags.

"Padre?"

"Yes?"

"Are you going to give him his last rites?"

Padre Imperio stopped the mule and turned to look at Clara.

"I'm going to help him die in peace."

Clara recalled the Saint Pantolomina of the Flowers card she had tossed behind the cans of peaches in the pantry all those years ago.

"I hope you get there in time," she said, staring into his dark eyes. "Goodbye, Padre."

The mule set off again. Bottles rattled in the saddlebags, and the priest's black cassock swayed, his hair tousled in the breeze.

"Goodbye, Clara." Padre Imperio's stomach knotted. He felt his red scar strangling him.

When Clara returned to Scarlet Manor, she set about shaving Bernarda in the kitchen. As she ran the razor over her chin, Clara blathered words so fast the cook could hardly understand. A pot of braised tongue simmered on the stove.

"No sad, lady. I know get daughter back."

"You know where Manuela is?"

"I get."

Bernarda picked up the pot with two towels so as not to burn her hands, then walked on tenterhooks around the house and through the yard. Out in the rose garden, her stomach aching from hunger, for she'd chewed on nothing but rose petals since hiding, Manuela smelled that aroma and thought Bernarda had come to feed her. But the moment she crawled out of her hole, she found her mother there, too. Clara grabbed her daughter by the ear and led her back to the house, tugging and scolding. Manuela Laguna swore she would never trust Bernarda again.

It was the Galician woman who treated Manuela's raw skin, applying cold cloths and antiseptic as she told the story of sailors lost in the fog.

Manuela rejoined brothel life as soon as she was better. Never again did she scour herself raw, but after every client she rubbed her body with the first thing at hand, a hairbrush, a string of garlic, or a negligee. Nor did she ever run away again, but they all knew that whenever Manuela was not in the manor or at the general store, she was in the rose garden, talking away her sorrow as she strolled the paths, conversing with the roses like her mother had once done with the dead before she found Bernarda's chin. Manuela washed centipedes in puddles, brushed them with dried petals, and laid them in beds of velvet. Every day she dreamed of the sea, the feel of cold waves as opposed to the warm hands of men.

Manuela's brothel career was short-lived, thanks to her complete lack of charm. "The only thing going for this Laguna is her age," they said in town. Whenever she went to the store for supplies with Bernarda, Manuela sat on the bench in the cart and stared at her feet or shawl. Once there, she simply recited the list to the shopkeeper. It was rumored her voice was as coarse as her skin and witch's eyes. Soon they began to call her "the ugly Laguna."

Manuela's only prominent feature was the Andalusian hair she inherited from her father, hair Clara Laguna combed with olive oil. But this was hardly enough for clients, who readily chose one of the two pretty young girls who had replaced Ludovica, Tomasa, and the shepherd's daughter when their flesh grew flaccid and they left for home. Manuela Laguna was rude to her clients, filling their pockets with cockroaches and spiders if ever they fell asleep. Clients even preferred the Galician, despite her age and expanding hips; at least she listened to them and indulged their heart's desires.

Some mornings Clara forced her daughter to sit under the purple canopy as she talked about the family curse, the icy misfortune that surged through bones, the tears that stabbed like knives, and the nausea of an empty body now that the soul was gone. She also passed on the Laguna witch's advice: "A cursed woman must die in church to die in peace," she said. "And keep a glass of water or wine nearby whenever you speak of curses—it makes a woman thirsty." But above all Clara taught the girl to wait for the Andalusian landowner. In Clara's dreams, his olive-black eyes had not aged, his lips had not been circled by wrinkles, and his legs were still firm and proud in riding breeches and boots as he strode through the door at Scarlet Manor.

"You have to know how to wait to take your revenge," Clara told her daughter.

"Yes, wait," Manuela repeated.

"In waiting, you learn."

"Yes, I'm waiting."

And so Manuela Laguna learned to wait, slipping away to the rose garden, imagining the sea in a yard full of petals and centipedes. She waited ten years, until the winter her mother could not get out of bed, syphilis consuming her pustule-ridden flesh.

When Padre Imperio heard of Clara Laguna's illness, he mailed her the violet-covered Bible from the past. Bernarda brought the package to Clara in bed, and she tore into it with skeletal fingers.

"Return it to the priest, but go in through the back door so no one sees you," Clara ordered. She lay back on her pillow, realizing there were no more tears to cry.

"As soon as you're back, I'll shave you."

"Yes, lady."

A few weeks later, another parcel arrived in the mail. This one was wrapped in colored paper and plastered with fifty stamps. This time Clara had Manuela open it. Inside was a silver-handled brush and mirror set from her most distinguished client, the diplomat, sent to her from a far-off land.

"So I can preen in my grave," Clara remarked, sitting up. "Brush my hair, Manuela. I don't have the strength."

Clara sat staring out the window, offering her now gray mane to her daughter. Streaks of snow slipped down the windowpane. Suddenly, Clara felt a death rattle in her chest, as if someone had thrown earth on her grave. She kneeled in bed, her lips pulled tight as she pounded on the icy glass.

"Open the window! Open it!" she begged her daughter. "Open it! He has to come. Now!"

"It's too cold. Your boils will freeze," Manuela said.

"But I have to see him," Clara moaned. "I've waited so long."

"You can always wait a little longer, Madre. You taught me a woman has to learn to wait." Manuela smiled.

Clara Laguna fell back onto her pillow. She recalled the words her mother whispered in the church just before she died: "Don't wait anymore. He'll never return; I saw it in the bones." Clara recalled the smell of holy oil, of sleepy incense. She recalled Padre Imperio's faith and his hands tracing crosses. For a moment, she wanted to beg Manuela to find the Saint Pantolomina image behind the canned peaches, then take her in the cart to church, where she could die a cursed woman at Padre Imperio's side. But a tremendous rage kept her from uttering the words: rage at the fate of the Laguna women; rage at the waiting daisies; rage at a life wasted on a revenge she saw on her deathbed was useless; rage at the Andalusian and the moonlight piercing the oak trees. Clara clung to the window and heard a *saeta*, smelled olive-soaked curls, and saw a slender young man with tomb-black hair, his boots trampling clumps of daisies. Life slipped through her lips like silt, the cobblestone drive empty of everything but the late afternoon, as the wind howled and the snowflakes swirled.

As Clara's body grew cold, it began to exude the smell of oak, an aroma that filled the room and never left.

It was the Galician woman who prepared the body for burial. No one else would touch that disease-ravaged corpse. According to Clara's wishes, she was dressed in the outfit she'd worn the first time she and the Andalusian made love. Manuela peered in from the doorway. Her mother had left her a prosperous brothel, a chronic revulsion for all physical contact, and the burden of her revenge. At the age of twenty-four, Manuela was now a wealthy but distant woman.

Clara's funeral service and burial were held in the privacy of Scarlet Manor. Despite Padre Imperio's efforts to have her buried in town, Manuela refused. Her wait was finally over. The brothel and her mother's remains belonged to her, and she would do with them as she pleased. Bernarda and the three remaining prostitutes carried the coffin on their shoulders, as if it bore a queen. Following Manuela's instructions, they brought Clara's body to the wild rose garden, where Manuela had dug a grave. Dirt speckled her eyebrows, her nails, her smile. Silence reigned as the women dropped the coffin into the hole, the sound startling birds into flight. When the cook began to shovel, Manuela turned to search for the olive-black eyes her mother had taught her to wait for from the age of fourteen. He'll come on the day of my death, if not before, she had repeated over and over again. But the only olive-colored thing Manuela saw was the scarf tied around the Galician's woman's sore throat. No man came to that remote rose garden that time, and resentment had twisted into a labyrinth of thorny paths.

All the while Padre Imperio was on his knees, crying as he prayed in the confessional of the Saint Pantolomina chapel, biting his lips, begging forgiveness for the soul he had not saved. "I didn't know how," he lamented, pulling the white hair at his temples. "Or I did," he tormented himself, "but I was filled with pride. God forgive the pain

I felt when she proved indifferent to my words or my presence." He wept until the sun set, old women in black shawls crowded around the closed confessional, spying on the priest crying as he whispered and clung to his rosary beads. Padre Imperio was too absorbed in his sorrow, this failure as monumental as his mission in the tropics, to notice. He began to age quickly, in his room next to the sacristy, his dreams tormented by a pair of yellow eyes that accompanied him until death.

After the funeral Manuela packed a suitcase, the excitement of freedom churning in her stomach. She would leave the brothel in the Galician's hands — she had been in charge of certain chores for the last several years, even though her body had grown fleshy — and go in search of the sea. But before she began her journey to the coast, Manuela headed into the rose garden one foggy winter morning to visit her mother's grave for the very last time. She had forbidden everyone from going anywhere near that mound of earth bearing nothing more than a simple iron cross without any name. Manuela bought it from a scrap merchant who'd passed by the same day her mother died. She hoped the thorns would devour and obscure Clara Laguna's grave.

Manuela walked quickly along the paths. As she drew near, the asphyxiating fog was split by a ray of sunshine that fell directly on the grave, revealing a woman kneeled before Clara Laguna's tomb. Manuela saw that it was Bernarda, lit up like a saint. In one hand she held fresh tomatoes and in the other a dish of salt, as if she were about to eat. The cook smiled and looked up at Manuela with docile eyes.

6

WHEN MANUELA LAGUNA first saw the flat sea on the horizon through the train window, she believed a field had frosted over and taken on a bluish tinge.

"What about the cows?" she muttered to herself. "They must have left in search of better grazing."

But as the train drew closer, Manuela could see the roiling waves, and the stories of her childhood burst in her chest. She pressed her hands and nose to the window, fogging up the glass, not moving until the train entered a tunnel and the view went black. By the time the train exited, the sea had disappeared, giving way to typical Galician country houses surrounded by vegetable gardens and farmland. Manuela sat back on the wooden bench, smoothed the wrinkles from her dress, straightened her spine, and placed her hands demurely on her lap, holding her bag. Her fingerprints, a nose print, even a smear of the outline of her mouth remained on the window. She glanced at them, gripped her bag tighter, and studied the passengers across from her, an older woman and her daughter. Manuela smiled despite the stern expression on the woman's face.

The train pulled into La Coruña station. Manuela's hands shook as she picked up her suitcase.

"Goodbye," she said to the woman and her daughter. "Have a nice trip."

Neither replied but Manuela continued to smile.

The moment she reached the platform, her legs began to shake, too. She teetered as if her knees were about to shatter beneath her dress. The engine whistle blew, spewing smoke, filling the platform with the smell of coal.

"Can I take your bags, señorita?" a porter asked.

"Not yet. Thank you."

Through the smell of burning coal, Manuela sensed a thick, salty aroma that stuck to her skin and knew at once he had come to greet her. She sat on a wooden station bench, suitcase on the ground beside her, and inhaled the humid breeze he sent. Around her, porters carried bags, women helped children onto train cars, men helped women, family members embraced, and lovers stared into each other's eyes. No one but Manuela was aware of the smell of the sea. It was noon on a gray day, and frothy clouds dotted the sky.

Manuela Laguna found a hotel near the port. It was small, inexpensive but clean — although at times the tarry smell of sailors lingered in the hallway. She had chosen this particular hotel because of its covered patio with a stone balustrade right across from the beach. There were tables and chairs where guests could read the paper or play cards, even when it rained. Manuela spent every afternoon there even though it was early February. The weather seemed warmer than where she came from, and she did not mind the dewiness; quite the opposite — she liked to feel it on her skin and in her bones for what it really was: the sea's icy, penetrating breath. Manuela's adolescence had taught her that love was uncomfortable, painful even, and her destiny as a Laguna woman was to suffer for love, that her soul would shatter, even though hers was already frozen.

At first she stared at the sea for hours, distinguishing the blue and green tones, listening to the sound of the waves. A staircase led down from the patio onto the street and the beach just across the way. Some days, even if the sun had already set, she would walk over, her boots sinking into white sand, salty wind whipping across her smile. Seagulls cawed in the sky, spiraling down to catch fish. Manuela envied them.

"You think you're the only ones who can touch it," she growled through her teeth.

One day she ventured down to the water. Waves crashed, soaking her boots and the hem of her wool dress. Manuela crouched down and touched and sniffed them, licked her fingers and savored the taste of the sea.

In the mornings Manuela wandered through the port, among the fishing boats. She liked to watch the women mend nets and unload the fish pouring out of them, with their glistening scales and deep-sea smell. She envied the fish, too, even though they were dead, their eyes blank, and she was alive to gut, scale, and cook them as she pleased. More than anything else, Manuela missed cooking alongside Bernarda. One afternoon, overcome by homesickness, she headed into the hotel kitchen, where she found the owner busily preparing a dish of red sea bream.

"Can I help?" Manuela asked, staring longingly at provisions scattered over the marble-topped table.

The owner studied her for a moment, this young woman who had been there for over a month and never spoke to a soul, this dark-eyed girl, plain and unattractive, wearing coarse country dresses and old-fashioned wool hats.

"I used to cook at home, far away from here, and . . ." Manuela began in her Galician accent.

"You're homesick," the woman said. "But you're from here or your parents were — it's clear from your accent."

"No, no. I just lived with someone from Galicia. If you have chicken, I could fry it with onions."

"I do, but I was going to use it in a stew."

"Then let me make it for you. I make a delicious clay-pot stew."

Manuela put on an apron. She plucked and cut the chicken with a dexterity that surprised the owner.

In spring Manuela began collecting shells and any other object the sea wished to give her. She kept them in boxes in her wardrobe, and at night, after her walk along the beach, she liked to sort them by color, size, and taste. She continued to befriend insects, too, trapping cockroaches in the hall and giving them perfumed baths.

One day, as she was walking through the streets near the port, Manuela came upon a store that sold wool and sewing supplies. She bought a petit point pattern of a rose and began working on it in the afternoons as she sat on the patio, listening to news the sea brought her. When she was finished, she bought one with a boat design, then another, until embroidery became a routine part of her life.

Summer arrived and with it bathers in swimsuits, children playing in the sand. Manuela was jealous of those who went into the sea, swam and leaped in the waves. She would watch from the hotel patio, annoyed by the racket, the shouting, the joy. More than one young man approached as she embroidered or walked through the port, wanting to talk or flirt with her, but Manuela was uniformly rude to them all. She had had enough of men forever.

One August evening Manuela set off on one of her walks along the beach, going almost as far as the port. Her slight shadow reflected on the sand. She was carrying her boots, her feet bare to step on the moon. It was humid. She could hear men singing as they stumbled out of a bar. The songs were in a foreign language. Sailors, she thought. Fishing boats from around the world moored in the port, the crew getting drunk before setting out again. The songs grew louder; Manuela knew the sailors were on the beach now. The songs became whistles and shouts. She could make out a few flushed faces, a shiny cap soaked with grease. She hitched up her dress and walked into the sea so he could protect her.

Manuela woke up in a sterile hospital room, in one of several metal beds lined up like the old women in her native town.

"How are you?" a flat voice asked. "Is there someone we can contact?"

Manuela shook her head no.

"It's over now. You'll be fine."

Manuela still had the taste of the sea in her mouth and sand in her teeth.

The hotel owner came to visit. They had grown close working together in the kitchen. The girl's a marvelous cook, the woman thought. I should hire her, but after what happened, she'll likely be scared and want to go home.

"Feeling better?" the woman asked, running a hand over Manuela's forehead. "I hear they were Norwegians off a boat moored here."

"Who?"

She recoiled at the tarry smell of the hotel wafting from the woman's dress.

Another day, strange men came to visit, asking questions she had no idea how to answer. They kept saying: "You were so lucky. You almost drowned!"

When she was discharged a week later, a smiling, bespectacled doctor said: "Now, you learn to swim. If not, no more diving into the sea, you hear? Promise me." He held out his hand.

Manuela stared at the man's skin, then asked for some gloves.

"What for?"

"To wear."

Manuela left the hospital wearing a pair of the gloves nurses used when tending to burn victims. At a store in town, she replaced them with white cotton gloves. Then, at an art gallery, she bought an oil painting of a calm sea, a boat, and seagulls.

The hotel owner was happy to see her. Manuela had dark circles under her eyes and bluish lips, as if the sea remained inside her permanently, using her body as a host.

"Would you like to stay and work in the kitchen? I'd pay you a small wage, and the room would be free. What do you say?"

Manuela accepted the offer. She cooked with her gloves on, never taking them off. She had to buy four or five pair on account of how quickly they soiled. The owner wanted her to take them off when she butchered chickens or rabbits — it wasn't good to be seen walking down the hall with blood-soaked gloves — but she didn't dare ask.

Manuela resumed her afternoons on the patio, embroidering petit point as she stared out at the sea. But never again did she go onto the beach at night.

One morning in late fall, when her dresses had grown too tight, Manuela left without a word, just as she had come, saying goodbye to no one, not even to the salty breeze that followed her to the station.

As inscrutable as ever, Manuela returned to Scarlet Manor. She had acquired two new features: the white cotton gloves she would wear until she died and a growing belly that settled between expanding hips. A few months later, Manuela collapsed on the bed with the purple canopy and, as her mother had done years before, called out to a now more healthy-looking Bernarda.

"Get between my legs and pull the baby out like you would a lamb!"

The cook grunted, spit on her hands, and rubbed them together.

At sundown, Manuela gave birth to an otherworldly little girl she named Olvido. The old women in town whispered about the provenance of a name that meant "forget," but they never learned whether it was chosen out of a desire to erase some event from her past or simply on a whim.

After Olvido was born, Manuela decided to dedicate her life and her daughter's to achieving one goal: the Laguna women were to become decent and garner the town's respect, something they had never had. Her first act was to light a sacrificial bonfire in the yard at Scarlet Manor. She burned the opera sofas, the silk damask curtains, the pictures of harem concubines, the garters, the satin dressing gowns, the *Il Seraglio* negligees and Moorish pants. She burned any potential reminder of the manor's past as an opulent brothel, and she did it before the eyes and noses of the town. They needed to understand that the era of Laguna whores died in those purifying flames.

Since she did not dare burn the girls who worked for her — though she did relish the thought of such sacrifice — Manuela gave them each a stack of bills and told them to go practice the profession elsewhere.

The Galician woman, who had acted as madam over the last year, believed she was safe from this inquisitorial cleansing. She was wrong.

Early one morning, as she ate breakfast in the kitchen, Manuela announced in her northern accent that she, too, must leave.

"But I've nowhere to go. I don't even remember the way back to the sea. This was my home, here, with you . . ."

"I'll pay you enough to jog your memory. Just go. My daughter and I are respectable now."

That night the Galician woman took a rope and hanged herself from the chestnut tree. Her body swung there until morning, like a censer perfuming the town with the eucalyptus exuded by her dead heart. Manuela buried her in the very center of the labyrinthine rose garden. Only she knew which winding paths led there: she did not want to share that grave or that place with anyone. There, multi-hued roses climbed up and over one another, creating a tower. The sun shone down on the earth, and Manuela felt at peace.

Bernarda was the only one to stay on at Scarlet Manor. Manuela was afraid to evict her for fear she'd hang herself from the chestnut tree, too. The town would accuse her of filling the streets with the smell of a horse stable.

When Padre Imperio heard news of the brothel's demise, he cried uncontrollably. Kneeling before Christ on the cross, he thanked God while lamenting, between snuffles and tears, that this destruction came too late. As he pounded his chest to stop his heart from aching with memories, he heard the clatter of uneven floor tiles. Someone had come up behind him.

"It's done, Father. I burned everything evil in Scarlet Manor."

The priest turned to find Manuela. He studied her carefully — her hair, her eyes, her lips, her slim frame — but could see not the slightest resemblance to Clara Laguna.

"Why are you staring? It's me, Manuela. Don't you recognize me?"

Not even her voice resembled her mother's. Clara's had been deep but beautifully melodious; Manuela's was rough, like Bernarda's grunts.

"You did what you had to, my child," Padre Imperio replied.

"Can I come to Mass now like the town nobles and respectable families?"

"God's house is always open, especially to those who need it most," the priest confirmed as he crossed himself.

Manuela Laguna's final act of purification was completed when she met with a lawyer with an office on the main street who'd recently arrived from Segovia. His business was inheritance law, wealth and estate management. Around forty, he had an air of modernity; the black automobile he drove was the envy of all. A man familiar with the region, who had sampled the Eastern pleasures of Scarlet Manor more than once, he was not of the opinion that money was in any way tied to morality and so agreed to represent Manuela. He would manage the fortune her mother had amassed, a fortune he invested in bonds and real estate far from the locals' forked tongues. The Laguna riches, and his own — for he kept a generous share of the profits — soon grew to a sizeable beast.

Manuela now decided to renovate Scarlet Manor. Decency should feel at home if it were to stay, she thought. She painted the smoke-scarred exterior a soft red and the shutters white. She decorated the bedrooms and parlor with flowered cornice moldings, bought a claw-foot tub for the bathroom, and installed a linen closet in the entryway. The only piece of furniture to survive the brothel massacre was the big iron bed, with the purple canopy and wool mattress that had witnessed her mother's carnal exploits, her own birth, and that of her daughter, Olvido. Keeping it was the closest Manuela had ever come to nostalgia.

7

EVERY SUNDAY THE Castilian town woke to the sound of church bells that announced the start of a day dedicated to God and rest. The doves that filled the bell tower stirred and took flight when the man they called "el Tolón" summoned the faithful to Mass, as he stood on piles of bird droppings. The smell of toasted bread, homemade soap, and freshly washed clothes began to flow through the streets and over the fields. Mass started at ten, but Padre Imperio opened the heavy doors at nine-thirty to silently let in parishioners — the rich in their veils, mantillas, and flannel, the poor in their patches and corduroy. The town square would empty, bereft of gossip, mules, and screeching children as the sound of the fountain with its three spouts lulled dogs to sleep, lying in ditches, their snouts pointed skyward. And yet, on that last Sunday in May, as the Republican flag flapped outside the town hall, a neoclassical building across from the church, the square was still full when the priest closed the wooden doors. Peasants and day laborers were protesting in their work clothes, demanding better pay and land reform.

Manuela had attended Sunday Mass ever since she burned the brothel luxuries and received Padre Imperio's blessing — despite Clara's warning that a cursed woman only ever went to church on her deathbed. Manuela rode into town on a cart pulled by a black horse without a name. She dressed in dark clothing, blouses that throttled her neck, wide skirts, shawls knitted in solitude by her gloved hands.

She was not yet thirty-two, but her face had aged—her eyes dull, her cheeks sunken, her lips scored by deep lines. No one, especially no one who had known her mother, could fathom why Manuela Laguna was so ugly. To top it off, she was losing her one charm, her Andalusian hair. Whenever she traveled by cart, mangy clumps would fall out and sail on the wind. Every now and then—and no one could ever explain why—they would appear on top of the maroon Bible on the church altar, floating in the mayor's breakfast bowl or the pharmacist's expertly prepared medicines.

That Sunday, Olvido Laguna went to church for the very first time. She had just turned six and had left Scarlet Manor on only a few occasions. Manuela kept her hidden away, washing her face with insect-infused water, scrubbing it with honeysuckle root and pig bristle, but none of those remedies worked, nor did any other Manuela invented. The child's inexplicable beauty, which her mother strove to eradicate with miracle potions, scouring, and poultices, was not only immune to it all but grew even more intense. The girl would wake up even prettier after these artisanal exfoliations, her skin even softer, her cheekbones more luminous, her lips more attractive with their blood-red curves, her eyes an even purer, more brilliant blue. Olvido's beauty was exceptionally disobedient.

After every failure, Manuela locked herself in her room and wailed with an adolescent fury. Sometimes she cried from morning until afternoon, and when her daughter softly rapped her knuckles against the door, she was startled that the girl was still alive. Manuela thought Olvido would suddenly die—no one could survive the burden of such beauty. The very thought of losing her daughter infuriated Manuela. She wanted to see her married to a rich, honorable man and bear children unencumbered by the Laguna name. Manuela believed this was the only way to earn the townspeople's respect, and until that day arrived, Olvido must live. After that, it didn't matter if her daughter died. After all, how dare she be more beautiful than her grandmother, the whore with the golden eyes?

On this Sunday, Olvido was wearing a new dress, thick wool herringbone. It swathed her from chin to heel as spring pricked at her skin underneath. What bothered Olvido even more than the welts that rose up from her incessant scratching was the blindness her mother imposed. On the way to town she could not see the rockrose in flower or squirrels jumping from branch to branch because a hat with an enormous brim covered her eyes.

When they arrived at church, Manuela helped her daughter out of the cart and smoothed her wrinkled dress before leading her into the 'shadow of the open doorway. Olvido walked into that place of worship and sat with her mother in one of the back pews, the townspeople's glances reeking with disdain. The Laguna family sins necessitated this distant pew. Sitting still on the hard wood, free of her tyrannical hat at last (Manuela had been forced to take it off out of respect for God), the girl watched candle flames flicker for the spirits of the dead, choosing to believe those little lights were fairies. She smiled at them, avoiding her mother's strained yellow grin, and dared to make a few wishes: Dear luminous fairies, please let someone play with me, let my mother's cane break and my father be rid of his fleas. Her hands interlaced, Olvido held her breath after every wish.

In the distance, at the altar, Padre Imperio spread his arms like the eagle he once was and recited from memory the Spanish Empire sermons that gave him his name when he first arrived from the colonies, full of the furor of youth. The church filled once more with Caribbean seas, ambushes amid coconut palms and tobacco plants, and swampy deaths. The devil reappeared in the form of a bayonet, a mosquito, a burning sun, and raging fevers. The old parishioners grew as emotional as ever, though some were still unsure after thirty years what it all meant. Others wept because they finally understood. Not even the young parishioners were immune to the glory and fear sparkling in the priest's dark pupils. They did not know the story behind his name, but tears still sprang from their eyes. Some of the girls suspected Padre Imperio was a distant relative of Imperio Argentina, the star of *La hermana San Sulpicio,* a film they had seen when the summer cinema came to town a few years earlier.

Padre Imperio wiped the sweat from his brow with a linen handkerchief, his white hair glowing like a halo, and crossed himself when he realized some of the pews were empty, that the church was not bursting with faith and the smell of sheep as it had the century before. He lowered his arms. There was no need for the censer to swing from side to side, leaving a perfumed wake among the faithful's prayers. He set his hands on the maroon Bible and sighed.

When it came time to sing the Gloria, Manuela Laguna joined in until all the others heard her and grew silent, a frosty insult rippling through the church. The song eventually returned to the parishioners' lips, but it was now an arctic hymn that would have turned Christ's lips blue. Padre Imperio then offered Communion, but Manuela stayed where she was; there was much to repent before she dared fall in line.

When Mass was over, Olvido was burdened by the weight of her hat once again. She did, however, take advantage of the spectacle before them — day laborers and peasants demanding their rights, chanting ¡Viva! for the new republic. She folded back the brim of her hat and smiled at a few people. Only one person smiled back, a boy playing between the adults' legs. It was the schoolmaster's youngest child. He was seven years old, had a cowlick of brown hair at the base of his neck, gray eyes, a dimpled chin, and plump lips. He curled up the corners of his mouth for Olvido to see, and she remembered that image forever.

"What are you doing? What do you think you're doing?" Manuela had just discovered her daughter's beaming face. "Never smile at strangers!" She squeezed the girl's thin arm. "Let's go home, where I'll teach you to behave like a respectable child!"

The two of them climbed into the cart. Restless, the black horse whinnied. The schoolmaster, a lean man with ash-colored eyes, stared. Manuela nodded, but he did not return the greeting. It's still too soon to forgive the Laguna women their carnal shame, she thought as she seized the reins, but one day they would acknowledge her. She lashed the animal's back. The horse's smell always made her hungry; she would make chicken in egg and almond sauce.

Olvido played with the memory of that gray-eyed boy as her mother raced home. Springtime accosted them as they came close to Scarlet Manor: bees buzzing, fields of poppy and bellflower, the breeze laden with pollen. Manuela took Olvido's hat off only when they reached the iron gate with its funeral bow.

"Get down and open it."

They heard a dog barking.

"I'll never smile at a stranger again. I promise, Madre."

Manuela gripped the reins with gloved hands.

"Be quiet. Wait for me inside."

Olvido walked down the drive worn by the force of Clara Laguna's gaze and waited in the entryway. She leaned against the linen cupboard, the smell of lavender sachets hidden between sheets and towels slipping out through the latticework doors.

When Manuela came in, she pulled out the cane used to beat rugs.

"Take off your dress. I don't want to soil it."

Olvido undid the buttons and the zipper along one side. "This child will cleanse the memory of this family," Manuela muttered as she studied the slight figure stepping out of her daughter's dress. "And if I need to cane her senseless to make that happen, then that is God's will." She brought the cane down on the girl's back. The sun perched high in the afternoon sky, its light mingling with the sound of tender young bones bearing the brunt of the lashes.

Once the cane was back in its bed of clean linen and lavender sachets, the smell of rain washed through the pine trees, and Olvido ran into the yard, to "her father," who lived among the hydrangea and morning glories. The girl liked to pretend a curse had turned her father into the scrawny black flea-bitten dog who frequented the yard.

"Papi, Papi! Look what I brought you!" Olvido pulled two slices of cinnamon cake and some chorizo out of a little pouch.

At the sight of such treats the dog's eyes sparkled and his snout grew wet, and he crept toward the girl wagging a tattered tail.

"Oh, Papi, I missed you," Olvido said, hugging him around the neck as he licked her face. "That tickles!" She opened her little hands and the dog gobbled up the treats, then she petted his head. "It's good, isn't it, Papi? You have to eat if you want to get better."

The dog licked her with a desperate love.

"Now rest for a while on your bed of leaves, and your fleas will soon be gone. I asked some fairies in church to get rid of them. Bye, Papi. I'm going to play with my friend."

Olvido walked away from the dog's dark eyes. She wandered through the tomatoes, lettuce, and squash in the garden, her back stinging all the way. The sun hid behind a raft of clouds as Olvido walked into the clearing surrounded by lush honeysuckle. It began to rain.

"Hi," she greeted the bushiest plant. "What do you want to play?" she asked.

There was a whisper of leaves and stalks rustling.

"You always want to play that."

Olvido picked up a long vine and began to jump rope. It started to rain harder, the water soothing her burning back.

"When I'm bigger, I'm going to learn magic and undo the spell that bewitched you and my papi. Then you'll have hands and feet again, and blond, blond hair that I'll braid for you." Her brow was damp and her shoes sank into rain-soaked earth.

Olvido returned home when the smell of chicken in egg and almond sauce filled the garden. Manuela had been preparing dishes from her childhood ever since Bernarda died a few months earlier in an accident in the stable. One morning, after finishing her chores, the cook decided to hide away among bags of alfalfa to suck on her greatest treasure: a scrap of Clara Laguna's shroud. The black horse inhaled the odor she emanated, mistaking it for a mare in heat. He rammed the stall door until it opened, then he shot out and kicked the bags of alfalfa in glee. Bernarda's skull shattered at the first strike, her brains lying naked on their yellow hiding spot, the scrap of shroud between her lips. They buried her at the cemetery in town. "After all, she never practiced the profession, and her simple nature shielded her from sin," Padre Imperio declared. It was winter, and snow streamed from the sky. The pine forest and hills around the graveyard reeked of mare for weeks.

Manuela moved down to Bernarda's room, next to the pantry, the room where she was raised. The smell of whitewashed walls and fresh provisions was comforting. She kept the straight razor her mother had used to shave the cook, which Bernarda continued to use in memory of her mistress. You could have been with me much longer, Manuela thought as she lightly fried the pieces of chicken, but you always did prefer her over me.

After lunch, Olvido went to her room on the second floor for a siesta, wishing time would speed up to her favorite part of the day. After dinner, she and her mother would sit in the parlor, in front of the fire, and Manuela would tell stories. Her voice lost its gruffness as she spoke of the sea, of beaches and cliffs. Although every now and then she would glare at Olvido and snap: "I did it for you."

"Did what, Madre?"

"Asked her to leave."

"Who?"

"She should have understood and never hung herself from the chestnut tree."

"Who did that, Madre?"

"Be quiet. You'll make it up to me."

Manuela would fill the fireplace with logs once more and recite another story to keep the flame alive.

Olvido grew up with Mass, her mother's stories, savory chicken dishes, remedies, and beatings. Manuela was sure her plans for her daughter would come to pass, but one thing did worry her: Olvido was illiterate. For several years Manuela tried to get her into school. Every September she put on her plainest dress and headed through town. The rows of women who had taken their mothers' place were now split into two camps. Their whispers had grown silent; they kept an eye out for traces of treasonous behavior instead. Whenever Manuela passed, they would simply look her up and down and purse their lips.

The school was a two-story ancestral home with mildewed walls and a vine-covered roof littered with cat feces — it was their favorite place to mate, screeching in a flood of moonlight.

"Your daughter doesn't need an education. No doubt she'll practice the same lowly profession as you, and there's no need to be literate for that," the schoolmaster said to Manuela Laguna year after year, his gray eyes flashing.

"My daughter will be respectable and must have an education!"

"I told you to go and never come back. As long as I'm in charge, there's no point wasting your breath or the soles of your shoes."

At that, Manuela would march down to the town hall to file a complaint.

"My daughter has a right to go to school," she would tell an official. "Times have changed. This I know, even if I can't read it in the paper."

"Place an X here," the middle-aged man would say, smiling. "I'll fill out the form, and you'll hear from us soon."

But no reply ever came to Scarlet Manor or anywhere else, as if the Lagunas did not exist — or no one wanted to admit they did.

The summer after Olvido turned eleven, several men seized the Republican flag flapping outside town hall and burned it in the square; meanwhile, red wine stuck like a blood clot in the craw of others at the tavern. Silence and sidelong glances clogged the air along with smoke from unfiltered cigarettes. The Spanish Civil War had begun.

In September the usual hunters did not come with their packs of hounds and handsome rifles. The town reeked of gunpowder from the killing of friends and relatives rather than stags and wild boar. Many, including the schoolmaster, enlisted to fight on the front. A kind-looking young miss was sent from the provincial capital to replace him. The minute Manuela heard, she went to town and waited by the door until school was out. The children stared at her white gloves as they left, certain they hid a wolf's claws.

"Good afternoon, señorita. I would like you to allow my only daughter into your temple of knowledge. She's eleven years old and can neither read nor write."

"Eleven years old and illiterate? That's atrocious!" The young miss glanced down at Manuela's cotton-sheathed hands. "Say no more. Bring her tomorrow and we'll straighten this out."

From the time her daughter turned six, Manuela had had everything ready for the first day of school: colored pencils, sheets of paper, a book bag, and, most important of all, a white cotton hat she had enlarged as each year passed and Olvido grew. Manuela was determined to hide the girl's face; life had taught her that nothing brought dishonor like extreme beauty, and school would be full of adolescent boys.

Manuela woke her daughter at dawn and led Olvido to her room. Armed with sewing scissors, she cut a swath of hair to create bangs that fell below Olvido's eyes.

"Now, listen very carefully: if you brush your hair from your face, I will cane you." Lilac-colored light from the yard infused the room.

"Yes, Madre."

Manuela put the white hat on her daughter's head; stiff strands of black hair poked through the lace border encircling her forehead.

"Now, go bathe and put on the clothes I set out for you."

"Yes, Madre."

In the pine forest a magpie cawed, and the sound of distant gunshots drifted on the breeze.

Olvido put on an ankle-length brown wool dress and slid her feet into boots two sizes too big. She had toast with butter and a glass of milk, then went into the entryway to wait for her mother. Standing on the clay tiles, watching her approach with a leather strap in her gloved hand, Olvido shivered. The smell of toasted bread still pervaded the house. Any thought of a caress or a kiss was swept from Olvido's mind. Silently, Manuela circled the girl's throat with the strap and sewed the ends to either side of her hat.

"I'll undo this when you get home."

"But it looks like the helmets soldiers wear to war."

"Don't be ridiculous."

A cool fog still lay across that September morning, and Manuela disappeared into it on her way to the stable. Olvido watched this phantom breath swallow her whole, afraid the morning might be only a dream. She so wanted to go to school and make friends. She rubbed the bangs across her eyes and said her name out loud. The horse's black head, with his crystal gaze and curly mane, emerged from the fog, then his square chest in its harness and his big horseshoed hooves that clattered like rain. Next she saw the cart and, on the seat, Manuela's blood-red shawl and spite-filled face.

The fog disappeared as they came into town. The horse's hooves on cobblestones sounded like a hailstorm. As the cart crossed the town square, a few women carrying laundry baskets watched it go down the street toward the school.

Children's voices drifted out through the window. They were reciting the names of all the rivers in Spain.

"Go on in. It'll be fine. It's respectable to learn how to read and write."

Olvido got down from the cart. Her mother snapped the reins and disappeared to the rumble of a pending storm. Olvido put her hand on the doorknob and pushed into the unknown. The door opened slowly. She walked down the hall to the room where the voices could be heard. Maps hung on the side walls, and a chalkboard was situated at the front. Sitting at their desks, her classmates stared. Olvido smiled, feeling every pair of eyes on her clothes, on her skin. As the teacher introduced the "new girl," Olvido walked toward her desk, but someone tripped her and she fell. A tide of laughter rippled through the classroom.

"Clumsy! You're a stupid, clumsy monster!"

The young schoolteacher helped Olvido to her feet, leading her by the arm to the last row of desks. Then, unable to control her students, she began to write a list of mountain ranges on the board.

Olvido Laguna crumpled over her desk and cried silently. Tears bounced on her desk as a sudden rainstorm pelted the windows.

"Monsters don't know how to cry, dummy! Don't you know anything?" the children taunted.

Olvido shut her eyes. She imagined she was climbing onto the thrashed back of her horse, burying her face in its black mane as she disappeared into the woods.

"Don't you have anything to say, stupid? Don't you know how to speak? Answer, ugly monster!"

A tall boy in the front row stood and shouted: "Shut up! Leave her alone!"

His classmates looked up in surprise. It was the schoolmaster's son, the boy who smiled at Olvido after church these last few years. His name was Esteban.

"You shut up!" Olvido replied, wiping away her tears. "I don't need anyone to defend me! I can take care of myself."

The boy's gray eyes traveled to the last row of desks to meet Olvido's enraged gaze. The second their eyes met, the young schoolteacher from the city forgot all about her list of mountain ranges, her naughty pupils, and their hateful parents.

That night, for the first time, Esteban did not think about trenches, rifles firing in the name of freedom, and bodies decomposing beneath the pines, put to death for treason. He did not think about his father or the war that hovered over town like a vulture. He did think about Olvido's eyes staring at him through strands of dark hair and what happened after school, when his classmates leaped on her, determined to rip off her white hat as she ate a piece of cinnamon cake. He remembered how fearful she'd been as he confronted the boys, yelling, "Cowards! Animals! You don't hit a girl!" He remembered their insults, the taunts, and the bared teeth threatening him. He remembered that pang he first felt at the church door, as she cowered like an animal trying to escape the rain in a cave, her body shoved against the mildewed wall, her lips dusted with cinnamon. He thought about how much he wanted to touch them but didn't dare, how he wanted to say,

"Don't be scared. I'll always protect you, and when I'm bigger, I'll enlist in my father's war." But he said nothing, just held out a hand to help her, which she refused, throwing the cake in his face and running off. "I don't need anyone to defend me! I don't need anyone!" she yelled.

Olvido ran home to Scarlet Manor through the pine forest. The leather strap had come undone on one side of her hat. The moment she saw her mother leaning against the iron gate, waiting for her under the funeral bow, she thought of the boy's gray eyes, big and brave, and the gloveless hand that offered help. Olvido cried not a single tear as Manuela caned her: the only thing that could hurt her now was if she never saw Esteban again.

The young schoolteacher from the city did not expect to see Olvido again, but she was wrong. Olvido continued to come to class, wearing her hat. Sitting at a desk in the back row, she covered sheets of paper with simple strokes at first, progressing to meaningless primer phrases such as "mi mamá me mima." In time, the taunts no longer bothered her. Whenever they were hurled, she felt Esteban's stormy eyes, his soldier's haircut, and his chin held high, defying them all.

"I told you chickens to leave her alone!"

"You leave me alone! I can defend myself!"

The boy's gaze would grow even stormier, and he would purse his lips, but he never gave up.

One morning in May of 1937, Esteban's father was found dead on the road that led through the pine forest to town. He was on his way home for a few days' leave, but someone ended that, blasting his torso open with a shotgun. For a time it was rumored that the other side not only killed him but ripped out his intestines as well.

Her face flushed, the young schoolteacher from the city announced the news in class.

"Our dear Esteban will not be in class today. Let's say a prayer for his entrails," she said, coughing, "for his father, I mean, who went to heaven in a warrior's clothes."

It took Olvido Laguna, who had just turned twelve, a moment to process what happened. Then, to the surprise of her teacher and class-mates, she stood and ran from the room.

Olvido headed through the square and up the hill to the cemetery. She found a place to hide among headstones and crosses, not far from where the schoolmaster's coffin was being lowered into his grave. The funeral cortège was a cluster of black surrounding the hole. The widow leaned against her daughter, the daughter supporting her mother's pain, and squeezed her son's arm with her hand, disfigured by years of mending socks. Behind the family were several townspeople. At the head of them all, Padre Imperio splashed holy water and delivered his words in Latin over the grave. The coffin bumped the ground as it hit bottom, and the group began to splinter. The only ones who stood firm were the widow and her daughter; even Esteban walked away. He would enlist, disguise his thirteen years in the vengeance of a sixteen-year-old boy, and kill the traitors who murdered his father. Olvido fol-lowed. Crickets sang as the sun burned the ground, which smelled like a mash of poppies and daisies.

"Hi." Olvido stepped out from behind a cross.

Esteban's heart fell onto the headstone of Paquita Muñoz, dead and buried at the age of six.

"They told us at school that your father died."

"They killed him, the traitors. It's different. What do you want?" Esteban was wearing a brown corduroy suit with a black armband.

"I ran here because I've never seen a funeral."

"Liar." The boy stuffed a hand into his pocket.

Olvido averted her eyes from his and stared into the furrow in his chin.

"And I came to comfort you because I thought you'd be sad."

"I'll be a soldier soon, and soldiers can't be sad. They have to be brave to go fight on the front."

"I think you must be a little sad."

"Even if I were, I wouldn't want your help. You never let me de-fend you."

"I can go if you like."

"No. The cemetery is no place for a girl. I'll walk you home. Soldiers have a duty to watch over women."

The breeze from the pine forest carried the smell of rockrose, thyme, and ferns up to the treetops. Esteban walked with his head down, while Olvido chattered about the honeysuckle that grew in her yard and the black horse that had the longest, curliest mane in the world. Esteban would glance at her every now and then, and every time he caught her staring at his hands. Worried, he glanced down to see whether his nails might be dirty. Suddenly, Olvido tripped over a rock and bumped into his arm.

"Sorry," she apologized, brushing her bangs from her eyes.

"That's all right. Do you want me to take your hand?"

Olvido had imagined his touch over and over again. She had even dreamed of it. Skin without white cotton gloves.

"I'll be fine."

"Gosh, you're stubborn."

"So are you!"

"I kept insisting because you did. A soldier shouldn't let a woman be insulted. Besides, you're not like the other girls."

"Look, there's my house."

The roof of Scarlet Manor filled the horizon. They walked in silence until they could see the front of the house, peeking out through the rain and the yard's fertile mist. A shiver ran through Esteban's body. His parents had told him about that hellish house, that wicked women lived there. He remembered how he and his friends would play a game that made the hair on their arms stand on end: "You're a chicken if you don't touch the gate at Scarlet Manor. Coward! Chicken!"

His mouth dry, Esteban would run to touch the iron bars and race back to his friends in the forest to celebrate his bravery.

"You'd better go. My mother will be angry if she sees you. She's got quite a temper."

The aroma of the dish Manuela had simmering on the stove floated out through a window.

"It smells delicious."

"My mother's making lunch. She's an excellent cook. If she didn't get so angry, I'd ask if you could stay for lunch."

"I have to go home to my mother and sister, but thanks."

A magpie flew overhead, cawing, followed by a hollow voice: "Olvido Laguna." Manuela appeared, jailed behind the iron gate. "What are you doing with this boy?"

"Madre, I didn't hear you. He, he . . ." Olvido stammered. "He's the schoolmaster's son. His name is Esteban. I went to his father's funeral and —"

"So you're the schoolmaster's son," Manuela interrupted, scrutinizing the boy. "Yes, indeed. You have his gray eyes."

"I was just leaving . . . My mother's waiting for me at home. See you tomorrow, Olvido," Esteban said, wringing his hands.

"Hold on, boy. Don't be in such a hurry. Would you like to come in for a minute and taste what I'm cooking?" Manuela smiled. "It's a very special dish."

"Thank you, but they're expecting me at home." Esteban's voice shook.

"Olvido, tell your little friend not to be rude and accept my invitation." Manuela's dark eyes narrowed.

"Please come in, Esteban. My mother's cooking is delicious; you'll see."

White cotton gloves wrapped around iron bars and pulled the gate open.

"I'll just have a little taste and then go home."

Esteban walked up the daisy-strewn cobblestone drive. He did not dare look around; it was as if the hydrangea and morning glories were stalking him, as if they wanted to sink their teeth into him, like prey. He followed Olvido and her mother into the clay-tiled entryway that smelled of herbs and garlic.

The kitchen was huge. In the middle was a wide table where Manuela Laguna eviscerated chickens by the light of the window. Up against the walls were cupboards, the dishes covered with blue checked cloths.

On top were straw baskets filled with fruit and vegetables. Pots and pans, ropes of garlic and onions hung from the ceiling.

"Come over to the stove, boy. It smells good, doesn't it?"

"Yes, señora." Esteban felt dizzy.

Manuela picked up a spoon and stirred the dish with delight.

"It's tripe with herbs and garlic. Be a good boy and try some." She scooped up a piece of meat, held it steaming in the spoon. She blew on it several times, offering it to Esteban with a smile. The boy looked at Olvido as he took a bite and slowly chewed. It was hot.

"Could I have another taste?"

"Of course, boy! Eat, eat till you're full," Manuela replied, handing him the spoon.

Esteban gulped down several pieces of meat.

"He's hungrier than a rat," Manuela murmured.

Olvido and her mother listened as the boy slurped up some sauce.

"Your daughter's right: you're an excellent cook," Esteban said with his mouth full. "But I better go. My mother will be worried."

"Listen carefully to what I'm about to say, boy. Tell your mother you've been at Scarlet Manor, and tell her what you ate. Oh, and don't even think about coming back. I don't want to see you near my daughter ever again!" Manuela's nose ended in a sharp point. "Now go before I gut you like a rooster!"

"Madre!"

Esteban stood staring at Manuela's white cotton gloves before racing from the kitchen without saying goodbye. He crossed the parlor, ran down the hall, into the clay-tiled entryway, and out into the yard. From deep inside he could hear the aromatic cadence of his father's voice repeating: "Go, son! Go and never come back! Run, run . . ." Esteban pulled open the iron gate and fled into the pine forest.

8

ESTEBAN LIVED IN a stone house with black balconies on a narrow street near the school.

"I'm not hungry. I have a headache," he told his mother and sister, waiting for him in the dining room before a soup tureen.

Esteban locked himself in his room, the scent of herbs and garlic trailing behind him. He slept or tried to sleep the rest of the day, twisting in the sheets as he thought of Olvido's eyes. He did not get up for dinner and spent the night sweating through nightmares of Manuela Laguna, until dawn broke into a purple blanket of wool.

A shepherd had already seen this in a foul premonition: just after noon, a bomb exploded inside the school. A few seconds earlier what sounded like the buzzing of a giant gadfly was heard in the streets. Up above the townspeople's gaping mouths came a low-flying silver plane. Several peasant women, who saw it first in their fields, confused it with those silver coffee sets sent by relatives, made of that precious metal the rich women had and that they coveted so, but it passed them by, continuing on to the town square. Women gathered around the fountain commented with trepidation on where that blindingly polished plane might have come from and how striking the pilot looked — this one was wearing a blood-red scarf, hair blowing in the wind, head tilted to one side, glasses shattered.

As the plane passed over the square, it lost a bomb attached to one side. A roar splintered the air and the school disappeared. The plane continued on its ghostly trajectory until it crashed into the horizon, its flames creating the most beautiful, fleeting sunset anyone had ever seen.

The plane itself was swallowed by the hills, but for a long while after, the school's ruins lay scattered about the town. Pieces of its vine-covered roof, cat feces, and mildewed walls stuck in the women's brooms, and they grew afraid to sweep with these constant reminders of death. One hot morning on his way to offer a parishioner his last rites, Padre Imperio felt thirsty and drank from the fountain in the square. Suddenly tormented by the purest terrors of his youth, he raced to the church and climbed into the pulpit that evening to announce that they were under surveillance by the devil, his bloody eye spying on the town from the fountain basin. Caught up by Padre Imperio's novena prayers, the town pharmacist rescued what scientific study determined to be a war trophy worthy of the highest honors: it was, without a doubt, the young schoolteacher's eye, with its bright, brown pupil. The woman had exploded along with the school, and her body rained down on the town like biblical hail.

"Thank God that plane dropped its bomb after midday when school was out," Padre Imperio declared. "Death is wise and in its wisdom decides when to attack."

Yet nothing could erase the smell of the bomb from that place. The townspeople did not want to rebuild on that piece of land. For years parents and grandparents took their young children and grandchildren there, to learn to recognize the smell of war.

Olvido Laguna was walking through the forest to Scarlet Manor when the bomb hit. She felt the pine tops and the branches of the beech trees shake. Throwing herself to the ground, she waited for war to come and kill her. But war was slow; it took its time. Bored, she stared at a pinecone resting on a bed of yellow needles. Niches without pine nuts, like a cemetery without any dead. Then Olvido thought she heard her name, off in the distance. She was afraid someone had ratted her out and war was coming to kill her, repeating her name with its long rifle larynx. "Olvido, Olvido." Her name drew closer, faster. She wondered whether the bullets would hurt when they entered her body, whether war would rip out her guts, like it did Esteban's father. She thought of the chickens her mother plucked and eviscerated, the soft whiff that lingered in kitchen corners, the color of blood on the table and floor tiles; she thought of Manuela gripping the knife and plunging it into the bird's flesh. Olvido retched, and her name fell behind her. "Olvido." She felt a hand through her blouse and knew that touch belonged not to war but to the gray-eyed boy. Drops of blood fell onto the pinecone.

"A bomb fell off a plane and blew up the school," Esteban said, reaching down to help Olvido stand. "The teacher was inside and exploded, too."

Olvido wanted to hold him, to plaster her life to his dirty shirt.

"I came to make sure you were all right."

"Your ear is bleeding."

"Oh, that." The boy raised a hand to his right ear. "Don't worry, it happens to soldiers when a bomb goes off nearby. My father told me in a letter, hoping it would stop me from enlisting. The only trouble is I'm a bit deaf right now, but I should be fine soon."

"Let me help you," Olvido said, pulling a handkerchief from her skirt pocket.

"Oh, okay. But just for a minute."

The breeze was heavy with human laments and the smell of war, but for Esteban, inhaling the nearness of Olvido, the tragedy had become a delight.

"You're not hurt?" he asked, wondering if he might be able to touch her, too.

"No. Just a little scared," she replied, raising her voice. "I got down on the ground in case a bomb fell in the forest. There. All better." Olvido put the stained handkerchief back into her pocket. "I better get home. My mother will be worried. Goodbye, then."

"Goodbye."

Olvido turned and took a few steps. Esteban stayed where he was. His hands were cold and his throat hurt. Suddenly, Olvido turned to look at him and said: "I was just thinking, if the school blew up and the teacher's dead, we won't be able to see each other again. My mother only lets me out to go to school."

"Maybe they'll find somewhere else for us to study and get a new teacher."

"But what if they don't?"

"Then we'll see each other at church, like the first time." Esteban smiled.

"Yes, but I'll never learn to read or write. Without a school or a teacher, and in wartime, who'll teach me?" Olvido brushed the bangs from her eyes.

"I could. When I'm older, when I get back from the war, I'm going to be a teacher like my father."

"Would you do that?"

"You'll be my first pupil."

"So you'll come to my house?"

"Scarlet Manor?"

Esteban could hear his father's booming words deep inside his head: "Don't go back there, son. Don't ever go back!"

"Of course. Where else?" Olvido asked.

"After your mother's threat, I don't think I should go back."

"She was awful the other day. I understand why you don't want to go. But she doesn't have to know. Every Thursday at five, she locks the door when she goes to see the lawyer on business. Then she shops at the general store and isn't back until at least eight o'clock." Esteban felt a blue noose around his neck. "We'd have plenty of time for lessons, and you'd never cross paths. What do you think?"

"Are you sure she won't find out?"

"Yes."

"What if she comes home early?"

"She never does. Trust me."

"All right."

As they went their separate ways, Olvido listened to each step Esteban took on the needles and ferns until she reached the gates with their funeral bow. He could not hear her footsteps but felt them in his gut until he reached the edge of town, where he faced the misfortune once again. Bits of the school lay in the streets, and an ashy rain soiled people's hair.

Esteban stayed in his room until Thursday. Hanging on one wall was a picture of his father in a corduroy jacket and black tie, standing proudly in front of the school.

"I tried to keep my word, Padre," he said, his heart full of sorrow. "I have to go. It would be rude not to. I promise I'll be careful."

An herb and garlic cramp twisted his stomach, and a forceful thrust of vomit rose to his mouth.

"Don't keep on about it, Padre. I have to go."

Esteban belched at his father's photo and fell into a deep sleep on a patched old mattress. In his dreams he was trapped among the hydrangea and morning glories at Scarlet Manor, unable to find Olvido in all that vegetation, unable to escape that floral embrace as it snapped at his penis, unable to die when Manuela Laguna appeared out of a sudden fog, her gloves stained with chicken blood as she stared at his crotch, dented by flowery tooth marks.

Esteban's mother attributed his behavior to the loss of his father. Mending socks with her daughter, she wondered if she should send him to the store or tell him to fix the leaky roof, work a good distraction for his soul. In the end, she decided to leave her son alone, continuing to baste her own life with determined stitches.

On Thursday at five o'clock, wearing his Sunday best and a cardboard cup fashioned to protect his crotch against plant fangs, Esteban did exactly as Olvido told him. He climbed over the stone wall that surrounded the yard, found the entrance to the rose garden but carried on, avoiding it, crossing the honeysuckle clearing and the garden with its tomatoes, lettuce, and squash. Accompanied by an entourage of bees, he reached the porch at the back of the house, where years before Clara Laguna had shaved Bernarda, where sofas and a wicker table now sagged under the weight of so many siestas.

"You came." Olvido's voice emerged from beside an ivy-laden trellis climbing the wall. "I was afraid you'd change your mind."

"A soldier always keeps his word."

Esteban brought his hand to the cardboard cup; he was finding it hard to breathe. Even though he had reached his destination free of leafy attacks or Manuela Laguna wringing his neck with bloody gloves, he still felt in peril.

Olvido was not wearing the hat with the cotton lace border she wore to school or the one with the wide brim she wore to church. Her bangs were pushed back from her forehead.

"We'll climb up to my window," she said, pointing to the trellis. "It's how I get out when my mother locks me in."

But Esteban was unable to move. Olvido held out her hand. He took it, blushing at her beauty. For the first time she felt his strong, sun-toasted touch, the texture of skin quite different from white cotton.

"Do you like my hands?"

"You have very long fingers . . ."

The springtime sky was bright. They looked at each other, unsure what to say. The breeze, sparkling with pollen, wrapped around them. Whispers of life could be heard from every corner of the yard. Cicadas, blackbirds, cats in heat. Esteban kissed Olvido on the cheek. She returned it with a kiss on the lips. The boy's cup crunched against his Sunday pants, and Olvido thought kisses crunched like the skin of crisply fried chicken.

"If you ever see a pot of chrysanthemums in my window, it means my mother's plans changed and you should go," Olvido warned as they climbed the trellis.

"I hope that never happens."

Olvido's room was large but simple. A blue rug on the wood floor, an iron bed against the wall opposite the window, an armchair with broken springs upholstered in floral fabric, and, in one corner, a desk with a chair and a stool she had put there that afternoon for her teacher.

"Don't you have any photos of your father?" Esteban asked.

The oil painting Manuela Laguna bought in Galicia hung over the bed. A calm sea, boats, and seagulls.

"I never knew my father." Olvido was ashamed to admit the only father ever to love her was a black, flea-bitten mutt now dead a few years.

Esteban stroked her hair. He could no longer recall how to read or write, his multiplication tables, or the Tajo River tributaries his father had made him write a hundred times. With Olvido Laguna, all Esteban knew how to do was look at her.

That September a temporary classroom was erected in a room with a leaky roof and flea-infested carpet inside the town hall. While they waited for another, more fortunate teacher to be sent from the city — a teacher who never arrived — Padre Imperio taught the children to read and write and gave a few basic lessons in geography and math. Olvido Laguna went back to school, but Esteban still tutored her at home every Thursday. The boy no longer took such monumental naps, but at night he still dreamed of hydrangea and morning glories devouring his member, of chicken necks dripping with blood. At thirteen, Esteban already knew everything Padre Imperio could teach and so did not go to the improvised school. Instead he spent his days in the hills looking for stray bullets and bits of bombs with the few children who'd remained his friends since the day he defended Olvido. He took his slingshot to hunt pigeons and rabbits his mother stewed in between mending sock after sock.

Esteban learned to live with the fear that Manuela Laguna might suddenly appear in Olvido's room and wring his neck with her gloved hands. But she continued to meet with her lawyer, one of the few men between the ages of fifteen and sixty still in town. His money and influence afforded him a medical exception, a case of chronic liver disease that prevented him from fighting on the front. He was still seen driving his black cockroach car, but the old women in black shawls no longer paid attention when they heard its futuristic purr. They stayed inside, twisting handkerchiefs or rosary beads, waiting for sons and grandsons to come home from war. Some nights, camouflaged by the darkened sky, they would slip from one house to another to exchange tales of woe, chickpeas for sugar, or rumors of trenches and fugitives in the hills.

In the spring of 1939, men in blue shirts in the back of trucks stormed the town square chanting victory. The Spanish Civil War had ended. Not a single piece of chorizo from the last slaughter or gallon jug of wine survived the night; they devoured everything that passed their lips and blacked out on the tables, snoring in their glory.

By now Esteban was fifteen, and his mother found him work as a carpenter's apprentice. He assured Olvido he would become a teacher, like his father, but — his studies interrupted by war and the destruction of the school — he would have to finish high school and move to the city to get a degree. A scholarship was the only way; he did not earn enough and his mother would never earn that much, no matter how many socks she and her daughter mended.

Esteban worked at the carpenter's shop from Monday to Saturday until eight o'clock. Every Thursday, as the hour of his meeting with Olvido drew near, splinters rammed under his nails and sawdust filled his mouth, settling on his heart. Sometimes it was as if the sea from the picture in Olvido's room speckled the workshop walls. He imagined the smell and sound of it as a distraction to keep from crying.

"What's the matter with you, boy?" his boss demanded. "Thursday is not your day! You don't get anything right. You sanded the wrong side of the wine-barrel boards." He slapped Esteban on the back of the head.

"Can I leave now?"

"Fix those boards and then you can go."

Esteban dove into the task with renewed energy. His hands shook and he sanded his thumbs instead of the wood, drops of blood signaling his misfortune. Consumed by thoughts of the girl he loved sounding out syllables, waiting for him, he simply licked it off and got back to work. When he was done, he threw on a clean shirt and raced through town, through the pine forest, until Scarlet Manor filled his view. He leaped over the stone wall and, through the arms of the vegetation, saw a pot of chrysanthemums on the windowsill, killing his joy. Dejected, he sat and touched himself among the honeysuckle that surrounded him every Thursday, multiplying in the heat of his adolescent juices.

On other days of the week, Esteban disobeyed his mother and went into the hills late at night, bringing cigarettes, red wine, and antiseptic for the wounds of his cousin, who was in hiding from the Civil Guard gendarmerie with others from the Republican Army.

"Can I carry your gun?" Esteban asked his cousin one night.

"Boy, don't play around with death," his cousin warned before handing it to him.

It was long and cold, smelled of gunpowder and decaying moss. Esteban set it on his shoulder. He imagined he was marching down a big city avenue, not stuck in the hills as the moon bared its teeth. Olvido was in the cheering crowd, her head free of any hat. He tossed her a kiss. She smiled and clapped.

School was still being held in the town hall, but construction had begun on a new building just outside of town; children should not study under the lingering odor of bomb. But since the municipal coffers had been emptied by war, Manuela Laguna donated the money. She hoped such generosity would help cleanse her family's sins and find her daughter the rich, distinguished husband of her dreams. Olvido, fourteen, had already learned to read and write, and where the Tajo River and Seville were situated on a map. Deciding this was sufficient for her to lead a quiet life of embroidery and social engagements, Manuela pulled her from school, keeping her locked up at Scarlet Manor once again. The girl's beauty now required the solitude of the garden and kitchen, where Olvido practiced the patisserie appropriate to the social position her mother dreamed she would achieve as a result of her donations.

Manuela continued to take Olvido to church on Sundays, still covering her with a hat. Until her daughter was of marriageable age, she would take every precaution to keep dishonor at bay. Never did she imagine that, tormented by Esteban's absence, Olvido sat on the pew at the back of the church fanning the flames of her love rather than expiating the Laguna sins. Olvido searched among the heads of the faithful for that brown cowlick, begging Christ to return the passion of her Thursdays. In a row at the front of the church, sitting stiffly next to his still-grieving mother and sister, Esteban felt blue heat radiating from the back of his neck. Instead of reciting the creed, he would recite Saint John of the Cross poems he had read in his father's books, and when he took Communion he devoured the host with sacrilegious gluttony because Olvido was the only taste that penetrated his mouth.

Outside after Mass, the fresh, biting air accelerated their pulses, which had been reined in by the holy. Gone were the days of childhood smiles; now they tried to pass each other, brushing an arm, a hand, a thigh, without being caught by the adults. And when their eyes met, sick from evenings alone and a surfeit of kisses, their desire caused the green-tinged church bells to ring. The townspeople raised their ignorance to the sky, congratulating Padre Imperio on Tolón's newfound mastery — after twenty years of standing over piles of bird droppings ringing those bells, he was suddenly able to play an angelic melody. The priest stammered at such praise and crossed himself under his cassock; he knew Tolón suffered from prostate problems and had a habit of running to relieve himself against the sacristy wall the moment the service was over.

In dark clothes and bright white gloves, Manuela Laguna walked over to congratulate Padre Imperio as well, nodding when anyone addressed her, offering a gravelly "good morning" now that she was the school benefactor. So absorbed in her joy was she that she failed to watch over Olvido. Not knowing whether she had looked or smiled at anyone, Manuela did not cane her at home but prepared her favorite cake, the cinnamon one.

Summer arrived as Manuela reveled in her joy. The honeysuckle at Scarlet Manor began to wither when Olvido stopped visiting every afternoon, like she used to. Instead she stayed in her room, reading poems by Saint John of the Cross from a book Esteban loaned her on his last visit, before the war ended. Manuela attributed her daughter's melancholy to her first menstruation as her body shed the last remnants of childhood.

But Manuela had no time to worry: in order to consolidate her new social position, she was organizing a tea at Scarlet Manor for the town's elite. The mayor's wife, the pharmacist's wife, the lawyer's wife, the wife of the largest landowner, and the widow of a notary from the city, along with others of lesser lineage, would repay her donation to the new school. Manuela bought sky-blue cards that smelled of ink and had Olvido write the invitations. She then placed them in matching blue envelopes and dropped them in the respective mailboxes, her hopes as high as those of a girl throwing her first birthday party. Manuela would offer the house specialties—boiled coffee and cinnamon cake—served in fine china cups and on silver trays. A week before the event, Manuela began ironing the Lagartera lace tablecloth, one of many presents the diplomat gave Clara Laguna during the brothel years. That Saturday morning, Manuela spread it on the table, setting it with silver platters piled high with slices of cake, the fine china coffeepot and cups. Then she scrubbed the house from top to bottom.

"Sit, please, ladies. Make yourselves at home. Mrs. Mayor, you sit here; it'll be better for your back." Manuela drank a cup of coffee in one gulp. "Yes, thank you, the yard is lovely." She drank another. "No, that was years ago." She ate three slices of cinnamon cake. "We no longer practice the profession. We are ladies now, like you." Her hands shook. She went to the kitchen for more coffee, pouring herself another cup. "A broken heart made my mother turn to prostitution." She shot back another cup, patted the corners of her mouth with a napkin. "I burned everything to purify this Christian home." She smoothed her hair pulled into a bun at the back of her neck. "Semen! Semen in the garden!" She nervously chewed a roll. "Never! Why, that's just malicious gossip!" She ate. She drank. "My daughter will be an aristocrat, you'll see . . ."

At six o'clock, just as the tea was about to start, a severe case of black diarrhea confined Manuela to the bathroom. It was Olvido who answered the door as servants delivered notes of apology from their mistresses, unable to attend due to an unforeseen indisposition: the mayor's wife, rheumatism; the lawyer's wife, toothache; the widow, a migraine; the pharmacist's wife, colic; the landowner's wife, cold sweats; not to mention the paltry complaints from those of lesser descent.

Manuela would forever associate this affront with the smell of coffee grounds in her feces. She considered asking the mayor to refund her money but at the last minute was afraid that would close the door on a respectable social life forever. Maybe I was rash, she thought; my mother's sins were many, and it'll take time to expiate them all. Besides, it wouldn't be seemly to demand the money now. There are other ways to repay such a slight.

Two days later, the pharmacist's wife was found dead on a group of rocks in the forest. Clutched in her hands were the stalks of rosemary she had gathered for her husband's masterly potions. Her throat was split by a wet, red smile, and a section of her bowel lay sizzling in the sun.

The Civil Guard immediately suspected the Republican soldiers hiding in the hills to escape jail or the firing squad. One of them must have dared come into town, seeking food or medicine, and been startled by the pharmacist's wife, slitting her throat to keep her quiet. What the Civil Guard could not explain was the viciousness of the attack, her belly torn open.

"People are hungry," mumbled one of the guards in charge.

"And it's only going to get worse," another replied.

They sent for reinforcements and organized a search of the hills crowning the town. The operation lasted two days. On the last night the guards came into the square dragging a man in handcuffs. He had a beard of moss and lichen, the strength of the countryside set in the wrinkles on his forehead. The prisoner denied any involvement in the murder. The guards tried to get him to reveal where his companions were hiding. The man ran a hand over his beard and spit on the floor. The next day orders arrived from headquarters: either the man revealed the whereabouts of his cohorts, or he would be executed.

Three shots rang out along the road just as the first stars began to shine. Esteban hid among the pines and ferns to see whether the prisoner was his cousin. He wanted to warn him when he first heard what the guards were planning, but his mother locked him in the cellar, shouting, "They're not going to kill another one of mine!" The man fell forward onto the ground; he was one of the soldiers who had been hiding with Esteban's cousin. He opened his eyes just before death, and the last thing he saw was the face of the boy who had pretended to march with a defeated rifle. The murder case was closed.

For the rest of that summer, none of the old women in black shawls was seen in the streets, not even when the sun faded quietly into the forest. If they whispered at all, it was before their increasingly miserly stews, with only the flames or a trusted relative to listen to them. The men drank watered-down wine and halfheartedly played cards or dominoes at the tavern. Very few ever stopped to speak in the town square; most hurried through as if pursued by the clatter of their own shoes on the cobblestones. Only on Sundays, before and after church, did the townspeople stop to chat. Manuela Laguna, on the other hand, passed the church doors unafraid and well fed, greeting the town's elite, demonstrating to herself and others that she bore no grudge.

It wasn't until the ghostly fog returned in late October that the old women left their homes and some Republican soldiers descended from the hills. The square filled with petticoats, swords, and frost, and the church with frozen lips. Shielded by a mist so heavy nothing was visible beyond their own hands, the old women and their daughters felt their way to the church, following the tenuous light of a candle. Tired of eating carob and hard rye rolls, there they found a black-market stall offering lentils, oil, and whole wheat bread. They occasionally bartered with one another but more often paid a king's ransom or traded a rabbit to the boy from one town over making a fortune on black-market goods.

"Lentils. Delicious lentils," he whispered from his stall hidden behind the big wooden doors.

The wind took it upon itself to spread the word through the fog.

But the old women and their daughters were not the only ones taking advantage of the sins those old souls had committed. Fugitives would come down from the hills under cover of night to doze in dark corners until the square filled with fog, then leap out to embrace a father, mother, or girlfriend offering not only love but often a dried sausage, a loaf of country bread, or socks to protect against the mountain cold.

Certain unwritten rules were soon established. You would touch the head of anyone you bumped into to make sure there was no tricorne hat. Once you were certain it was not the Civil Guard, you asked the reason for his visit. People thus helped one another find the black-market stall or the relative they were hoping to meet. No one ever gave a real name, using aliases instead. That fog the townspeople had respected for centuries and most had feared became an ally of hunger and love. The dead old souls could no longer purge their sins in peace and sometimes tried to rid the square of intruders, turning their steely wind into gale-force gusts.

"Enough, you bastards!" could be heard in the thick of those souls. "We're all outcasts here."

Padre Imperio, well aware of all that went on in the fog through the confessions of widows, wives, and mothers, in an act of compassion ordered Tolón to ring the morning bells as late as possible. Some days the square cleared when the sun had already lost its red hue and the priest had to open both church doors to allow the souls back into their tombs, to harbor both fugitives and the black-market boy in the cellars until night, when the dark and cold of October concealed their escape.

One day after church, when Manuela was distracted, Esteban asked Olvido to meet him under the cover of the fog, but she was afraid there'd not be enough time and her mother would notice.

Manuela still rose at dawn to begin her chores, just as Bernarda had raised her to do. She tended the garden, took care of the animals, cooked roasts, and made stews. Hunger did not find its way to Scarlet Manor: Manuela had enough money to buy almost anything, and the garden continued to disobey the seasons. Despite the chill of fall, there was more than enough produce to meet their needs after they had given the required quota to the government official in charge.

"Come to my room on Thursday night," Olvido proposed instead. "Wait until midnight, then climb up to my window."

Esteban felt a vomit as white as Manuela's gloves rise in his throat.

Just past midnight the following Thursday, the moonlight pierced Esteban's face.

Olvido was waiting by the open window. Esteban jumped off the sill, and the two embraced.

"You smell like cedar," she said, stroking the sawdust behind his ears.

"I made a cupboard today. And you smell of lemons." His breath was cold.

"I made marmalade with my mother."

"You've grown." Olvido's larger, firmer breasts pressed into his chest.

"My mother says I'm a woman now."

"You are."

Olvido felt the taste of snow in her mouth. Her hair suddenly fell down her back into his hands, which rested on her bottom.

"I should have come sooner," Esteban murmured between kisses. "We'll never be apart this long again. I'd rather die," he said as an image of Manuela Laguna's yellow smile filled his mind.

Their desire slipped through the pine forest, triggering the green-tinged bells, which began to play an angelic melody, just as they did after Mass. Padre Imperio startled awake. Who but the devil's minions could be ringing those bells, announcing their master's arrival? Several townspeople, wrapped in blankets and with sleep in their eyes, came into the street, plodding along underneath the stars, shuffling to the church. They hammered on the doors, demanding that the Glorias and hallelujahs stop. A pair of policemen from the Civil Guard came armed with rifles, fearing a Republican Army fugitive was ringing those bells, inciting rebellion. The priest opened both wooden doors with three scapulars around his neck, mistaking the guards and his parishioners for Satan's soldiers.

"Who's ringing those bells, Father, and why?" the Civil Guard corporal demanded.

"An envoy of the devil himself," Padre Imperio replied.

"We'll see about that."

"It must be the wind. It's really quite strong," the other guard mused. "And the bells. They're old and run-down. We'll take them down tomorrow."

"Not a word about what we've seen here!" the corporal ordered Padre Imperio.

Esteban returned home a little before dawn, and the town fell quiet. That morning, not a single inhabitant could properly perform his job, and it was decided at a special town hall meeting to melt the bells to make a statue of General Franco.

Esteban returned to Olvido's room every Thursday night. He had never cared about the curse on the Laguna family and the misfortune foretold for any man who dared break it—not when he was a boy and could not understand, certainly not now as a young man nearly sixteen years of age. Olvido would never suffer for love, he told himself, because I will never abandon her. Her family's disgrace means nothing to me. I will marry her. I will marry the Laguna with the hats, as she's known. Not even her mother's gloves can make me change my mind.

After leaving the carpenter's shop, Esteban crouched among the pine and beech trees until midnight. He trembled with fear and impatience, sometimes spitting a frothy, salty liquid like the sea. At the first cry of an owl, he would come out of hiding, leap over the breach in the stone wall, and climb the trellis. Olvido would be waiting by candlelight to read verses by Saint John of the Cross. ("O night that has united / the Lover with his beloved, / transforming the beloved in her Lover.") The new church bells, which Padre Imperio subjected to three days of exorcisms and novenas before they were hung, never again rang as they kissed. Meanwhile, Manuela Laguna snored in her first-floor bedroom. Though still not that old, Manuela suffered from arthritis and, every evening at dinner, splashed laudanum into her wine to ease the pain and allow her to sleep.

Olvido told Esteban that after the tea fiasco, though she swore she was over it, her mother killed more chickens than ever to placate her anger. She would march into the kitchen during midafternoon and pluck them alive. The birds' shrieks swarmed through the rooms like ghosts until Manuela deigned to wring their necks. She did not even cook them then, but stayed to savor the taste of death.

One afternoon in early January of 1941, fleeing the hens' torment, Olvido disobeyed her mother and slipped into the loveliest room in all of Scarlet Manor. It had not been used since the death of Clara Laguna, that woman neither Manuela nor the townspeople could or would forget. The door creaked as it opened, and Olvido held her breath. Wrapped in half-light stood the great iron bed, still hung with the disheveled purple canopy that had danced to the beat of her grandmother's revenge. The room did not smell of sex or seclusion; it did not smell of cobwebs or mothballs. Every corner of the room exuded an aroma it took Olvido a moment to identify. Only when the wind escaped from the yard and the door blew shut did she realize the smell was oak.

Olvido crept over to admire the blue arabesque washbasin. It was there that Clara Laguna had washed away her tears for the Andalusian landowner. It was there, too, that Bernarda had washed Olvido's newborn body. A terrified squawk rose up to that room, and dusk hurtled toward the window like a knife to a chicken's neck. Olvido walked over to her grandmother's dressing table. A silver-handled brush and mirror sat on a yellowed lace doily. The metal shone enticingly. Olvido picked up the brush and began to pull it through her long tresses. No one had ever described Clara Laguna's face, but Olvido saw it reflected in the oval mirror: chestnut hair sprouting daisies and golden eyes turned to stone. Olvido continued to brush her hair. The whisper of a river could be heard in the walls, and Olvido's stomach cramped. That was not just any river, she suddenly knew, but the river running through the oak grove. A voice ordered her to go there with Esteban, for nowhere else on earth was as perfect for lovemaking.

Olvido proposed this to Esteban during one of their clandestine meetings. Now that the snow had come, he said, the river would be covered in a cap of ice as brittle as burnt sugar and the wind would buffet their love until it froze. "I'll take a blanket and hold you even tighter," Olvido assured him, pressing her lips to his. Lost in her kiss, Esteban began to think it might be a good idea to meet in the oak grove, far from Manuela Laguna. He would rather be taken by the sweet pins and needles of snow than by that woman's bloody gloves.

At midnight the following Thursday, Olvido climbed down the trellis into the yard. She ran past the wilting squash and avoided the roses — for their perfumed tongues told Manuela everything that happened nearby — crossed the honeysuckle clearing, and jumped through the breach in the stone wall. Esteban was waiting for her in the pine forest.

"Can't we just stay here, Olvido?"

"Let's go to the oak grove, please."

Hand in hand, they walked to the hill a dapple-gray horse had climbed one stormy morning carrying the Andalusian and Clara Laguna. From up there, the oak trees seemed to have been swallowed by the valley. The night air was heavy and humid, and the moonlight plunged into the river, scattering like silver droppings.

Esteban leaned into the trunk of an oak tree carved with an old heart. He held Olvido, caressing her neck with his lips. Inexplicably, he suddenly had the urge to sing a *saeta* and Olvido wanted to twist his hair, which suddenly gave off an odor of olive oil, around her fingers.

"Tomorrow I'll hunt partridge and give them to you so you can stew them in sauce," he said.

"I'll make the dish more delicious than anything you've ever tasted."

A cold breeze brushed their foreheads, their lips, their cheeks. The grass crunched as if someone were walking on it.

"Is someone watching us?" Esteban asked.

"Who?"

"Your mother?"

Olvido peered into the dark between tree trunks.

"Something's moving over there," she said, pointing to a shadow. "It looks like a woman."

"Let's go back to the pine forest." The boy trembled as he thought he saw bloody gloves reflected on the river.

"No, wait." Olvido was struck by a cramp like the one she'd felt the previous day in Clara Laguna's bedroom. Her eyes turned yellow and her tongue bore the taste of a secret grave. "I'll go up to the attic tomorrow and find the chest engraved with your name."

"What attic? What chest?" Esteban stared at her in fear.

She gave no reply but walked to the river, shedding her clothes: first her coat, then her sweater, her blouse, until she was wearing only her bra.

"Olvido! Come back! You'll catch cold!"

Esteban looked at his beloved's naked back, saw the white skin, the scars left by the thrashing of a cane. When he caught up to Olvido at the river's edge, she seemed disoriented. He handed her her clothes, and the blue slowly returned to her eyes. She shivered as she dressed.

"Does she still hit you?" Esteban asked.

"Sometimes. But now when she does, I think of you and it hurts much less."

That was the first time Esteban considered killing Manuela Laguna. He would smash her skull with a rock until his hands ached.

9

THE ATTIC WAS FILLED with junk organized according to the whims of nostalgia. A mountain of white porcelain bedpans teetered in one corner. They were used by the prostitutes who lived at Scarlet Manor all those years ago, but only Manuela Laguna knew why these pans, joyfully corroded by urine, had survived the death of the brothel. To the right was always the smell of gunpowder. Propped against the ruins of a French-style chest of drawers, the hunting rifle continued to weep its victories. It had been there since the Andalusian gave Clara Laguna the estate, but no one knew to whom it belonged, how old it was, or how many it had killed. Across from the chest of drawers were shelves with pots the Laguna witch used to brew her potions to cure evil eye. On the back of one shelf were mummified letters the landowner had written Clara, some of which she used years later to try and lure him back. Also surviving the dust on the shelves were the rigid sack containing the bones of a cat, the thread for repairing hymens, and a few jars of magic ingredients.

In another corner of the attic stood a metallic object. It was only up close, under a cascade of cobwebs, that the ecclesiastical lines of a candelabrum could be discerned, one that had graced the parlor in Scarlet Manor when it was bursting with whores and opulence. Perhaps Manuela thought its holy provenance would not sully the honor of her home. She used to peel the rivers of wax as she waited, with neither courage nor panties, for her next client to arrive. Manuela had also kept her daughter's crib. It sat among several pieces of furniture draped in mothball-smelling sheets. On the urine-stained wool mattress sat a child's sewing basket, now a refuge for moths. On rainy days, water dripped a lullaby onto the crib.

That roof had leaked for more than a century. A builder once came from a neighboring town to repair it. It was a spring day, and the sun beat down on his back. He climbed onto the roof with his toolbox and began to belt out a *saeta* as he replaced the broken tiles. Clara Laguna, relieving herself on the daisy-strewn cobblestone drive, heard the builder singing his Andalusian folk song. For a moment she thought her mother's spell had brought her lover back, though his voice must've grown rough over time. When she raised her eyes skyward to thank God, she realized her mistake and felt hate drip onto her calves. Clara reached for a stone and threw it at the builder's head. He fell from the roof.

On orders from their mistress, three prostitutes buried his body under a rosebush, while Bernarda cleaned the blood-spattered porch. His toolbox was walled up in the attic. For weeks they waited for the Civil Guard to come asking after the dead man. Every woman in the house was warned to deny the builder had ever been to Scarlet Manor. Clara had also prepared certain exclusive services to help ensure that the authorities believed her. But no one ever came. Time and the fatigue of flesh caused them all to forget. They only ever remembered the builder on spring days, when the sun baked daisies on the drive and the hammering of little metallic voices could be heard in the second-floor bedrooms.

Late-afternoon sun slipped in through the small round window, illuminating a basket of treasures from the sea: conch shells, strings of algae, the skeletons of little fish. Once the light faded, a rush of fireflies filled the attic, like little golden soldiers celebrating victory in battle. This was the best time of day to visit the attic, the most picturesque of all. But Olvido could not go up there until midnight, when her mother was snoring off the splash of laudanum. Barefoot, carrying a candle, she climbed the rickety stairs. Though it was the first time she had ever been in that part of the house — her mother had always forbidden it — it was as if she knew the way. Guided by the breeze of the oak trees, she knew what she was looking for and where to find it. When she entered the attic, stars crowded against the small window.

Olvido walked over to the mountain of bedpans and set them on the floor, one by one. Every bedpan had the name of one of the prostitutes on the handle: Tomasa, Ludovica, Petri, Sebastiana . . . Olvido's eyes misted over with a yellowish tinge. As she removed Petri's bedpan from the pile, the others came tumbling down. A clamor of white porcelain buried her feet, but Olvido stood perfectly still. A small chest appeared with the name Clara engraved in bronze on the lid. Inside were the only possessions of her grandmother's to survive the terror of respectability. Olvido lifted the lid, a puff from a woman's grave caressing her face, and pulled out the undergarments Clara Laguna wore the day she gave herself to the Andalusian. They were stained from her first time. Olvido then pulled out an ornamental comb inlaid with silver, her grandmother's favorite, and a leather-bound book. Her stomach cramped and she knew this last item was her destiny. She stroked the cover. A face appeared in the window, among the stars and misty moonlight. It was one of Clara's clients: a bald diplomat with round, gold-rimmed glasses. Olvido opened the book to the first page, made of silk, and found a dedication: "For the most exotic pubis in the world. Forever yours, wherever I might be, my concubine, my Clara." Olvido's hands were as white as death. She flipped through a few pages, feeling daisies sprout between her thighs. She flipped through a few more. This book, written in a foreign language, contained drawings of a naked man and woman, exquisitely profiled in ocher ink, coming together again and again in different positions. The candle flame flickered. Olvido closed the book with a smile and pressed it to her belly. She replaced the pile of bedpans and returned to her room, her discovery hidden in the pleats of her nightdress.

· · ·

Olvido dreamed of those drawings over the next few nights. When the day of their secret meeting in the oak grove arrived, she placed the book in Esteban's hands as she glanced at him.

"Is it a present?" he asked.

"Not really; it's not mine to give. It belongs to my grandmother Clara."

"But she's dead, isn't she?"

"Sometimes."

"What do you mean sometimes?" the boy insisted.

"I don't know. Look at the book."

"Is it about dead people?"

"No."

"Is it poetry?"

"No."

"Is it a novel?"

"Just look!"

Esteban read the title, written in Gothic print.

"*Ka-ma Su-tra.* Is it by Shakespeare?"

"I don't know. Flip ahead a few pages."

When Esteban came to the drawings, Olvido kissed him on the lips.

The two of them curled up in their bed of mud along the river's edge. He caressed the scars on her back through her blouse, she his strong carpenter's chest, until their passion defied winter and they were half-dressed, shivering with cold and with love, under Esteban's coat. As the blood-red veil of dawn arrived, their bodies, exhausted by snow and inexperience, came together in the first position.

They practiced nine of the positions from January through the middle of March. They lit a fire underneath a giant oak and wrapped themselves in a blanket. They smelled each other, kissed to melt their frozen loins. The grass beneath them was dead and the river frozen, but their desire was like a chronic cold.

One afternoon, after they practiced position number ten, Esteban made a decision without talking to Olvido. He thought about it all day at work, amid sneezes and feverish chills. As the sun sank into the pines, he hung up his hammer and his saw; he washed his face and his armpits, wiping away any sawdust that might affect his image; he changed out of his dirty clothes, into a clean shirt inherited from his father and a new sweater knit by his mother, and he headed to Scarlet Manor. Along the way, he recalled the day Manuela Laguna invited him in to try that stew. He could taste the herbs that had tortured him afterward, could hear his father's deep, aromatic voice begging him to run far, far away from that cursed house and the women who lived there. Esteban picked up a sharp rock, slipping it into his pocket.

Manuela Laguna was eviscerating a chicken at the big kitchen table when Esteban knocked on the front door.

"Good evening, señora."

Her cotton gloves dripped blood.

"Do I know you, young man?" She studied his face.

"Yes, señora." Blood splashed onto clay tiles. "A few years ago you invited me in to taste one of your stews. I'm the schoolmaster's son."

"I see that now. How could I forget those eyes? You've grown . . . But what do you want?"

"Well . . . Forgive the late hour . . ." Esteban stuttered, reaching into his pocket to grip the stone. "I just got off work, and I've come to ask for your daughter's hand."

Manuela narrowed her eyes.

"And what is your job?" A scarlet puddle oozed over the clay tile floor toward the boy. "Are you deaf?"

"I . . ." Esteban felt the rock in his hand. "I'm seventeen years old and a carpenter's apprentice. But when Olvido and I marry, we'll move to the city and I'll study to become a teacher."

"So you want to follow in your father's footsteps, become as worthless as he."

"My father was an honorable man who died for his country!" The taste of that stew began to fill his mouth.

"What do you know about his death! You were just a miserable child. You still are!"

"You're wrong. I'm a man and I love your daughter." Esteban formed a fist around the rock.

"Don't be ridiculous . . . you love my daughter. You've never even seen her face. All you want is the fortune she'll inherit one day." A tuft of Manuela's hair fell into the puddle of chicken blood.

"That's a lie. I've even seen her naked. More than once. You should know we've practiced those positions in that book of your mother's. That's how well I know her!" Esteban let go of the rock as the confession slid from his throat.

"Listen to me, boy, if you don't go back to where you came from right now, I'll rip out your guts. I should have done it the first time you were here." Manuela's white cotton gloves shone in the moonlight.

Esteban fled toward the pine forest, tasting his father's warning like that very first time.

In the half-light of the entryway, Manuela pulled out the cane for beating rugs. The smell of lavender wafted up to Olvido's room. Drowsy with fever, she did not hear the knock on the door or the conversation between her lover and her mother. Olvido saw the face of the moon through the window. Manuela burst in and caned her, then examined her hymen with a magnifying glass, as closely as if she were an entomologist.

"I'll get a folk healer to restore it. This would be much easier if the Laguna witch were still alive. But you were born a whore like your grandmother. You will not leave this house until you are twenty! As for that depraved sex fiend who came to ask for your hand, to rub what you've done in my face, I will rip his insides out."

Anyone else would have stayed away, but Esteban was too enamored and returned. The night had grown steely, with only a few stars. He climbed up the trellis to the window; he did not notice the moon hanging itself with its own white rays. Kneeling on the sill, he rapped on the glass as a star plummeted to its death behind him. Olvido heard something but hesitated. The wind was blowing, the wooden shutters bashing into Esteban. "Olvido! Olvido!" The girl recognized her name. She let Esteban in, then slapped him across the face.

"I'm sorry. I don't know what I was thinking. It was the fever, the cold, kissing you in the snow just once a week. It made me crazy. I'm sorry," he repeated. "Did she cane you?"

Olvido lowered her eyes.

"I'll kill her. If you ask me to, I'll kill her right now and we'll move to the city." Esteban felt the rock in his pocket, Olvido's finger on his lips, followed by a kiss.

Off in the distance, the new church bells began to ring in the frozen air — not a glorious melody, more of a funeral march. Suddenly, a cloud of gunpowder filled the room. Wearing nothing but a clean pair of gloves, her breasts hanging down to her belly, Manuela Laguna stood holding the rifle from the attic.

"So you've come back to fuck the honor of my home, have you, boy? All right, if that's what you want, we'll take this as far as it goes."

Olvido stared at her mother's pubic hair.

"If you let him go right now, I promise I'll never see him again," she begged, placing herself between Esteban and her mother.

The boy gripped the rock in his pocket so tightly, a sharp edge cut his finger.

"Shut up. Clearly you inherited Clara Laguna's bad blood, and it's going to cost you dearly."

Manuela clicked off the safety and brought the gun to her shoulder. "Move."

"Madre, please. Let him go."

"Not on your life."

Manuela slammed the rifle butt into her daughter's temple, and Olvido crumpled to the floor. A small stream of blood obscured her vision. It's all a dream, she thought; I'm lying in the honeysuckle clearing. Esteban's voice attacked Manuela: "I'll kill you, you witch! I'll kill you!" A shot rang out, gunpowder speckling the seascape on the wall. Maybe it's a battle between pirate ships, Olvido thought. It's all a dream; tomorrow we'll kiss in the oak grove on top of the snow. The springs in the old chair creaked. Her mother had sat down with her legs spread and was delivering an ultimatum: "Fuck me or I'll kill my daughter." Shot in the arm, the boy pulled down his pants, today I made lemon pie but it burned because I was thinking of you, Olvido murmured, tomorrow I'll make apple pie and bring you a piece at work, but he was rubbing his penis with a reluctant hand, you'll savor it and I'll lick the crumbs from your lips. The boy walked toward Manuela, quaking, tomorrow we'll forget all about this, come, kiss me, tomorrow we'll bathe in the river no matter how cold it is, Olvido begged, a bullet entered the rifle chamber, her mother fired and the bullet punctured the ceiling, I said fuck me, boy, he vomited and backed away from Manuela toward the window. Don't worry, my love, tomorrow the church bells will play a love song, come, let me lick the sawdust from behind your ears, let me lick your splinters, he opened the window and the late-March cold cleared out the gunpowder, come, let me kiss the whorl at the back of your neck, let me kiss the dimple in your chin, the rock fell out of his pocket onto the floor, Manuela laughed, you were going to hit me with that, I'll teach you how to kill, another bullet entered the rifle chamber and she shot him in the gut, come, come, Olvido screamed, Manuela approached with the rifle aimed at the boy's chest, when no more than a breath away, she threw it on the floor and pushed Esteban out of the window, his skull smashing on a rock below, tomorrow . . . Olvido moaned . . . in the oak grove, you'll look at me with your gray eyes . . .

10

THUNDER CRACKED AND split the sky, clouds piled one on top of the other, night closed in darkness. Olvido walked over to the window. Rain pelted her face and a gust of wind froze her cheeks. She started to shake when she saw Esteban's body in the yard, immobile, a red halo around his head, sanctifying his death. She furrowed her brow — wanting to tear anger, pain in two — and a permanent crease formed between her brows, a crease that transformed her into an adult beauty. Olvido felt dizzy. She closed the window and contemplated the moonless sky through the glass, Esteban's body being mourned by the shrouded stars. The cut on her temple still bled, dripping onto her chin, her dress. She crumpled to the floor, fainting.

Her mother had left the room, slamming the door in triumph. She would go back to bed on the first floor and sleep soundly now that there were no more gray eyes in town to ruin her plans for the future. Manuela finished grooming a cockroach she had set in perfumed water before undressing and heading to Olvido's room to restore her honor. She tied a crimson leash around the insect's swollen body. Then she pulled the drapes closed and crawled between stiffly starched sheets. It was then she sensed it for the first time, rising from her stomach to her breasts, that smell of fear, that smell of sex the boy exuded.

Dawn came earlier than usual that winter morning verging on spring. It was as if the sun, after the moon's suicide, did not want to leave the world orphaned any longer. An orange glow slowly lit up the wintry mountains, turning white as it hit Scarlet Manor, wrapping the boy's body in a shroud. Esteban already belonged to the yard. A gleaming puddle lay coiled on his belly, and a poppy sprouted from his lip. His blood and thick brains were frozen on the moss like morning dew. The storm that assaulted the night was still reflected in his eyes.

Olvido felt a stabbing pain in her temple when she woke. A trail of dried blood ran down her face to her neck. Her lips trembled to the tempo of memory; her teeth began to chatter. The light of a new day flickered in her icy, mourning heart. She got up and stumbled over to the window. Her mother was coming down the stone drive in the cart, the black horse trampling daisies. Behind her was another, larger cart. A beam of sunlight fell on the two occupants. They were thin and dressed in black. This procession shattering the dawn stopped beside Esteban's body. Manuela got down from the cart, pointing to the boy's pants around his ankles. Her mouth contorted in hate. One of the men took notes, while the other stared at the body being consumed by that yard. A daisy sprouted from Esteban's inner thigh. A few minutes passed before the men dared wrap the body in a blanket the same color as their mules. Esteban left the yard to the bump and creak of wood, but the abstract painting of his death remained on the moss for a long time to come.

The morning remained pale. Olvido pulled a chair to the window and sat cross-legged, holding vigil over Esteban's absence as a wintry river seized her bones. She heard the pines rustle and recalled her first outing with Esteban on a bed of needles. She had no desire to eat or drink; she did have to pee but refused to move. Urine soaked her buttocks and thighs with a warm sense of well-being. She listened to the caws of a magpie that coveted her tears. The fruit trees and wild roses shook in the yard.

By afternoon, Olvido had begun to shake. Her damp nightdress clung to her skin. She wanted to get up and change, but her limbs had fallen asleep after so long in the same position, consumed with sadness. When she did manage to rise she decided to go out into the yard, and nothing would stop her. She pulled off her nightdress, pulled on a wool dress and coat. From the hallway, she could hear the crackle of wood in the hearth. Carrying her boots, she walked down the stairs and into the yard. She kneeled on the moss stained by her lover's remains. She pulled out a pair of scissors and cut her bangs, then the tresses that hung to her waist. Clumps of hair fell on the icy red moss. The wolf's howl returned, as did the steely cold. Olvido knew it was useless to look for the moon. Clouds crowded the last light of day, and she gave in to exhaustion. She laid her head on the moss, and death pricked her cheek. I will never forget you, she thought, pressing her body deeper into the moss, and I will never live again.

Manuela Laguna told the Civil Guard she'd heard noise and shouts coming from her daughter's room; that's why she went in with the rifle, only to find the boy trying to rape Olvido. He was strong and threatened Manuela with a rock. She fired twice: once in self-defense and once to defend her daughter's honor. The boy opened the window to escape but fell into the yard. In order to guarantee this version of events and ensure that the guards did not interrogate Olvido as a minor, Manuela donated a good stack of pesetas to the municipal coffers. But despite being locked in by her mother, Olvido escaped early one morning and went to the station on a narrow street just off the town square. She was wearing only a nightdress, a wool coat, and boots with the laces undone.

"My mother killed him," she told a policeman. "She killed him because he loved me and I loved him."

The policeman looked at this girl, thinking she was the most beautiful thing he had ever seen, even if her blue eyes were glazed over and her skin pale.

"He didn't, the boy didn't try to hurt you? You know, rape you?"

"He was my lover," Olvido replied, and she left the station, shuffling her feet.

After that, Manuela had to give even more money to the municipal coffers for Esteban's death to be deemed an accident. According to the police report, Manuela Laguna found the boy in Olvido's room late one night with his pants down and believed he was trying to rape her. The boy threatened Manuela Laguna with a rock, so she was forced to shoot him.

The townspeople learned of the secret relationship between the Laguna with the hats and the schoolmaster's son, but it did not tarnish his name and he was given a Christian burial next to his father.

By the end of that winter, the cemetery groaned under the weight of snow and all the headstones for fallen soldiers. Magpies sat in cypress trees, waiting for funeral processions. Local legend said that their feathers grew shinier the more pain they observed. Like the birds, Olvido spent two days waiting for the town's most recent casualty. She slipped out to the cemetery at dawn, even though her mother had caned her when she went to the Civil Guard, and the town learned that this Laguna, shielded from dishonor by her hat, had a secret lover. She spent the day among headstones, crosses, and family vaults, filling her stomach with snow, reading Saint John of the Cross. She walked back to Scarlet Manor by starlight and curled up in Clara Laguna's bed, with at least the smell of oak to keep her company. On the morning of the third day, the funeral procession appeared at the cemetery gate. Olvido sat in the same spot where she had watched the schoolmaster's funeral, observing the cluster of black as it gathered around the grave. Esteban's mother and sister formed an impenetrable wall once again. Only this time the boy constricted in his corduroy suit and mourning armband was not there. Instead he was in a wooden box being lowered into the hole as Padre Imperio, his hands shaking with age, swung the silver mace and spat Latin.

When only the magpies remained, Olvido stared down at daisies left on the grave. High in the sky, the sun illuminated the remnants of a white winter and mildewed headstones. Esteban would have to get used to the damp of infinity. As magpies soared over family vaults, their wings like mirrors, Olvido threw herself onto the grave and lay there for hours, feeling the earth's heartbeat, listening to the whisper of the worms. Only when the sun set did she gather a handful of daisies and go home to Scarlet Manor.

Manuela Laguna was working on her needlepoint in front of the fire when she heard her daughter arrive. The girl's icy steps crossed the tiled entryway and climbed up to Clara Laguna's room. Manuela wanted to grab the cane and throw Olvido out of that forbidden space. A log disintegrated on the fire, and Manuela sensed in her chest the Galician woman's black braids, her eucalyptus heart, her stories, and settled back onto the couch. Later, she thought.

Meanwhile, Olvido placed a bouquet of daisies on the bed and said: "Abuela, I brought you flowers from Esteban's grave."

In the garden it began to snow. Olvido let her wet clothes fall to the floor. She sat under the canopy and opened the window Clara had gazed through as she waited for the Andalusian landowner.

"I've come here to die, with you."

An icy wind carrying swirling snowflakes assailed Olvido's nude body as she lay calmly on top of the daisies. That last winter storm would return her to her lover's arms. Several minutes passed as the purple muslin danced like it had in brothel times, as Olvido laid shivering, clutching daisies to her chest and belly. Traces of Clara Laguna's silk robe rose from her dressing table as two yellow eyes shone in the wind lashing the room and the window slammed shut. The sound of the river in the oak grove bounced off the walls like a loud roar of laughter. Olvido sat up, her stomach cramping furiously. Only then did she realize it had been two months since her last menstruation.

"You're expecting his daughter." Olvido recognized her grandmother's voice clawing her insides, and one word erupted in that oak-filled room: *revenge*. The mirror on Clara Laguna's dressing table shattered. Olvido furrowed the now permanent crease in her brow. She had to live for the child she was expecting — the child who would ensure that Manuela Laguna never forgot what she did to Esteban. She pulled the heavy quilt over her body. "That's it. Save yourself to exact your revenge," Clara Laguna said inside. "Flaunt your pregnancy in town, up and down the streets, up and down, with no hat to hide the truth of your eyes, your cheekbones or lips. Let the old women in black shawls and their daughters see you, let them whisper that the curse continues, for another Laguna is pregnant and lovesick."

Olvido curled up on the pillow. "You're right, Abuela. The dreams Madre had for my future will never come true. There'll be no marriage to an aristocrat or children whose last name is not Laguna. It will be as you wish: our family legend will cause tongues to wag once again."

"Yet another Laguna alone and pregnant," one old woman will say to her daughter, adjusting her shawl.

"Probably a girl, too."

"And the schoolmaster's son is the father."

"Dead now."

"Yes, father and son both dead."

"Maybe they kill them after they mate."

"But aren't they condemned to suffer for love?"

"Serves them right, the whores."

"Yes, and all because Manuela prances around town like a lady, smiling and offering donations to mask her shame. Twenty years ago, she spread her legs for five pesetas."

"They always were expensive."

"They do say the house was opulent . . ."

"Wicked women . . ."

"And who is Olvido's father?"

"Manuela might not even know!"

"That's what the old women will say to their daughters," Clara Laguna whispered into her granddaughter's heart.

"Yes," Olvido replied, her skin covered in goose bumps. "That's what they'll say."

And that's what they said when winter and spring ended and July crashed in, when Olvido Laguna's belly was now swollen. The gossip whirled as well behind the windows of whitewashed stone houses and in small chairs placed outside when the sun set. They gathered in groups of two or three, at most, to avoid suspicion of trafficking in black-market goods or treason. The girl wore a mauve dress, tight across the hips, and shoes with a bit of a heel that clicked over the cobblestones, her hair loose, floating on the breeze that filled the town square and narrow streets in the evening, cooling off her sweaty temples.

Meanwhile, in the entryway, Manuela Laguna waited for her daughter's return, armed with the cane. For months they had shared Scarlet Manor in a long-suffering silence. An invisible divide separated the rooms and their feelings. Sunset fell on Manuela's dressing gown, her white gloves, her mouth with its taste of insects. Olvido appeared on the cobblestone drive, her eyes and cheeks puffy. She saw her mother waiting.

"Give me your hands, your hands, your hands," she murmured softly and erratically. "So strong, how strong they are." She saw the weapon shaking in her mother's gloves.

"Don't you dare; I won't let you!" Olvido walked slowly, her shoes gripping the stones, the daisies, Clara Laguna's amber gaze. She saw the menacing shadow of the cane, saw her mother's murky eyes, and stared into them with contempt. The cane leaped toward her belly, but before it made contact, Olvido ripped it from her mother's hands, spat on it, and threw it into the yard. It lay on the sand, covered in dust. Manuela Laguna had never felt as alone as she did that instant, not even when her fourteen-year-old body lay dying under the butter maker from Burgos. She had lost her power to a pair of gray eyes, and she cursed them.

Olvido headed into the kitchen. Ever since Manuela discovered she was pregnant, Olvido was afraid her mother would try to make her miscarry, stirring potions into the pots she left on the stove for Olvido to eat from, and so she decided to cook her own meals using the recipes her mother had taught her. According to Manuela, a good housewife knew how to make not only cinnamon cake and lemon pie for her husband but also the most delicious savory stews. At sixteen, Olvido had not had time to learn all of Bernarda's culinary wisdom, but she had learned enough to not die of hunger.

More important, it was there in the kitchen that she found the perfect place to exhume the body of her beloved Esteban. The desire to feed her hunger soon gave way to the desire to remember, the desire for pleasure. Rope braids of garlic and onion, potatoes, tomatoes, and red peppers piled in straw baskets on top of cupboards, bay leaf, mint, sage and other herbs, the bloody meat of chicken, river trout—any ingredient, Olvido made love to it first. She washed it, sometimes, she kissed it, always, she smelled it, before the kiss, she caressed it, then she cut it, crying, warming it between her hands or on the open flame until it climaxed.

One early-August afternoon, Olvido was cooking lamb when a liquid flooded her legs. Her daughter was ready to come into the world. Olvido left the kitchen clutching her belly and slowly made her way upstairs. She would give birth in Clara's room. Everything was ready, waiting. On the dressing table were clean towels and the scissors she had used to cut her hair the day after Esteban died. The fragrance of that room intensified as the birth of another Laguna girl drew near. The child's first breath would fill her lungs with the smell of family.

For hours, Olvido's hair and face were soaked by perspiration as she lay naked on the bed in labor. Downstairs, on the sofa in front of an empty hearth, Manuela sat embroidering. When the horizon slipped into darkness, Olvido squatted on the floor. The purple canopy shook as if performing an Eastern dance in the evening breeze. Amid gushes of blood and urine, Olvido screamed her lover's name and pulled out a gray-eyed girl. She cut the umbilical cord at precisely the same moment as, downstairs, Manuela snipped her excess thread. Olvido walked over to the washstand and lowered the baby into the basin, washing her under the watchful gaze of two amber eyes. The church bells began to play a joyful melody. Since Esteban's death, the bells had only ever rung on Sunday before Mass, on civic holidays, or when a wealthy family celebrated a wedding.

The little girl began to cry. A scarlet puddle lay on the wooden floor. Olvido wrapped the baby in a towel. I will call her Margarita, she thought, after the flowers on the cobblestone drive. Margarita Laguna. Olvido staggered toward the bed and collapsed as her daughter suckled at her breast.

I I

~~~~

WHEN MARGARITA LAGUNA was six months old, the kitchen at Scarlet Manor began to take on the odor of puréed food. It was never clear whether the girl's sensuality — apparent from her first streams of urine — came from the pleasure and heartache her mother cooked at a low fire or the Eastern influence of the *Kama Sutra* that led to her conception. Margarita, at her young age, was already dark, toasted by steam from the cooking pots and exposed to the air. She was always tearing off her clothes: from diapers and christening robes to cotton underpants and dresses with bows. How she hates anything but the wind on her skin, Olvido thought, and she never feels cold, wrapped as she is in a cocoon of love.

Hidden in corners or behind the windows' shutters, Manuela Laguna spied on her granddaughter's nudity. She had hated the girl long before she was born, but one afternoon, when Olvido was distracted and Manuela peered over the side of the bassinet to find gray eyes she thought she had eradicated forever, she spontaneously went about a chicken massacre to calm her rage. From then on, whenever she saw those gray irises she delved into some new savagery. Armed with the kitchen knife, Manuela would guillotine giant roses, drown cockroaches and centipedes in perfumed water. But she knew the only thing to soothe her ire would be to cane her granddaughter's little body until it simply disappeared. Perhaps then she would be free of that torturous smell, that smell that lay inside her like death since pushing the school-master's son from the window, that smell of his genitals and fear.

Olvido knew exactly what her mother was thinking and feeling. She had learned to read hate in the light of those eyes, in those hands gripping that lavender cane, long before she was ever given her first elementary school speller by her long-gone teacher. Olvido spent day and night watching over her daughter: as they played among the honeysuckle and daisies, as they napped in Clara Laguna's room. If at last she succumbed to sleep, Olvido dreamed of small white coffins and sun-faded photos of little girls on headstones as her skin exuded the fragrance of the produce she cooked.

One day in mid-August of 1942, when Margarita was a year old, Olvido took her out for a walk through the pine forest. There they came upon Padre Imperio's mule behind a large rock, bottles of holy oil clinking in the saddlebags as the priest lay on a clump of ferns, a gash on his forehead trickling blood. Olvido lifted his shoulders and set his head on her lap. At seventy-some years of age, he had lost his healthy complexion from his time in the colonies, had become an old man with fragile limbs. Olvido cleaned his cut with a handkerchief as Margarita played in the pine needles. It was early afternoon, the sun intensifying Padre Imperio's distress. His priest's collar was suffocating. Olvido removed it, undoing the top few buttons of his cassock, revealing the scar that crossed his once firm, now saggy neck.

"We must resist. Courage and faith in God! They were up in the palm trees, the bastards. Ambush! Ambush!" Padre Imperio ranted.

His eyes were again the color of the Caribbean Sea.

"I'll take you to the doctor in town." Olvido tore a strip off her slip and tied it around the old man's head.

"Leave me to God's mercy, soldier. Save yourself! The red ants are attacking as well."

Margarita Laguna sat pricking the priest's hand with pine needles. Olvido chastised her daughter, who tumbled laughing into the ferns.

Meanwhile, lost in the jungle of his delirium, Padre Imperio grabbed his throat: a Cuban rebel had just slit it with the whoosh of a machete. He patted his cassock, searching for the canteen that hung from a soldier's uniform. He found it, invisible, cleansing his wound with holy water, the medicine of miracles that stopped the bleeding just as it had forty years before.

"Can you put your arm around my neck, Padre?"

By now the sun had roasted him to the brink of starvation among lianas and soft earth, until the Santeria priestess found him, fed him cassava jam, and smeared his throat with a yellowish poultice. That color wedged in the chaos of his memories. He looked at Olvido for the first time when she helped him up, but he saw her grandmother instead. In his delirium, the priest traveled back to the dreams that had tormented him for years: that girl burning in the amber flame of her own eyes. Through parched lips, he called her Clara. A breeze stirred in the pines, ruffling their hair, calming the light of the insect bites. Olvido put the priest onto his mule, and as he sat tall for a mere instant Olvido stroked his red scar with fingers not her own. Padre Imperio slipped deeper into the past, remembering his own broad shoulders, dark hair, and the spark of determination in his eyes.

"Do not ruin your life for revenge. Help me save you," he said before falling onto the beast's neck.

Olvido picked Margarita up and secured her to her waist in a shawl.

"Hold on tight to the mule, Padre, and don't say another word. Save your energy." She took the reins and headed for town.

The saddlebags swung and clinked. The breeze died down and the heat of the afternoon intensified.

A week of mourning was decreed when Padre Imperio died of a stroke two days later. A priest was sent from the city to officiate at the funeral. In his thirties, Rafael Arizpicoitea was a big man with a ruddy complexion.

On the morning of the funeral, Manuela Laguna climbed into the cart and waited for Olvido and her granddaughter to do the same. Though they had not spoken since the night Esteban was killed, they still went to church together. Thanks to her many donations, Manuela now sat in a front-row pew, while Olvido chose to remain in the back with little Margarita.

Padre Imperio is gone, the women in mourning veils and mantillas whispered as they milled outside the church. Gone, and there'll never be another like him to draw faith through tears and crocodiles, standing in the pulpit with arms spread. Manuela walked among the elite of society, acknowledging their greetings with all the dignity of a queen. Olvido, on the other hand, still searched among the parishioners for Esteban's gray eyes so the church bells would play an angelic melody. All of the women looked at her accusingly, as if she and her own supernatural beauty were responsible for the priest's death — after all, she had been seen leading the mule that carried his battered body. No longer did they call her the Laguna with the hats; now she was the Laguna of the dead boy. All of the men, however, studied her with the curiosity of desire and sat over a cup of red wine in the tavern after Mass, wishing she sold herself like her grandmother with the golden eyes.

When Padre Imperio's funeral was over, August cooled with a sudden rain that turned to hail overnight. Hunger grew more acute in stomachs as the townspeople wept to the pounding of ice pellets, unsure whether their grief was over the loss of that magnificent man or the misery of this time of weevils and brown bread. The boy with the black-market stand was seen jumping over the cemetery wall when the moon rose; it was even rumored that fugitives came down from the hills, taking advantage of the dark and the bad weather to say good-bye to the priest who offered a safe haven from the Civil Guard in the church basement. Rarely in the week after his death was Padre Imperio's grave unattended. The Sunday faithful went during the day, the outlaws at night. Until, that is, the Civil Guard set up watch; then only magpies sought the shade of the headstone when the hail stopped and

August returned, leaving the policemen no choice but to go back to the station without a single prisoner, just star-flecked tricorne hats.

The constant coming and going in the cemetery prevented Olvido from visiting Esteban in the grave next to his father's. BELOVED SON AND BROTHER, REST IN PEACE, read the epitaph engraved on a headstone sticking up from the earth like an ornamental comb. When the undertaker locked the gate at six o'clock, Olvido and her daughter slipped out of their hiding spot in a nobleman's vault. At first the magpies squawked, nearly tearing their beaks apart, trying to warn the undertaker, who lived in a hut not far away, of this intruder. Olvido threw stones at their wings until they came to tolerate her. After closing, they flew up and down the cemetery paths in search of shiny objects dropped by grief-stricken mourners, while Olvido sat on her lover's grave, earth warmed by decomposing kisses. She rested her head on the tombstone, stretched out her legs, and read Saint John of the Cross out loud in the cool of the spirits, while Margarita raked dirt into little piles she then knocked over. Sometimes Olvido would stop reading and play with her daughter; at seventeen, she herself was still a child. The grave was piled with little mounds harboring memories. One held the smell of sawdust from behind Esteban's ears, another their icy embraces beneath the giant oaks.

When evening nodded off and the cemetery filled with the sounds of nightfall, the bones of the dead sparkled in the ossuary like giant fireflies, headstones glowed purple, and cypress shadows roamed the paths with their lances. Olvido lay on the grave, one cheek against the earth, and told Esteban about Margarita's new teeth and the stews she made as she thought of him; in tears, she swore she would never forget him. Only when Margarita complained of hunger, demanded her dinner, did Olvido sweep the grave smooth and replace the bunches of flowers so as not to be discovered. Under cover of darkness, she jumped the lowest part of the wall with her daughter holding tight to her neck. Once, outside the church, Esteban's sister threatened to tear

Olvido's hair out if she ever discovered Olvido was disturbing her brother's grave at night.

"You are nothing to him, not you or your bastard," she snapped, peering at the child as her mother looked on from a distance, wringing a black handkerchief.

But Olvido could not stay away from Esteban's grave. That ground whispering memories is what kept her alive — that dirt, the love she bore for her daughter, and the revenge she inherited. She would not let Manuela Laguna forget what she did to Esteban. Even so, after countless sleepless nights watching over her daughter, Olvido began to consider leaving Scarlet Manor and that town. In the wee hours, recalling Padre Imperio's words as he sat on his mule, Olvido sometimes packed their clothes into a dusty old suitcase she found in the attic, then unpacked them again in the morning as she watched her mother eat gizzards for breakfast. As long as we're here, Olvido thought, she'll be reminded that her dreams will never come true. We are the face of her failure.

Later in the evening, her youth trembled as she hid in the vault, waiting for six o'clock. Margarita napped on her eternally frozen stone as a mountain breeze carried the fresh smell of pine and fern.

The only one to ever discover Olvido in the cemetery was Padre Rafael, who stayed on after his predecessor's funeral. The old women in black shawls called him Padre Gigante. Not only was he big and broad-shouldered — his cassocks had to be made to size — but he was also exceptionally tall. Of Basque origin, with blue eyes and blond hair, Padre Rafael nearly fell from the pulpit during his first Sunday sermon, when the floorboards cracked under his beast-of-burden weight. The floor had to be reinforced with a steel plate, and even then, many a Sunday parishioner paid more attention to the possibility of his skull cracking on the tile floor, as the wood groaned and nails worked their way out, than to his quiet sermons. But Padre Rafael's sermons and his nature were the only quiet things about him. In every other respect his time on earth was a cacophony of noise and tremors. Fields, cobble-

stones, and floors shook with his steps. He was never able to go anywhere without an elephantine thunder announcing his presence, as if
the very earth echoed every footfall. The day he walked into church to
officiate at Padre Imperio's funeral, more than one parishioner thought
an earthquake was coming. The maroon Bible shook on the altar,
along with the host in the ciborium and the mourning rosettes on the
pews; even the wine swirled in circles, all harbingers of telluric energy.

Although they tried, the townspeople never got used to the labori-
ous rattle that followed Padre Rafael wherever he went.

"Here comes the giant," the old women would say in the street as
their few remaining teeth swung from their gums.

"Here he comes," they said as they hid in their homes during those
difficult times, hurrying to keep clay stew pots from falling off shelves.

Once they were sure the pulpit would hold the priest's weight and
the town would not shake as if an earthquake were happening, the parishioners began to miss Padre Imperio's lively sermons, especially
those who'd listened to them for years and now nodded off to the all
too calm, clear words of Padre Rafael.

The ruckus that accompanied Padre Rafael contrasted sharply with
his affable nature. He was a slow, practical man who loved science and
abhorred all physical exercise. Not once did he venture into the hills
on Padre Imperio's mule — it could not have withstood his weight —
to give last rites to shepherds or parishioners who lived outside town.
When autumn came and the fog of spirits returned, Tolón rang the
morning bells precisely on time and the church doors remained closed.
The priest thought such legends were nothing but a meteorological
phenomenon, and the boy offering black-market goods, the old women
bartering lentils, and the fugitives seeking the embraces of loved ones
were forced to find somewhere else to hide when the noblemen's souls
disappeared.

The day Padre Rafael came to the cemetery after six o'clock, his
steps caused seismic waves that shook graves, rattling the bones of the
dead in their coffins and creating a sinister clatter that tarnished the

evening. Playing in the dirt on her father's grave, Margarita Laguna began to cry inconsolably. Cypress trees swayed, magpies flapped off course, headstones wobbled. Olvido recognized the priest in that thunder, picked up her daughter, and fled to the vault. But guided by Margarita's cries, the priest stood before them in no time at all.

"The cemetery is closed, señorita," he said, stonefaced.

"We brought flowers to a family member and lost track of time. It's a good thing you found us."

"The desecration of a grave, young lady, is a terrible thing." The priest had seen the dirt under Olvido's nails.

"Her father is buried here," Olvido replied, stroking her daughter's hair.

Margarita had stopped crying and was studying Padre Rafael with wide, wet eyes.

"Her father's remains belong to God and the earth now. I do not want to see you here after hours again, or I will have to call the police."

Padre Rafael walked them to the gate, then returned to investigate the rain damage to several vault roofs, not realizing his own presence might be more destructive.

For some time following Padre Rafael's warning, Olvido stayed out of the cemetery after the undertaker locked the gates. But her need to be close to Esteban forced her to return, despite her fear of being arrested and having her daughter left in the care of Manuela Laguna. That idea was so horrific that she limited her furtive visits to once a month.

As Margarita grew, so did Manuela's hate for her. When the girl turned six, Olvido was so exhausted by insomnia and worry that she decided it was time for her daughter to go. She was school age, anyway, and Olvido worried the local children would be as mean to Margarita as they had been to her. It made no difference that the new school was built thanks to a donation from her mother; their family was still cursed, still carried the stench of dishonor. To execute her plans, Olvido asked the lawyer who managed the Laguna estate for help. By now he took his drives around town and the countryside in a brand-new silver car with a horn that startled the donkeys and gave chickens the runs.

Olvido saw the lawyer for the first time just after Margarita was born. He arrived unannounced at Scarlet Manor, with urgent business for Manuela. Olvido opened the door in a flowered dressing gown that could not contain her milk-filled breasts, her hair grazing her shoulders, her eyes stormy and blue. From then on, the lawyer besieged her with letters declaring his admiration, his wish that they meet in secret. He sent gifts — bouquets of daisies and roses, coral necklaces, silver thimbles — and showed up at Scarlet Manor with any excuse to delight in the goddess-like attributes that had charmed him so. Olvido did not reply to a single letter, returned all of his gifts, and ignored him whenever he came. However, on her daughter's sixth birthday, praying to God for rain, enough to flood the world, she sat down and wrote the following letter:

Dear Sir,
Please advise my mother that I will be sending my daughter, Margarita Laguna, to a boarding school in the capital, where she will remain all year long except for Christmas and summer vacations. I would also ask you to help choose a school where my daughter will receive a decent education.
Yours sincerely,
OLVIDO LAGUNA

The lawyer, now a stooped man in his sixties, received the letter first thing in the morning a few days later. His maid set it on the silver tray with his breakfast. Having devoured a piece of garlic toast drizzled with oil, he absent-mindedly read the return address. Instinct brought his hand to his groin, staining his silk robe. He huffed angrily and choked on the smell of garlic.

"Get this peasant fare out of here, and bring me buttered toast and marmalade!" he shouted at his maid.

Spellbound, he turned back to the fine handwriting in the letter.

He thought of the color blue, hips like a mountain stream, breasts like big, ripe figs . . . His hand went back to his groin, staining his robe yet again.

A few hours later, dressed in an alpaca suit, he wrote Olvido a note to say he would be pleased to comply with her request, yours with affection, honor, and humility, the undersigned—on gold-embossed letterhead.

The boarding school the lawyer chose for the youngest Laguna was run by Augustinian nuns on the outskirts of Madrid. He told Manuela the news at one of their Thursday meetings. She rubbed her white gloves together and smiled: not seeing her granddaughter's gray eyes and distancing Olvido from the shame of being an unwed mother was the best she could hope for at this point. But Manuela still wished to one day regain control over her daughter, and this seemed like a unique opportunity.

"I'm glad you approve of the arrangements I made."

The lawyer, too, was celebrating Margarita's departure. He pictured the young mother naked on satin sheets, with nothing but gratitude and time to spare.

Because the lawyer had complied so completely and expeditiously with that request, from then on, any time Manuela and Olvido had something important to say to each other, they did so through him. He read Manuela the letters from her daughter and, when she spat a reply, asked Olvido to come to his office in town—always at the end of the day and always through the back door—so as to have the pleasure, my dear friend, of advising you in person of your mother's wishes, yours always, affectionately, honored to be of service, the undersigned—on gold-embossed letterhead. P.S. I devotedly adore you . . .

From behind a mahogany desk, strangled by a white shirt and Italian tie, the lawyer recited Manuela's decisions to Olvido as if they were verses from *Don Juan Tenorio,* condensed desire sweating from his bald head and nose.

"My dearest Olvido." He pulled open a drawer. "Please accept this modest gift." A leather case was placed on the desk.

"You've done more than enough for me already." Olvido's eyes darkened.

The lawyer stood from his large Spanish armchair and came to place a fleshy hand, speckled with age, on her exquisite forearm.

"Ask anything of me, my dear. Just ask. I only wish to please you . . ." he whispered.

"If you would be so kind as to divert some of my mother's funds into an account in my name, I would be forever grateful. After all, I am of age now." Olvido's lips grazed his ear.

"But my dear, you must understand that——"

Olvido continued her ardent, whispered plea.

"Yes, Olvido, my dear. I cannot deny you any longer. Yes, I will help. Your daughter will want for nothing. Yes, I know you know how to repay me." A trickle of drool fell onto his lapel. Then, as if she were yelling from a cave, his wife's voice called him to dinner.

The boarding school run by Augustinian nuns was housed in a small stone palace with pointed windows that had belonged to King Philip II's secretary. It stood alone on a hill, and its silhouette from the road below looked like that of a medieval abbey. It was surrounded by a wall where daisies, cotton thistle, and clumps of lilac grew, where neighborhood dogs came to howl and mate after night fell. The main door — which the nuns closed from midafternoon until after matins — was spiked with square nails, like a torture device. The grounds behind the wall were large and sunny. There was a rose garden and a vegetable plot out back where tomatoes, lettuce, and shallots grew. There was also a grassy meadow with weeping willows where the girls skipped rope or sewed in the melancholy shade of the trees, as well as a dirt field for hopscotch and relay races.

From the very first day, the grounds inside the wall were Margarita Laguna's favorite place. She would wander out at recess to inhale the fragrances that took her back to Scarlet Manor. But when autumn came and the grounds fell silent with nary a flower, she knew for the first time what it was to be sad. Margarita had to wait until spring— through afternoons of rain and lined notebooks—to smell those memories again.

Margarita celebrated the return of the poppies, geraniums, and hydrangea in April by pulling off her gray skirt and navy blue sweater to lie naked in the meadow by the willows. Before her classmates found and taunted her, before a nun in a wimple bent to cover her with the rough sacristy blanket the cats used to sharpen their claws, Margarita Laguna felt like she was home, her eyes closed, the sun playing on her skin. The wimpled nun led her down a hall past snickers and insults to see the headmistress. Such indecent behavior was a serious breach of discipline; do it again and she would be expelled.

The next morning, when Margarita felt the sun's caress and inhaled the flowers' perfume, she had to stifle the desire to strip naked and lie on damp earth. She spent all day scratching as her body was suffocated by clothes, but by nightfall she had an idea. The nuns had forbidden her to take off her uniform but said nothing about her underclothes. From then on, Margarita Laguna decided not to wear panties again. Her pubis would grow free, at the mercy of the wind and sun that found their way there, mocking her uniform.

Margarita Laguna came home to Scarlet Manor for the summer. Olvido waited at the train station, a few miles from town, to meet her. The lawyer had chosen a suitable matron to chaperone the girl on the trip. Margarita jumped from the first-class car, ran down the platform and into her mother's arms. The chestnut hair she inherited from Clara Laguna was pulled into two braids, and her gray eyes sparkled at being back in the land where her father lay. The locomotive belched smoke. Men in green Civil Guard uniforms appeared, there to inspect any basket or suitcase considered suspicious, in search of black-market foods.

"I missed you so much!" Olvido was crying.

The suitable matron stepped down with Margarita's suitcase, which did not raise suspicion among the guards, recounted the details of the trip to Olvido, and sat on a bench to wait for the next train back to the city.

"Mamá, Mamá, can I sunbathe naked this summer?"

"In the honeysuckle clearing, the way you like to, yes."

"Good!" Margarita clapped. "At school they don't let me."

"No, at school you should never do that. Only at home."

"I know. At first I was sad, but then I realized I could go without panties under my uniform, and no one ever found out," she replied, lifting her skirt just a little. One firm, pink cheek flashed on the platform.

"You little rebel," Olvido said with a smile. "Just like your father. She told him not to come back, but he did."

"Back where, Mamá? Who told him not to?"

"Stories of the past, my darling."

"You don't have to tell me if you don't want to." Margarita walked along, holding her mother's hand. "How is Abuela?"

"In more pain every day. Her arthritis is very bad."

"Ar-thri-tis. That's a hard word. Do you think she'll speak to me this year?"

They left the train station. A flock of swallows crossed the sky. The old cart was waiting with the dapple-gray horse that had replaced the black one, dead of old age.

"It's best if your grandmother stays away from you and you stay away from her. Don't love her. She'll only break your heart."

"If she's so awful, then why do you live with her?"

Cicada trills rose from nearby fields.

"So she'll never forget."

During summer vacations, Olvido and Margarita read stories and poems as they sat on the porch in the midafternoon light. At first it was Olvido who read to her daughter, but once Margarita learned to read, Olvido would beg her to — especially if it was Saint John of the Cross. She loved to hear Margarita's voice, so like the burbling of a river, as her blue eyes stared off toward the cemetery. The two of them baked cookies and cakes, went for walks in the oak grove, braided honeysuckle and daisies into each other's hair, like wood nymphs. They planted tomatoes, lettuce, and squash, and sunbathed naked in the clearing, of course—even though men from town fell and broke bones climbing the rock wall to watch the most beautiful woman in the world bronze herself alongside her bastard child.

Meanwhile, stripped of her power, Manuela Laguna watched from a distance so as not to arouse suspicion. Her chicken massacres continued and were so brutal that the birds whimpered in terror whenever Margarita came home to Scarlet Manor. Manuela's other victims—centipedes, cockroaches, and roses—were more fortunate; they were attacked less often. Their executions were not nearly as bloody and so did not soothe her as easily. What the arthritic old woman wanted most was to regain control over her daughter. Olvido was not yet thirty; there was still time to marry her off to a rich man.

Margarita's vacations passed all too quickly for Olvido. Year after year, as the day of her departure approached, she considered keeping her daughter home. But then she would be tormented by dreams of small, white coffins and photos of dead little girls pasted to headstones. "Let her go back to Madrid," Olvido would say to herself as the dough for cinnamon cake rose in the kitchen. "She'll be safer with the nuns. No one can hurt her there." A few days later she would take her daughter to the station, handing her over to the respectable matron who would chaperone her to school. The locomotive would whistle white steam, and the train would set off. "Goodbye, darling," Olvido would whisper, lost in a cloud of dust. "Be happy." The rails would squeal and the car windows would observe her. The entire station would begin to smell of moss, rain, and lavender.

Olvido would race to the cemetery, hide in the vault, and, after six o'clock, lie on Esteban's grave until magpies woke her in the morning. With a mouth full of soil and fingers perfumed by flowers, she would go home to Scarlet Manor. Manuela, stationed in the kitchen plucking chickens, would hear her climb the stairs to Clara Laguna's room. She let her go again, Manuela would think, delighted, sharpening a knife. "Well done, dear. Maybe next time I'll have the opportunity to take care of her once and for all," she'd murmur, licking the droplets of blood that speckled her lips.

Manuela followed through on her threat when Margarita Laguna was thirteen. The cinema came to town that summer, like it had before the war. There was no more rationing, and the taste of white bread, not brown, of lentils, not weevils, returned to the old women's palates. The Civil Guard no longer hunted fugitives in the hills, and young people could afford to spend a little money on a film. There was only one showing, Saturday evening in the town square. A recently released prisoner set up the folding chairs, a man who drank what little he earned to wash away the taste of bullets and prisons walls. Manuela saw him drinking a bottle of wine by the fountain one morning. She waited until dark, hauled her arthritic body up into the cart, and headed for town. This time she found him sleeping in an alley, half-dressed and drooling. The town was immersed in the magical half-light of the cinema. *Welcome, Mr. Marshall!* was playing. Manuela kicked the man awake. When he opened one hazel eye, she tossed a wad of bills onto his chest.

"Crush her skull with a rock," she said.

"Who, señora?" The man patted the money with a shaky hand.

"Crush it," Manuela insisted. "I want to see if it's the same excrement inside like her father."

"That's awful, señora. I might be a wretch, but I'm no murderer."

"Tomorrow at noon you will be," Manuela replied, flipping more money in his face. "All this will buy a lot of wine, whiskey even. You will kill her tomorrow without fail. Now, let me tell you who and where to find her."

The man took a long pull of wine from a bottle and stuffed the money into his flea-infested pants pocket.

That Sunday burned hot from dawn, and the August heat stuck to the skin. Near midday, sparrows gathered in the treetops in search of shade as bees fainted onto roses. The nearly adolescent body of Margarita Laguna lay sunning in the honeysuckle clearing. The drunk Manuela hired found the gate open and stared up at the words on the funeral bow: WELCOME TO SCARLET MANOR. He could not actually read them, but he shivered all the same. In between swigs from a new bottle of wine, he entered that fertile yard. He tried to remember the directions Manuela had given him, and he left the daisy-strewn drive behind him. The closer he got, the more his heart demanded wine. He stopped in front of the house several times. No one saw him. Finally, after circling it and crossing the vegetable garden, he found a clearing where the smell of honeysuckle was more intoxicating than good cognac. In the midst of that paradise, he saw who he had come to kill. He saw her long, pink back; he saw the outline of what would be a breast; he saw raised calves and feet casting shadows on two round buttocks; he saw chestnut hair; he saw the tip of a tongue following a nib as it moved across the page of a sketchbook . . . Instead of pulling the sharp rock out of his bag, he stuffed the wine bottle in and approached the girl as he undid his pants. A cloud hid the sun and the air grew nauseating. Margarita heard leaves rustle, turned—a triangle of light-brown shadow below her stomach—and found a stranger with his pants around his ankles. She did not feel afraid. She dropped her pencil and stared at his greasy hair, his wine-stained shirt, and that thing rising between his legs. Shots rang out. The man fell to his knees, staring at Margarita through the eyes of a newborn, reaching out—wanting to touch that skin as smooth as glass—but died before he made contact, on top of the girl's drawing of a farm with ducks and cows.

Olvido Laguna stood holding the rifle. Her breathing was rapid and steam rose from her temples. She had seen the man from her bedroom window, weaving his way toward the clearing.

"He fell on my drawing." Margarita cocked her head, narrowed her eyes, and looked down at the dead man reeking of wine.

"You can make another."

. . .

At sundown Olvido dug a hole at the base of a pear tree and buried the body. Streams of sweat ran down her skin. Her arms hurt, her back hurt, but she could not rest.

Manuela was removing her dressing gown when she saw her daughter waving her cane. She did not part her lips — pride would not let her be the first to shatter their long-standing silence — but looked into Olvido's eyes — sword blue — looked at the cane — resplendent in new hands — and waited. The bedroom curtains were open. Manuela felt the cane on her back just once, startling at the dry crack on brittle bones. She did not scream. Moonlight poured through the window, and Olvido let the cane fall to the floor. Its sound as it hit the ceramic tiles made Olvido nauseous, and she stalked off to Clara Laguna's room wishing for only one thing: death.

The summer cinema left town that night. Several employees searched the tavern and the streets for the man who'd set up the chairs.

"He must be sleeping it off wherever he happened to fall," one of them said.

"We're better off without him," the owner declared. "The rows were crooked whenever he drank too much, and customers hate that."

The man rotted beneath the pear tree. The only time Olvido thought of him was after a nightmare in which her hands were covered in gunpowder. From the moment she killed him, she promised to keep Margarita away from Scarlet Manor even more. Olvido now spent Christmas at a guesthouse in Madrid, where she slept soundly. Her daughter was allowed back only on summer vacation. But before Olvido left for the station to meet her, she set the cane next to the fireplace in the parlor. Her mother needed to know the cane now belonged to her, and with it, all power over their cursed home.

12

THE SUMMER MARGARITA LAGUNA turned eighteen she graduated from boarding school. One late-June morning she came down
the steep staircase from the dormitory into the entryway adorned with
saints and crucifixions. She held a suitcase in each hand; her hair was
curled with an iron, her eyes big and stormy, her lips painted pink.
Margarita was not as gorgeous as her mother but still very beautiful.
She was wearing a white blouse with lace trim on the sleeves, a wide
plastic belt, and a lizard brooch. An A-line beige skirt and stiletto heels
completed her outfit.

When Olvido Laguna saw her daughter, she leaned back against a
drawing of Saint Lucia and wanted to cry.

"You look lovely . . . and so grown-up, darling."

"Mamá! I'm so happy to see you." Margarita laced her fingers with
Olvido's. "There's something I have to ask. It can't wait. I'm too excited . . . My entire future depends on it."

The girl's gaze burned brighter, and her mother glimpsed Esteban's
stubborn nature.

"And what is it?"

"First, you need to know that if you refuse, I'll die." Margarita
pouted.

A ray of sunlight bounced off Saint Lucia's crown of angels, illuminating the crease between Olvido's brows.

"Then I'll have to visit your grave and eat your favorite cinnamon cake, just to make you jealous."

"Mamá, I'm serious. My life is in your hands."

A tremor ran through the scars on Olvido's back, and she knew that, sooner or later, they would come to bear on her daughter's destiny.

"That's quite a responsibility, then," Olvido whispered.

"It's about Paris," Margarita said. "I want to go to university in Paris. It's the only place to study art. All of the great modern masters lived there. Painting is in the very air. Do you understand what I'm saying, Mamá?"

The wood paneling gave off the warm scent of varnish. Engrossed in the upside-down crucifixion of Saint Peter, Olvido Laguna repeated the name of that city: Paris, Paris. Paris is so far away. Good, she thought. For months she had been unable to sleep, unable to concentrate and give her cooking the passion it required. She worried Margarita would want to come back to Scarlet Manor after graduation. And yet, on that summer day teeming with swallows, all of her fears disappeared at the sound of one word: Paris. Nothing could reach that far, not Manuela's claws, the town's disdain, or the Laguna curse. She'll be so far away, Olvido lamented. I won't see her often. Olvido then mourned for the blood pouring from Saint Peter's wounds. But she'll be safe, studying art. Olvido smiled. The martyr's face radiated peace, the kind that came through dying for a loved one.

"Are you all right? Say something, please." Margarita had just noticed her mother's rapt contemplation. "Sister! Bring me a glass of water. My mother's lost in a trance!"

The Augustinian nun, confined to a box of a room to watch the door during Mass and rosaries, looked at Olvido Laguna. Rather than the glory of God, she saw the cobwebs of nostalgia in her eyes.

I'll have to meet with my dear friend the lawyer, Olvido thought, completely unaware of her surroundings. I'll need a lot of money for her tuition, lodging, food, and other expenses. I'll have to keep him happy.

"Drink, Mamá!" Margarita took the glass of water the nun handed her.

"Paris," Olvido blurted out. "That's an excellent idea, darling. You'll go to Paris and you'll study art."

Margarita dropped the glass, water miraculously splashing onto the illustration of Saint Lawrence burning on an iron grill, and curled up in her mother's arms.

For two years Olvido and her daughter wrote each other every week. All around the seascape on Olvido's bedroom walls were postcards of the Eiffel Tower, Notre-Dame, Sacré-Coeur, the Invalides, bridges over the Seine. In many of them Margarita apologized that she would not be home for Christmas or summer vacation. Some seminar or class trip always came up to prevent her from returning to Scarlet Manor. "You're doing the right thing, darling. Don't come back. You'll never be happy here. Don't come back. Enjoy your freedom in Paris," Olvido murmured as her life passed in slow motion, like a dying river.

Olvido spent mornings in the yard, even when winter encased her heart in a blanket of snow; she tended the tomatoes, lettuce, and squash, their aroma permeating her skin; she read Saint John of the Cross next to the mossy stone where Esteban's skull had shattered; she swept the cobblestone drive. The only place Olvido never went was the rose garden. That tangle of thorns and giant petals belonged to her mother.

When it was time for the midday meal, Olvido went into the kitchen to delight in cooking her recipes, even though Manuela still left pots on the stove. Over the years, however, with Margarita gone, the contents of those pots went from nothing but scorched leftovers to delicacies Manuela prepared hoping to soften her daughter's resentment. Olvido would sometimes find gifts as well: gold rings, silver bracelets, and crystal baubles accompanied by a note in the lawyer's hand. "There will be more if you marry me." But Olvido never accepted a thing.

Afternoons belonged to the lust of cooking. Olvido spent hours and hours remembering Esteban in that sanctuary of taste. Esteban's features — the dimple in his chin, the cowlick at the back of his neck, his gray eyes — and his young body — firm thighs, sun-toasted hands, soldier's chest — became more present in her mind. The only thing that bothered her was the smell of fresh blood from chickens massacred on the wooden table, an area she avoided in disgust. Olvido and her mother shared the kitchen but always used it at different times: Manuela in the mornings, Olvido in the afternoons. And there were certain territorial limits. Her mother was not allowed to set any entrails on the countertop where Olvido brought her ingredients to climax, and in exchange, she did not clean the sacrificial altar in case the smell of innards that reminded Manuela of her childhood should disappear.

One or two afternoons a month, Olvido had to leave her culinary paradise and go to the lawyer's office. Dressed in flannels and silks, he kissed her neckline while confirming there were more than enough pesetas in her checking account to cover Margarita's expenses. But as time went on and age was not kind, he grew more and more demanding.

"My dear," he said, licking her cleavage, "if your mother finds out I am diverting funds to you and your daughter, I will be in a great deal of trouble. I'm afraid that, next time, if you don't" — he slipped a hand under Olvido's skirt only to find a petticoat as rigid as iron — "if you don't come less heavily attired . . . You understand? I mean, it's like you're wearing a chastity belt. Yet we all know you have a daughter, and children, my dear. Well" — he pinched her thigh — "you know what I'm trying to say. Either you come prepared for the act — I cannot wait any longer — or the money will stop."

"How much does my mother allow for Margarita's expenses?"

"One quarter of what she needs. Your mother is not very generous with her fortune and even less so with her granddaughter. Therefore, if you do not want the girl to be mired in the hell of poverty, then come here next Monday without that chaste armor and our private arrangement will continue."

Out in the street, Olvido took a handkerchief from her purse and wiped down her neck. Between the rooftops, autumn was beginning to show. Hunters had returned. Exhausted packs of hounds relieved themselves on the stone fountain in the square as their owners, rifles on shoulders, the smell of the hills saturating their green attire, sat drinking in the tavern. It was almost six-thirty. Olvido sat down on a bench.

Drawn by the current of modernity that surfaced in the late 1950s, Padre Rafael had set up a public address system in the church. At that time of night several speakers attached to the church and town hall as well as several lampposts along the main street would broadcast a program on religion, culture, and social concerns. The first time sound boomed through town, the old women — who watched the speakers and cables being installed, who heard Padre Rafael announce this invention at Sunday Mass — thought for a moment the good Lord himself had come down from heaven to speak, as dogs and cats scampered into ditches, eardrums aching. Excited by these new times, microphone in hand, sitting still so the reverberation of his life would not disturb the waves, Padre Rafael reminded parishioners of times for catechism, Mass, and funerals, commented on the latest film — *La gran familia* — or delighted listeners with cassettes of Gregorian chants. Once they grew accustomed to the priest's tinny voice, the packs of hounds snuggled down and snoozed to the sacred music. Olvido had become a fan of these programs — a distraction from her solitary existence — and tried to be there for both the noon and evening shows.

"May I say that you are the most beautiful woman I have ever seen," a hunter said to Olvido that day.

Sitting on the bench, she looked up at his damp cloak, the cartridge belt hugging his waist, his pants tucked into tall boots, his black hair and dark green eyes. A desire not her own stirred inside. Olvido thanked him for the compliment and set off for Scarlet Manor, pressing her purse to her chest to contain the tension rising in her throat as Padre Rafael's words were lost on a liquid wind.

The next week Olvido walked to the lawyer's office through the pine forest. She had not put on a petticoat or underwear. He sat waiting for her behind his mahogany desk in a houndstooth suit.

"Sit, my dear Olvido," he said, scratching between his legs. "You're looking lovely for the occasion."

Olvido took off her coat, sat across from his desk, spread her legs, and shimmied her skirt up to her waist. The lawyer adjusted a pair of round silver glasses on his nose.

"Your secret is almost more beautiful than your face, and that is no easy feat." His hands shook. "My dear Olvido, how often I have dreamed of this moment."

Faced with that universe opened lusciously before him, the lawyer pulled down his pants and boxers ironed with rose water. But nothing else happened. His member shrank at such beauty, at the sight of pink mounds softly rising and falling, surrounded by a thoroughbred's crimped mane.

Seven times, on seven different weeks, the lawyer tried to sleep with Olvido Laguna. And seven times, confronted by his own age and such divine topography, the lawyer was overcome by a wave of impotence that left him prostrate on the couch, sipping lime blossom tea. Olvido breathed a sigh of relief. Every morning she washed her vulva with well water, scrubbed it with a poppy and citrus blossom paste to enhance its magnificence, leaving its mounds as smooth and radiant as a bride's skin.

But her nightmares were what helped Olvido break free of the lawyer for a time. Ever since her daughter moved to Paris, Olvido had dreamed of Esteban's blood. She would wake drenched in the scent of squash and crawl under the covers, shaking. Every now and then she vomited a clear moonlight-colored liquid.

One Sunday night a blizzard thrust the smell of pines into the hearts of sleepwalkers and insomniacs alike. It ripped Padre Rafael's speakers from the front of the church and blew open the kitchen window at Scarlet Manor just as Olvido was about to make cinnamon cake. The blizzard carried the death of leaves, the damp of mushrooms, and the solitude of a land only just recovering from adversity. The bottle of cinnamon shattered on the floor, and its perfume filled the room with the memory of Margarita. It had been years since Olvido had kissed her, held her. Olvido Laguna knew she had to visit her daughter before the nightmares engulfed her forever.

The next morning, as the town surveyed the destruction wrought by the blizzard, Olvido wrote to the lawyer:

My dear friend,
Please advise Manuela Laguna of my immediate departure to
see my daughter in Paris. In the name of our mutual friendship,
I must trust you to finalize the financial details of this trip, if
you understand.

With heartfelt thanks, yours truly,
OLVIDO LAGUNA

"You can't leave just when we're becoming intimate," the lawyer protested from behind his desk.

"I'll be back soon, I promise. My daughter is in trouble. She needs me. Surely you understand a mother's obligation."

"Well, I spoke with your mother yesterday, and she did not approve your trip. Without her consent, there is no money for you to go. And if I give it to you, she will discover our secret."

"Tell my mother that, if she gives me the money, I will marry whomever she chooses when I return."

"What madness is this, my dear Olvido? Who would want to marry a woman with your reputation?"

"My mother will do whatever it takes to find him. Someone will want me."

"I haven't offended you, have I? I adore you, Olvido, but I am constrained by a fifty-year marriage, seven children, ten grandchildren."

"I know. I wasn't thinking of you. Propose this to my mother. Find me a good match, and I will repay you once I return."

Three weeks later Olvido Laguna was on a plane to Paris. Looking through the window of this amazing contraption floating among the clouds, she recalled her mother's smile as she left. "I'll be here, waiting for the wedding," it seemed to say. "I'll do my petit point, tend to my roses, and butcher my chickens — and find you a husband, of course. Come back soon!"

Margarita was waiting at the airport when she arrived. This time it was Olvido who walked downstairs with a suitcase in each hand. She was thirty-seven years old, and for the first time since Esteban died, she wanted to live.

"Mamá! I don't want us to be apart ever again. Stay with me here!" Margarita said as they embraced.

"As you wish, darling. I give in. I'll do whatever you ask."

"Then it's settled. You'll stay." Margarita kissed her mother's cheeks. "And how is Abuela?"

"Her arthritis has worsened."

"*Arthritis*. I used to repeat that word at boarding school as I went to sleep. The other girls thought I was praying. Tell me, Mamá, does Abuela know how to write?"

"No, she's illiterate."

"Are you sure?"

"Yes, of course. She doesn't know how to read or write."

"And is there anyone who can write letters for her?"

"Only her lawyer . . . Why do you ask? Have you received a letter from her?"

"No! I've told you a thousand times, I just feel sorry for her. I wonder how someone like that can get by." Margarita was pensive for a moment. "I also wanted to ask if one day you'll tell me about my father."

"What's gotten into you, darling?" Olvido asked, stroking her daughter's hair. "I've just arrived and——"

"I want to know more about my family. That's all, Mamá. You never tell me anything. It's as if you have something to hide."

The stench of gunpowder filled Olvido's nose. How could she tell Margarita the truth about her father's death? How could she tell her she was born into a family burdened by a curse that would chill her bones?

On the taxi ride into the center of Paris, Olvido admired the beauty of the city. The sorrow she'd felt moments earlier began to dissipate.

Following his client's instructions, the lawyer had booked a five-star hotel. Manuela wanted to make sure Olvido was happy, that not a single complaint would derail her plan to marry off her daughter. The lobby floor was tiled in pink and white marble; on the walls, mirrors and paintings glittered in the light of a crystal chandelier. Three women shuffling on rags were polishing tiles in step to a military beat.

Margarita checked her mother in at reception. A bellboy carried both suitcases, leading them to Olvido's room. It was large but a bit dark, classically furnished with heavy green curtains. Margarita tipped the bellboy as he left.

"Mamá, can I ask you a question about my father now?"

"Of course."

"Did you love him a lot? I mean, did you love him like in the movies?"

"I did, darling. I loved him like that and more. Your father was everything to me."

"And then he fell out a window."

"It was an accident."

"Do you think he died just because he loved you?"

"Of course not."

"I'm never going to fall in love." Margarita plunked down on the double bed. "I've decided."

"Well, that's a shame. Besides, you should know by now it's not something you can stop. It just happens and that's that."

"But you were unlucky and I'm sure I will be, too."

"That makes me sad, darling." Olvido took her daughter's face in her hands. "There's no reason the same thing will happen to you. Your life is completely different from mine. And I was lucky; I was so lucky to know your father. He taught me to read and write. It was wartime, and a bomb destroyed the school. Now, is this on your mind because you like someone?"

"No." Margarita sighed and looked at the clock. "I've got to go, Mamá. I have a meeting at university. Rest, and I'll come back in a few hours for dinner."

Olvido took a shower when her daughter left. She turned the water hot, letting it cascade over her memories. In the distance, she thought she heard a bomb explode.

The phone rang at nine-thirty that night.

"Hello?"

"Mamá, were you asleep?" Margarita's voice crackled.

"No, just resting."

"Something's come up at university, so I won't make it for dinner. I'm sorry."

"Do what you need to, darling. I'll eat here at the hotel and see you tomorrow."

"See you then."

Olvido had no appetite. She walked over to the window. Through lace curtains she could see the silhouette of a full moon, lighting the sky over Paris with a milky halo. Olvido shivered. That moon was just a phantom. She knew. It couldn't fool her, even if it did illuminate the rooftops and chimneys with its melancholy obesity. "As far as I'm concerned, you died that icy night," she whispered, narrowing her eyes as she recalled Esteban's last kiss and how it tasted of fear. That moon was rotting in some celestial graveyard.

Margarita spent so much time at university that Olvido had to get used to being alone again. Every day she would walk along the Champs-

Élysées, around the Eiffel Tower and the stunning Invalides, carrying a newspaper or magazine in a language she did not understand. Longing for Esteban's grave led her to wander through Père Lachaise Cemetery from the time it opened until it closed. She was fascinated by the vaults, the sculptures that adorned tombs, anchored by thick foliage. She liked to sit on one with the statue of a soldier on his knees, his jacket open to receive imaginary bullets. Olvido stuffed the soil from Père Lachaise into the pockets of her raincoat, the weight of death preventing the Parisian wind from lifting her airborne, as if she did not exist. She also spent time at the Louvre and some galleries Margarita recommended. At sunset she would sit by the window in a Montmartre café to admire the domes of Sacré-Coeur or paintings set up on easels in the square, and feel Paris gaze upon her. She would drink one, two, three, four glasses of wine, damning its blood-red color as moss from the yard at Scarlet Manor grew thick in her mouth.

One day in late February, the day dawned to a mass of clouds that unleashed a mountain rain, and Olvido's luck changed. Margarita phoned to ask her to attend a party one of her professors was holding. Olvido noted the address and lay back in bed to wait for nightfall.

The professor lived near Notre-Dame, in an apartment overlooking the river. As Olvido descended from the taxi, the church towers looked like a pair of bat ears. A sparkling fog lay over the Seine. The temperature was dipping down near zero. As she walked up the stairs into the old apartment block, Olvido realized this was the first party she had ever attended. Before ringing the bell, she smoothed her hair; it hung loose, the first strands of gray appearing in the dark tresses. Margarita opened the door with a glass of wine in her hand.

"Mamá, I'm so glad you came." Margarita kissed her on both cheeks. "Let me introduce you to two of my classmates from Spain so you'll have someone to talk to."

Olvido followed her daughter into a room thick with cigarette smoke and young intellectuals. She took off her jacket, hanging it on a rack. A record was playing French music. In the middle of the room, several pale girls with black-rimmed glasses were dancing and smoking with eyes closed.

"The first thing you've got to do at any party in Paris or anywhere else is loosen up," Margarita said, pouring Olvido a glass of wine.

Olvido gripped the glass so tight her fingertips ached.

"Let me introduce you to Juan Montalvo and Andrés García."

Two young men with bloodshot eyes reached out to shake her hand.

"Have fun, Mamá!" Margarita disappeared down a hall.

"All mothers should be as beautiful as you," one of the men purred. "I hope you don't mind my saying so; I'm just trying to be friendly."

"Thank you." Olvido drank her glass of wine in one gulp and moved on, using the excuse that she was going to get another.

A slow song was playing, and several couples held each other tight as they danced. Olvido picked up a bottle of red wine and went to drink it near a couple kissing in the corner. The wet sound of their lips caused her heart to race. The smell of a carpentry shop slipped through that home like a ghost. On a sofa, surrounded by young, red-lipped French girls, the host was carving a piece of wood. Shavings whirled at his feet. Olvido could not take her eyes off him. And as he gave form to his piece, the green-eyed man stared back. His name was Jean, and his female students said he had the most handsome arms in all of France. He taught sculpture at the university, and when not in class, he was carving at home.

The song ended. Olvido heard the bells of Notre-Dame play a somber melody as a young man changed the record. Feeling dizzy, she left the room. She walked down the hall in pursuit of the smell of wood and came to the kitchen. There, on the icebox, was a carving of a male foot. Olvido continued to the bathroom, where the towel rack was a torso of a Greek god made out of cedar.

By the time the host was able to get free of French lipstick and look for her, Olvido had reached the bedroom. He walked toward her like an adolescent approaching his first love. He took the bottle and glass from her hands, replacing them with a champagne flute. Olvido took a sip of that liquid reminiscent of Clara Laguna's eyes and stroked behind the professor's ear. She found what she was looking for—sawdust—and kissed that pale powder. The host returned the kiss on her lips, as if his mouth were a knife testing wood with a first cut, then slowly began to carve. After a moment, he pulled back from his piece and said: "Jean, c'est mon nom."

Olvido's lips were a brilliant sculpture.

At dawn, Olvido tasted wood beside her, the taste of a man. For a split second she thought that frozen night with the voice of a wolf and a celestial suicide never happened. She thought the gunpowder and her mother's smile never happened. He was alive. He would open his leaden eyes, always darker on waking, and stroke her back. When she realized that more than twenty years had passed and the lips on her shoulder were not Esteban's, she startled. She could not remember who this man was. Her head ached and champagne bubbles still fizzed in her stomach.

Olvido slipped out of bed, trying not to wake him. She gathered her clothes from among wood shavings on the bedroom floor and got dressed in the bathroom. She did not take a taxi, choosing to walk along the Seine to her hotel instead. As she skirted the frost sleeping on cobblestones, one word came to her lips like a prayer, the word *Jean*.

Jean woke to the ringing alarm. It was eight o'clock and he had to teach. He reached out for the woman who had spent the night. He wanted to hold her, kiss her, but the bed was empty. Disappointed, he headed for the shower to scrub away his hangover. He went back into the bedroom to dress, and in the closet, the image of a slave's scarred back assaulted him from between shirts on hangers.

In the metro, he tried to remember her name but could not. As he walked up the stairs to the fine arts building, the fleeting belly of a woman appeared on every step. He walked into a room full of sleepy students. He said good morning and opened his briefcase; between the leather dividers, rosy crests bordering that perfect fissure lay in wait. He rubbed his eyes and began to explain certain techniques for mastering perspective. Champagne bubbles slipped out through his lips. Two breasts hovered over the room, aureoles spread like sails. He had to stop his lecture and swallow. He began again, this time writing on the board as his students looked on inquisitively, but the visions continued. On that scratched green surface was the outline of two thighs. Jean went to his seat behind a solid professor's desk. He could not remember where he was in his explanation, could not remember a single thing about techniques for mastering perspective. A pair of hips sashayed toward him.

He canceled class and went down to the cafeteria. The body of that woman assumed various poses as he drank a cup of tea. He had to see her again. He hurried to find Margarita as she was leaving class, asking her mother's name and where he might find her. Margarita hesitated. On the one hand, she was happy Olvido had left Scarlet Manor and was enjoying herself, but on the other, she was annoyed that her mother had been with the most sought-after professor in the entire university after just one night.

"Olvido Laguna. Hôtel la Madeleine," she said at last with a frown. "*Merci.*"

When Jean knocked at the door, Olvido was reading Saint John of the Cross. She had used her nail file on a bedside table, and her bare stomach held a little mound of sawdust.

"Margarita, is that you?"

Olvido heard a man speaking French as she reached the door and thought it must be a hotel employee.

"Je suis Jean." The professor's cheeks were rosy from the Parisian cold, his lips set in a tortured grimace.

Olvido silently repeated the word: Jean.

"Depuis que je me suis réveillé, je n'ai pensé qu'à toi," he said.

Olvido went to the door and motioned for him to come in.

"Partout j'ai vu ton corps et tes yeux." He stared at her lips.

"I don't understand. I don't speak French."

"Olvido."

"You know my name . . . Maybe I told it to you, I don't remember. I'm afraid I had too much wine, too much champagne."

Jean's eyes took aim at her heart.

"Champagne," he replied, smiling.

"Yes." Olvido inhaled his aroma, a combination of wood and cologne, and kissed him on the lips.

He ran his hands over the body that had tormented him so, caressing it as if it might disappear at any moment.

They left the hotel arm in arm at noon. Both spoke words the other could not understand, and out on the sidewalks of Paris, eager for spring they kissed. They decided to have lunch at a bistro. Jean ordered two sandwiches, Olvido two more—pointing at the menu as Jean nibbled her neck. They needed to regain their strength. Later they had coffee and Jean showed her how to smoke a Gauloise. Olvido inhaled, opening her mouth to let the smoke escape. She coughed and they both laughed. The two walked back to her hotel late that afternoon, but Olvido did not ask him up to her room.

"I have to speak to Margarita," she said.

"Margarita, oui, demain je viendrai te chercher."

Margarita Laguna came to the hotel around eight o'clock that night. She was not wearing any panties, like when she was a child.

"I've been thinking about Scarlet Manor all day," she told Olvido. "I suddenly realized how much I miss it. I think I'll go back with you."

"What are you talking about, darling? Your studies are here, your friends are here."

Margarita slumped back on the bed.

"This doesn't have anything to do with what happened at your professor's party last night, does it? Before you answer, I want to apologize. I drank too much champagne, and that man . . ." A smile escaped. "I couldn't help it. That smell, it reminded me so much of your father . . ."

"Really?"

"He smelled like wood, too, with sawdust behind his ears. He was working as a carpenter's apprentice until he could become a teacher."

"So that's why you got together with Jean?"

"I liked him. Plus, as I said, I had too much wine. And that yellow nectar, champagne, it was the first time I'd ever tried it."

"That's what my Spanish friends said. They said you drank too much and were rude, leaving Juan hanging when he was just trying to be nice."

"I'm sorry, darling. It was my first party and I was nervous. Are you ashamed of me?"

Margarita paused before answering.

"No, what do I care what they say. All I care is that you're happy."

"It won't happen again. I promise."

"That's all right. Besides, it can't happen again if we go back to Scarlet Manor."

The next day Olvido Laguna packed her bags. She dressed in a suit with a dark gray jacket and called down to reception for a taxi.

It was a sunny morning that smelled of daisies and fresh-brewed coffee. The taxi was waiting.

"À l'aéroport."

"Oui, madame."

Olvido pulled a sheaf of hotel letterhead out of her purse and, in a script that bumped along with the car, wrote:

Darling,
The lawyer was in touch this morning to say your grandmother's arthritis is worse. I have to go home. You stay in Paris.
This is your place. Be happy. Tell Jean it was a pleasure to meet him.

With love,
MAMÁ

13

WHEN OLVIDO LAGUNA returned to Scarlet Manor, her mother was waiting with a suitor to marry her. The man was a friend of the lawyer's from a nearby town and met all of Manuela's criteria. He had a spotless reputation, not even a hint of scandal that might tarnish it, as well as plenty of money and property. Widowed four years earlier, he was looking for a woman to ease the sorrow and solitude of retirement. The candidate was seventy-eight years old. But as far as the lawyer and Manuela Laguna were concerned, age posed no problem as long as the other two conditions had been met. It was unlikely Olvido would give the candidate children, a fact he did not mind in the least: with eleven children and twenty-seven grandchildren from his first marriage, the last thing he needed was another descendant to carry on his name.

The lawyer met with the candidate at his local tavern, listing not only Olvido's beauty but also her culinary skill and fondness for good conversation. The suitor asked how such an extraordinary woman was still single, an opportunity the lawyer used to reveal that Olvido had a twenty-something daughter, the result of rape when Olvido herself was not much more than a girl. She had spent her life raising her daughter, who now lived in Paris, so Olvido could now look for a good man who would accept her past and keep her company.

The suitor came to Scarlet Manor one rainy afternoon in a fancy chauffeured car. The lawyer sat beside him in the back seat. The man's face was jaundiced, and he leaned on a wooden cane with a silver handle. Olvido had spent the night weeping on Esteban's grave, swearing between heavy sighs and earthen kisses that she was committing this sacrilege purely for Margarita's sake, that she would hate her future husband whomever he might be. And yet, as she watched her suitor shuffling through the entryway after her mother and choked on the medicinal cloud surrounding him, she felt compassion.

Manuela Laguna showed him the house, peppering the tour with all manner of anecdotes about the aristocratic Laguna family. She seemed not to notice her future son-in-law's precarious health, just as she ignored her own trembling white gloves. Fifteen days had gone by without her butchering a single chicken, and Manuela's nerves were on edge. She had decided there should not be a whiff of fresh blood in the kitchen lest Olvido's suitor think the house smelled of death.

Over coffee in the parlor, it was agreed that the wedding would take place in one month's time. The lawyer gobbled sweets and slurped coffee. Given the groom's poor health, he knew the marriage would last only a few months, but he suddenly realized that if Olvido were to inherit any money after her husband's death, she would no longer need him to keep Margarita in Paris. His power over Olvido was in jeopardy.

A trip to the city was planned for the following week to finalize the paperwork and buy both the bride's dress and her trousseau. Olvido's suitor left Scarlet Manor feeling more alive than ever. He had fallen in love at first sight. On the ride home, he swore to always protect Olvido Laguna. Wanting nothing more than to make her happy, he decided a few days later to begin training at a brothel. The man had lost count of how long it had been since he was last with a woman, and on their wedding night he wanted his bride to forget her past trauma and take pleasure in the gentle passion of a loving man. His health proved too precarious, however, and he was found dead in a brothel bed a few hours later. The "pick-me-up" tonic he had taken erupted in the last orgasm his poor old body could handle.

Disguising his joy, the lawyer brought Manuela and Olvido the news. He proposed they postpone the search for another candidate at least a year, out of respect for the deceased. Olvido, who was saddened by the death of that man as jaunty as he was jaundiced, replied that she no longer intended to marry; she would not be introduced to every terminally ill old man in the province. Hearing this, Manuela flew into a rage, immediately butchering two roosters with reddish combs. The strain in the relationship between mother and daughter intensified. Manuela left charred pots of leftovers on the stove instead of delicacies and reduced Margarita's allowance even further. The only reason she did not eliminate it entirely was because the bastard might decide to come home. In spite of this, after one more year of solitude, silence, and stews, that is exactly what happened.

The first sign announcing Margarita Laguna's return was a stirring among the honeysuckle, the plants recognizing her touch the moment she stood under the gate with its funeral bow. It was a July morning, the air swarming with swallows and wasps. Eight months pregnant, Margarita walked down the daisy-strewn drive and knocked on the door. Her chestnut hair hung loose in the joy of summer, and her cheeks were damp with perspiration.

"Mamá, Mamá! Hug me if you can!"

Olvido could barely stammer her daughter's name.

"I know I didn't tell you I was expecting in my letters, but it was a surprise. I wanted to come home to Scarlet Manor and give birth, here, with you. Aren't you happy?"

"If you are, darling, then so am I." Olvido hugged her.

Then she saw him.

Tall. Strong. He was striding down the drive with a suitcase in each hand, tromping on Clara Laguna's daisies.

"Who's that?"

"Pierre Lesac, my boyfriend and the father of my child."

Two big black eyes fell like a disaster on Olvido's face.

"It's a pleasure to meet you," he said with a French accent, extending a hand.

There was a Gothic beauty to this young man of no more than twenty-five. He had a thin moustache that dripped over either side of his mouth to meet a neatly trimmed goatee. Olvido withdrew her hand, but Pierre's touch remained, a touch she suddenly felt burrowing under her skin like a tick.

"Mamá, aren't you going to say anything to Pierre?"

"Welcome."

"Merci."

He was wearing a beige shirt and beige pants. The sun shimmered on his short, dark hair, and his lips were plump.

A cough came from the entryway.

"Abuela?" Margarita asked.

The scent of lavender puffed out of the linen cupboard.

"Marriage certificate," Manuela demanded, stretching out a white glove.

Those were the first words she had ever spoken to her granddaughter, and her bitter face awaited a reply. If this young gray-eyed thing had married, it might have been the start of a new era for the Laguna women.

"I'm not married and won't ever be, Abuela. Things are different now, and that would be a step back. But Pierre, the father, is here with me."

"You're all the same," Manuela growled, and marched back to her room, relieved. She would not have to stop hating that girl.

"She'll never change, will she, Mamá?"

"No, it's too late for that. I hope she didn't upset you."

Mother and daughter hugged again, and Olvido felt Pierre's eyes on her.

Margarita's baby was born premature due to a series of events all related to romantic desire. It started when Olvido encouraged her daughter to see the gynecologist who had just opened an office on the main street in town. His name was Antonino Montero.

A sultry heat lay over his building, the sun lighting up the doctor's white sign, creating a mirage.

The sky would screw the earth if it could, Antonino Montero thought, imagining the sexual cataclysm. Humans would die, crushed between nature's moist flesh. He trained his glasses, like black television sets, on a fifty-something vagina, but startled when he heard his nurse shout.

"I told you! The doctor will not see you without an appointment. Now, go!"

The gynecologist came out of the examination room and into reception.

"What's going on?" he asked.

The nurse adjusted her cap as her boss's robust figure approached.

"It's these two, Doctor." She waved a scornful hand at Olvido and Margarita. "They want to see you, but they don't have an appointment. I told them there's no way. We're completely booked."

A wave of murmurs rose up from the waiting room.

Antonino Montero studied Olvido. Her breasts were like those ripe mangoes he had eaten in that Caribbean city, at a conference on mammary gland tumors — before he was accused of wrongful death at his practice in Madrid, before he was forced into exile in this grungy town. Antonino continued to stare at her. Her waist and hips were as curvy as the road that dropped down to the beach, where clouds formed in the shape of thighs.

A girl stood beside her, arms crossed over her belly. Antonino Montero coughed inscrutably and said to his nurse:

"It is my duty as a doctor to examine this young woman whether or not she has an appointment. She is quite clearly far along in her pregnancy."

"But, Doctor . . ."

"I must be true to my Hippocratic oath and would ask the ladies waiting to please understand. Have these two come in as soon as I'm finished."

The murmurs in the waiting room grew louder.

"Thank you for seeing us," Olvido said when they were seated across from the single, balding, forty-something gynecologist in his office.

"No need. It's my duty." Antonino smiled and saliva filtered into the channels of his jaw.

"My daughter is eight months pregnant, and I'd like you to examine her, make sure everything is all right."

"How can this be your daughter? I thought she must be your sister."

"I had her when I was young . . . Things were different back then."

"You live in that lovely estate on the outskirts of town, Scarlet Manor, if I'm not mistaken. I haven't been here long or had a chance to meet everyone yet."

"Yes, that's right, Doctor."

Antonino recalled the story about Olvido's grandmother that the pharmacist had told him over a game of cards at the tavern — about a prostitute with golden eyes named Clara Laguna who used to dance in an enormous bed covered by a purple canopy.

"May I ask how old you are?" Saliva pooled in the corners of his mouth.

"Thirty-nine."

"I thought you were young. And tell me, how old were you when you had your daughter?"

"Doctor, I didn't come to talk about me. We're here to see about Margarita."

Antonino did not hear her but was again savoring the stories he had heard at the tavern about the Laguna family. He pictured Olvido undressing by candlelight in the old carpentry shop. It would seem the pregnant girl was the result of her mother's forbidden love with the carpenter's apprentice, a boy found with his skull smashed and his pants down in the yard at Scarlet Manor. Yes, without a doubt, she was the Laguna of the dead boy.

"Since you're here, let me offer a free checkup. I imagine it's the first one since your daughter was born."

"That's not necessary. Again, I only came so you could see my daughter."

"No, no. I insist."

Antonino Montero now imagined himself in the yard at Scarlet Manor, surrounded by its devilish fertility, where Olvido Laguna mounted the dying boy. The doctor was spellbound by the grinding of her hips, the straight black hair cascading down her back, becoming entangled in twining plants.

"If you would like me to examine your daughter and attend the birth, then I will have to examine you first to determine whether there are any hereditary conditions." His words were dictated purely by imagination.

"I see."

"Go next door and undress from the waist up. First I must check the state of your breasts."

Olvido stroked Margarita's hair as she dozed in the chair. The trip from Paris had exhausted her.

"Rest here. I'll be right back," Olvido said.

The room was painted a soft peach color designed to soothe his patients' nerves. An examination table was covered in a sheet, with a stool and a lamp at the far end. Olvido took off her blouse and bra, then sat on the edge of the table. The gynecologist came in — and explored her breasts with feverish fingers.

"Excuse me." Antonino sucked in his stomach and hurried to the bathroom in the hall, where he spilled his pleasure all over the blue tiles.

Heat constricted his heart. He splashed water on the back of his neck, sucking clear droplets off his fingers, possessed by an unusual thirst.

When he returned, Olvido was dressed and waiting with her daughter. Margarita had taken off all her clothes, ready to get this exam over so she could nap in peace. Antonino Montero had her lie on the table and examined her under Olvido's watchful eye.

"The entire family is in excellent shape," he said to Olvido, his brow soaked in sweat. "Here is my home number if anything unexpected should occur, but I hope that won't be for a few days."

That afternoon, Olvido cooked dinner. She kissed each raspberry, washed them all, crushed them in the mortar, and threw them into a simmering pot of water, sugar, milk, and cinnamon. She gazed outside as she stirred and saw Pierre Lesac, pretending to be out for a walk in the garden. She turned back to her bubbling sauce. The sound reminded her of the river as it passed through the oak grove in spring. She sighed, turned off the heat, and set the pot aside, then began to cut up a piece of lamb. When she was done, her cheeks speckled with tiny drops of blood, she chopped a few onions. Tears fell from her eyes, drawn to the wet, pungent smell of the bulbs. Meanwhile, spying from between planted rows, Pierre watched her place the onion and lamb in a clay pot, then set it on the stove. He watched her sauté the meat; he watched her moisten her lips with a tongue he imagined like silk; wrapped in the glow of sunset through the pines, he watched as she left the clay pot on the stove and dropped her house robe to her waist. He felt ablaze at the sight of those breasts. Nothing would ever be the same again. The horizon began to meet the sun, and pierced by violet light, Olvido inhaled the smell of the cooling raspberry sauce, smearing a bit on her left nipple, then on her right.

"The perfect temperature and consistency," she said aloud.

Olvido used this culinary trick with most of her recipes; it never failed her. Nipples were the perfect chef's tool for tasting. She poured the sauce onto the meat, and that is where Antonino Montero's desire came to rest. Pierre Lesac waited for Olvido to leave the kitchen before he entered, plunging his fingers into the clay pot and licking them clean. His yearning merged with the doctor's. The moment Olvido poured the sauce on those slices of lamb, there was no going back.

· · ·

By dinnertime, the moon had filled the dining room with a cosmic silence. A porcelain platter of steaming lamb sat on the lace tablecloth the diplomat had given Clara Laguna.

Olvido served Margarita four slices of meat. Margarita attacked them with fork and knife, resorting to her hands whenever any bits close to the bone resisted. She stared at the strands of meat as she brought them to her mouth, wolfing them down with a primordial hunger.

"Mamá, four more," she said, holding up her plate.

"You shouldn't eat so much after dark. It'll take forever to digest in your condition." Olvido glanced at Pierre.

"I've got a stomach of steel," Margarita assured her mother, sopping up sauce with a piece of bread. "Isn't that right, Pierre?"

He nodded.

"Can't you just say yes? Would it kill you to open your mouth and pronounce a single syllable?"

Pierre nodded again.

"Can't you just forget your stupid circle of inspiration until I've given birth?" Margarita exclaimed. "I can't stand that you won't speak to me. I need you."

Pierre Lesac slowly chewed a piece of lamb.

"Talk to me, I said!"

He shook his finger no.

"You shouldn't get so upset," Olvido said, serving her daughter two more pieces of lamb.

"Give me two more, Mamá."

"It won't sit well, darling. Be reasonable."

"Either you give me two more pieces, or I will throw myself on that platter."

Olvido served her, and Margarita tore the pieces apart with her hands, barely chewing before swallowing. She then ripped the loaf of bread in half and began to sop up more sauce.

"This is divine. Just divine." A raspberry moustache stained her upper lip.

Olvido decided to take the last piece of meat into the kitchen before her daughter consumed it.

"Where are you going, Mamá?"

"Darling, please don't eat any more. Let Pierre have this piece."

Again, the Frenchman shook that finger Olvido would grow to hate forever.

"The only thing you care about is your damn circle of inspiration. Well, tomorrow you'll want me to speak to you, you'll beg me, but I won't say a word."

"I'll eat it, then," Olvido said. "I'm still a bit hungry."

"Don't you dare! That's mine." Margarita speared the piece of lamb and gulped it down. "Now give me the platter. I want more sauce."

"Please, darling. I know it won't agree with you."

"Don't be ridiculous. I said give it to me."

Olvido let the platter fall to the floor.

"You did that on purpose!" Margarita yelled as she stood from the table, her face flushed. "I need some air. I'm going outside."

"Do you want me to come with you?"

"No, I'd rather be alone. You two stay here. You" — Margarita looked at Pierre — "and your circle of inspiration can go to hell. And you" — she looked at her mother — "you and your childish games."

Margarita hauled herself out to the porch in search of oxygen.

Pierre Lesac had begun to draw as soon as he could hold a pencil. He colored the silk walls in his mother's room, the servants' legs, the Belgian lace tablecloths. He colored the desk of the banker who was legally his father and the floor tiles in the basement, where the banker locked him when he was bad. Hiding out in his mother's room, he colored her stepbrother's pants and the back of the satin-covered sofa. He colored the pews at Notre-Dame in Paris as darkness fueled his eyes and his mother wept in prayer, repenting her forbidden love. He colored the palms of his hands as he filed out of church, a distraction from the terror instilled by those gargoyles. He colored the curtains in the stepbrother's parlor as he listened, yet again, to his mother's pleasure. He colored his little bed, surrounded by the loneliness of parents at war. It was not until one morning, when the banker told him his mother had left with her stepbrother, that Pierre Lesac began to color on white paper. He was nine and his eyes were dark as sin.

In late adolescence, Pierre graduated from colored pencil and paper to oils. He left the banker's house behind and with it a taste for still life: jars, fruit, tables. From then on he specialized in portraits. The first one he ever painted was thanks to the magic of memory. He spent an entire day in silence, searching for his mother's features. When he found them in a corner of childhood, unable to forgive, he transferred them to canvas and sold them to an art gallery for more than he'd expected.

Ever since that exorcism—and as a result of its success—he decided not to speak for twenty-four hours prior to starting any portrait. Eyes, nose, lips, breasts, collarbone, waist, hands, profiles, forearms, eyebrows—among many other features and postures—would race through Pierre's body and mind to be imbued with inspiration. Since this journey began and ended with his heart, the organ that guided the master's hands, its complete path traced a circle Pierre called the circle of inspiration. He explained this extraordinary process to Margarita when they first started dating. She thought it a charming approach that set Pierre apart from all the other painters in Paris. Margarita had always respected his silence, but that night, eight months pregnant and struggling to digest a whole lamb poisoned by desire, her boyfriend's silence unhinged her. She waddled back from the porch struggling to catch her breath.

"Mamá! My stomach hurts!" she yelled.

Olvido, in the kitchen doing dishes, came out to meet her.

"Mamá! It hurts so much!"

"Take a deep breath." Olvido stroked Margarita's hair. "Let's go into the parlor so you can lie back on the sofa."

Margarita plodded along.

"Pierre, where are you? I need you, Pierre," she whined before falling onto a cushion, her legs spread.

Pierre Lesac, as tall and thin as a church spire, came in through the kitchen door.

"Sit beside me."

His dark features moved toward the Laguna women.

"Breathe deeply, darling. Nice and deep." Olvido wrung her hands.

"I'm scared, Pierre. Talk to me. I need to hear your voice. Speak to me in French. Tell me everything will be all right."

The Frenchman sat next to Margarita and caressed her cheek but said not a word.

"Speak to me, damn it! Speak to me!"

Pierre could not break the circle of inspiration, could not allow it to escape through his lips. All that accumulated desire, all those many nights longing for this moment. Twenty-four hours with her inside his body, racing through it, saturating it—ever since that night in Paris when he saw her photo on Margarita's bedside table and her beauty became an obsession.

"Has your damn circle made you deaf? I demand that you speak to me!" A viscous liquid ran down Margarita's legs.

"Your water broke! My God, the baby's on its way!" Olvido cried.

Leaning on Pierre and her mother, Margarita made it up to the second floor. Olvido guided her to the room where the iron bed awaited the birth of another Laguna girl. Olvido had cleaned the room every week since Esteban's death and would sometimes spend afternoons under the purple canopy, where she could smell the oak forest.

"Why here?" Margarita asked, panting.

"This is where you were born. And besides, it smells of family."

"I'm going to have a girl, aren't I? It's the curse. Abuela told me everything in a letter the lawyer must have written. I didn't want to tell you when you came to Paris, in case it made you hate her even more."

Fear rose in Olvido's throat.

"I'm going to have a girl and Pierre will die, like my father. We're fated to suffer for love and bear only girls who will suffer, too."

Olvido looked at the Frenchman; news of his imminent death did not seem to affect him in the slightest.

"I shouldn't have fallen in love. Abuela warned me in the letter. 'Stay pure,' she said. 'Stay pure and do not reproduce. The curse is in your blood, and you will kill the man you love.' I tried, Mamá. I swear I did. But I couldn't resist Pierre. I couldn't, Mamá. I couldn't. Je t'aime, Pierre." Margarita caressed his face, but all that mattered to him just then was feeling the circle, completing it successfully.

A contraction pushed Margarita onto the bed. Olvido pulled back the covers, revealing the scent of lavender in the sheets.

"I'm going to call the doctor. Please look after her, Pierre."

Inhaling the smell in that room, he stared at Olvido's lips, taking them into his veins.

From the bottom step, Olvido watched as her mother dipped a glove into the liquid that had run down Margarita's legs. She then sucked the cotton, recognizing the taste of life. Olvido shot a threatening glance as she passed her mother on the way into the parlor. It had been a year since the lawyer convinced Manuela Laguna to install a phone so she would not have to go into his office every Thursday. Manuela was reticent at first — not trusting the communicative power of an apparatus that looked more like donkey balls — but later agreed. It was becoming increasingly difficult to drag her arthritic bones into town.

"Dr. Montero, this is Olvido Laguna." A few tears fell onto the early-sixties black rotary phone. "My daughter's water broke. Come quickly, please."

"Olvido Laguna?" Those words meant little to the doctor beyond two breasts that had left him spent.

"I beg you. Come to Scarlet Manor. I need you."

"In that case, señora, how can I refuse? I'm on my way."

He hung up the phone and groomed his pubic hair with a fine-tooth comb. Any knots and he simply could not feel prepared. He picked up his bag and left for Scarlet Manor without a care for what people might say.

From the moment the baby was born, it harbored the sweet taste of Olvido's nipples on its tongue. Antonino Montero picked the baby up by the ankles, held it upside down, and smacked it on the bum. An angry wail rose up.

Olvido was wiping her daughter's brow.

"Doctor, does that cry mean she's all right?"

"She?" Antonino Montero arched his brows. "My dear, take a look at what your little granddaughter has between her legs."

Dawn shone in through the balcony, casting its light on the newborn's genitals.

"It's a boy," Antonino affirmed, "with two perfectly round testicles."

"Indeed, it is a boy," Olvido said, confirming there was no inherited vagina hidden in a fold on her grandson's little body.

"Margarita, you had a boy. A Laguna boy! How extraordinary. He is so beautiful . . ."

"I just want to sleep, Mamá."

"You wash him while I tend to your daughter," Antonino Montero said to Olvido.

Olvido bathed the baby in the blue arabesque washbasin, just as she had Margarita. She thought of Esteban, the cowlick at the back of his neck, his stormy eyes, his grave damp with memories. When she kissed the baby on the lips, he smacked in response, and she wrapped him in a towel caressed by the cane used for beating rugs. Olvido put him into Margarita's arms and headed to the guest room, where Pierre Lesac was resting with his circle of inspiration intact. Olvido did not notice two gloved hands hiding behind the bathroom door, waiting for her to leave Clara Laguna's room. In them was the cane. Sunlight burst in through the balconies. Manuela came out of hiding and moved down the hall. Olvido knocked on Pierre's door.

"Are you awake? May I come in?"

Manuela found the granddaughter she hated lying in bed.

"Pierre, you have a lovely son."

The Frenchman was still dreaming. He was painting a portrait on the face of Notre-Dame, in between Gothic relief and rosette windows.

"Pierre." Olvido touched his shoulder, and he opened his eyes.

"I'll start painting today. The circle of inspiration is complete."

"Your son was born."

Pierre sat up in bed. The illusion of the gargoyles he feared so much still circled him.

"It's a boy?"

"Yes, the first Laguna boy."

"Would you like him to take my name?"

"That's for Margarita to decide," Olvido replied, hurrying out of the room.

"Olvido . . ." Pierre heard the door close and felt the gargoyles threaten, pulling the sheet up over his face. Before he could rise, he had to repress the desire to paint the furniture, the blankets, the walls . . .

Morning moved across the yard at Scarlet Manor. Olvido opened the balcony doors to let the scent of honeysuckle in to greet the man of the house. Instead, the summer breeze brought the perfume of roses.

"Mamá! Mamá!"

The door to Clara Laguna's room was ajar. From the hallway, not all of Margarita was visible. Olvido could see only half her face, half her nightdress. On the bedroom floor was the cane.

"Mamá! Mamá!"

Olvido raced in to her daughter, feeling hate refresh her face. At the foot of the big iron bed, Manuela Laguna was holding the baby as Antonino Montero rubbed his head with a pained look on his face.

"What happened?"

"This crazy old woman came in and hit me."

"That's my mother. I'm sorry. Would you be so kind as to tell her to hand the baby back to my daughter unless she wants me to cane her brittle bones."

"Mamá! Don't say such horrible things!" Margarita seemed to have recovered her strength. "Let Yaya hold Santiago."

"Yaya? Santiago?"

"Yes, Yaya." Margarita pronounced that term of endearment with a satisfaction hidden for many years. She had always sought her grand-mother's affection. "Yaya asked me to call him Santiago, after the apos-tle James, and I agreed."

There were tears on Manuela Laguna's face, a child's tears. It was the first time Olvido had ever seen her mother cry.

"Margarita, tell your mother the curse has been broken." Manuela's voice sounded different. The bitterness that had characterized it since youth was gone, and it sounded as if it belonged to someone who might harbor a soul. "A boy has been born to the Lagunas." She stroked San-tiago's genitals. "He will redeem this line of women fated to sin and suffer for love." Her chin trembled as an undying love suffused her face.

"Mamá, don't you see? If the curse is gone, that means Pierre's not going to die and I can love him with no regrets."

"He doesn't have to die, darling. It's enough that he break your heart, like what happened to your great-grandmother Clara," Olvido explained.

"Tell your mother to let go of the past for the sake of this child." Manuela had removed her gloves, and her soft, wrinkled fingers were caressing the baby's skin.

"Would you two just speak to each other! I refuse to be in the mid-dle any longer. Pierre! Pierre!" Margarita had just noticed her boy-friend leaning against the door. "Come, kiss me, Pierre. Come see our son!"

"Olvido, are you all right?"

Olvido did not hear the Frenchman speak. Her mother's words— *let go of the past, let go of the past*—beat in the heart she had consoled for so long through cooking. Olvido felt Esteban kiss her in the oak grove; felt his icy face the night the moon died in the sky; felt dizzy as she looked out the window, at her lover's ancient eyes, their goodbye, red vomit on moss; felt the mournful grave of that man buried under the pear tree, her hands chafed by gunpowder; felt Margarita's gray gaze through a train window, moving away; felt the lawyer's hungry lips, the smell of medicine surrounding the jaundiced suitor who once shuffled through Scarlet Manor, leaning on a cane . . . For years she had lived solely for these memories, and now she had to let them go. Olvido sat on the foot of the bed, her gaze lost in an invisible purgatory.

"Mamá? What's wrong?"

But Olvido had fallen fast asleep, curled up on the lavender sheets.

14

RIGHT AFTER HER great-grandson was born, Manuela Laguna placed a mantilla over her hair speckled with dried insect corpses and went to town to announce — this time to both the rich and the poor — that the curse of the Laguna women had ended that iris-strewn morning. Divine Providence had at last brought a boy to this line of illegitimate girl-children, and what's more, he would be named after the apostle who traveled to Spain. Everyone was invited to witness this remarkable event.

The first visitors arrived at Scarlet Manor midafternoon, hate folded in their pockets like a snot-filled handkerchief. Manuela made them wait a few minutes in the entryway — her teeth ached from gnawing on such joy — before leading them to where Santiago slept. On the second floor, she pointed out the bathroom, saying: "As you can see, we even have a porcelain clawfoot tub."

A soft murmur rose up as they continued to the bedroom.

"Now gather around the cradle," Manuela ordered.

She slowly undid Santiago's diaper and lifted his genitals with a stick for all to see. The baby remained fast asleep.

"They're too round," one masculine voice let slip.

"Because they are French, my dear man. His father is a direct descendant of that Napoléon fellow."

After the ladies contemplated the miracle of the Laguna boy, Manuela invited them to stay for coffee, but none accepted. Some said they had lentils already simmering on the stove; others complained of a migraine. Alone in the kitchen, the old woman slurped coffee as resentment marched through her bowels yet again.

It was a very hot summer. Manuela Laguna rose at dawn, made Bernarda's gizzard recipe for breakfast, and slipped up to her great-grandson's crib to take him into the yard, tucked in the little burrow she prepared between her chest and robe. Once there, she headed for the rose garden. It had grown more twisted and intertwined with each passing year, becoming a giant, labyrinthine knot. No one but Manuela knew how to reach its center. No one knew its secret: a grave covered in roses as black as the deceased's braids. Sliced by spears of light, Manuela carried her great-grandson there, where she pulled him out of his lair, revealed his male member, belched the taste of innards and garlic — a second helping of affection and breakfast — and, in her northern accent, begged the Galician woman to look at this little boy who would redeem the family name. Every now and then, Manuela would notice a centipede crawling on the ground and her lips would swell with desire. Should she leave Santiago on the rose tombstone just for a moment to catch it? No, she told herself, swallowing the sinful urge. She would keep him in her arms, rocking him to the beat of menthol puffs exhaled by that grave.

But before Manuela reached the rose garden, she had to cross the vegetable patch outside the kitchen, where Olvido stood preparing breakfast and caught sight of her mother's hunched silhouette. The old woman kicked at the plants, glancing every which way, distrusting even the growl of butterfly intestines. Someone might discover her, demand her hidden treasure. Olvido slipped out through the kitchen door and followed her mother at a distance.

"I will not let you hurt that boy. This time I will be ruthless. I would even kill you, Madre. Although, by some miracle, you do seem to truly love him. I've never seen you so happy, never seen you touch anyone the way you touch him. Never once have I felt a single caress from you." Olvido rubbed her tear-filled eyes with her fists. "But still,

I don't trust you. I will keep my eye on you, Madre. I will not leave you alone with my grandson for even one moment, much less in this cursed place, where your hate vomits up roses as big as calf heads."

By the time Olvido entered the rose garden, she realized Pierre Lesac was stalking her. What she did not yet know was that behind him, naked and in love, hurried her daughter, Margarita Laguna.

Pierre began to paint what he considered his masterpiece the day Santiago was born. He erected a stand with an enormous canvas on the porch. There he would capture the face and body that gave him not a moment's peace. After dreaming of a lyrical tumble with his muse, he woke with lips as blue as a dead man's and blisters on his member that began to ooze what looked like sea foam as soon as the first rooster crowed. Pierre set out on his silent pilgrimage to the kitchen. A flood of light illuminated his way across the clay tiles, dust-speckled rays falling on his hair.

Olvido, who began using the kitchen in the mornings once her daughter arrived, sensed the Frenchman's footsteps and black eyes.

"Good morning, Pierre. I'll bring breakfast to the dining room. Have a seat and wait for me there."

But instead he stood watching her. His muse was preparing coffee and toast; her hair tumbled over her shoulders and arms, her throat pulsed like the ocean, her eyes blank, her house robe wilted by the July heat.

"You know I need to watch you. An artist must spend as much time near his model as possible, and you refuse to sit for me. But that's all right. My work will be perfect, like you."

Pierre's torso was bare; paint-spattered pants hung reluctantly on his hips, displaying young muscles that reminded Olvido of Esteban.

"Don't stop on my account. I won't say a word or bother you." Pierre placed a hand on his lips, then moved it away and said, "I prom-ise."

Olvido ignored this half-baked vision, the long, strong fingers, the smooth palm.

"Would you like some cake as well as toast?" She was not, however, afraid to look him in the eye, for they were not gray but as dark and melancholy as a solemn chant.

"No."

"Go into the dining room."

"That's not possible."

"Is my daughter still asleep?"

"I don't know."

"Go on now."

But Pierre only moved closer to observe her face, filled with the pleasure of remembering. His tongue sketched on his palate as he thought, This afternoon I will put more vermillion on the precipice of her neck, a stroke of garnet in the corner of her right cheek. Neither of them suspected that, behind the kitchen door, Margarita was spying, her face ravaged by brutal insomnia, eyelids puffy, and underneath her eyes, two furrows the color of mud.

After giving birth, Margarita did not move out of the big bed where Clara Laguna devoted her body not only to the Eastern exoticism of the *Kama Sutra* but also to certain postures of a more Castilian nature invented to exact revenge on her Andalusian lover. Margarita did not mind offering her breast to the baby every three hours, did not mind that, shortly after falling asleep, she was woken by a golden-eyed woman's laughter. She did not mind that the room filled with the smell of wine consumed a half century earlier or that moans and shouts of ecstasy sprang from the walls. The only thing she minded was the complete absence of a certain Frenchman. Pierre Lesac needed solitude to focus on his masterpiece.

"You don't love me anymore. You don't kiss me like you used to," Margarita complained.

"Je t'aime, mon amour. Je t'aime."

"Ever since our son was born, I disgust you. Yes, that's it . . ."

"My love, I need to work on my masterpiece. That's all. I'll sleep next to you when I'm done." His skin gave off a faint smell of a large, white Paschal candle.

"You're lying. You smell like a church."

"Don't be silly . . . I smell of paint. Blue paint. As pure as your mother's eyes."

"My mother! My mother! I'm sick of you and of her . . . and this house . . . and your masterpiece! I want to make love in Paris . . . Are you listening to me, Pierre?"

But the Frenchman was only thinking, mesmerized, of the painting of his muse.

"Pierre . . ." A heavy afternoon air hung over the porch. "I love you. I'll love you until the day I die. I would die for you, Pierre . . ."

"A little more pink in the corner of her lips? No, it's fine as is. *Merci,* my love. Your help with my masterpiece is indispensable."

"I hate you! Do you hear me, Pierre? I hate you!"

In the mornings, Margarita Laguna waited impatiently for Pierre to wake. If Santiago began to cry, she would recite the prayer the nuns taught her in the silence of the Holy Sepulcher, rocking the boy, disgusted by the oak smell surrounding her. The moment she heard Pierre leaving the guest room, she would lay her son in the cradle and follow him down the hall. His hair's messy after another night without me, Margarita thought; his eyes still lost in dreams, where I no longer exist, she lamented; his chest so smooth, just as the fried eggs in the American breakfasts I used to eat in Paris. She licked her lips. And wet patches on his shorts. Who could he have desired to cause those traitorous ejaculations, she wondered, hammering a fist on the wall.

The memory of honeysuckle flowed in through the window, and for a few brief seconds, Margarita remembered how happy she had been drawing among those plants as she bathed naked in the sun. But now her destiny lay in the kitchen, with her mother, with Pierre, until the hunched silhouette of Manuela crossed the vegetable garden. Olvido followed her mother, and Pierre his muse. All that remained on the kitchen floor was a few drops of milk as Margarita followed the three of them, her breasts agitated by the to-and-fro of suspicion.

Every now and then, whenever she heard a rustling of the thorns, Manuela would interrupt her conversation with the Galician woman.

She stood alert, cradling her great-grandson, but carried on a few minutes later, convinced the sound was only the July heat as it lay heavy on the roses. Meanwhile, those hiding behind her were scratched by thorny stems, and scarlet-colored cuts opened up.

Before heading back to the house, Manuela made the sign of the cross and warned the Galician woman: "Don't you dare leave here. I told you to go and you died, so dead you'll stay. And don't send your putrid menthol smell out beyond the last rose. I have to protect my great-grandson's reputation. Oh, and by the way, I tried to kill the chestnut tree you hung yourself from, pouring three bottles of bleach right into its mouth. I know you know, but I like to tell you so you'll see how I try to protect you, too."

At lunch, they all gathered around the delicious meals Olvido prepared, glancing at one another's scratches, silence floating between them.

Afternoons were even quieter. Manuela Laguna sat in the parlor embroidering, as she recalled the Galician woman's stories. These were for Santiago now.

Olvido read poetry in her room, the older books belonging to Esteban. She laid one by Saint John of the Cross on her chest, like a tombstone, and imagined her body surrounded by damp earth. Later she returned to the kitchen. Her cooking had never been so prolific. Every lunch and dinner there were dishes upon dishes: squash soup, ham and leek soufflé, chicken mousse, hens stuffed with foie gras and pine nuts, vegetable salad with raisins, steamed sole with butter and herbs, truffle Bavarois, honey-soaked pastries . . . Olvido was possessed by a fertility of biblical proportions. Yet no one ever knew if this had anything to do with the plague of miniature violets that began to fill the yard, eventually spreading into the house.

A clump of these violets took root on Pierre Lesac's masterpiece, right on the chest of his muse. Infuriated at first, he later fell asleep on the porch sofa, like he did every afternoon. Margarita was not nearby, watching him breathe.

. . .

They all gathered for dinner.

"Magic, Olvido. Your dinners are magic." Pierre ran his tongue over his juice-soaked moustache. "What a banquet! It's like a wedding feast."

"Well, I don't think you cook nearly as well as you used to, Mamá. All quantity and no quality. The chicken is salty"—Margarita spat a piece onto her plate—"and the bread is as hard as a rock. You really can't cook French recipes. They don't taste anything like what we ate in Paris, do they, Pierre?"

"You're so cruel, *mon amour*. Don't mind her, Olvido. Your French cooking is wonderful, like everything else you—"

"No, Pierre. Margarita is right. I can't cook French dishes no matter how hard I try. And the chicken really is very salty."

"Mamá, why don't you let Yaya cook?"

Manuela Laguna pulled her teeth back from a chicken leg. Ever since Santiago's birth, she had stopped eating alone in the kitchen. It was hard for Olvido to see her so near Margarita. But the only thing the birth of a Laguna boy did not change was the silence that reigned between Olvido and her mother. Neither was prepared to give in.

"I'll fry up some nice gizzards with garlic and pepper, and sweetbreads with rice. You'll lick your fingers clean." Manuela opened her mouth, and a chortle of stones escaped.

Olvido noticed her mother had only three teeth left in her upper jaw, but their ridged edges looked like they could tear apart an ox.

"Mind now, I can't make this crap from France. If the cook who raised me ever saw this . . . What do you call it? Cluché?"

"Soufflé, Yaya. It's soufflé." Margarita smiled.

"Well, this fluché thing. If she ever saw it on the table, she'd have flogged the horse for having shat where it shouldn't."

Margarita burst out laughing.

In mid-August there was a downpour. The sun did not set when it should have, was still high in the sky after ten o'clock. The townspeople sat down to dinner in its rays, but hardly anyone ate. They stared out the window with empty forks, tore bread into little pieces on the table, checked their clocks. Perhaps nature had taken a break. The old, toothless farmers consoled themselves by chewing on their tongues.

Suddenly, without a hint of warning, the sun plunged into the pines. Most animals were startled and fled into the oak grove. The sky turned black, not a single hue on the horizon. A half-moon reluctantly appeared, tired of waiting for nightfall. A few hours passed as giant clouds filled the sky. The townspeople had by now gone to bed. There were one or two flashes of lightning. No stars shone, however much they were missed. More lightning. One flash struck the rose garden at Scarlet Manor, and the yard filled with the smell of charred earth. The half-moon disappeared behind a cloud. The breeze that had assaulted the town every evening died, and a stillness crept in through the townspeople's navels, causing bouts of insomnia. But no one turned on a light. House fronts remained dark, though the people were there, immobile behind bricks, eyes open, necks bathed in perspiration, bodies wrapped in sheets, imprisoned, unable to escape their fate, a fate that grew more and more humid. Another flash struck rockroses in the pine forest. Resin clumps on tree trunks looked like strings of incandescent drool. The rain came. Not a few drops to start but a deluge unleashed by the sky, enveloping houses, yards, and hills. For hours, falling water was the only sound that night. Not a soul dared get out of bed; hands grew slick with cold sweat, eyes fixed on windows and balconies. The storm battered everything.

Margarita thought Clara Laguna's window might burst and glass shards would pierce her face. She saw herself covered in blood, the purple canopy splattered by the tragedy, and felt an overwhelming desire for Pierre Lesac, his black eyes and skin, but suppressed it calmly. Santiago grasped his pacifier between his fingers. Downstairs at Scarlet Manor, it smelled of damp whitewash. A tide of water streamed down one spongy wall in Manuela Laguna's room. The old woman could hardly breathe, sure such oppression could only be God, and muttered an an illiterate prayer. Her gloves lay stiff on the sheets; if only she stayed still, misfortune would pass her by. There was a blue flash of lightning, followed by a roll of thunder. The half-moon melted over the fields, over the tops of the pines. Face-down on her mattress, Olvido could feel the sting of childhood scars on her back and bit down on her pillow. The yard was not visible through her window, only the face of the deluge.

A section of the church roof collapsed onto the altar. The sound of rubble tumbling was quickly gobbled by that of rain, until every corner of town was under its spell again. Dawn did not come. Only a wafer of moon remained, and clouds were battling to overtake it. The weathervane at Scarlet Manor, a cock on one leg, spun crazily, pointing north, then south. An icy wind blew. Curled up in a tangle of sheets, Pierre Lesac listened to water rushing through the gutters. He tried to think about his masterwork helpless on the porch. He tried to get out of bed and save it from the storm but could not, held captive by his childish fear of the gargoyles at Notre-Dame. He remembered their jaws, their feet and daggerlike claws. They could rip off his head and devour his heart. Unbidden, a memory of his mother came to him, of the dark cathedral and the word *sin* she repeated so often. He remembered her stepbrother's pants, the toast with plum jam the banker made him eat the morning his mother left. He wanted to vomit, but it was caught in his throat. For the rest of the night, as the storm spewed its torment, he felt the gargoyle's stone touch.

The rain ended toward morning just as it had begun, suddenly. It was cold for August. Patches of frost lay on drenched grass. The young man who had replaced Tolón rang the church bells. The Christ on the altar was broken — a rotten beam had fallen on its back. The sacristy echoed with Padre Rafael's restless pacing. Outside, it smelled of rain corpse. The sun began to shine. The road to the city had flooded; so had the winding path through the pines, beech trees, and rocks, and the oak grove. The labyrinthine rose garden had flooded, too, its twisting paths now canals transporting thousands of petals. They floated white, yellow, red, blue, black . . . making the rose garden a multi-hued cemetery. The deluge had dismembered rosebushes and left their bodies limp.

As always, Manuela was the first to rise. That morning she did not have breakfast but went straight into the yard, her feet infected with limestone, her stomach growling. She had to get to the rose garden. The vegetable patch had become a small lake. The water reached mid-calf, and her feet sank in the mud with every step. Legions of grasshopper corpses floated in that pond. Manuela scooped a few into the palm of her glove; they were stiff, their little legs bent into their shells. She tossed them back into the watery grave and looked up at the sky. The sun lacked warmth, struggling with the clouds, fighting to impose its rays. When Manuela reached the rose garden, she stopped on one path and fell to her knees. Water rose up to her waist as she cried. The body of a centipede stuck to her arm; she thought she could see its insides through its skin. She squeezed and it disintegrated. She crossed herself, rose, and went toward the center of the rose garden. The sight of skeletal rosebushes was almost too much to bear as colored petals sailed down flooded paths. The old woman was afraid she might find the remains of the Galician woman floating aimlessly, afraid they might slip down a drain and disappear from her life.

That morning no one followed Manuela. She felt every dead insect that bumped into her and clenched her teeth. She did not want to see them. She just wanted to reach the mentholated grave but got lost in the labyrinth. She took a wrong turn, followed a path she had never taken, a forbidden path whose secret only she knew. Desperate, she searched for a centipede. There were grasshopper and cicada corpses bobbing in the sun, as if the canals were tributaries of the Ganges River, but none possessed the amber chill of the insect she yearned for inside. She smeared the remains of the one she'd squashed moments before onto one finger and sucked it greedily. Manuela had never let anyone see her commit this shameful, savage act. Sometimes, after grooming a centipede, she would eat it for the taste of quince it left in her mouth.

Manuela wanted to cry. Before her was the cross she'd bought from the scrap merchant for her mother's grave. She never wanted Clara Laguna to escape that mound of earth, never wanted anyone to visit her. She never wanted a soul to drop the weight of even one memory on those bones, and that is why she buried her on this secret path. Manuela kneeled down and water once again bathed her waist. Like an accusing finger, a single ray of sun illuminated the letters engraved on one arm of the cross. Manuela retched. She never wanted that name — Clara Laguna — written on that grave. The Galician woman had told her that, if a grave does not bear the name of the deceased, the spirit will not dare leave, for when it wants to return it cannot find its way, remaining forever lost and alone. But there it was in the rust, scrawled in a shaky hand. Someone had written her mother's name on that iron cross. Though she could not read, Manuela recognized those two words from all the documents at the lawyer's office, those two words that had outlived her memory: CLARA LAGUNA. She kneeled in the mud like a rock, a rock that meandered down rose-filled canals. Her mother's spirit could wander through the yard, through the house, through the oak grove, and return to that grave marked by her name.

The moisture from the storm only intensified the plague of violets that had assaulted Scarlet Manor in July. Bunches grew on mattress corners, on the whitewashed walls of Manuela's room, on the staircase banister, on the seascape in Olvido's room, on the carpet in the parlor, on the purple canopy, on little Santiago's crib. Scarlet Manor was filled with the smell of wild shoots.

Pierre Lesac woke in a bad mood. He felt like he was waking in his childhood bed at the banker's house. What if he went down to the kitchen and found toast smeared with plum jam? A colored pencil lay between the fingers of his right hand. It was blue. He tried to suppress the desire consuming him: he wanted to color the walls, the sofas, the tablecloths . . . Pierre Lesac needed to color everything in his path. And if that weren't enough, a miniature violet had sprouted in the thicket of his masculinity. He locked himself in the bathroom for nearly half an hour. When he opened the door, the pencil was gone from his hand and the violet lay on the tile floor. It was not alone; next to it was a clump of hair and three big drops of pleasure. That had freed him of the burning sensation and weeping blisters, the gargoyles disappearing from his life with the very first stroke. Next he put on his paint-splattered pants and was ready to face what the great storm had done to his canvas.

The porch had become a vibrant lake, upon which his former masterpiece, now a funereal platform, was floating. He brushed off the crickets and cicadas, could just make out the curve of Olvido's lips, their vermillion unscathed. But his muse's eyes were dying beneath the mire. He vomited what had stuck in his throat the night before. It was mid-August. Olvido, I still have you, he thought; real, beautiful. Olvido, I can still watch you while you cook. I can still eat what first grazed your nipples and mouth. I can still follow you down the perfumed twists and turns of the rose garden. I can still . . . He left the porch, running to his muse's room. Stained with paint and mud, his bare feet left prints on clay tiles that would remain for years to come. Olvido. Pierre wanted to become that name, wanted that name to devour him. Olvido.

The window in Olvido's room had blown open in the storm, and the yard's damp breath drifted in. For once that yard had succumbed to the weather. For once it suffered the same misfortune as the town that hated it. Pierre found Olvido in bed, face-down, the sheet swirled around her knees, naked. Hypnotized by the power exhaled by her flesh, he stood staring, as if she were not a woman but an extraordinary, shapely sculpture. He blinked in vain. A flock of birds flew low through the yard. Their chirping caused the narrow abyss between Olvido's legs to softly stretch. She moaned. Her black mane smudged her face; in between strands were two sleeping eyes, parted lips, cheeks flower pink.

It was then Pierre noticed the scars on her back. From that moment on, he no longer cared that Olvido's arm was curled lovingly around her pillow, that her neck was damp with the perspiration of dreams. All that existed were those scars coiling along her back, those serpents dead beneath her skin. He moistened his lips and sat on the edge of the bed. He wanted to touch them, kiss them, trace them with his tongue. He reached out and ran a hand over the outline of one crimson scar. Olvido's body sighed. Suddenly, her thighs began to part and her waist to navigate an invisible sea. Pierre's touch lay enamored; if only that scar were her heart. Thunder rumbled. Pierre thought the storm was returning. The August rays that minutes earlier had lit up the room were being swallowed. He wished they were winter rays, softer, whiter. A dry leaf blew in the window, traveling on a wind that did not know how to forget. Pierre kissed another scar. The moon that poked out above the clouds was small and pale, ghostlike, but the sky exploded in blue.

Someone pushed the door open. Pierre had left it ajar. Olvido's flesh ensnared him, leaving him without the strength to close it. What was a doorknob compared with that explosion of skin? he would ask himself years later, crouched in the shadow of Notre-Dame. Margarita Laguna, her hair loose, eyes tempestuous, breasts exhausted from nursing, found Pierre licking her mother's scars. She watched his tongue move down the one he had chosen as his favorite, shaped like a wave and seemingly brimming with foam. She watched her mother's naked body reflected in Pierre's face when he startled, raising his head from that deformed delight, looking at her without fear. Margarita knew she was going to kill him. She cursed in French and moved toward the bed. Olvido woke and said her daughter's name, feeling a trace of something wet and sticky on her back. Beside her was Pierre Lesac, his lips sparkling. Suddenly it turned cold. Winter settled over Olvido's heart and hung from her icy legs. Margarita slapped Pierre.

"It's only art, my love," the Frenchman replied.

The smell of wax filtered through the room. Margarita's nostrils flared. She knew he was lying. He loved her mother. He desired her mother.

"Since when?" she screamed, hammering his chest with her fists.

"Ever since I saw her photo. She is an artist's dream," Pierre confessed. The taste of her scar still lay on his tongue.

Margarita dropped her fists and fell to her knees. Milk spurted from one nipple, leaving a stain on the carpet. Olvido remembered she had dreamed of pirate ships that night. She stood, wrapped herself in the sheet, and held her daughter. Margarita was rigid, frosty.

"It's nothing," Olvido whispered into her hair. "Let's sunbathe in the honeysuckle clearing today."

Margarita pushed her away. She had spotted a letter opener on the desk and within seconds was waving it wildly. She aimed for Pierre's heart but found only his hand. Blood dripped on the carpet.

"Enough, darling. Enough!" Olvido tried to wrest the letter opener from her daughter's hand.

Margarita smashed the handle into her mother's temple. Olvido brought a hand to the wound and felt the whisper of blood, like she had on that frigid night.

"Enough, darling. Enough!" she repeated.

But Margarita was struggling with Pierre by the open window.

Olvido wanted to go to them, protect them from the abyss that had swallowed Esteban, but there was no time. Margarita pushed and Pierre fell out.

"Don't look!" Olvido begged her daughter. "You'll remember that sight forever, even in your dreams."

There came the ghostly howl of a wolf, and Margarita hurled herself into the yard.

Silence and the caustic smell of tragedy filled the room. Olvido hid her face in her hands. Her life was being torn in two along that pious crease in her forehead when someone stroked her hair. The touch was rough and smelled sweetly of ivy. Olvido raised her eyes to confront death's desire, give in to it, but instead saw the silhouette of a man as tall and thin as a church steeple. It was Pierre Lesac. He had managed to grab the wooden trellis and climb back into her room. Olvido raced to the window.

"No," Pierre said. "Not her."

Margarita Laguna lay on her father's memory, her skull smashed on a rock.

15

OLVIDO LAGUNA WALKED down a muddy path through the pine grove. Dressed in black, she was wearing thick stockings, a dress secured at the neck with a safety pin, and a veil over her hair. She hurried along toward town, sure of her sorrow. It was Sunday morning, and the smell of rain still hung in the air. Countless dead ants and grasshoppers floated in puddles, and the surviving squirrels dozed on tree branches. Olvido walked on without stopping. Every now and then she would coo to Santiago in her arms. He was hungry for a breast; he missed the heat of skin perfumed by new motherhood and the heart that beat beneath it. Manuela wanted to wring the last harvest from that now dead chest but did not dare, afraid Olvido would discover her, accuse her of defiling Margarita's body; afraid her bones would then smell of lavender; afraid of losing her great-grandson.

On the horizon, the town's first roofs and church bell could be seen. Olvido began to walk faster. The baby started to cry. She knew what he needed and stopped to unbutton her dress. As she offered her breast to her grandson, she heard the same enormous magpie caw as the day Pierre Lesac arrived. She felt Santiago's lips tugging on her nipple. She closed her eyes. It was Margarita in her arms. It was her daughter sucking on memory, and her insides drowned in happiness lost. A gust of passionate wind rustled the treetops. Santiago had stopped crying. His grandmother's breast gave no milk, but it did harbor the taste that led to his birth.

After buttoning her dress, Olvido resumed walking. The smell of damp plaster, rain-soaked clothing, and furniture permeated the town. No one toasted fresh bread, and no one wore clean clothes or washed with fragrant soaps. The church bells rang nine times, misfortune hauling on the ropes as the new Tolón slept off the flood. There would be no Mass that Sunday; their Christ lay dying under a rotted beam. The church was a jumble of mantles, candles, and piles of rubble dripping water. Padre Rafael was in the sacristy, mourning the loss of his public address system. Anyone who wanted to receive Communion that morning would have to go to the neighboring town, where heaven's tide had left the church unscathed.

Olvido walked down a narrow street and came into the town square. There was no one, the only sound coming from the fountain spouts. All of the dogs had fled. Donkeys dreamed of storms in flooded stables. She left the center of town and headed into a neighborhood of humble dwellings. One old woman was sweeping water out her door. Olvido Laguna's mourning collided with her own. The woman set down the bucket and hurried up the street to tell her friends that one of the wicked Lagunas had shrouded herself in black, covering up her shamelessness and beauty.

Olvido soon came to a filthy porch where petunia pots had cracked in two. She rapped on the door.

"Come in," a sad voice said.

The room was silent. It reeked of winter, although it was August. There was hardly any furniture: a round table covered in an oilcloth, two wicker chairs, a threadbare sofa, and a coal stove. On top of the table was a heap of socks and stockings. Behind it, the balding head of an old woman, glasses perched on her nose. She did not bother to look up; she did not care who was there. She kept her head down, mending. For years her life had been nothing but a row of perfect stitches. Water had seeped into the room and rose up to the old woman's ankles.

"Leave your stockings on the table and come back the day after tomorrow—or tomorrow, if you like. With no Mass, I'll work all day . . ."

"I haven't brought anything to mend. I've come to talk to you about a grave."

The old woman took off her glasses. Olvido Laguna was easy to recognize under the modesty of that veil; the blue eyes and beauty that had killed her young son were just as vivid as ever. The woman wanted to tell her to leave the house they were forced into after her husband was murdered, but she was intrigued by Olvido's state of mourning.

"Who needs a grave?" she asked.

"Your granddaughter."

"I never had a granddaughter." Her voice turned vicious. "You're mistaken."

"Her name was Margarita Laguna, and as you well know, she had your son's eyes."

The old woman chewed on her lip.

"What've you got there?"

"Your great-grandson. His name is Santiago. Santiago Laguna."

"I know. Manuela made sure to announce it all over town, as if an heir to the throne had been born. But we're not interested in a relationship with you, no matter how rich you are." Her hands and lips trembled; her voice was a sharp thorn. "Everyone knows where he came from . . ."

"Would you like to see him?" Olvido held out the baby.

An infant's sigh was heard.

"Bring him closer. I just want to see whether your kind actually gave birth to a boy."

Light shone in through the dirty window.

"Better let me hold him. Can't tell anything if I don't actually touch him."

The old woman took Santiago in her arms, and he gave a sleepy smile. Her heart felt the weight of soft bones, the warmth of newborn skin, the caress of talcum powder.

"I've come to ask whether I can bury my daughter with Esteban. She should be near her father."

"Don't even dream of it," came a harsh, unrecognizable voice.

Olvido turned. It was Esteban's sister. She had aged since the day her small, bony frame supported her mother's grief over that gaping hole in the cemetery.

"You will not bury your bastard with my brother." She strode through the room as if a lake were not covering the floor. "And let me tell you something else: if I hear you've spent one more night on Esteban's grave, eating flowers, like a savage, you'll have to deal with more than me. I'll have you locked up—in prison or an insane asylum."

"If you want me to beg, I will," Olvido replied.

"Take your mourning and your new bastard, and get out of my house."

The old woman's cheeks burned as her eyes pleaded with her daughter.

"Return the baby, Madre. He's got nothing to do with you."

Olvido took Santiago from her two old arms.

"Let me see him for a minute." Esteban's sister took the baby's face in a hand wounded by pinpricks and frostbite. "If it weren't for your age, I'd swear he was yours," she spat. "He's got your demonic eyes."

Even though it was Sunday, the lawyer had the mortician come from the city to repair Margarita Laguna's disfigured face. They had laid her out in the dining room, in a white coffin with a bleeding Christ on the lid.

"Get me the plot as close to Esteban's as possible," Olvido begged the lawyer. "That way my daughter won't feel so alone. Cost is no issue."

Manuela nodded when the lawyer looked to her for approval.

"She'll be buried where you want, don't worry," he replied, regretting the veil, the safety pin, and the thick stockings on the woman he desired.

Olvido sat next to the coffin, watching how that man from the city used brushes and creams to erase the truth of Margarita's death from her face. Behind Olvido stood Pierre Lesac. No one noticed, but he had painted a dagger on the coffin.

When night fell, and the lawyer and the mortician left Scarlet Manor, Olvido locked herself in her room and bricked up the window both Esteban and her daughter had fallen from. Never again would the sun shine in that room with its seascape; never again would her dead loved ones peer in from that outline on the moss. That room would forever remain in shadows, despair eventually filtering out through the gap she left between two bricks.

They had to wait three more days before Margarita could be buried. The cemetery had flooded, and inscriptions and bones drifted through the neighborhood. The ground was too soft to hold the recently departed.

Olvido found a large leaf left over from Palm Sunday in the attic and like a Nubian slave began to fan the body. The August heat was accelerating the decomposition. Accustomed to the presence of death, Manuela Laguna continued her petit point in front of the hearth, while Pierre Lesac spent hours wandering through the house with a clothespin on his nose and a blue pencil in his hand. Hiding in corners, he would murmur prayers in French and stuff himself with sweet peaches to keep the rotten stench of Margarita's body from sticking to the back of his throat.

On the third night, hot and remorseful, Pierre ran into the yard. He was sorry he had betrayed Margarita but sorrier still that his muse had scorned him ever since. More than once he tried to take her hand or kiss her cheek, whispering apologies and declarations of love, but she rejected his touch, his breath, his words.

Lying on the damp porch, Pierre watched Olvido walk barefoot toward him.

"Go," she demanded. "Go back to France."

He was soaking wet, like a shipwrecked sailor.

"Et l'amour?"

"The only woman who loved you is inside a box."

"Perhaps in time . . ." His right hand ached to hold a pencil.

"Even a thousand years from now, your touch will remind me of my dead daughter. Go. I'll look after Santiago."

His shouts and wails reverberated in the garden for hours.

By dawn, the only trace of Pierre Lesac at Scarlet Manor was a colored pencil, a helpless pencil abandoned on the tiles like a motherless child.

Margarita Laguna was buried with the first echoes of evening. She lay naked in the casket, surrounded by honeysuckle flowers. Padre Rafael, with his shaking of earth and spitting of Latin, did not attend; nor did the lawyer, or anyone from town. Only the undertaker was there, in rubber boots, his three teeth chewing a wad of tobacco with each shovelful of earth. When the coffin disappeared from view, Olvido felt a strange warmth on her shoulder and turned to find a cotton glove clutching her grief. It was immaculate, not a drop of chicken blood on it. Olvido held her breath for a moment, savoring this maternal weight. The sun sank into a row of headstones. The sky was cloudless and the heat of August had abated.

At that moment, Scarlet Manor entered an era of peace. Olvido and Manuela sat together on the porch every afternoon. They bought chairs and a table, burning what was left of the old ones after the flood—burning Pierre Lesac's painting, too. Manuela embroidered while Olvido read poems and tended to Santiago.

"I think fall's come," Manuela said one day, after twenty-some years of not speaking to her daughter. "It's going to be a cool one this year."

"We'll need more wood," Olvido replied, turning back to Saint John of the Cross as if reading it for the first time.

From his mother, Santiago Laguna inherited a passion for lying among the flowers; from his father, an obsession with coloring everything in his path—when he was four, they gave him a blue pencil from France; from his grandmother Olvido, her extraordinary beauty; from his grandfather Esteban, a love of poetry; and from his great-grandmother Manuela, a taste for tales and for death.

Santiago learned to cook from a very young age. He loved being in the kitchen with Olvido, helping her prepare the recipes she invented over years of dreaming about the past. They spent their days handling squash, peppers, any ingredient to be used in their stews. Olvido taught him to love boiling water, the bubbling like a river in spring; the aroma of acorns; the color of ash where chestnuts roasted, for it was the same color as his mother's and grandfather's eyes. She taught him that well-trained nipples could become a chef's best tool and that the family's most cherished recipe was cinnamon cake, served with boiled coffee. After a day of affection and games, Santiago would sink into the clawfoot tub, where his grandmother would scrub away the flour or oil spattering his body. Sometimes she joined him in the tub, and Santiago would stretch his little feet out and slowly walk them up her skin in a tickle.

At dinnertime, they would sit at the dining room table with Manuela to savor the dishes they had prepared. Manuela no longer cooked; the arthritis in her hands was now complicated by Parkinson's, and she could not hold a pot without spilling it, peel a potato without skinning a finger. She could barely eat by herself. It was little Santiago who brought food to her mouth with the patience of a saint. Manuela's ailments resulted in unprecedented longevity in the chicken coop, and the smell of entrails faded from the corners of the kitchen.

After dinner the family would gather before the embers of the fire — the heat from the smoking bricks warming their faces — to listen to the stories Manuela told choked with memory.

"In far-off lands they say that many years ago a phantom ship sailed the northern seas, terrorizing sailors and captains alike. A cold fog as thick as the manes of the dead blanketed water and sky so nothing was clear, not even whether it was day or night. Few dared head out on such seas, but those who did and made it back alive told that, from out of the fog came the monstrous silhouette of a galleon fitted with mermaid cannons. The foam parted reverently and a vast silence reigned.

They all knew what would happen next and covered their ears in vain, hoping to escape the terrible threat: the red bell that hung from the mainmast, as brilliant as fire, was rung by a shadow as the name of one sailor was pronounced. No matter how that poor man cried and begged, the captain was forced to hand him over to the specter unless he wanted to suffer the same fate. For that phantom ship, once it filled its hold with victims, would set sail for hell." Manuela bared her teeth in a smile.

"One day or night—no one knew which—a young man arrived on these northern shores with horseshoes on the soles of his boots, like a mule. Tattooed on his tongue was a list of his exploits and glories across the many seas. Eager to add one more, he assured the people—cowards, he called them—that he would free them from the threat of the phantom ship in exchange for three barrels of gold. 'All you have to do is take the red bell,' he said. 'The next time it rings with the name of some poor sod, I'll go in his place and take it.' And so he did. He took the bell no problem, but once it was in his hands, before the frightened eyes of the entire crew, he became a fabulous galleon that replaced the phantom ship. His neck stretched until it was as long as the mainmast, with the red bell hanging there. They say the fog disappeared and the man-boat sailed into the horizon, his tongue now a flag flapping in the breeze.

"A hundred years passed before they saw him again, on stormy nights, when the sound of his approach is like mule hoofs on the earth, and sailors tremble in fear. They know he will have to make the bell ring and steal their souls."

Santiago Laguna's introduction to society came at the age of six. The town needed to meet and learn to accept the first boy in that family of cursed women. He went to church on Sundays, sitting in the front row with Manuela. (Olvido still preferred the last row.) The Christ whose back had been snapped by a beam years ago had been fixed and stood resplendent on the high altar. A gold plaque on the pedestal reminded readers of the catastrophe and how the great storm had damaged the church. The chapel to Saint Pantolomina of the Flowers, however, had remained unscathed.

Santiago then started at the school built on the outskirts of town with Manuela Laguna's donation. It was a brick building with a slate roof, where no cats ever mated by moonlight and no weeds ever grew. Santiago's grandmother walked him to school the first day. They crossed the pine forest bright and early that morning. Olvido had bought him a new pair of boots, a canvas book bag, and a white shirt with a striped tie; there was no hat with a lace border on his head or black bangs to cover his eyes. On the way, his grandmother lectured him on all the things he should not do at school. Among other things, he was not to take off his clothes in the schoolyard, no matter how much they might itch; he was not to color the desks, walls, or chairs with felt-tip pens; and he was not to fight with his classmates if they said mean things.

Olvido watched him walk excitedly into the school. She did not go back to Scarlet Manor but waited for the mothers of the other children to leave before peering in through a window to see whether Santiago was receiving the same treatment as she had on her first day of school. Santiago had sat in the second row, next to the fruit merchant's son, and was drawing a squirrel on his hand. I should've told him not to color his classmates, Olvido thought. When he was done, the girl in front held out a coquettish arm for him to draw another. It was the pharmacist's granddaughter.

At recess, Santiago was looking forward to eating the cinnamon cake he and his grandmother had made but found himself surrounded by girls. He drew dogs, roosters, cats. As he walked home to Scarlet Manor with Olvido, a smile danced on his lips.

"Did you have a good first day at school?"

"I did. My classmates are nice, especially the girls."

"What about the boys?"

"One of them stared and said I looked like a girl."

"Did you fight?"

"There wasn't time, Abuela. All the girls defended me. They said he was just jealous."

"Tomorrow, why don't you ask if he wants to be friends?"

"No! He should ask me."

That afternoon the Laguna family sat on the porch. Santiago wrote rows of vowels in a lined notebook, while his grandmother peeled potatoes and his great-grandmother monitored his penmanship.

"Make them all nice and neat, Santiago. You have to be head of your class and go to university, become an engineer or a doctor, the most honorable profession of all. You're the family savior—don't ever forget that your birth was a good omen."

Three years later the town fell prey to an extremely long winter. At the end of March the pine forest was covered in a blast of snow, the treetops becoming white roofs. Even their scent hibernated among the branches, dreaming of warm spring air. The beech trees looked like icy wraiths blanketed in early-morning frost. The road to town was impassable, and Santiago stayed home from school.

One night, Olvido came in from the stable with her cheeks aglow; the dapple-gray horse was dying.

"I'll try to reach the veterinarian's; it's less than a mile from here. Maybe there's something he can do."

"Just let him die. He's no good for anything anymore." Manuela was dozing in front of the fire.

"If only the phone worked . . . But this damn snow has knocked out everything."

Even Clara Laguna's daisies had frozen on the cobblestone drive.

"Go on if you want, dear. I'll look after our little treasure."

Olvido wrapped a shawl around her shoulders and headed for the pine forest but soon realized she would never make it. A frigid wind buffeted her every step. If the horse gets worse, I'll use the hunting rifle from the attic to put it out of its misery, she thought as she turned for home. Her lips were covered in snow, and her teeth chattered.

The clay-tiled entryway lay in shadow, a shadow tainted by a sweet perfume that reminded Olvido of her childhood. The linen cupboard doors were open, the lavender sachets out of place.

"Madre? Madre!"

Manuela Laguna appeared in the hallway, lit by the glow of the fire. She looked at her daughter and wanted to smile. Rising up out of her mother's glove, Olvido saw the cane.

"You couldn't get there in this foul weather, could you, dear?"

"Did you cane him, Madre? Did you dare cane him?"

After years of being locked up with the tablecloths, sheets, and towels, the cane skeleton glowed happily in its master's claw.

"I had no choice. His penmanship was sloppy, and he knows he has to apply himself if he's to be our savior," the old woman replied with a smile, baring yellow teeth.

"Where is he?"

"He went to his room to redo the part he did poorly. Don't worry, dear. He'll learn soon enough."

Santiago's was the guest room where Pierre Lesac had stayed at Scarlet Manor. It was smaller than Olvido's and much smaller than Clara Laguna's, but it got more hours of sun. Olvido found the boy on his stomach in bed, writing in his lined notebook.

"That's enough homework for today. You've worked hard," she said, stroking his hair.

"But I have to practice so Bisabuela won't get mad again. Tomorrow morning, I'll show her this page I just finished. It's nice and neat."

"Don't worry about your penmanship, sweetheart. It doesn't matter if it's messy."

Olvido had lifted Santiago onto her lap and was rocking him like a baby.

"It matters to Bisabuela."

"I'll take care of your great-grandmother. I'll make sure she won't ever get mad at you again," Olvido assured the boy, kissing him on the forehead.

"So, she won't cane me?"

"No, she won't ever be able to cane you again. I promise."

Heavy snow fell from a moonless sky. Olvido led Santiago to her room, where she treated the welts on his back. Wind hammered the bricked-up window, the onslaught bringing back the memory of death on icy moss.

That night Santiago fell asleep in his grandmother's bed as she told him a story. Insomnia then took over Olvido's body and mind. Eyes wide open, she delighted in the warmth of her grandson's breath. Hours passed. Hours filled with shadows. Just before dawn, Olvido thought she saw a face from the past in the bricks. It was a face she had seen at church. Dark, proud, with gray eyes, that face belonged to Esteban's father. Little by little, the smell of a dish Olvido recognized filtered through the room. "Tripe with herbs and garlic," she murmured. It was a recipe Manuela adored. Olvido could taste the strong flavor of entrails seasoned with rosemary, thyme, and garlic. She protected Santiago, still asleep, shielding him from the phantom stew and the face of the schoolmaster floating in the bricks, until the first ray of sun forced it out through the gap. Olvido wondered why that man appeared to her. According to her mother, he refused to admit her to school. She wondered, too, how he knew that recipe and why he would remind her of it with his presence. Manuela made that dish often, but the first time was when Esteban was still a boy and had just buried his father. Manuela invited him in to try it. He ate several bites before running out.

The snow had stopped. A bright winter morning illuminated Scarlet Manor, but the strong wind that had blown all night continued to shred the daisies and roses.

Manuela woke in her room with its damp whitewash and got out of bed feeling more sprightly than she had for days, maybe even months or years. Her gloved hands shook less than usual. Clearly, being reunited with the cane was good for her health. She did not open her window and so did not see the fistful of black petals that traveled on the wind and came to rest on her windowsill. She put on her dressing gown and headed into the kitchen. She would tell Olvido she wanted gizzards with garlic for breakfast.

Manuela found her daughter cleaning the hunting rifle that lived in the attic. For a moment, she thought Olvido might aim it at her, rip her chest apart with a single shot. She felt lightheaded, as if she were falling into her grave.

"I just killed the horse." Olvido said.

"I didn't hear the shot."

"I held the gun to its head."

"It was a good-for-nothing old hack. It's better off dead."

"Yes, since he wasn't good for anything, he's much better off dead." Olvido looked into her mother's dark eyes.

"I want gizzards for breakfast." Manuela blinked in anger.

"We don't have any. I'll make toast with olive oil. And for lunch, tripe with herbs and garlic. I know you love that dish."

A gust of wind blew the kitchen window open, and a whirl of black petals surrounded Manuela.

"This storm is killing my roses!" she cried, batting the petals away. "It's the first year they've succumbed to the wind and the snow."

"Yes, it's been a long, hard winter. Not everything will survive."

Olvido closed the window. The petals fell to the floor at Manuela's feet.

"Do we have fresh tripe for you to cook today?"

"No, but I'll get some at the farm next to the veterinarian's. That way, if I see him, I can ask him to take the carcass away."

"Good." Manuela rubbed her gloved hands together. "Hurry home, and make the stew good and tasty. That recipe brings back memories. By the way, are you going to take our little man with you?"

"Yes. A bit of sun will do him good."

"You spoil him too much. But yesterday he learned that in this house, you have to work hard." Manuela rapped her knuckles on the wooden table where years before she had massacred chickens.

It was nearly noon by the time Olvido and Santiago returned from buying the tripe. As they walked into the house, the boy smelled the perfume of his beating filtering through the linen cupboard latticework.

"Don't worry. It all ends today."

"What ends, Abuela?"

"The lavender, sweetheart. The lavender."

They began to prepare lunch. Together they washed the tripe, their fingers touching under the running water. Together they cut the onions, studying the bright drops sparkling in their identical eyes, the fresh herbs and garlic. Together they mixed the ingredients in a clay pot they handed over to the flames on the stove.

Once the stew was ready, Olvido served three bowls, filling one more than the others and taking it into the pantry. Santiago could hear the clink of porcelain and glass. His grandmother was searching among the bottles he was not allowed to touch, bottles out of reach to a nine-year-old boy. The wait for what was to come dragged on. He ran a hand over the butcher's block, got caught up in the irreparably rough touch, the grooves left by a knife. Clouds filled the sky. It would rain soon. Olvido came out of the pantry, a white powder on her cheeks. Her hands shook. Santiago hurried to take the bowl before she spilled it and wiped her face with a cloth.

"I hope it tastes as good as it smells," Manuela said when the boy walked into the dining room with the steaming bowl.

"I'm sure it will, Bisabuela."

He sat next to the old woman and, smiling, cut the tripe, smothering it in sauce before bringing it to her lips. After lunch, Manuela told him a story as he looked into her eyes, waiting for the silence.

As it grew dark, a spray of black petals pelted the window in vain. The crackle of the fire slowly swallowed Manuela Laguna's voice. Her hands no longer shook. The memory of a dead adolescent vanished from her stomach and chest, as if, in this final moment, all was forgiven. She took off a glove and caressed her great-grandson's face, flushed by the wait, until her voice disappeared in a whisper of eucalyptus. The only noise was the sound of the fire clearing its throat. Santiago thought: It's done. A trickle of poison, as blue as the sea in one of her tales, spilled from Manuela Laguna's mouth, ran down her neck.

The next day Olvido walked to the Civil Guard station to report that she had found her mother dead. An autopsy was performed, determining the cause of death to be an overdose of the prescription painkillers she took for her arthritis. They also found traces of laudanum and rose fertilizer in her stomach, but no authority wanted to investigate the case any further. According to the official report, these had been ingested accidentally. No one cared who killed the old whore who for years sashayed around town, putting on airs. No one cared if the Lagunas destroyed one another. Besides, when her great-grandson was born, Manuela had amended her will, and the town would inherit a sum of money to build a sports complex to be named after Santiago Laguna. The mayor wanted the case closed to receive those funds posthaste. All he cared about was exactly how fat the municipal coffers would be and how to keep that damned name off a public building.

Olvido prepared a funeral fit for a queen. She had a carriage sent from the city, pulled by two sorrels with plumes rising from their heads, cinches with silk tassels, and manes braided with silver thread. The mahogany coffin with Manuela Laguna's remains paraded through town behind the municipal band as musicians puffed a requiem on trumpets and saxophones. Dogs poked their noses out of the ditch and old men jabbed the sky with their canes as the cortège passed. Once it reached the square, the procession circled the fountain with its three spouts as church bells rang, honoring the memory of the departed. A blond boy, the son of a town councilor, then appeared on a city hall balcony to read the eulogy to all the onlookers who had filled the square, wondering what those words might mean.

At noon the funeral cortège made its way up the hill to the cemetery. Wearing a mauve brocade cloak, Padre Rafael strode through the graveyard to the pounding of drums and the rattle of bones. Holding the silver vessel, he quietly sprinkled holy water on the coffin. Two altar boys attended, as well as the mayor, the pharmacist, and other illustrious members of society. Olvido even hired mourners from neighboring towns, dressed in black, to wail themselves hoarse and tear their hair before Manuela's grave, as if she had been loved.

As they lowered the mahogany coffin into the hole and earth fell on it like rain, a mason began to erect a pink marble mausoleum.

Once everyone left the cemetery, Olvido laid a handful of eucalyptus leaves on her mother's grave. Another afternoon of snow was visible on the horizon.

16

THANKS TO MANUELA LAGUNA, Santiago grew up believing he was born under the halo of the chosen. At the age of seven, after catechism class with Padre Rafael one day, he nearly drowned in the river that crossed the oak grove. Convinced of his messianic gifts, he wanted to show Olvido he could walk on the dark water. But the autumn wind thrashed the trees' firm stance, and the boy sank before resurfacing and paddling to shore, thankfully only a few feet away.

"If you dare try anything like that again, you will not be allowed to cook with me," his grandmother warned once he was safe and panting on the moss. "Being a Laguna boy is extraordinary, but that's as far as it goes."

Even though Olvido did not believe her grandson possessed any divine attributes, over the years she did come to suspect a miracle: Santiago was blessed with a wide range of talents that would eventually redeem the family's social standing. His friendship with Padre Rafael from the age of two helped him achieve what at first appeared to be his destiny. The priest had a soft spot for the blue-eyed boy who was never scared of the commotion caused by his movements, the drumroll of the earth, the shaking of trees. While other children burst into tears and hid behind their mothers' legs, terrorized by the giant ruddy-faced figure, Santiago would smile and tug on his cassock, babbling incomprehensibly. Momentarily reconciled with the anger he felt toward the uproar of his own body, the priest would crouch down and offer a caress, his hand completely engulfing the little boy's face.

When Santiago turned eight, Padre Rafael happened to hear him sing and discovered an angelic voice. With nary a thought for curses — such a golden voice could never be sullied — he dressed the boy in a white tunic and sent him onto the altar dais to sing the Gloria and the Ave Maria, to the delight of his parishioners. The first few Sundays, the old women in black veils crossed themselves when they looked at that boy burdened by his grandmother's beauty. They squirmed in the pews as if bitten by ants, and the phlegm of bitterness stuck in their craws. But the celestial melody he intoned tempered their bile and memories of disgrace. Within a few Sundays, they were moved by his songs. Some even smiled at him after church, while others patted him on the back in congratulations. The only woman who did not succumb to Santiago's voice was his aunt, Esteban's sister. She wrung her hands, narrowed her gaze to cast evil eye on her nephew, swore into her veil, and spat insults.

During Holy Week, with a purple cord around his waist and a face contorted by the fervor of suffering, the boy sang a *saeta*. Padre Rafael's eyes filled with tears, and the hair on the parishioners' arms stood on end, straight through their lightweight wool clothing. After Mass, in the sacristy, the priest wrapped the boy in a hug, and Santiago felt all the air squeezed out of his chest.

"Where did this talent come from, you little Castilian devil?" Padre Rafael asked, ruffling his hair.

"I don't know, Padre."

No one in town remembered that Santiago was the great-great-grandson of that Andalusian hunter who mesmerized Clara Laguna with folk songs and *saetas*.

Santiago's artistic abilities did not end there. After Manuela Laguna died, the boy read the parable of the wheat and the tares from the book of Matthew during catechism, and Padre Rafael discovered his oratorical skills. The priest had not abandoned his passion for modern technology when the public address system was ruined in the great storm. This time he set up a radio station that broadcast all over town from a little room next to the sacristy. He immediately decided Santiago would take one of the afternoon religious programs. The boy would come twice a week, after school, to read passages from the book of Matthew, Romans, and Corinthians, and poems by Saint Teresa of Ávila as the townspeople had their *café con leche* and sponge cake or bread and bacon. It was then that they stopped referring to him as the Laguna boy and began to call him the Laguna prodigy.

Olvido bought a transistor radio just to hear her grandson as she sat in the kitchen, the pots in the cupboards, the vegetables in the baskets, the knives in the drawers, and silence in her hands so nothing could distract her from that child's voice praising God. When the program ended, she climbed into the cart to pick up Santiago in town.

"Did you hear me, Abuela? Was I good?"

"Better than good. If I weren't a believer, I would be after I listened to you."

"You always have to listen because I think about you when I read, just like when I sing."

Olvido hugged him as the jolting cart carried them, with their identical black hair and identical ocean-blue eyes, into the horizon. Evening was settling over Scarlet Manor, the daisies on the drive enveloped in shadow. The kitchen waited for them to make dinner.

Santiago sank his hands into a porcelain bowl of flour. He felt its warmth, felt it growl softly as he held it in his fists. He let the flour sift through his fingers, smiled, and watched his grandmother in front of the counter, silhouetted against the window like another star embellishing the night. Olvido was preparing sole, caressing the skin, kissing the tail as rough as sideburns. Her hair was pulled into a ponytail with strands of pewter. The circles under her eyes looked like boats pulled up on the beach, small against the blue horizon of her eyes. Her supernatural beauty remained, as immune to time as it was to Manuela Laguna's potions and poultices.

Santiago flicked flour into her hair.

"I'm going to turn your hair even whiter, Abuela."

Olvido furrowed her brow, waving the sole like a weapon.

"Only if you can, young man."

She caught the boy and tickled his ribs.

"I give up!" Santiago laughed.

After dinner they sat together in front of the fire: Santiago in his great-grandmother's chair and Olvido in another beside him. The fire crackled and flushed their cheeks. It was Santiago who told Manuela Laguna's tales; it was he who let them float up into the air of their happy lives. Fingers entwined, they rode the waves that filled the parlor, listened to the fishermen's hoarse voices, the mermaids' bubbled song. Together they were startled by the storms, the vengeance of sperm whales, and dozed to the romance of sand and tar. Night had fallen and darkness curled up behind them when Santiago paused and kissed his grandmother's hand. It was she who always told the end of the story.

The summer Santiago Laguna turned twelve, a six-by-three-foot package arrived at Scarlet Manor. Tied with seven or eight pieces of twine, some thicker than others, it was wrapped in cardboard stained by lichen and grime from all over Europe. Stamps from post offices in London, Lisbon, Paris, Brussels, and Amsterdam, among other cities and towns, were smudged by the rain, the journey, or the porters' sweat. It smelled of cat piss, tulips, french fries, and mayonnaise, rancid chocolate, train soot, and filthy boulevards.

"Sign here, señora," the postman said to Olvido Laguna, holding out a receipt.

"What did you buy, Abuela?" Santiago looked at the package, curious.

"Nothing," she replied with a shrug.

The boy went to get the tree shears. Some of the twine was stiff with a layer of dry grease, while other strands melted like butter, rotted by mildew and time. Once Santiago had removed all the twine, he used a knife to split the tape that held the cardboard together. Olvido helped him peel it back from the corners to reveal the portrait of a stunning woman. It was painted in oil, the strokes full of pain, pastel colors, and memory infused with love and abandonment.

"It's you, Abuela."

Olvido's cheeks burned in anger. On the bottom right-hand corner of the painting was a black signature resembling a dead cricket.

"Don't you like it?"

Olvido said nothing. She had noticed a letter at her feet; it must have fallen out when they opened the package. Her hands shook as she tore open the envelope.

"Who's it from, Abuela?"

"Your father."

"I knew it." Santiago smiled.

The paper was crinkled, spotted with yellow and perfumed like lemonade.

"What does it say?" the boy asked.

"It's illegible." She pursed her lips. "It must have gotten wet. All you can make out at the bottom is your father's name—Pierre Lesac—and the date."

"Can I see it?"

Olvido passed the letter to Santiago. It was dated two years earlier. The painting had been touring Europe ever since, either lost or cheating fate.

"It's the first time I've seen my father's work. I love it. He seems like a magnificent artist. Can I have the letter, even though it's smudged? I'll keep it with the others."

Every year at Christmas Pierre Lesac sent his son greetings from Paris, sometimes even a photo. Occasionally he remembered his birthday and would send a postcard. The postscript always read, "Give your grandmother a kiss and take good care of her."

"Do you think he was writing to say the painting's my birthday present—not this year's, but when I turned ten, only it's late arriving because it got lost?"

"I'm positive it's your birthday present." Olvido caressed his cheek.

"Where'll we put it?"

"How about in the attic, to keep it safe?"

"No, Abuela. We'll hang it in the parlor. You're so pretty in it . . ."

From then on, Pierre Lesac's painting accompanied their evening stories. Olvido tried not to look at it so the end of the story would not fade on her lips, so the vine of memory would not creep up her tongue.

That summer, Santiago Laguna began to develop another of his artistic abilities. He could draw well and had loved to do so ever since he was small, but by the age of twelve it was clear he did not have his father's skill. Santiago preferred writing poetry. Lying in the honeysuckle clearing, in nothing but his underwear, he would sun himself next to his grandmother. She reread Saint John of the Cross while he drafted his first poems in a notebook. They dealt with a nostalgia he had not yet felt, a nostalgia he observed and intuited in nature. The branches of honeysuckle resting gently on top of one another seemed to be waiting for someone who was gone, seemed to be waiting for a return that saw them dry out and bloom again. They lived and died waiting, over and over again, in a never-ending cycle of snow, parched leaves, and sunny laments.

Santiago, on the other hand, was a boy who wanted for nothing; he had everything he desired. He made friends that first day of school, though he was never particularly close with anyone. He liked to play bottle caps, painting them various colors, and soccer, their ball a chickpea or a marble. Sometimes they played hide-and-seek in the square or dodge ball on the outskirts of town. Once, during a game, the undertaker's son dared call him cursed. Santiago crossed his arms, laughed in his face, and said: "*You're* the one who's unlucky. I'm the only one in town born in the light of the angels."

"Well, my mother says your great-grandmother was a whore, and your grandmother, too."

Santiago punched him in the eye and kicked him in the shin. In pain, the boy tried to fight back, but Santiago shoved him to the ground. None of the other boys defended the undertaker's son; none dared go up against Santiago Laguna, the tallest among them and the only one with supernatural ancestors.

Only one girl dared call him cursed and pick on his family: the florist's granddaughter. Santiago shot her a blue-eyed stare, bit his tongue, and walked away, determined to punish her with the power he discovered early on that he held over the opposite sex. From then on, he would wink at her as he sang in church, offer her wildflowers, do her science homework. When she was besotted and begged forgiveness, he spat: "I guess you're the unlucky one now."

That was the only problem Santiago ever had with a girl. Most of his female classmates were dying to be his girlfriend. Not only was he the best-looking boy in town, he was also the funniest and sang like an angel. But Santiago never settled on anyone, though he did quite like the pharmacist's granddaughter, a delicate girl with blond ringlets and bark-brown eyes who had been crazy about him since the age of six, when he drew a blue squirrel on her arm. On afternoons when he did not have his radio show, they would go into the room behind the pharmacy where Santiago would help with her homework — she pretended to need help in literature, biology, and chemistry, all of his favorite subjects. In that room with its sparkling tiles, he would set aside the books and convince her to concoct poultices to cure mange in dogs, anise and rose water enemas for constipated cats. The room would fill with the vapor of his elixirs, bits of herbs floating in the fog of his own invention, as the girl watched him stirring.

What Santiago most desired, however, was his grandmother's love; he was her world, too. Padre Rafael's affection, as immense and resounding as his presence, replaced that of a distant father who never came to visit.

By thirteen, Santiago had perfected his poems to the extent that he began to read them on the Saturday-morning culture show he hosted on the radio. Padre Rafael was so proud to hear him recite his poetry on air. The priest had aged but still looked ten or fifteen years younger than he was. The men in his family were known to live to a hundred, dying not of old age but of boredom. Most were in excellent health right until the end, marred only in some generations by a nasty case of incontinence. This had just hit Padre Rafael. It rattled his nerves, and every chance cough, sneeze, or laugh tied him to a porcelain bedpan. He was therefore forced to teach Santiago how the radio transmitter worked. More often than not, it was the boy who played the Gregorian chants or read the sermons Padre Rafael wrote in pages and pages during sleepless nights, summarized in the light of day and prayer. Santiago spent so much time in that little room next to the sacristy that he began to miss his grandmother. He suggested that the priest expand the cultural programming to include one on cooking, which Olvido Laguna could offer. Padre Rafael thought it was an excellent idea.

The first show was broadcast one Saturday morning. Olvido agreed only because she could not deny Santiago anything. Sitting before the microphone, an eggplant across her throat, she began to talk about batters. Her hesitant speech lugged the solitude of years spent in the silence of meat, fish, and vegetables but grew stronger as she delved into her recipes. Tears, revenge, nostalgia, laughter: all these left the kitchen at Scarlet Manor to explode over the airwaves in that little room next to the sacristy. Olvido's voice was a rushing stream that soaked the microphone; she had tasted the sweetness of communication, and nothing could stop her now. The women from good families licked their lips and nibbled on their pens as they jotted down recipes, refreshed cheeks with a cool hand, and rolled their eyes in lace-filled parlors over *café con leche*. The old widows, meanwhile, gathered around the one transistor radio owned by the wealthiest among them, eyes cemented with gossip, tongues clucking, nodding malevolently.

Olvido Laguna's social life slowly progressed from polite conversation when Santiago began to sing at church to a clamor of culinary exchanges. The women and cooks from noble families, the wives and daughters of merchants, and those of lesser standing would stop her in the square, in the narrow streets, at the pharmacy, to congratulate her on the program and clarify doubts about sautéing or rabbit stew. At the store they began to sell squash and cabbage with a sign that read:

ESPECIALLY FOR OLVIDO'S RECIPES. Her beauty seemed to have been miraculously forgiven. Her curse disappeared among batters and fresh poached cod. She was invited to dine with the undertaker's family and once even to the mayor's estate. They stopped calling her the Laguna of the Dead Boy and began to call her the Laguna Chef. The women in black shawls greeted her with a nod as she passed, as if now they understood her story. Manuela Laguna twirled with glee in her pink marble crypt. Esteban's sister, however, grew more resentful amid heaps of pulled stockings.

It was around then that construction was finished on the sports complex Manuela Laguna financed through her last will and testament. A municipal edict — approved by almost everyone in town — declared that, out of respect for the deceased, it would be named after Santiago Laguna. To celebrate such an honor bestowed on a boy his age, the pharmacist's granddaughter kissed him on the lips as he prepared a rosemary and mint poultice to treat horsefly bites. Santiago enjoyed the warm feel of that small mouth. He savored it like an apricot, pried it open with his tongue, as if to remove the stone, and explored until he captured her tongue with his own. All thought of the poultice escaped him. With paste-covered hands, he held tight to that adolescent waist, sensed the mass of curls, intimate desire slipping out through feminine cheeks.

"I love you," she said. "I've loved you for so long."

The girl's ardor condensed on the tiles. Santiago kissed her again, pulling her to him, her breasts like Sunday paella mussels cleaving to his chest.

"Will you write me a poem?" she whispered in his ear.

That night, alone in his room, keeping the day's events from Olvido in case she felt betrayed, Santiago wrote a poem not to the ringleted girl but to the kiss, which had become a thing unto itself, floating in the room.

17

EVEN THOUGH SANTIAGO LAGUNA believed he was born free of the curse, the Sunday he met Ezequiel Montes after Mass, an icy effervescence surged through his bones. The man smelled of lavender soap and the sweetness of sheep, a smell that had permeated the wrinkles in his forehead and neck, a smell that remained no matter how much he bathed. Santiago shook his hand, rough and cold from the October air. Ezequiel smiled at him. He was wearing a black suit as stiff as armor and a white, collarless shirt. His short hair was thick and brown, curls brushing his temples. At sixteen, Santiago was taller than him, a handsome young man as tall as a church steeple, just like his father.

"I'm so happy you two have finally met," Olvido said after introducing them.

Ezequiel Montes looked deep into her eyes, his own tinged green from staring at meadows. Olvido responded with a tender glance. It was then Santiago discovered that, instead of bones, rivers flowed under his skin, and he cursed blackberry cakes, blackberry bushes, and sheep bells. For the first time in his life, he felt like the unluckiest boy in the world.

One mid-September morning, when Santiago was in school, Olvido went to pick blackberries in the hills to make him a cake. Fate or a rock caused her to trip and lose her balance. She fell into a bramble-filled ditch with the most luscious end-of-summer crop. Bruised and pricked by thorns, Olvido watched as a sheep with a bell around its neck appeared at the edge of the ditch, followed by another, and another, their round eyes glazed as they chewed the grass. Behind them towered the powerful silhouette of Ezequiel Montes. Olvido had occasionally seen him at church or the general store but never paid much attention until he stood staring down at her, his feet spread, a bag slung across his chest. He reached down to help her up, taking her arm when she faltered. He offered his name with the scruffy solitude of the country and, trailed by foggy bleats, led her to his hut to tend her cuts.

"Let me put some ointment on those scrapes." His voice rose hoarse from his throat.

It was a small stone hut with a slate roof. Ezequiel Montes decided not to take Olvido inside, where there was only an unmade cot, a little table, and a hearth for heat and to cook his meals. He helped her down onto the grass, by the door, and placed his bag under her head. High in the sky, the sun cast its midday light. He went inside and soon emerged with a jar of ointment, a clean cloth, and a cup of milk.

"Drink this. It'll do you good."

Olvido sat up to drink the milk, then lay back down.

"I'll pull the thorns from your legs."

"Thank you." Olvido hitched her skirt above her knees and pressed her thighs together.

She felt Ezequiel's thick fingers pluck the thorns out one by one, felt the burning sensation that remained.

"It's the first time anything like this has ever happened to me. I've walked these hills all my life."

"That ditch is dangerous. One of my sheep fell in not long ago and tore up her legs. Uh . . ." He paused, a look of concern on his face. "You're much better looking than any sheep, of course. I didn't mean to compare."

"That's all right." Olvido smiled.

The shepherd cleaned her cuts with the cloth and applied rosemary ointment but did not dare go any higher than her knees.

"Now for the scrapes on your arms and face."

He leaned over her. Nature had been his only company for weeks, and his stomach fluttered. He avoided looking into her eyes, avoided looking at her lips, concentrated on her cuts. An invisible haze emanated from the shepherd's chest, soothing Olvido's pain.

"Can you roll up your sleeves?"

"Of course." Olvido's skin began to tingle as she uncovered her arms.

"Do you live far from here?" Ezequiel asked.

"The estate by the road." The shepherd had big, weathered hands. "The one called Scarlet Manor. I'm sorry. You've been so kind, and I never even told you my name. I'm Olvido Laguna."

"Let me walk you home, Olvido."

"Oh, I've kept you long enough." She slowly got to her feet.

"Can you walk?"

"Yes." She took a few steps. One leg hurt and she limped a little.

"I'll go with you."

He put the sheep in the pen, leaving two dogs to watch over them. Then he took Olvido's arm in his, telling her to lean on him, and they began to walk down through the meadows, bright with bellflowers and poppies. In the distance they could hear the bleating of other flocks that disappeared in dusty cane fields and along enchanted paths, their metal bells honing the breeze. Out of habit, Ezequiel walked in silence; at forty-four, he had been a shepherd all his life.

"I won't be able to make that blackberry cake today after all. I left my basket in the ditch," Olvido said.

"I'll pick more tomorrow so you can make your cake."

Beech leaves had begun to fall from their branches. The air was warm and limp by the time they reached Scarlet Manor.

When Santiago arrived home from school early that afternoon, his grandmother told him what happened. Concerned, he washed and disinfected her cuts before bed, thinking his grandmother meant the shepherd Saturnino, a big old oaf who drank too much on Sundays and belched all through the town square. The next morning Santiago wanted to stay home to look after her, but Olvido insisted she was fine, and he finally left for school. Just after eleven, there was a knock at the door. Olvido felt it in her belly and knew it was Ezequiel Montes. Freshly shaven, his leathery skin brought out the soft green of his eyes. His hair shone and he stood wringing his hands, red from milking animals in the misty dawn. Olvido invited him into the kitchen.

"I found your basket." The shepherd handed it to her, filled to the brim with blackberries.

"I'll have enough for at least two cakes now," she said, setting the basket on the counter. "Would you like a cup of coffee?"

Ezequiel accepted and remained standing to watch her. He knew the story of this beautiful woman's past, the story of her family and the lavish brothel housed there in the early 1900s. But his soul had been cooled by mountain air for more than forty years; caring nothing for gossip, he listened only to his feral heart.

"Are you feeling all right?"

"My scrapes hardly hurt and my leg is much better after a night's rest. You really were very kind." Olvido handed him a cup of coffee, and they sat at the white table that had replaced Manuela's butcher's block.

"Do you work the estate alone?"

"My grandson helps me. He just turned sixteen, nearly a man now."

"I'm a widower. My wife died of pneumonia before we had children." Ezequiel took a sip of coffee, bitter on his tongue.

"I know what it is to lose a loved one. I'm sorry. We're never the same again . . ." The taste of graveyard earth filled her mouth, and Olvido lowered her eyes.

Ezequiel Montes set down his cup. He would have liked to stroke her hair, caress her cheek, but merely squeezed her hand.

"A wolf takes one sheep, but the rest still need tending."

Olvido looked into his eyes. The shepherd's touch felt good. She liked inhaling the invisible cloud that rose up from his chest.

"I should go. Thank you for the coffee and the chat. Sometimes I go weeks without seeing another soul." Ezequiel withdrew his hand and stood.

"Come back whenever you like."

Ezequiel Montes seemed to be in a hurry. Olvido walked him to the door and watched him walk down the daisy-strewn drive.

When Santiago came home, he found his grandmother baking a blackberry cake and chastised her for going into the hills before she was better from her fall.

"The shepherd brought them," she said without a second thought.

"That Saturnino's going to great lengths for you."

"It wasn't Saturnino but another shepherd. You don't see him in town very often. His name is Ezequiel Montes."

Santiago vaguely remembered him. He was a big, silent man rumored to have the looks and instinct of a wolf.

"I was going to pick blackberries for you this afternoon." Santiago furrowed his brow. "It was nice of him, but if you see him again, tell him there's a man in this house already." He left the kitchen, climbing the stairs to his room two at a time.

Olvido washed the berry juice off her hands and followed her grandson.

"What's wrong?"

Santiago was lying in bed with an absent look in his eyes.

"I don't want anything to happen to you, don't you see? I want us to be together forever."

Olvido sat next to him, stroking his hair. Santiago put his head on her lap and held her tight.

The next day, when Santiago left for school, Olvido prepared lunch, worked in the garden, and went to look for Ezequiel Montes. On this foggy morning the meadows looked like mirages and the memory of the shepherd seemed like a dream. When he was not by the ditch, Olvido continued to his hut. She walked leaning on a stick, careful not to drop her cake. The sky had begun to clear by the time she arrived. She saw Ezequiel sitting on a stool by the door, lost in a book. He looked up, set the book on the grass, and smiled. A gust of wind came down from the mountains, ruffling Olvido's hair and the flounce of her skirt.

"I brought you a blackberry cake."

Her cheeks were flushed from the effort, her back damp with sweat. But when Ezequiel Montes approached her, she began to shiver.

"Are you cold?"

"A little." She was about to blush and looked away before handing him the cake.

Ezequiel thanked her, taking it into the hut, setting it on the table by the hearth. He came back out with a sheepskin coat and placed it on her shoulders.

"There's a real bite to that wind."

"What are you reading?" Olvido asked as she sat on the stool.

"The Bible."

The cover was black leather, the pages turned brown by time, by lonely hands and nights and howls of wild beasts.

"It belonged to my father."

"Do you like to read?"

"Only the Bible. I learned to read with it, and it's as far as I got."

"Have you tried to read anything else, if you don't mind my asking?"

"I understand your curiosity, but no, whenever I try, the letters all jumble up and I can't understand a word. Still, I've read the Bible twenty times at least, without any trouble at all."

Ezequiel sat on the grass, pulled out a blade, and stuck it between his lips. He began to tell Olvido about his father, the young priest of a small church in Soria who hung up his robes when he fell in love with a girl, a dressmaker's apprentice, who came to light candles for her ancestors every morning. The light from those short wicks designed for remembrance dancing on her cheeks and in her wild cat eyes were his father's introduction to physical love. Ezequiel could not remember those feline eyes: infectious tuberculosis took his mother when he was just four. After the funeral, his father moved back to where he was from and became a shepherd, nurturing his son, his sheep, and his sorrow in the mountains. Ezequiel never went to school; his playmates were the lambs and the dogs. He learned to read with the Bible and to count with the sheep: he added when lambs were born, subtracted when they were taken by wolves. The Civil Guard killed his father in the late 1940s, accusing him of selling milk and cheese on the black market. They shot him on a path where poppies and cotton thistle had grown ever since. Ezequiel found the bullet casings in the mud and carried them for a time in a little leather bag. He would never have looked for them if he hadn't been so young, but it was as if they could bring back what he had lost. He slept with that little bag under his pillow, the shells exploding in his dreams, filling the hut with gunpowder and terror. In the meantime, wolves ate his sheep as he did nothing to stop them. Until one night, the shells no longer burst, and Ezequiel killed his first wolf with a man's rifle. At dawn he went back to the path and buried the little bag under a clump of poppies.

The shepherd cleared his throat. It had been years since he had talked that much, years since a woman had listened to him. They said goodbye just after noon. The slow tinkling of bells, the bleating of sheep, the pastures saturated with a green quite different from Ezequiel's eyes, spurred him on to ask her if she might visit another morning.

"I'll make you some cheese."

Nature, however, was the first thing to come between Olvido and Ezequiel, when it rained passionately for several days. Ezequiel's cheese soured in the hut as a result of the wait. The milk fermented impatiently, mold appearing on the rind as often as the shepherd went to the window in search of a woman's silhouette in the storm. One afternoon he crushed the round with the butt of his rifle and set about preparing a fresh batch. When it was ready the next morning, he put on his oilskin coat, sheltered the cheese next to his heart, and left the hut. He walked down through the pastures and cane fields until he came to the thick stand of pines and arrived at Scarlet Manor.

The rusty hinges on the iron gate squeaked and the daisies were crushed under his boots. The gold knocker shaped like a woman's fist rose up, slippery in his hand. Olvido opened the door to find the shepherd under an old, wide-brimmed leather hat.

"The cheese couldn't wait."

He pulled it out of his jacket as Olvido invited him into the kitchen. Olvido took the round in her hands and felt it throb against her fingers.

"Thank you," she said, but nothing more.

Olvido did not dare tell him that she'd tossed and turned all night dreaming of gunpowder the last few nights, unsure whether it came from the rifle Manuela used one winter night or the casings the shepherd had placed under his pillow. She did not dare tell him that, when the moon appeared, she would lie under the purple canopy while two yellow eyes laughed at her restless wanderings through meadows and flocks of sheep. She did not dare tell him about mornings when her eyes were lost in the clouds, her hiking boots ready by the door, her raincoat on the hook, anxious to reach its destination. She did not dare tell him about the squash that died in her hands as she cooked them wistfully thinking of him, unsure how it had happened. She did not dare tell him about her sorrow as she watched the rain, the sorrow in her grandson's voice or hers at lying to him for the first time ever.

Ezequiel Montes took off his oilskin coat and drank his coffee. Olvido told him about her annoyance with the bad weather, about her garden blessed with prodigious fertility, about her cooking show on the local radio. She even turned the radio on to listen to Santiago recite a poem by Fray Luis de León in a hoarse voice, a sign of his future torment.

"Will you come see me when the weather clears, to continue our chat?" Ezequiel looked at Olvido intensely.

"I'd like that."

They heard coals crumble on the fire. Afternoon was dissolving in the sky as darkness timidly stuck out its tongue of stars. Ezequiel put on his jacket and hat. Outside, it continued to rain.

"See you soon." He smiled.

Olvido stood in the doorway, watching.

Ezequiel spent his time reading the Bible until the skies cleared a week later. He rememorized the story of paradise in Genesis, and, when night fell and sleep would not come, trapped in thoughts of a woman's hair, he read by candlelight how God's people wandered through the desert. The day it cleared, Olvido headed straight for his hut. It was very early, the first scratches of dawn just visible on the horizon. Santiago had stayed over at the church to help Padre Rafael, whose incontinence had grown worse in recent years, so Olvido did not have to wait for him to leave for school. The dogs barked as they came to meet her, wagging their tails, announcing her arrival. She was carrying a book under her arm, *Legends* by Bécquer. Ezequiel Montes was milking the sheep, unshaven, his shirt untucked. He knocked over the bowl of milk when he saw her.

"It's such a lovely day. I woke early and felt like taking a walk," she said.

"You're welcome here anytime." The shepherd ran a hand over his face, wishing there were no shadow of stubble, and hurriedly tucked in his shirt.

"I brought a book, in case you might like to read it."

"Oh . . . thank you. Have you had breakfast?"

"Just a little fruit."

"Then I'll make toast with cheese and a cup of fresh milk."

They ate together sitting on stools outside the door to his hut. Though Olvido wanted to help him toast the bread and cut the cheese, Ezequiel insisted on doing it himself. The inside of the hut smelled like a bachelor's home, the cot still unmade, last night's dishes all over the table by the hearth. After breakfast, they chatted about the hunters arriving in town, the condition destroying the priest's kidneys despite his strength, and the domino tournament at the tavern in a few weeks' time. Ezequiel planned to enter; his father had taught him to play when he was just a boy, and it had been a passion ever since.

"We could play if you like. I sometimes play with my grandson," Olvido said.

"Why don't you read me a few pages of the book you brought?"

"Wouldn't you like to try? Perhaps I could help."

Olvido handed Ezequiel the book that had been sitting on her lap. Instead of reading it, he stroked the cover as if it harbored the soft touch of the woman now smiling expectantly at him. If the written word had seemed like rows of marching ants before, with Olvido beside him the ants piled up into a thick mane of hair hanging down a naked back. His face flushed, his lips trembled, and he recited a verse from Genesis by heart: "This is now bone of my bones, and flesh of my flesh: she shall be called Woman, because she was taken out of Man."

"Let me read it, then."

"No, please. Another time. I can't concentrate right now," Ezequiel begged, setting the book on the grass.

"What's wrong?"

Olvido felt Ezequiel's hand in hers. They kissed, slowly at first, then in great crashing waves, as if they wanted those kisses to last until sleep, to last until death. They embraced and fell to their knees like penitents. Kisses dripped down their clothes, his shirt, her sweater; they dripped down her skirt and his pants, falling onto the pasture, creating a river where bellflowers rustled on the shore. It was not air they breathed, but lips. They touched as if they had found each other, touched as if they were thousands of miles apart. They lost their balance and rolled in each other's arms. They continued to kiss, bathing in the river of kisses until Olvido could not catch her breath. She stood, brushed off her skirt, and ran from her own kisses, like a teenage girl, toward the pine forest.

By the time she reached the square, Olvido thought her heart would leap from her chest. She furrowed the crease in her brow and climbed the hill to the cemetery. The undertaker was weeding between headstones to keep roots from scratching the dead. He watched her walk past, pale, panting louder than the magpies' caws.

"Something wrong?" he shouted.

Olvido said nothing, continued to weave her way between rows of crosses and dusty wreaths to the old part of the cemetery where Esteban was buried. She had stopped hiding in the crypt once she began to care for Santiago, but she still went every week during regular visiting hours to pray at her daughter's grave, clean the headstone, and lay flowers.

MARGARITA LAGUNA. REST IN PEACE. Olvido read the epitaph and crossed herself before kneeling on Esteban's grave. She gathered two fistfuls of earth and held them tight. Slowly, she opened her palms and brought the dirt to her lips. The magpies heard her talk to it, heard her kiss it with all the affection of eternity, heard her cry over it until the perfume of rain slipped through the cemetery. Olvido lay down on the grave and closed her eyes.

The next morning, through the kitchen window, Olvido saw the outline of Ezequiel Montes pacing outside the iron fence, an apparition that maintained the robust form of the living. She busied herself washing seeds out of a pepper, frying onion, cutting chicken, until Ezequiel's silhouette disappeared. She ate alone in the kitchen, staring out the window, promising to go out and meet him if he returned. She had no room for dessert, her stomach full of the memory of what happened the previous day. She wiped chicken grease from her lips, wrapped a shawl around her shoulders, put on her hiking boots, and left.

She found him sitting on a rock in the meadow that led from the hut to the ravine. He was holding the Bécquer book like a lump of stone.

"I was afraid you wouldn't come back," the shepherd said as he got to his feet.

"So was I," Olvido replied.

The book fell to the ground, the river of their kisses flowing over it. They walked to the hut. Embers from the logs that had comforted Ezequiel's sleepless nights still crackled in the hearth. They kissed against the wall, undressed on the unmade cot that groaned under the weight of love, the weight of bodies now come undone, and the smell of a man who lived alone drifted out the door.

18

THE CASTILIAN TOWN was unprepared for Santiago Laguna's fall from grace. The townspeople had watched him grow up on that altar dais in the church, singing Glorias and Ave Marias in an angelic voice that may have lost purity and gained gravity with the onset of adolescence but continued to fill hearts with faith, raising the hair on arms swathed in their Sunday best. (Some even remembered him lying in his crib, sleeping like a baby, as Manuela Laguna lifted his genitals on a stick to display proof of his exceptional birth.) They had grown used to hearing him recite sections of the Gospels or saintly poems on their radios, their hands greasy with bacon, a *café con leche* moustache over their lips. No one made announcements like him: times for Mass, times for catechism, times for retreats flowing out over the waves. "The boy speaks so clearly," they said, "with such joy and conviction." They had grown used to his poetry about honeysuckle, geranium, and morning glories every Saturday morning. Young girls sucked on lollipops as they thought about petals; older girls confused pine needles with wintry branches awaiting the return of an uncertain love; old women were invigorated as they made vegetable soup. They had even grown used to his beauty, adopting it as theirs, making it the pride of the town. "Shame there are only contests for the best-looking calf around here. If there were one for boys, our Santiago would win them all," the old women in black shawls would comment in the late afternoon when they saw him pass by, offering a smile. It no longer mattered that his beauty came from Olvido, she who had given them recipes to soothe their longing for the dead. It no longer mattered that his saint's name was followed by a last name sullied by a curse. Without a doubt, he had been born to put an end to that curse, to squash it with his prodigious gifts. So said Padre Rafael, who loved him like a son.

But once Santiago saw the way his grandmother and Ezequiel Montes looked at each other that October Sunday, his Glorias and Ave Marias were suffocated in a mantle of grief and rage that clouded any godly love in the hearts of the faithful. This affliction—inflamed on holiday afternoons when Ezequiel Montes drank boiled coffee and ate cinnamon cake in the parlor at Scarlet Manor, sitting between him and Olvido—also affected his ability to write and recite poetry. Santiago read the Gospels halfheartedly, like a simple instruction manual; he attributed verses by Matthew to Luke, and Luke's to a nonexistent apostle. He recited sacred poems in fits and starts, with the intonation of a dying man, and he constantly mixed up the times for Mass, catechism, and retreats. Afternoon teatime became dull, cups of *café con leche* unsteady, and slices of bacon disappointing. Old women went to church in time for First Communion catechism, while children, excited by the prospect of holy wafers, arrived to hear talks on living with Christian principles after a spouse has died. The poems Santiago wrote for his Saturday-morning programs were no longer filled with nature's nostalgia but steeped in eulogies to times gone by, to rough traitors who stole love and died poisoned by laudanum and rose fertilizer.

Padre Rafael began to do what he had never done before—censor Santiago's poems—until there was nothing left to read, nothing but pursed lips before the solitude of a microphone. Fraught by the anguish of his love and incontinence, the priest wound up buying a mammoth collection of religious music to replace Santiago on the air until he was cured of the ill consuming him, an ill the priest attributed to nothing but a furious attack of adolescence.

October unfurled in the mountains, fields, and pine forests. Nights began to smell of snow, carpets of dry leaves were picked up by the wind, and the ground grew hard with the first frost.

The traitors who invaded Santiago's poems appeared in Manuela Laguna's stories as well. At Scarlet Manor, as night grew thick after dinner and Pierre Lesac's portrait over the fireplace flushed with shadows, the Atlantic Ocean grew choppy between Olvido and Santiago, schooners splintering to pieces, waves flooding eyes, and the traitors the boy invented were the cause of all misfortune, of all the sailors' laments, of all the losses in the world, as if they controlled nature itself. When Santiago fell silent, waiting for his grandmother to tell the end of the story, his cheeks would furrow with sad creases. But Olvido paid no attention to the traitors, treating them as if they did not exist. Nothing had or ever could change between them, she seemed to be saying to her grandson as she recounted the end of the story just as she had heard her mother tell it many years before.

Santiago fell ill and stopped going to school. In the mornings he would vomit the dinners he and his grandmother had made, now without laughter or games, dinners of silent squash, grief-stricken tuna, and bitter potatoes, dinners seasoned with the same question — "Is he your boyfriend?" — and the same answer — "For now he's just a good friend." But she was lying, even if it was to save him from hurt, to let him slowly get used to Ezequiel Montes on the periphery of their lives.

Santiago knew it was a lie. Olvido's eyes sparkled when she talked about the shepherd; before they had only ever sparkled when she talked about him. Santiago twisted in his sheets, afflicted by cramps that filled him with joy, for as long as he was home, his grandmother could not meet Ezequiel in the meadow, could not walk in woods that had always been theirs. Olvido brought him chamomile tea, fed it to him by the spoonful, kissed his forehead when he was done, and he was as happy as when nothing stood in their gaze. Didn't Ezequiel Montes know *he* was the one chosen to save his family? Didn't Ezequiel Montes know who he was up against?

Olvido had had the occasional suitor since her cooking program opened doors to a social life. Santiago knew that Agustino, the widower from the fabric store, invited her to the summer cinema one day, but she offered apologies, saying she was going with her grandson.

That night Agustino sat drinking wine in a corner of the plaza, fuming as he watched them laugh at the movie, arm in arm against a star-speckled sky. Santiago had also watched as the lawyer's son — who had inherited the business after his father died of prostate cancer — tried to caress Olvido's hand when he indicated where she was to sign. As she moved toward the paper, pen in hand, he was waiting with the vile sword of his fingers. It was not war they were seeking but love, and she knew it, a feverish Santiago thought, and would surreptitiously move her hand, leaving the office holding her grandson's hand, squeezing it to include him in what had just happened.

The new doctor in town, a young blond man afflicted by alopecia and extreme myopia requiring thick glasses, came to Scarlet Manor to diagnose Santiago. Long fingers examined Santiago's stomach, finding it contracted, as if wanting to escape his touch. He examined Santiago's tonsils, as red as cod gills, and his ears, where he found a wax plug he extracted with a silver instrument and a gush of water.

"The boy is healthy," he told Olvido at last. "The vomiting is a case of nerves. Make sure he gets out for fresh air, and if symptoms continue, give him a glass of water with baking soda and three drops of lemon every eight hours. If his nerves don't settle on their own, they'll need to be purged."

That night there were no stories by the fire, replaced by baking soda purgatives. Olvido went to bed early in Clara Laguna's room, wanting to avoid the bricked-up window in her room and hoping her grandmother might offer advice to help the boy understand her friendship with Ezequiel Montes. Olvido pictured the shepherd reading the Bible, lonely as a wolf, unable to eat, unshaven and in love, the candle nub melting onto the table, him lying on the iron cot, waiting for her. It had been over a week since she had seen him, since Santiago had grown ill. Sunday teatimes were suspended, as were Ezequiel's visits during the week to bring them cheese and fresh milk or have a cup of coffee in the kitchen.

The baking soda and lemon revealed a new dimension to Santiago's stomach, filled with longing for Olvido. Unwell, he went to her room, but not finding her there, he continued on to Clara Laguna's. He stood for a moment, staring at his grandmother's shape beneath the purple canopy, then climbed in silently beside her. He wrapped his arms around her waist and fell asleep as a lace dressing gown swished down one wall.

Fire. That was the first night Santiago dreamed of flames surrounding him, choking him. But the dream ended there. He woke in a cold sweat, his gaze lost in the purple canopy. He clung to his grandmother, who calmed him with kisses, rocking him as she had when he was a boy and the nightmare of Manuela Laguna drooling a blue sea of poison startled him awake. They held on to each other for over an hour, sharing secrets in the silent dawn filtering in through the window. Later, over a breakfast of toast, Santiago thought those flames must belong to the very hell Padre Rafael spoke of from the pulpit armored against his prehistoric weight. Santiago felt guilty about leaving the priest to his fate surrounded by bedpans, the theological treatises he wrote in the clarity of morning, and records of Gregorian chants, requiems, and solemn Masses. He refused the glass of water with baking soda and lemon and had no trouble with the previous night's dinner or the morning slice of bread and butter.

"I'm going to church, Abuela," Santiago said after drinking the last of his milk. "Padre Rafael needs me. I shouldn't have left him like that."

"I'm sure he understands. He loves you very much . . ."

"And tomorrow I'll go to school."

The day dawned to black clouds, so Santiago put on a raincoat and rubber boots. He went to stay goodbye to Olvido, busily skinning a rabbit for lunch, and found her smiling down at the blood and clumps of fur that escaped her knife.

Santiago headed down the gravel road. He knew Olvido would go see Ezequiel Montes and felt a stab in his chest as his bones became a mountain stream once again. But he needed to see Padre Rafael and resolve this issue with hell. As the first drops of rain fell, he began to think about the pharmacist's granddaughter, his ringleted classmate whose breasts had grown from paella mussels to frosted cupcakes. They still kissed and caressed in the room behind the pharmacy amid balsams, bottles, and concoctions, though he had never dared tell Padre Rafael or his grandmother. Santiago thought he might be able to give up those afternoons that engorged adolescence in his pants, if in exchange God would separate Olvido and Ezequiel Montes. After all, Santiago told himself as rain pelted his forehead, this is all just a mistake; I wasn't born for misfortune.

Padre Rafael was so happy to see Santiago that he had to race to the bathroom. The church echoed with his footsteps, but not like before, his illness softening both him and his journey through the world. Santiago waited for him in the small radio station room. It was more organized than he could believe. A new shelving unit stood in one corner, housing the collection of sacred music Padre Rafael had bought, the records arranged by choir or composer.

"How are you, my boy?" the priest asked when he came back from the bathroom wearing an oft-mended cassock.

"I want to help with the radio again, and with Mass if you need me. I don't feel like doing my radio shows yet, but I could play the music."

"I'm so happy to hear that, son. I was considering finding someone else — just until you were better, of course."

"No need, Padre. I'm here. But I have to tell you, I dreamed of hell last night."

"Such a place was not made for you, Santiago," the priest replied, ruffling his hair.

When he arrived home for lunch, Santiago found a rosy-cheeked Olvido in hiking boots.

"You went up to the meadow to see your friend the shepherd," Santiago said.

"In a few days, when the fog of the dead arrives, he'll take his sheep to Extremadura and won't be back until spring."

Olvido knew shepherds led their flocks to pasture in Extremadura because of its warmer winter and returned once the cold weather was gone. Still, she had never paid attention to it until that morning, when Ezequiel Montes announced his departure. She would miss their conversations sitting by the door to his hut, their walks through the meadows, their hugs and kisses on the messy iron cot.

"Invite him to tea this Sunday to say goodbye," Santiago proposed.

The boy was thrilled to see just how quickly God listened, taking Ezequiel Montes away. The second half of fall and one full winter seemed long enough for his grandmother to forget. Now he had no choice but to hold up his end of the bargain and stop his games with the pharmacist's granddaughter.

Ezequiel Montes came to Scarlet Manor in his stiff suit, his hair neatly combed back with cologne. He watched Olvido pour the coffee and arrange the cinnamon cake on a porcelain platter. He spoke of his trip, the excellent pastures free of snow, and oak groves that turned the landscape into a world of giant shadows when night fell. Santiago was friendly that evening. He asked the shepherd how long it would take him to reach Extremadura, what towns he would pass, and other details that interested him not at all.

Just after eight o'clock, Ezequiel said he should go. Santiago said goodbye in the parlor, letting his grandmother walk the shepherd to the door. Hiding in a corner of the hallway, Santiago watched them hurriedly kiss, reach up to touch a face, as if hands were memory to be recalled later, and embrace as a blade of dark sliced their bodies through the half-open door. It took everything in Santiago to forget this painful image, and after dinner, when he and his grandmother sat in front of the fire to tell their stories, he had to fight the desire to inject a traitor responsible for the deepest sorrow.

The next day, when the first church bells rang, Ezequiel Montes set off with his flock and his dogs, leaving the town behind like a cloud billowing up at dawn.

November crept deep into the mountains and forests. Winds blew, making lime trees sing, mountain ash burn bright, beech trees turn yellow, ferns grow brown. Autumn marched wet and multi-hued into winter.

Santiago's bones were bones once again. He sang at Sunday Mass once again, up on the dais with a voice still recovering, deeper but also more beautiful. He recited the Gospels and sacred poems once again, announcing times for Mass, catechism, and retreats without any mistakes. The only thing he could not do was write poetry, neither about nature nor traitors. Santiago asked his grandmother to pick him up from school a few days a week and accompany him in the room next to the sacristy for his radio shows. She would sit and watch him recite into the microphone, but every now and then Santiago sensed her gaze was far away, lost elsewhere, though her eyes were fixed on his, and it pained him to think that she might have traveled to Extremadura, to that rough man off in some pasture. Yet Olvido showed no sign of missing the shepherd.

The only noticeable change was that she went to the cemetery more often. Olvido always visited the graves of Esteban and her daughter, and sometimes Manuela's mausoleum. It was a hexagonal, pink marble shrine held up by Ionic columns, a gloved goddess rising from the center. The townspeople whispered that it was a fitting grave for the life she had led: a whore who rose high because the flesh was weak. In winter no one was ever at her grave, but in spring and summer, entomologists from all over the province, even the capital, visited the mausoleum. At that time of year, thousands of insects—primarily centipedes and crickets—would pilgrimage there. Scientists had yet to discover a reasonable explanation for this phenomenon. Endless rows of insects climbed the hill with religious obstinacy, despite children throwing rocks to break their military formation, stray dogs sniffing them with wet snouts, and funeral processions stomping on them to avenge their pain.

By the time the first snow fell, Santiago noticed that his grandmother had become more absent-minded. She would forget her stews on the stove, burning them; use dessert ingredients in first and second courses, adding cinnamon and sugar to garlic soup or cooking meatballs in lemon cream. It was then she began to tell her grandson about Ezequiel Montes, his life, his childhood adding lambs and subtracting them, his extraordinary ability to read the Bible when he was illiterate before any other book, the little bag where he kept the shells of the bullets that killed his father and how for years he slept with them under his pillow.

Santiago's bones ached and the vomiting returned; so did the traitors in Manuela Laguna's stories and fire in his dreams. But this time Santiago did not fear they were the flames of hell. Even though they still surrounded him like that very first dream, now they were suddenly extinguished by a ray of moonlight. This heavenly glow bathed him in an albino fire, and it was in those fresh flames that the face of a woman appeared. Over several nights all Santiago could make out was a mass of wavy chestnut hair. But as the dream took root inside, one night he distinguished a smooth forehead, another night a pair of sorrowful black eyes. The next day Santiago was obsessed with the lumps of coal in the stove; he gorged on black olives and squid in its ink that Olvido prepared, surprised by her grandson's sudden desire to consume anything dark she set before him.

Several days passed before Santiago was assaulted by the dream again. He had tried to sleep wherever he could, slumped over his desk at school, listening to the Gregorian chants and requiems he played on the radio, as his grandmother told the end of a story. He was no longer afraid of the fire. Instead he was anxious to decipher the woman's whole face, anxious to see what lay beyond those eyes that held him captive.

One afternoon, after the radio show, he curled up on a pew in the chapel to Saint Pantolomina of the Flowers, and the veil of moonlight fell from the woman's black pupils, revealing a small, straight nose. Santiago made it a habit to nap there, and a quick snooze offered up geometric cheekbones and ears one stormy night when he could not go home to Scarlet Manor. The more features Santiago saw, the less he recognized her and the more beautiful he found her.

When only her lips and chin had yet to be discovered, Olvido decided not to mention Ezequiel Montes until spring but to nurture the love she had given her grandson for the last sixteen years. Back were their games and jokes in the kitchen, nipples smeared with sauce, walks in snowy mountains, and afternoons gazing at each other in the room next to the sacristy. Meanwhile, the shepherd, alone in Extremadura, counted the days before he was to return to Castilla, and the ringleted girl dissolved in tears among elixirs in the room behind the pharmacy after Santiago approached at recess one morning, eating a piece of cinnamon cake, and simply said: "We can't fool around anymore. We can't even do homework together. I've had to sacrifice everything for something greater, but you'd never understand."

Santiago's dreams of fire simply ceased, and no matter how he tried to bring them back, he failed. And yet, the incomplete face of that woman crouched deep down in his heart.

Nothing could stop the sun's rays from bringing an end to winter, lime trees bursting into bud, sparrows throwing themselves into the world with a manic trill, bees buzzing among roses like nannies to the dead. Faced with these inescapable signs of spring, nothing could stop Olvido Laguna from heading to the meadow one afternoon, where she found Ezequiel Montes, still smelling of cane fields. They slowly said hello, as if they hardly knew each other, months of silence standing firm between their eyes.

"How was your trip?"

"I thought of you and thought it would never end."

It was only seven o'clock, but behind the treetops, the moon gave way to clouds. The weight of a storm lay heavy in the sky. The months of silence disappeared, and Ezequiel took Olvido by the waist, kissing her on the lips as lightning flashed. They walked arm in arm to his hut. Firewood crackled in the hearth, the room smelled of evening, and the shadow of the cot wavered large on the wall. Their clothing was soon unbearable. Ezequiel looked stronger, after months on the road. A torrential spring rain poured down on the mountain.

But before it soaked everything, Santiago arrived home after his radio show; not finding his grandmother there, he set out for the meadow. He crossed the pine forest with freezing hands. He climbed hills not caring that the sky spat rain down on him, until he saw the outline of the hut with its black smoke rising from the chimney, the gleam of fire escaping through the window. Water poured from his hair, plastering his clothes to his skin with the icy chill of a curse, but he trudged up the last bit that separated him from his suspicion. Santiago shook when he opened the door. A blade of wind and rain cut across the naked bodies making love on the cot. Santiago shook when he heard Ezequiel Montes propose marriage at the precise moment he arched his back, pulling away from his grandmother. Santiago grew deathly pale. Night descended over his throat and the ferocious mountain, and Santiago left the door open and ran across the puddle-strewn meadow.

By the time Olvido reached Scarlet Manor, the house was dark, the entryway dead. She climbed stairs that creaked under her feet. The second-floor hallway opened up, shadows filtering in through balconies, silence like snowfall. She found Santiago in Clara Laguna's room, seeing him first through the haze of yellow eyes: lying on the bed, his body curled up like a fetus, unmoving, reeking of sorrow.

Olvido held her grandson's name on her lips before approaching, finding his eyes swathed in sleep, his skin bright where raindrops had crystallized, smooth and frighteningly cold, his clothes stuck to his skin. It took some doing to undress him; his arms and legs were stiff, and he raved with fiery breath. When she wrapped him in the sheets and quilt he began to tremble, his blue lips pursed, his eyelids grew smaller. He seemed consumed by nightmares. Olvido took off her clothes and, in the skin of another, lay down beside him, pulled him to her, held him tight to offer warmth. Tears snaked from her eyes. The boy's heart raced in the frenzy of tachycardia, and she wondered what would become of her if she lost him. She pictured her grandson dead, drenched by rain, the reflection of a new absence, a new grave on which to converse with worms. She felt like a heartless wretch for having hurt him, having found him as cold as an icicle. She covered his face with kisses, drowning in the desperation of the steely night; she kissed him more, lost all composure and reason, a moan escaping her throat that brought their bodies together, the same old story of "suffer no more, my child" as he woke from his delirium, his lips heavy with two generations of love, and pressed them to hers over and over again, falling into delirium once more, dreaming of a fire with no ray of moonlight, a fire that burned with such vigor it hardened desire, and he woke, recognizing his grandmother in those caresses, and he cried, and she cried more, they consoled each other in a whisper of kisses, the suck of two bodies that should never, ever touch. They merged in a tumble of "I can't live without you," of "nor I without you," of a search for all the hidden corners of flesh, of loving each and every one of them. Stars filled the room, illuminating a premonition: the purple canopy danced as it had when Scarlet Manor was a brothel, and in a corner Clara Laguna smiled, adjusting a garter on an invisible leg.

At six o'clock in the morning, Santiago woke with lips raw from the dementia of fever, love, and rain, but the space beside him in bed was empty. His naked reality shattered when he called out to his grandmother in the light and shadow of what he thought was dawn. He heard no reply. Suddenly, he sat up. A whiff of smoke was drifting into the room, choking him. He went to the window, and the dream he thought he was living became a nightmare. The stable was on fire, a fire so big it threatened to devour the clouds.

Santiago's eyes clouded with fear. He searched for Olvido in every room on the second floor, calling out to her, his soul shouting itself hoarse. He did not find her. The silence became black smoke creeping in through every crevice. He went down the stairs two by two, stumbling at the bottom, falling onto clay tiles, skinning his knees. He ignored the scrapes and limped to the door, tried to open it, but it was locked from outside. He ran as best as he could to the kitchen, clicked the deadbolt on the door into the garden, filigrees of blood shining on the lettuce and squash. He heard the loud crackle of stable walls, the whinnying of the horse that someone had freed from its stall and was trotting through the yard, its mane inflamed by the wind. It criss-crossed in front of Santiago as he stumbled toward the heart of the fire, as if ordered to stop him from reaching the flames. The boy dodged it and moved forward as his skin boiled, became charred by the smoke.

Near the stable doors he recognized Olvido's robe and slippers in a pile on the grass, as if she had wanted to offer herself naked to death. He picked them up and held them to his chest. Four sheep ran past, having escaped from the corral; Santiago watched them and their apocalyptic bleating disappear. The stable walls fell in a burst of fire, and he sat hard on the ground, staying there until firefighters arrived with their sirens to stop the house, the rose garden, the woodlands, from burning.

For days, wrapped in the blanket they had thrown around his shoulders, finding not the slimmest ray of moonlight to extinguish the fire in his dreams, he watched the entire town parade before his grief, offering condolences, staring into the grave where the most beautiful woman in the world must lie. For all that they searched, no body, not a single scorched bone could be found. Padre Rafael gave him food and water, cleaned the grief from his wounds, watched over him at night, waiting patiently for Santiago to be ready to come and live with him.

There was now not a single Laguna woman left to be saved, just a young man sitting on soft earth.

19

"THEY SAY THAT a long, long time ago, a young man named Esaín challenged the sea, chaining him to a eucalyptus tree for one hundred days. They say that from a long, long time before that, there was an alliance between the sea and the men of a great town. Every August full moon, the town chief would set a fisherman's clothes on the golden beach. The sea would arrive in a giant wave after midnight, soak the clothes, and assume human form. Stuffed into flannel pants and a puffy, white shirt, he would walk through the streets and squares; he would drink the wine from any barrel he passed and lay with the most beautiful women. With the first rays of dawn, he would return to the beach and shed those magic clothes, his body, still drunk on wine and flesh, dissolving into a wave. In exchange, the sea had given people the gift of tears to be cried whenever they were sad — for nothing alleviated misfortune like tears — and a promise to respect the lives of all fishermen.

"One tragic year, the town chief died and was succeeded by Esaín, his firstborn son. He was a brave young man, known since youth for his skill and strength in hand-to-hand combat, as well as his noble heart. Esaín had a younger sister. When their father died, already orphaned of their mother, Esaín had to take care of her. The girl had a name pronounced differently in four separate languages and, at just eleven years of age, was possessed of unparalleled beauty and a voice that could bewitch the mermaids themselves. In the primitive light of dawn, she would go to the golden beach to sing and dance on its dunes, bells on her ankles and ribbons on her wrists. The sea would watch her through its waves—her svelte figure, dark hair in the breeze like a pirate flag—listen to her laugh, listen to her dream with dark eyes that never left him. In the evenings, when the girl returned home to a stone house surrounded by eucalyptus trees high on a hill, the tide would leave the beach, traverse the streets and squares to arrive at her door like a thin, silent tongue, climb the wall to peer in the window and watch her sleep curled in her bed. The townspeople knew it was the first time the sea had ever fallen in love. Knowing this, Esaín feared that, when dressed as a man, the sea would possess his sister, take her to his depths, and he would never see her again. And so, when the August full moon came, he left a vagabond's rags on the beach. As always, shielded by the moon, the sea soaked the clothes, but his body remained liquid and cold. Furious at this betrayal shattering their alliance, he flooded houses, streets, and fields in a tempest, asking the townsmen with a frothy throat why such deceit after centuries of living in peace. Fearing for their lives, they confessed who was to blame and where he lived but refused to say any more in case the sea's fury were to grow and destroy them in his waves.

"The sea immediately recognized the traitor's house as belonging to the girl he adored, but this time he climbed high on the hill in a roaring wave, tossing bits of algae in the air. Esaín and his sister had run into the eucalyptus forest to escape him. Towering cumulous clouds swirled in the sky, and the moon grew as pale as the face of a dead man. The sea followed them through the woods, trailing seashells, froth, and gasping fish among the treetops. He had no trouble following their trail, for the girl was crying in fear and the sea could smell her tears, made, as they were, of his water. He reached them near a cliff where the forest ended. Esaín hid his sister behind some rocks and came out to confront the monster howling with a hurricane wind.

"'If you want to be a man, then fight like one,' Esaín said, tossing the magic clothes he carried into a sack.

"The moon grew even more pale as waves broke against the

clothes, submerging them in a foamy crash, and the sea became a stout man with an icy gaze.

"'Here I am, boy. Now you'll pay for having kept me from your wine and warm flesh.'

"They dove into a ferocious battle. Even though Esaín was strong and skillful, the sea surpassed him, for his arms held all the power of storms. He threw the young man onto the ground and choked him. That's when Esaín's sister came out from her hiding place to stare with dark eyes at the sea. The sea felt love weaken his arms. Esaín flipped him over and held him to the ground.

"'Dance!' he ordered his sister.

"The girl danced like she did on the sand at dawn. The sea's flesh turned fiery. Esaín let go so as not to be burned and ordered his sister to stop. Then he spoke in the language of the trees to a great, ancient eucalyptus, which pulled its roots out of the ground and bound the sea to its trunk. The next morning Esaín circled the sea's arms and legs with chains, holding him prisoner at the mercy of the sun and the wind.

"The townspeople soon suffered the consequences. As each day passed, the vast surface once occupied by the sea blurring into an ephemeral horizon became a desert where not even a weed could grow. Fishing boats became skeletons of wood and salt, and men lost all memories of their lives as they forgot the taste of fish. Their grief was worse than ever before, with no tears to cry. The town elders grew invisible when a famine as silver as the August moon gripped homes and the hearts that dwelled inside. After one hundred days, men gathered outside Esaín's house high on the hill and begged him to let the prisoner go. He was suffering the same fate and gave in to their pleas.

"Up on the cliff, Esaín found his sister, dancing and singing around the sea as he cried crusts of salt and his chains grew red hot, singeing his human flesh. For one hundred days, the girl had been the only one to keep the sea alive. She had fed him spoonful by spoonful, offered him drink, protected him from the sun with a straw hat.

"'Go home,' Esaín ordered his sister. 'I'm going to set him free.'

"She slipped into the eucalyptus woods but, rather than obey her brother, hid behind a tree. From there she could watch Esaín remove the chains and the roots release the sea. A late-winter afternoon, warm and weak, hung over the cliff. The sea's body fell to its knees on the ground, spent. The girl wanted to run to his aid but feared this would anger her brother and stayed hidden behind the minty aroma.

"'You're free,' Esaín said. 'You can go.'

"'You will pay dearly for your audacity,' the sea mumbled, looking at him for the last time as a man.

"The sea shed his pants and white shirt and, when not a thread remained on his skin, dissolved into an immense ocean that dove off the cliff. Esaín thought it was all over but soon heard his sister scream from the woods.

"'Watch out, Esaín! Behind you! Behind you!'

"He turned and saw that the sea had silently climbed back up the rocks to take his revenge. Esaín jumped into the puffy shirt and flannel pants. Before his sister's frightened eyes, he became a frothy wave and threw himself off the cliff, with the sea.

"They say the girl ran to the edge and watched as one wave swam in the opposite direction of all the rest. They say that to alleviate his loved one's sorrows, the sea gave tears back to men, though fishermen never set sail with them. They leave them at home, in the care of their mothers and wives, so the sea cannot track and shipwreck them. But they also say that if, despite this precaution, the sea does find them, a wave will sometimes break on the horizon, pick them up, and carry them safely to shore."

Standing on a dimly lit stage in a Madrid café, Santiago Laguna listened to the applause. Cigarette smoke swirled around young faces at tables, rising to the ceiling, where fans sliced it to ribbons. "Tell your great-grandmother's stories to the world," Padre Rafael had said on his deathbed, patting his hand. "You were born to be an artist." And Santiago had listened.

During the agonizing months the priest was confined to bed with kidney failure, reduced to the size of a normal man, the only thing that soothed his pain was Manuela Laguna's stories. Santiago sat by his bedside day and night as the replacement priest, just out of the seminary, kindly set himself up in a little house next door. Padre Rafael insisted on dying in his own bed, and neither his doctor's recommendation that he be admitted to the hospital nor orders from his ecclesiastic superiors could change his mind. It was shameful enough, the priest thought, to die at seventy-five when men in his family died in their hundreds and women as old as tortoises, without ever going to the hospital in their lives.

The doctor would pay house calls when the priest could no longer stand—much less wreak havoc as in years past. He would listen to the priest's heart and take his pulse, looking at Santiago with eyes that eliminated any hope. After the doctor left and they were alone, as they had been these last two years, the boy would sit next to Padre Rafael's bed and tell him a story. The sea bubbled into the parish bedroom, and the priest could sense the irascible Cantabria of his youth, the squawking gulls, the salty breeze, and smell of fish in the market. That first day, Santiago did not tell the end of the story but stopped all of a sudden as tears welled up in memories.

"Go on, I want to know how it ends," the priest said.

"I don't know, Padre."

"Man of God, how can you not know? And if you don't, then make it up. Just don't leave me hanging." He squirmed in pain.

"Easy now, or it'll only get worse."

Santiago began to tell him another story, which he also left unfinished, interlaced with another and yet another, none of them finished. Padre Rafael fell asleep, bewildered by all of these storms, fishermen, and mermaids. The next day, after breakfast, when Santiago asked him if he would like to hear another story, the priest said no, not unless it was told from beginning to end.

"I tossed and turned all night, caught up in nightmares, trying to figure out how yesterday's stories ended."

His face contorted in a pain that would not be eased by pills.

"I'm sorry, Padre. You see . . . she was the one, my grandmother, you know . . . I would stop just before, and she would tell the end of the story." He closed his eyes and felt fire in his heart.

"Go pray, my child, go pray." The priest reached for the boy's hand and gave it a squeeze.

"I'll tell you a whole story as soon as I'm back. Rest now, Padre."

Santiago left the room and headed for the sacristy. There, instead of praying, he drank the last drop of consecrated wine and any unconsecrated he could find. Meanwhile, the priest huffed and puffed to sit up in bed, peed through a tube that terminated in a bag, and writhed in pain, caused not by his illness but by a confession secret that had troubled his soul since the night of the fire.

That day, with his mouth tasting of the bread and cheese he had eaten to disguise any trace of wine, Santiago Laguna told Padre Rafael a complete story. But before the end, he paused for a minute, as if waiting for Olvido's voice to come back from the deepest recess of death. That silence, which from then on preceded the end of every story, grew shorter as the weeks and months passed but never disappeared entirely. Even after one August night, when Padre Rafael reached up and held the boy's face in his hands, leaving this world, the bitter taste of an untold secret on his breath, and Santiago began to work as a storyteller, that silence continued to float among the public in cafés and halls, sometimes only for the briefest second it takes to drop a flower on a grave.

Santiago lost his voice after the fire. Days passed as he sat staring at the smoking remains of the stable, petrified by misfortune, leading to an elephantine chill that left him shaking with fever and gibbering insect obscenities for over a week. Padre Rafael, who gave him cough syrup and menthol steam baths, cooled his forehead with a handkerchief soaked in holy water, came to believe the boy would not survive such sorrow at just sixteen years of age. But one day Santiago woke with no fever, and the blond doctor with alopecia assured the priest that the danger had passed. Santiago's recovery was considered nearly miraculous. Even so, he rose from bed smelling like earth after a rain, an odor that never left him.

When Sunday came and Santiago climbed up onto the dais to sing the Gloria, a mechanical warble like a cricket chirp had invaded his baritone. He stepped down from the dais before the hymn was done, before the expectant eyes of the townspeople who for the first time ever felt sorry for a Laguna, and never stood on it again. Padre Rafael had the doctor examine the boy's throat: the inflammation in his tonsils was gone, and there was no physical reason for the warble. It was then Padre Rafael realized that an infirmity of the soul had stolen Santiago's melodious voice.

Santiago moved into the broom closet, where Clara Laguna had taken off her harem attire to put on the charwoman's clothes while Padre Imperio waited in the chapel to Saint Pantolomina of the Flowers. There was no other place in the small parish house, with its one small kitchen, bathroom, the priest's austere room, and the room next to the sacristy with the radio station; catechism classes and seniors' retreats were held at the town hall. The priest proposed they shut down the radio station, sell all the equipment, and make that Santiago's room, a place from his childhood where he would feel at home. But the boy needed the distraction of the radio programs. He would rather sleep in the other room, a room that, after a thorough cleaning, a fresh coat of paint, the addition of a hard old bed, a chair, and a folding table, became a Cistercian six-by-six cell. The boy's clothes were divided between Padre Imperio's wardrobe and the wardrobe that held the ecclesiastical clothes for important celebrations.

Santiago read the Bible and religious poems on the radio with such mystic determination and care that, when the old women listened on the communal radio, they were sure he would be ordained a priest despite his illegitimate, cursed beginnings. The young girls, however, had doubts about this vocation. Just as his grandmother Olvido had licked her nostalgic wounds by cooking the memory of her lover, and his great-grandmother had placated her arrogant fury by slitting the throats of chickens, Santiago placated his guilt and loneliness by fornicating in a crypt near the cemetery, where it was said Knights Templar had been buried. Even though not a bone or medieval strand of chain mail remained, it was a magnificent place to frolic, maintaining the temperature of the earth's core all year-round. The crypt was reached through a secret passage starting at a trapdoor in the floor of the chapel to Saint Pantolomina of the Flowers that Padre Rafael showed the boy, hoping to distract him soon after he moved into the parish house.

An aura of torment had surrounded Santiago ever since the fire, intensifying his good looks and the blue of his eyes. As if that were not enough, his movements had acquired a French charm inherited from his father, and this distinguished him from the other boys in town. He spoke to his conquests with the intimacy of a deep voice that had fallen from grace, and though as a child he did not allow anyone to think of him as "cursed," it was how he described himself now. And so — he explained, rippling their skin with the vapor of his breath — loving him would only condemn them to being unlucky in love and total social disgrace. With such a fate, they were left no choice but to lie like beasts in the secret of the crypt, without reason or conscience, accompanied only by the flicker of candles for the dead, made from bits of wax Santiago took from the church and placed on little zinc platters all around the bed of passion he built from sacks of straw covered by Clara Laguna's quilt. Thanks to these preparations, the rocky oval of the crypt filled with a familiar aroma.

The first to smell it was the pharmacist's granddaughter. After forgiving Santiago for abandoning her in the room behind the pharmacy, she threw herself into consoling him with a fervor that could only have been stoked by the fires of love. At seventeen, she was willing to condemn herself to any misfortune as long as her breasts remained in this young man's hands, where they had grown, her mouth on his, her body in blue eyes that contemplated her naked even if they were thinking of someone else.

The pharmacist's granddaughter soon learned she was not the only one, and she slapped Santiago, scratched him, pulled his hair, but came back to him because her heart had no choice. She learned to share him in exchange for those moments when, after their amorous romp, Santiago would twirl her golden ringlets and they would talk of their childhood adventures like two old lovers. They would laugh in the complicity of plasters and potions for one-eyed cats, and this—she dreamed—he could never have with another. Afterward, in the monastic silence of his room, Santiago wished he could love her, blaming himself in tears when his affection cooled with the first song of dawn.

Santiago did not dream again of that fire extinguished by rays of moonlight or the woman who appeared to him afterward. He tried everything to bring her back. He gorged on black olives, even peppercorns and bitter chocolate, trying to attract the dark he did not find in any other woman's eyes. He gave in to endless naps on a pew in the chapel to Saint Pantolomina of the Flowers, thinking of her as he slept, reconstructing the pieces of her face like a puzzle, hoping that dreams would provide the missing ones: her lips, her chin, her neck . . . He went to the oak grove one night and got drunk on eau de vie under the waterfall of a full moon, invoking her like a pagan goddess. In an alcoholic stupor, her tore off his clothes, lit a fire, and was about to sacrifice himself in memory of Olvido when a shepherd found him and knocked the inebriation right out of him. Santiago lamented that it was this savage beast who'd saved him and not the woman whose lips he had just invented.

It was then he decided to paint her. No one had ever told him about Pierre Lesac's circle of inspiration, but the day before he began the portrait, he told Padre Rafael he was ill. He did not go to class or help with the radio programs. Locked in his room, he spent hours thinking about her, feeling her features travel through his veins, devising potions to dream about her. When night fell, he placed a glass of water on the windowsill, right in the moonlight's path. At dawn he drank it all down and lay back in bed, waiting for a dream that never came.

Unlike his father, Santiago painted the portrait in charcoal. Her wavy, chestnut hair, her sad, black eyes, her prominent cheekbones, her small nose. He did not dare draw the lips he had imagined. Leaving the portrait unfinished, he hid it among his books and, for weeks, would stare at it before bed, expose it to lunar winds, all to no avail.

A little more than two years passed since that fiery spring before Padre Rafael became terminal and took to his bed. It was early summer. Santiago was almost nineteen and had finished school with good grades. The new priest arrived in town with camphor hair and tight lips. The radio station was closed, the technical equipment and sacred-music collection driven away from Santiago's life in a van, destined for parts unknown. As he stood in the square to watch the van go, the rumbling of its epileptic motor took what was left of his soul.

Santiago cloistered himself in the church to care for Padre Rafael during the dog days of summer that dulled the senses. He put an end to his frolics in the crypt, and the pharmacist's granddaughter had to content herself with seeing him only on Sundays after Mass. She would slip into his little room and wait impatiently for him to come and hold her, desperate for consolation after the impertinence of Ezequiel Montes's eyes, fixed on him as a little leather bag, pinned to the shepherd's pants, wafted a fine putrefaction between them that smelled like the ashes of death. The censer swung from one side of the church to the other as a mustard-colored wind slipped in through the cracks in the walls and panes of glass, baking both the faithful and Padre Rafael, who, aided by an ear trumpet, strained to hear Mass from his bed.

Santiago began to write poetry again as the dying man slept. The two of them shared the same medicinal air, the same suppurating heat. Padre Rafael's snores were interrupted by nightmares and hallucinations when, in Latin and in Basque, he would recite that bitter confession secret his vows forbade him from revealing to the boy sitting lucid and awake beside him.

"Easy, Padre." Santiago mopped the priest's brow.

"Do you understand? She thought there was no other way," the priest insisted in the language of his dreams.

"Who?"

"Her, her." Pain clouded his eyes.

"Easy now, Padre. Please."

"Morituri te salutamus," Padre Rafael burst out, smiling.

Secrets merged with the Roman movies he adored and with his own death. Once Padre Rafael had calmed, Santiago drank all of the sacristy wine; later the new priest would find it missing.

A plague of cicadas had come to town, riding the mustard-colored air like a flying carpet. Santiago found them buzzing in the corners of the priest's room and killed them with a broom, then sat down at his bedside to write poems filled with nostalgia for a body and name stained by the green eyes of a traitor. Every now and then Santiago would succumb to the sacramental torpor of wine and fall asleep. He dreamed that hundreds of cicadas were humming a requiem and woke in a fit of tears, clinging to Padre Rafael's torso as if it were the one from yesteryear, big and ebullient, not the scrawny mass it had become. Still half-asleep, the priest consoled him in Latin, until the boy's sorrow faded and together they said the afternoon prayers.

One suffocating midday in late August, Padre Rafael watched his mother's spirit killing cicadas covering the windowsill and knew God would come for him at sundown. He asked Santiago, who had not seen the Basque woman in farm clogs squashing insects, to take an envelope with red and blue airmail lines out of his drawer. Before handing it to the priest, the boy saw the words *Paris* and *France,* and his heart began to gallop.

"Santiago, God willing, I'll soon be gone to bathe in his glory in heaven. I worry about you even though you're of age and can live comfortably on your inheritance."

"You're not leaving me yet."

"I would love to stay, son. Truly I would. But don't worry; when I go, you will not be alone in this world. This letter is from your father, Pierre Lesac. He lives in Paris, as you know, and he wants you to go to him there. You can study whatever you choose at university, like your mother."

Santiago stared at Padre Rafael as his skin exuded the scent of moist earth.

"I wrote him before I took to bed," Padre Rafael went on, "and he is so sorry for hardly communicating all these years. But God—who is all-powerful, never forget that—showed him the way, and now your father is a priest in that cathedral in Paris, Notre-Dame."

"He never answered, so I stopped writing when I was young. I always got a Christmas card, sometimes a birthday card. Once he even sent me one of his paintings, a portrait of my grandmother. It made me so happy. My father was an artist and I was proud. But I haven't heard from him since I was fifteen."

"He is repentant and has joined the priesthood, as I said. He deserves another chance."

"How did you find him?"

"Your grandmother gave me the last address she had for him." Padre Rafael choked at the mention of Olvido.

"When?" The stable fire burned in Santiago's cheeks.

"Years ago she begged me to look after you if anything ever happened to her, and if I couldn't, then I was to do everything possible to find your father. She gave me a letter to send to Pierre Lesac, and that's what I did."

"Do you know what it said?"

"Of course not, child. I don't make it a habit to read other people's mail."

"It doesn't matter."

"Will you go to Paris when I'm gone? Please say yes so I can die in peace. It's for the best. After all, he is your father."

"You're the only father I have." Santiago burst into tears. "You're the only father I've ever loved, and when God takes you to him, I'll be left with nothing, nothing . . ."

The priest bolted up, his catheter coming out, and hugged Santiago with all the strength he had had when his weight cracked the wooden pulpit floor.

The woman in charge of cooking and cleaning brought their lunch on two trays, where she found them praying. Later Santiago told Padre Rafael one of Manuela Laguna's stories, and the priest fell asleep. Afternoon slipped toward death as the boy held Padre Rafael's hand, glancing at Pierre Lesac's letter on the bedside table.

When the first stars began to shine at twilight, Padre Rafael's mother came back to kill the cicadas and it was over. The blond doctor pronounced the priest dead, and the undertakers took his body to prepare it for burial. This, however, was delayed three days, the time it took—spurred on by the speed of decomposition—to make a pine coffin large enough, for Padre Rafael's body had suddenly recovered its size from when he was in his prime. Overcoming illness, death had granted this one final grace, and Padre Rafael would go to his grave as he had been in life, a giant Basque who had made the ground tremble.

All the while, the new priest watched Santiago wander through the church and parish house like a sleepwalking animal. Everywhere it smelled like damp earth. The new priest checked the windows, running a hand along the edge, expecting it to be wet, finding only the dry heat of mustard-colored air. He was going mad, tracking this stormy consequence through side chapels, the sacristy, the little room that once housed the radio station, only to find Santiago at the end of every trail, his blue eyes bewildered by pain, reciting Saint Teresa of Ávila poems by heart, holding piles of cicadas embalmed in wax, palms open as if in offering. The new priest and his superiors agreed the boy was to leave the parish house right after Padre Rafael was buried. When he went to give Santiago this news one evening, the priest found him in the old broom closet with a half-naked, blond-ringleted girl, drawing woodland creatures on her skin with a blue marker as he recited a chapter of Revelations.

It took years to wipe that image from his mind.

"Tomorrow, after the service, you are to leave and never profane this house again," he said in a voice mesmerized by ire.

"Don't worry, tomorrow I'll leave forever."

Meanwhile, with no living Laguna there, Scarlet Manor slowly succumbed to spirits and the yard surrendered to the weather. The hydrangea and morning glories dried up with the furor of summer;

the chestnut tree grew pale; the roses shrank; honeysuckle branches snapped; lettuce, tomato, and squash rotted in the garden, refusing to sprout. Its prodigious fertility waned with Santiago. Only the daisies continued to sputter in hate.

Padre Rafael was buried in late afternoon to escape the high-summer, mustard-colored heat. Since the coffin would not fit in the hearse, arrangements were made for it to be brought to the cemetery in a cart pulled by two draft horses. The entire town was there. It took thirteen men to carry the coffin to the grave. "There goes Padre Gigante," the widows murmured. "Our teeth and dishes will rattle no more." It then took that many more to handle the ropes that lowered the coffin into the ground. The afternoon wound down on a red horizon of Our Fathers, and the townspeople hurried home under the threat of a downpour. But by the time night came, not a drop of rain had fallen and the wind had grown drier.

Santiago decided it was the perfect time to die. Evading the new priest who had by now moved into Padre Rafael's room, he slipped into the chapel to Saint Pantolomina of the Flowers. He lit the two candles that illuminated the portrait of the saint and burned the letter from Pierre Lesac. The flame reflected in his pupils, and he was brought back to that night. His mouth tasted of ash. Santiago went to the sacristy to wash it away with wine, then returned to the chapel in silence. Light from a full moon filtered in through the windows and cracks in the wall like liquid silver, puddling on the stone floor.

Like the cursed man he thought he was, Santiago decided to die in church like his ancestors — even though Manuela Laguna had taught him to scorn this tradition. Sacramental wine swirled in his head, forcing an unconscious smile. Below Saint Pantolomina's portrait, in a glass reliquary, was her right middle finger, not a scrap of flesh on it, its two bone phalanges pearly with the glitter of the divine. Santiago crossed himself before opening the little lock of the reliquary with the key he had taken from the sacristy. He picked up the finger and lay on a pew. The relic narrowed to a pointed ivory tip. Saint Pantolomina had been dismembered by infidels, her bones broken to crush her faith, and only that finger had been saved. In times past it was said to possess the curative power of miracles. Santiago used it to slit one wrist, and his blood began to flow. Just as he was about to cut the other, a ray of moonlight fell across his wound, solidifying the blood in silver bubbles, moving on until it struck the stone wall, where he watched the face of a woman appear.

The image was blurry at first, and he thought it must be Saint Pantolomina of the Flowers revealing herself in the pallor of a miracle. But as the image grew more distinct, he realized this was not the martyr: her hair was entwined with irises and as blond as God's embers, her light-colored eyes reflecting the resurrection of the dead. Instead, the woman floating on the white wall had the chestnut hair, sad black-olive eyes, and small nose that Santiago had seen in his dreams. A shiver brought him to his knees to contemplate the features he had sought for so long: plump lips, an oval chin, and svelte neck. The smell of ink and hundred-year-old parchment perfumed the splendor of the moon. The woman's lips parted, and Santiago heard these words: "Take me to Scarlet Manor." As if waking from a dream, the woman disappeared. The wall grew dark with shadows, and Santiago's blood flowed again, dripping onto his pants and the stone floor as wine calmed his mind, inflaming his heart with uncertainty. Had he fallen asleep?

20

CIGARETTE SMOKE GREW thick in the July heat at the Madrid café. A Mecano song animated conversations, and candles on the tables highlighted the lurid eye shadow licking some of the girls' brows. Santiago had left the stage to applause and cheers of "¡Tío bueno!" Sitting down at the bar, he drank his whiskey and cola under the admiring gaze of the bartender, a young thing just barely twenty, a brunette, her bangs teased up into a cresting wave.

"Want to go downstairs for a bit?" Santiago asked when his drink was done.

She had a waiter in a black T-shirt take her place.

She and Santiago walked through a graffiti-scrawled door near the bathrooms and down a set of stairs. The subterranean world cooled their skin. The cave that served as the café storeroom was lit by only one bulb. They had sex in between cases of Pepsi and Orange Mirinda, on a mammoth sack of peanuts crushed by their passion as bottles of olives and pickles rattled on the shelves. The smell of fluorescent rat poison and insecticide seeped out from the corners, quite different from the romantic perfume of oak and the bones of Templar Knights in the crypt where Santiago had cavorted with local girls.

The bartender tucked two polyester shoulder pads under her bra straps and put on her T-shirt, her bright blue eyelids half-closed. That color so like the sea and shoulders as square as a soldier's jacket reminded Santiago of his military service in Valencia. He had received his papers when lodged at the hotel in town. Dominated by the obsession that drove him, he spent his days in the chapel to Saint Pantolomina, staring at the wall where the chestnut-haired woman had appeared, his nights wrapped in immaculate white sheets, searching for her amid a jumble of dreams.

When the blood started to drip onto his pants that night, Santiago staunched the flow by tying his shirt around his wrist and burst in to see the doctor, who stitched him up without too many questions. There was no way Santiago could kill himself now that she had finally revealed herself in full: her face, her neck, her breasts. He believed that Saint Pantolomina, dismembered and miraculous, had rescued her from his dreams so he could search the world for the flesh-and-blood woman. The very thought of having her before him, being able to touch her, drove him mad. For now he would content himself with dreaming about her, slipping out from his wrist like smoke from the moon, like a genie out of a bottle. The only thing that unsettled him were her words: "Take me to Scarlet Manor."

When his military papers came, Santiago took it as a sign telling him where to begin his search. Besides, he thought, in Valencia he could finally see the sea that figured in all of his stories. A wave rippled in his chest, and he felt this was another reason to live.

Santiago cut his hair, put a few changes of clothing into a kit bag, along with the charcoal drawing he had finished after he let her features course through his body for more than twenty-four hours. The afternoon before he left, he went to Scarlet Manor. The yard began to stir when he reached the gate with its funeral bow; the hydrangea and morning glories woke, the honeysuckle reached out, a rosebud the color of his eyes sprouted, and a squash revived in the garden. But Santiago could not walk through the rusted gate, where the stable of ashes stabbed at his heart. The flames of that night burned in his cheeks, the sheep with their terrible bleating, the horse mad with freedom. As so often before, he imagined his grandmother, naked but for her perfume of squash, more beautiful than ever, walk into the stable, set fire to the straw, and sit on a bale, waiting for heat to inflame his caresses, bubble up, and burst in purification. Santiago fell to his knees, gripping the iron bars, and wept tears of guilt, anger, sorrow; he vomited the smell of earth and rain, and would have hanged himself from the funeral bow — WELCOME TO SCARLET MANOR — if night had not cast the memory of the moon, the woman with the chestnut hair, and his trip to the seashore. He walked down the road with two crickets perched on his back, and the garden fell dark so the spirits could shine once again.

At first light the next morning, Santiago said goodbye to Padre Rafael at the cemetery, praying at his mastodon grave, a favorite of the magpies. He had planned to steal Saint Pantolomina's finger on his way to the church but changed his mind at the last minute out of respect for the memory of Padre Rafael, who would have flushed with shame at such a despicable act, and out of respect for the townspeople, who adored their saint and loved him. "Good luck, handsome Santiago," the widows said as he walked down the narrow streets, his kit bag over his shoulder, on his way to the train. "Do your country proud, Laguna prodigy." The mustard-colored wind blurred their faces amid trilling cicadas, and he could just make them out, like toothless wraiths.

From the very first day, Santiago used the rigors of military service to purge his despair. He enthusiastically crawled over Mediterranean earth with a CETME assault rifle; hiked twenty-five miles with a backpack that felt light compared with the stones of his memories; acted as reserve guard, he and his machete listening to the snores, flatulence, and dreams of young recruits; and practiced maneuvers on hills, skewering invisible enemies with his bayonet. Whenever possible, Santiago volunteered for cleaning and kitchen duty — his fingertips cracked from scrubbing latrines, wiping down tables, scouring pots so big they could boil a man, taking out heaps of trash — and guard duty. When winter came, up in the pigeon loft of a guard tower, wearing a wool poncho and rain cape, he shivered in that cold so different from the harsh, dry Castilian climate, a cold that seeped into your bones with marine timidity. His favorite was guard duty at night, and Santiago would pay a hefty sum of pesetas to trade for it when the moon was full. They wound up calling him the Wolf Man. On those nights he would offer up the scar on his wrist and implore Saint Pantolomina, praying the chestnut-haired woman would appear on the grubby, peeled-paint wall, but she never did.

Almost every month he received a letter from the pharmacist's granddaughter, the pages wrinkled by tears and lipstick kisses, plus a few photos of her with fashionably disheveled blond ringlets. When fellow soldiers asked if she was his girlfriend, he denied it. They knew Santiago was an orphan, that he never went home on leave like they did, bringing back strings of chorizo and blood sausage; they knew he was obsessed with dark-eyed brunettes — he never looked at any other type of woman on their weekends in the city — but never seemed satisfied with his conquests: none was the woman he was searching for; they were just easy-to-forget substitutes. They also knew of his passion for the sea. The first time Santiago saw it, the resemblance to him and Olvido was clear. Strong, beautiful, hypnotic. Sitting on the beach, he could stare at it for hours, whether frozen in winter or broiling under a summer sky that melted into its waves.

Santiago's fellow soldiers suspected he was religious — taped to his locker door was a holy card of Saint Pantolomina of the Flowers, one he'd found when he was fifteen, creased and filthy on the pantry shelf where they kept cans of peaches, and whenever the sergeant called "Squad, cadence count!" on marches, he would hum Glorias and Ave Marias in his cricket warble — but they never discovered his newfound love of holy relics. During his service, Santiago saw most of the relics housed in cathedrals: the mummified arm of Saint Vincent the Martyr, one thorn from Christ's crown of thorns, the holy chalice, threads from the Blessed Virgin Mary's veil, the incorruptible body of a Holy Innocent massacred by Herod, and various other bones and objects belonging to martyrs and saints, all of which he begged for help in his search. Santiago bought every reliquary card available, hiding them in a secret pocket sewn into his kit bag.

When Santiago was discharged, he returned to the austere Castilian climate of Ávila, tired of being stiff with cold and drawn by the number of Saint Teresa of Ávila relics there. He stayed at a hotel near the city walls for several months, eating his fill of roast lamb and *yema* sweets, getting drunk on red wine and every chestnut-haired woman he passed, reciting the saint's poetry to them. He got his first job as a storyteller at a downtown café and was so popular the owner proposed he move to Madrid, where he had another, bigger venue. And so Santiago arrived in the capital with his kit bag of clothes and a pocket filled with reliquary cards, determined to keep looking for the woman whose charcoal portrait he kept there, too.

The Madrid café was abuzz with conversation and pop music, thick with smoke and the smells of beer and sweat.

"I'm on again the day after tomorrow. I'll see you then," Santiago told the bartender when they came up out of the cellar.

He kissed her goodbye and stepped onto the street. Night exhaled light from the street lamps. It was Thursday. He walked up Calle de las Huertas. Every now and then a bar door would open and music would spill out, like a shout, and maybe a vendor carrying bright pink toys. Santiago's footsteps echoed on the sidewalk, on asphalt cooked by the sun.

"Got a smoke?" a kid asked with his lighter flickering.

Santiago passed him one as the flame wavered in his eyes. He continued up the street. At Plaza de Matute the noise of a garbage truck was deafening. Santiago crossed quickly and came to Calle de Antocha, where he had just rented an apartment after living in a hotel.

The second he arrived in the city a few months earlier, Santiago had been struck by a sudden longing for nature and chose a small hotel across from the botanical gardens, then bursting with spring. He would often wander down lanes of exotic trees, into tropical greenhouses, and around the duck pond. For the first time since leaving home, he missed the calm of the yard at Scarlet Manor, especially lying in the honeysuckle clearing to read or write poems. Though Madrid was a paradise of chestnut-haired beauties and churches filled with relics, the roar of traffic and jackhammers cracking sidewalks and the lightning-fast pace of life filled him with an unease only soothed by nature's proximity.

Santiago met his only friend at the botanical gardens. One mid-May afternoon near closing, he slipped into a greenhouse and stayed out of sight until he heard the plants breathing in the quiet of night. He walked over to some rows of potted dahlias. Sipping on a flask of whiskey and smoking cigarettes, he began to scrawl poems in his notebook, waiting for sleep to rain down from the stars.

A guard with a thick moustache found him early the next morning.

"Get up out of there, pal, unless you want me to call the police," he said.

Santiago stretched awake. A yellow petal was stuck to his lips, and his eyes were swollen with pollen.

"You'll get one hell of a fine for crushing the flowers. Get up, you hear me? And pick up that flask . . . I thought it stank like whiskey."

"Is it late?"

"The sun's been up for ages and will burn that binge right out of you."

Santiago smiled at him.

"What are you doing sleeping here, anyhow? You're young, but you don't look like a delinquent."

"I'm new to the city and was lonely. I missed home . . ."

"So you go and sleep in a garden? Do they sleep with plants where you're from?"

"I was born in a town in Castilla."

"Go on. As far as I know, everyone in Castilla sleeps in a bed — a good, sturdy one at that . . ." The guard clucked his tongue.

"Would you like to hear a good story over breakfast?"

"Son, I had my coffee and churros hours ago."

"I promise you'll like my tale. I'm a storyteller, did you know?"

"Yeah, that's exactly what this is: a cock-and-bull story. Come on, pal, get up. We open soon and there are two school groups today. I don't want the kids finding a dopey young man — not much of an example."

"You'll see. I usually tell stories about the sea when I perform, stories my great-grandmother told me when I was little, but I've got one I just invented for you. It's amazing. It's about women who are cursed . . ."

The guard, a soap opera aficionado, scratched his head.

"All right, kid, I'll listen as I walk you out. And if I like your story, I just might not call the authorities."

"You'll love it. I tell a fantastic tale."

Santiago and the guard walked down leafy lanes, exotic treetops bending down to better hear the stream of words. The guard, a man near fifty named Isidro, walked more and more slowly as Santiago got to the heart of this story of passions. They took several trips around the duck pond, went in and out of the greenhouses three times before the tragedy came to an end. The guard honked into his handkerchief and wiped tears from his eyes, blaming it on allergies, before shaking Santiago's hand goodbye.

"Come by when you've got another story to tell — but this time during regular business hours."

From then on, Santiago would often visit before closing. He would accompany Isidro on his rounds, entertaining him with ocean waves and eucalyptus as fragrant as a prostitute's heart. They began meeting outside the gardens as well. Isidro was single, childless, and his life consisted of TV and a passion for sports lotteries and the Atlético de Madrid soccer team. He was also devoted to the saint whose name he bore, one in a long line of Isidros that ended with him and his cousin, a priest at San Isidro Church. The guard was happy to learn that Santiago liked prayer, whiskey, and gardens, that he could recite the Gospels as if blessed and went in search of holy relics. The boy would kneel down and pray that his wish be granted, that he meet someone whose identity he did not reveal, someone — Isidro suspected — who tormented his soul, just like a Venezuelan soap star. Santiago was perfect for the part: impossibly good-looking, an orphan with a fortune — that's what he told Isidro — working in the bohemian world of the theater, breaking the hearts of dark-haired beauties, the darker their eyes, the better. Isidro witnessed this one memorable June day that began with a favor to his cousin, going to view the incorruptible body of Saint Isidro the Laborer, followed by a fast as they sat in the Plaza de Oriente, needing time to digest the grace of such a relic, a day that ended in a bar hop toasting miracles and sampling tapas with a group of women tourists from Andalusia.

Santiago would occasionally attend an Atlético game with Isidro. The guard was convinced his hobby — the shouting, the goals, the frittata sandwiches and insults hurled at the referee and linesmen — helped Santiago forget, for a while, whatever was tormenting his soul. But when he saw Santiago perform, he realized the boy would never quiver at a tremendous penalty-kick save or midfield goal quite like he did up on that stage telling his stories. Whenever he performed, Santiago felt as if he were up on the church dais at home, during those messianic years when his voice could raise the hair on the arms of the faithful, when he believed his happiness was destined to last forever.

Their friendship grew as the months passed. In late July, when an apartment came free at the house on Calle de Antocha where Isidro lived, Santiago was easily persuaded to rent it.

"Living at a hotel that long will only make you feel uprooted," the guard assured him. "If you're not going back, then you'd better find a home somewhere else."

"The home I want is impossible, Isidro. I'm only moving because I've missed having a kitchen where I can make my grandmother's recipes."

The garbage truck finished its work at Plaza de Matute and turned into Calle de Antocha. It passed Santiago, rumbling on in search of garbage cans. A full moon hung low over the roofs, as if it had come loose from the sky. Building façades looked bathed in milk, and bats flew into streetlights. When Santiago reached the house he had moved into just that morning, irises stirred in his chest. There were two great big wooden doors and a long, uneven cobblestone passage that carriages had once bumped down to the building that was now more than two hundred years old. The superintendent's apartment was through a set of glass doors, with rusty mailboxes lined up outside, waiting for the postman. Santiago climbed a bleached, gray stairwell. The newly polished banister was attached to each step by an iron bar ending in a lion's head. Like a child's ice cream cone, the walls were two colors: vanilla from the ceiling halfway down and chocolate from there to the floor.

Santiago stopped on the second-floor landing before a door with a gold metal peephole in the shape of a rosette. That was where Isidro lived. Santiago considered ringing the bell to see if he wanted a drink but looked at his watch and saw it was late. He continued up to the fourth floor, where his apartment was. He had liked it the moment he saw it: the large entryway with honey-colored floorboards, plaster cornices with a flower motif along the ceiling, like in some of the rooms at Scarlet Manor. The similarities did not stop there. White shutters on the windows and balconies, a turn-of-the-century boiler streaked with grime resistant to all cleaning, and a white clawfoot tub in the bathroom that brought to mind happy steam-filled afternoons that smelled of soap and his grandmother's skin.

Santiago walked down a creaking hall to the bedroom. Since the apartment came furnished, all he'd brought was his kit bag with its cards, toiletries, and a change of clothing. It lay on the floor, next to a double bed in a white iron frame. He left the light off; moonlight streamed in through the window, illuminating the room, comforting him. He stroked the scar on his wrist and lay down in his shorts.

All of a sudden, he felt a tomb pressing down on his heart. It began to smell of wet earth. Santiago stood, trembling, dizzy with an invisible omen. He opened the window with a shaky hand and inhaled the night air. Among the pipes crisscrossing the narrow inner patio walls were rows of windows aligned in the dark torpor of dreams—all but one, that is, the one directly across from his bedroom. A small lamp illuminated a desk covered with books and papers. A woman sat with a quill in hand, writing what Santiago sensed in the pit of his stomach were the hieroglyphics of his destiny.

He stared at the woman's profile, the ribbons of chestnut hair falling down over a turquoise robe. The smell of ink and parchment paper wafted up like a strand of life and death. The woman set the quill on the desk, picked up a cigarette, and placed it in a long holder, lighting it, the smoke smudging her face for an instant. Santiago reached into his kit bag, pressing down on his toiletries, his razor slicing the tip of a finger, which began to gush blood. Leaving that trail of memories behind, he crept to the window and found the woman at hers, reaching into the sky in search of nonexistent rain. The moon, reflecting off TV antennas on the roof, flooded her face, and Santiago could watch her without being seen. He grew sick with ecstasy, affection, and fear. This woman had been resurrected from his dreams: the sad, jet-black eyes he had sought for so long, the small nose, the geometric cheekbones, the thin neck, the full breasts peeking out from her half-open robe. Santiago stood still, his extremities numb with an intense heat, blood dripping onto his chest, his knees, his shorts, absorbed in the splendor of reality until the woman left her window, lay back on a cushioned divan near the desk, and began to quell the heat with a peacock feather fan.

21

WATCHING HER, SANTIAGO fell asleep standing up and woke on his knees, his head resting on a spot of dried blood. The cut on his finger was proof of the previous night's reality. He got to his feet with the sound of nutshells cracking as his spine fell back in line, then he stretched and leaned against the wall, smiling. He was afraid to go to the window and find her. First, he wanted to savor events alone, internalize them, die with them if necessary. He recalled her writing, smoking, looking up at the sky, fanning herself. He fell into bed, curled up in the delight of what was his, the delight of the wait and eventual encounter. He prayed fervently to Saint Pantolomina, showering her with praise, gratitude, and precious stones; he prayed to her virginal irises and her serious eyes; he prayed to the blessed body of Saint Isidro, to the splinters from Christ's cross, and fell back asleep muttering a series of Our Fathers.

At three o'clock that afternoon, Santiago was awakened by a shout that suddenly hung in the room.

"Paco! Mari's on the phone!"

It was a woman's voice, coming from the courtyard. For a moment Santiago had no idea where he was. Flashes of anxiety exploded in his mind: He pictured himself in bed at Scarlet Manor, curled up to the heartbeat of vegetation as it climbed the trellis; he pictured himself in his cell at the church, his fingers sticky with Padre Rafael's medicine; he pictured himself in his military cot, dazed by the flatulence and sweat of strangers; he pictured himself in his Madrid hotel room, botanical garden dahlias under his pillow. Until he sat up in a swirl of sheets, Santiago did not recognize that house with its window open onto paradise. He wondered whether the voice might be hers, though it sounded different from the one he'd heard in the chapel to Saint Pantolomina. This one sounded rude, angered by the day-to-day minutiae of life. He wondered whether she lived alone, with a girlfriend or family, whether she was married or had children, and the sting of impatience, of needing to know, pricked his chest. He slipped over to the open window and scanned the inner patio. The desk lamp was off. A pyramid of books that might have been dictionaries or encyclopedias had grown up around it, but papers continued to dominate. Over the divan lay the fan and the turquoise robe.

His mouth was parched. Santiago went into the large kitchen decorated with vanilla-colored furniture. He let the water run and poured himself a glass. Heat led him to open the window, desire to search for the woman in the window across the way, and destiny to find her in the kitchen, her windowsill filled with potted petunias, eating what looked like a chicken sandwich. The thrill that coursed through him when he realized she needed to eat like every other human, to drink a cola as she seemed to do with near-adolescent enthusiasm, caused him to let down his guard and be seen. He smiled when she did, after licking a drop of mayonnaise from the corner of her mouth. He smiled unaware of the tears in his eyes, the rain-scented sweat coursing down his body. A cramp of hunger brought him back to this world. He moved away from the window, slid down a cabinet until he was sitting on the floor in a fit of laughter.

Since there was nothing to eat in the kitchen, he went back to his room to breakfast of a cigarette and a few loose pieces of gum he found in the bottom of his kit bag. He had planned to go shopping that day, but evening was already dismantling the sky and he had no intention of leaving home, no intention of letting her out of his sight as long as he lived.

Santiago's tenacity nearly made him sick. He spent hours spying on the woman from the bedroom, from the kitchen, taking great care not to be discovered again. He stalked her like an animal his prey, running from one room to the next, barefoot, panting. He watched her smoke with her long cigarette holder, write with the quill dipped in violet ink, consult the books on her desk, fan the heat while sitting on her divan in a blur of peacock feathers, and dance with her arms like a swan's neck, her body's undulations leaving him crazed in a puddle of sheets. He was fascinated by her short pants and the shirt that left her bellybutton bare. He was even fascinated by the fact that she had to relieve herself; her bathroom window was next to his, and though he could not see her, he felt the fury of the chain and peed at the same time, laughing. When overcome by weakness, Santiago would give in and smoke, utter the names of books of the Bible named after women, and recite saintly poems, transcribing the verses on his arms to forget his hunger.

Before it was completely dark, someone rang his bell. Santiago assumed it must be Isidro but decided not to answer — he wanted no one to disturb his joy. I'll drop by tomorrow, he thought. Before long he realized the guard might know who she was and was overcome by another wave of delight. Something as simple as her having a name seemed almost supernatural. A name by which to remember her, a name that contained her entirety. Santiago's dreams seemed dull, tedious, soulless, compared with a life with eyes wide open. Still, he did not go see Isidro but spent another night watching, for she worked until dawn. As he watched he imagined names, discarding some with a laugh, savoring others, as if he might discover the answer in the way the syllables rolled off his tongue.

Her name was Úrsula Perla Montoya, and she wrote romance novels. When her first book was published, she insisted they include her middle name in homage to her grandmother, a Persian poet who at the turn of the century fell into the arms of a Spanish archaeologist excavating near Persepolis. He brought his bride back to Spain years later, a converted Christian hauling a trunk of secrets and Eastern garments, not to mention a longing for the desert locked in her dark eyes, a longing only ever satisfied on holidays in Almería. She had looked after Úrsula until Úrsula was twelve, when death took her like a sandstorm, sealing her heart with an infinite dune that Europeans insisted was angina. Only her granddaughter understood the reality of this loss, which sent her to a Catholic boarding school in Valladolid while her parents, classical actors, toured the world. At her grandmother's wake, Úrsula took diabolical pleasure in sharing one last secret with her: the reason the deceased's lips remained parted, melancholy puffs of superfine sand and salty dust slipping out, causing sneezes and hot flashes in the mourners. Ever since then, though not a woman easily drawn into the hurricane of nostalgia, Úrsula Perla Montoya fell asleep to the droning of the muezzin calling the faithful to prayer that her grandmother had sung like a lullaby, overwhelmed by the cataclysm of a soul that never ceased being Muslim, telling her woes to a stone the size of an egg and dancing a thousand-year-old dance whenever she was troubled. It was her grandmother who taught her Persian, the language they spoke together, and Úrsula translated from and into whenever not immersed in the literature of love, an emotion she considered a tool of her trade.

When she ran into Santiago Laguna on the fourth-floor landing that Saturday morning, she recognized him as the young man she had seen through the window at lunch the day before. This time, however, she saw his eyes up close, and a poem of her grandmother's sprang to mind. It was about a young man who bathed in a sacred lake and was punished by a genie, forever condemned to bear the weight of the lake's turquoise water in his eyes. Úrsula smiled stiffly; an invisible string between her stomach and her lips tugged at the sight of the handsomest man she had ever seen standing before her.

"I'm Santiago Laguna, your new neighbor," he said, unable to hide his idolatry.

His voice sounded timid—gone was the depth with which he usually dominated his conquests. She was the only thing left in his heart, sheathed in a strappy dress. The entire world was reduced to their two stomachs. Úrsula thought he looked like an enchanting bird, though there was an air of torment about him, as if he had been locked in a cage.

"I'll see you around, then."

Santiago's scar began to throb. Úrsula's voice, asking him to take her to Scarlet Manor, pounded in his temples. He was lost in memory as she walked to her door, jingling her keys.

"Wait. Will you sign this for me?"

Santiago hurried to pull Úrsula's most recent book, *Evening Passions on the Divan,* out of his grocery bag and hand it to her. He had bought it that morning after breakfast with Isidro, after contemplating Saint Pantaleon's still-liquid blood at the exact moment he asked the guard to reveal her identity, first hearing her name before that glorious relic.

"Have you read my other books?"

"No, but I've heard of you. I mean, I've seen you before."

"Really? Where?"

"You know, I'm going to bake you a cake — I'm an excellent cook. I'll bring it over and tell you everything then." The Santiago with a sheen of arrogance from his messianic days was back.

Úrsula wrote "May the genie never take pity on your eyes" as she glanced sidelong at him.

"What genie is that?"

"I'll tell you when you bring me that cake."

Santiago's hands were soon immersed in a bowl of egg yolks. He opened the window wide. The last time he'd cooked was when Olvido was alive. He added flour, sugar, and a pinch of salt to the yolks, his hands mixing the ingredients, transforming them into a dough. He dipped his right index and middle finger in, smeared a bit on one nipple to test the consistency. It was perfect. He kissed that bit of dough and combined it with the rest. He knew Úrsula was watching from her window, in plain sight. She watched him with interest at first, becoming more intent on the ripple of his hands, the thickness of his lips, the drops of sweat on his brow, an anatomy she began to intuit by staring at his temples, his cheekbones, his chin. She was sweating, too, as late-July heat baked the courtyard with its silent pipes. She, too, could feel the soft dough. Santiago opened a mesh bag of lemons and grated one until a little mountain of zest formed. He stared at it with awe, as if observing a landscape he could run his fingers through, smell, and suck. So he did. Then he put the zest in the dough and rolled it out on the counter, painting Úrsula's face with more yolk. She had never seen such technique; this was a ritual that made her want to eat the cook, not the cake. She had never seen anyone bake with such love, a love that was solid, liquid, and gas, a love that crossed the inner patio to enlarge the corollas on her petunias, her windowsill becoming a jungle that gave way to the inevitable.

That night, on his way to perform at the café, Santiago felt as if someone nearby was weeping bitterly for him. The unexpected drama made him feel uncomfortable, caused his skin to tense, turning it frosty under the asphyxiating embers of bats plastering the Madrid sky. Walking down Calle de las Huertas, he wondered if it were scientifically possible for the dead to cry in a process to eliminate waste or something like that. He mused on whether only the recently departed could cry or those who had been dead for a long time, cemetery subsoil becoming secret marshland. These were the thoughts consuming him when he arrived at the café, his skin still icy cold. The usual bartender served him his whiskey and kissed him on the lips. Santiago took several gulps as lights flickered onstage, a reminder that they were waiting for him.

He climbed onto the stage and told a story about the sea. He rushed through it, accelerating storms, making mermaids capricious, drowning sailors without any consideration at all. He even introduced a traitor, like when Ezequiel Montes came into his life, someone to blame all misfortune on and finish the story before it was done. He felt the scar on his wrist burn with impatience under the moonlike warmth of the lights. All he wanted was to get home and bring Úrsula the cake. He had napped while it was in the oven, then showered, put on a shirt to look more like a man than a boy, and brought it to her. He rang the bell. No answer. He waited and rang the bell again, listening to the most painful silence through the door. He looked for her through the windows, seeing nothing but the jungle-filled sill. He was so frightened by the thought of her sudden disappearance that he had to fight the desire to cut himself to prove this was not a dream.

From his place onstage, Santiago saw Isidro on a barstool with a beer, looking like the good, solitary man he was. Over the years, the security guard's eyes had grown bigger from watching TV, his soul Caribbean from countless soaps. Santiago suspected a rocky young love in his past, for his skin would become striped like a tiger's whenever he heard a romantic story, an unmistakable sign of melancholy that could be cured only by shouting himself hoarse at Atlético matches. A woman with a white scarf covering her hair had sat down beside Isidro but kept her back to the stage. Santiago was annoyed by this gesture, as if his story was of no interest to her at all, and for a moment that not even he noticed, his chest began to sweat an earthen smell.

Santiago told the end of his story, stopping first for a few seconds, just long enough to drop a flower onto a grave. He got down from the stage and walked over to the bar amid applause that slashed ribbons of smoke and alcohol vapors. The woman in the white scarf finished her orange soda in a single gulp and jumped up from her stool the moment Santiago arrived to greet Isidro. She bumped into his arm as she hurried out, not turning to look at him or apologize. The door slammed shut, and Santiago stood watching through the window as her slightly stooped figure melted into sultry Madrid. His skin turned cold once again, overcome by a reptilian omen warning of something, though he had no idea what.

"Oh, how that poor woman cried," Isidro said, burning with compassion. "Tears as big as pears."

"Do you know her?"

"I only just saw her profile, but no."

The bartender walked over to Santiago, smoothing her teased hair.

"Can I get you anything, love?"

"No, I'm heading home."

"You're such a bore sometimes," she said, stalking off to serve two patrons in rock band T-shirts elbowing each other at the opposite end of the bar.

"Walk with me?" Santiago asked Isidro.

"Sure. I'm not up for any high jinks tonight either."

Night plunged Santiago into an Úrsula paralysis yet again, and he forgot everything else. She was a pier that could stop any stormy wave the past might toss at him. Isidro saw the boy shiver before the blood of Saint Pantaleon when he pronounced her name, as instructed. When he overheard Santiago inject the suffering of Úrsula Perla Montoya into his prayers, Isidro's lips drained of all blood. He took Santiago by the arm and marched him out of church, crossing himself with his other hand, afraid such sacrilege would cause hell to swallow him right there. Ever since, every time the guard looked at his friend, his face constricted in worry.

"She's too old for you," Isidro said as they walked up Calle de las Huertas.

"She's only ten or twelve years older. That's nothing."

"It is when you're only twenty-one. You're just a kid and she's an experienced woman. This is a bad idea. I'm telling you this because I know things, things I shouldn't but I do. Our building is a small community and that courtyard a showcase of shame."

"I don't care what you know."

"She's like a praying mantis—beautiful, yes, but her beauty attracts her prey. They say she uses a man for every novel she writes, leaving him when she's done."

"Well, she'll write the rest of her books with me. She'll never leave me once she knows."

"Once she knows what? That you fell in love like a dog after seeing her through a window?"

"Once she knows I've been searching for her for five years, that for five years she has appeared to me both asleep and awake."

The two walked the rest of the way in silence. Isidro now understood all those times when Santiago kneeled before the relics of saints and martyrs, praying to find Úrsula, praying she would fly into his life on the same miraculous wings she had used to enter his dreams and visions. A shiver ran up the guard's spine as his mind wandered to a series of soap opera arguments about lovers with miraculous destinies.

When they said good night on the second-floor landing, Isidro put a hand on Santiago's shoulder and said: "I'm here for you, kid." He sighed. "If only you'd been born in Venezuela . . ."

The light in the stairwell went out, but Santiago had no intention of fixing it. He took the stairs two at a time, traversing blades of moonlight as they penetrated open windows. He arrived home ready to track Úrsula Perla Montoya through the courtyard. This time it was easy; she was in her kitchen with a man in his early forties. He was uncorking a bottle of wine, and she, wearing her turquoise robe, was taking two glasses out of a cabinet as they chatted rather intimately, Santiago thought. Santiago picked up a knife and reopened the cut on his finger, but blood was not what confirmed this was real. Instead, his ears, the back of his neck, his chest, all began to burn as his head filled once again with green-eyed traitors. Then he noticed the cake crowning a white porcelain plate on the counter and decided to take it to her.

Úrsula opened the door with her mass of chestnut waves falling over her shoulders and down her back. The two looked wordlessly at each other, sensing each other's heat.

"Now will you tell me what genie should never take pity on my eyes and why?"

"I'm busy, but thanks for the cake," she said, snatching it from him. "Good night."

Úrsula Perla Montoya walked down the hall to the kitchen, knotted by an anxiety so powerful it caused her hands to shake.

"What's this?" the man asked when she walked in with the cake.

"A nice neighbor made it for me."

"It smells delicious. Cut me a piece — I'm hungry."

"No." Her cheeks burned. "It's not at its best yet. It has to sit until tomorrow."

"Then I'll come back again tomorrow." He had taken Úrsula by the waist and was whispering in her ear.

"Take the wine and wait for me in the living room. I'll be there as soon as I put this away."

"Hurry." He kissed her on the lips.

Alone with the cake, Úrsula recalled how Santiago had caressed the ingredients — the egg yolks, the flour, the sugar, the zest — how he had smelled them, kissed them; how he had mixed them with his hands, the dough hanging from his nipple, his lips parted, drops of sweat licking his brow. She was aroused by the love that went into its preparation, aroused by the love now inside, there for her to eat. She took a few crumbs and savored them slowly, pressing them to the roof of her mouth. The taste of Santiago was on her tongue. She pinched off a bigger piece, then another, spiced with a touch of cinnamon, alive, smooth, and a barely perceptible aroma of sugar and rain inflamed her breasts.

The man's voice interrupted her tasting, calling out to her from the living room. Úrsula covered the cake with a tea towel and left the kitchen.

"You were taking too long." He was settled into the loveseat.

"I couldn't find the right container."

Úrsula sat beside him and took the glass of wine he offered but drank not a drop. The man pulled her toward him and began to talk about the book he was translating from Greek. Úrsula was not the least bit interested in his problems with verbs or stanzas or the musicality of poetry. She had chosen him almost by accident; her most recent novel, *Afternoon Passions on the Divan,* was selling well, and her editor was pressuring her to write another. Úrsula needed a fling, and it was then she saw him in the library. They had gone to university together but lost track of each other after graduation. He was attractive. He had been living in Greece for five years, the last two on a small island where he grew pear tomatoes and translated nature poetry. Úrsula thought his sun-toasted face and Adonis profile might inspire a Greco-Latin passion filled with Cupid's arrows and demigod lovers. But right then the taste of her neighbor, kept safe in her mouth, was the only thing to inspire passion, even if it was cannibalistic.

"You're not listening," the man complained. "Your mind is elsewhere."

"I'm sorry. I was translating Ferdowsi until late and am exhausted."

He stroked her hair, recited verses from *The Odyssey,* and tried to kiss her, but Úrsula's lips were shut tight.

"I said I'm tired. Let's do this another day. I really need to sleep."

She said goodbye with two quick kisses on the cheek and headed into her room, sensing it would rain that night. The smell of mud and grass filled her house. It slipped in through the open windows and advanced on invisible steps. Úrsula looked in her dresser mirror, opened the neckline of her robe a little further, loosened the belt to show a slip of belly, lifted her arms, put her palms together, and shook her torso just as her grandmother had taught her. She was ready to find him now.

Santiago Laguna, his elbows on the bedroom windowsill, naked in that starry and noxious night, shook with rage when Úrsula appeared, fanning herself with peacock feathers.

"Can't sleep?" she asked, leaning on her windowsill with the air of an empress.

"I don't want to dream."

"I can't sleep either." She ran her tongue over her lips, the roof of her mouth, and rows of insects seemed to march up and down Santiago's body.

"I thought I saw you had company."

"An old friend, but he had to go." She closed her fan, resting it in the palm of one hand. "I didn't let him taste the cake."

"Good. It was just for you." Santiago's voice cracked and his knees buckled as his anger gave way.

"That's what I thought. I loved it."

"Tomorrow I'll make cinnamon cake and palmiers—a family specialty."

"Do you come from a family of bakers?"

"No." He smiled. "I'm the only male in a family of cursed females."

"So the men aren't cursed?"

"No, we are, too."

"And as a cursed man, what is it you do?"

"I tell stories in cafés."

"A profession right out of *The Arabian Nights*."

"Would you like me to tell you a story?"

"I'd rather you tell me about your family, what sort of curse you suffer from."

"I'll tell you how it all began so you can better understand."

"Come over, then. We can get comfortable on the couch."

The moon had dropped in the sky, balancing on clotheslines that crisscrossed the inner patio, and come to rest on her face. The neckline of her robe formed a V.

"Don't move," he begged. "I'll tell you the story here."

"All right."

"Late in the sixteenth century, in a cottage along the coastal lagoon of Valencia lived a couple who dreamed of one day having children. For years they asked God to bless them with his grace, but the woman was now over forty and had yet to conceive. Their neighbors felt sorry for the couple, with no one to help them in their fields or bring joy to their home through laughter and games.

"One spring morning the farmer's wife, a robust, cheerful woman, disappeared from the cottage without a trace. She returned a few days later, telling her husband she had been to a beach where an old woman sold her a spell to get pregnant. Nine months later, the farmer's wife gave birth to a lovely little girl. The neighbors heard the news with some suspicion. How could a woman that old, that unattractive, have had such an extraordinarily beautiful child? It was only when the girl turned one that they denounced the case to the Holy Inquisition and the extent of her beauty led to disaster. The farmer's wife was accused of having fornicated with the sea in a satanic ritual. The proof was irrefutable, for the girl possessed all of her progenitor's attributes: her eyes were the color of water, her hair like the darkest deep sea, her skin as pure as the froth that forms in waves, and her lips coral red.

"They burned the farmer's wife at the stake for being a witch, but though the farmer was judged, he was found innocent. He had fallen prey to his wife's cunning; she had cheated on him with nature. The problem of what to do with the child arose. Upon seeing her, no one wanted to order her death, even if she was born out of witchcraft. They agreed the girl would be sent to a convent and raised under the watchful eye of the nuns. Yet no religious order would accept a girl with a background such as hers. They therefore wrapped the girl in a scapular and handed her back to her father. Having succumbed to drinking, he locked her in the stable with the calves.

"A gentleman dressed in fine attire came to the cottage a few months later.

"'I'll pay one silver coin if you let me see the daughter of the sea,' he said to the farmer.

"The farmer stood perplexed. He went to the stable, unchained the girl from a post, washed her face, and showed her to the gentleman. The sight of such beauty, which had only grown over time, satisfied him so that he paid two silver coins, not one. From then on, men and women would come to the coastal lagoon just to see the half-human, half-marine creature. The farmer squandered the money on wine and women, while the girl — whom he called Mar or Sea in public but who was in fact baptized Olvido — grew wild with the stable animals. One evening when a duchess was admiring the girl, now twelve, she pointed to the woman's magnificent yellow silk dress and spoke these words: 'Lanai ursala.'

"The duchess paid the farmer one more coin than agreed because the daughter of the sea had spoken to her in the language of the waves.

"Around this time, a handsome young linguist from Castile traveled to the coastal lagoon and, one clear night, came upon the girl hiding in tall grass.

"'I'm looking for the girl who knows the language of the sea,' he said warmly, so as not to startle her.

"The girl pointed to her chest and replied: 'Mar.'

"Do you know if her cottage is this way?"

"The girl reached up to the biggest star burning in the sky and said: 'Ursala.'

"Her face was covered in dried dung. She was wearing rags that stank of the stable, and one of her legs was bloody, as if she had escaped from a trap. Feeling sorry for this creature, the linguist pulled a handkerchief out of his frock coat and wiped her face in the light of the moon. She reveled in his touch through the silk handkerchief.

"'You are, without a doubt, the daughter of the sea,' the linguist said, admiring her beauty.

"She again pointed to her chest and repeated her name.

"'Speak to me in the language of the waves,' he begged.

"The girl pointed to the moon and said: 'Saluma.'

"'Saluma?' the linguist repeated, confused, as the girl smiled and pointed again at the moon.

"It was then the young linguist realized the truth: the girl spoke not the language of the waves but one she had invented, since no one had ever taught her a civilized tongue.

"For more than four years, the linguist taught her language and the ways of men while the farmer was at the tavern or the brothel.

"On the evening of her sixteenth birthday, the captain of a pirate ship came to the cottage determined to learn the secret to outwitting storms. The girl replied in perfect Spanish that she was unable to help for she did not know the language of the waves; her father was not the sea but that farmer who tried to con him. The captain beat the farmer mercilessly. The girl did not treat her father's wounds, did not help him to bed, did not give him water to drink, did not answer the question that escaped his throat as he lay dying—'Who taught you to speak, you traitorous bitch?' She simply waited for him to die. When the linguist arrived for their lesson, she told him what happened and they immediately left for Castile.

"Once there, the linguist found work at a school and the girl completed her education with piano and sewing lessons.

"By the time she reached legal age and was introduced to society with her real name, the girl's beauty had surpassed all reason and desire. On her birthday, as asked, the linguist gave her a yellow silk dress and, thanks to acquaintances, secured an invitation to celebrate at a ball at the Duke of Monteosorio's palace. There the girl was captivated by the sumptuous furnishings, not to mention the jewels worn by the women dancing in the salon, for they shone brighter than the stars. And so, when Alonso Laguna, the duke's son, fell in love with her at first sight and proposed, Olvido accepted.

"Upon hearing the news, desperate, the linguist confessed his love. Olvido threw herself crying into his arms and kissed him passionately. They made love all night long, but the next morning, when the linguist wanted her to write to break her engagement, she refused. 'I'll marry him,' she said, 'but you'll come and live with us. That way our love will go on and we'll be rich.'

"The wedding took place at the duke's palace a few weeks later. A great banquet was prepared as well as a majestic dance that lasted until morning. The most illustrious citizens were in attendance, noblemen, even an envoy sent by the king to congratulate the couple on his behalf. During the celebration, Olvido could not forget the dark strands of hair that fell over the linguist's brow, his firm chest peeking out through the flounce of his shirt, his cognac-stained lips as he said goodbye. When the party was over, she slipped out of her nuptial bed and galloped to the house she had shared with the linguist only to be met by the dark of night, for he had left forever.

"Time, the tyrant of life, gave Olvido ten years of dances, banquets, and dresses, not to mention a little girl. Perhaps guided by nostalgia, she named her María del Mar. Perhaps also guided by nostalgia, one spring morning when her husband was away on business, Olvido felt the urge to travel to her birthplace on the coastal lagoon. From behind the safety of carriage curtains, she peered out at rice fields misty in the dawn, stocky farmers, and the blue, frothy face of her father. When the carriage stopped in front of the cottage, she got out and walked to the stable. She missed feeling wet calf snouts on her legs, missed hearing their soft, sad mooing. Although the stable was filled with the half-light of sunset, she saw a man curled up in a corner. Strewn around were empty bottles of cognac. He was wearing a farmer's pants, and his chest was covered with sores and parasites.

"'Get off my property,' she ordered.

"'Salima, ursula,' the man croaked.

"Olvido searched for the vagabond's eyes amid strands of greasy hair and discovered they belonged to the linguist.

"'What have I done to you, my love? What have I done?' she lamented, taking him into her arms.

"'Salima, ursula,' he repeated, his eyes glazed.

"Olvido Laguna tore a cross on a chain from around her neck and threw it onto the ground.

"'I,' she declared in a burial voice, 'daughter of the sea, renounce the God that robbed me of my mother and ask Satan to curse my name and that of my descendants. May my daughter's honor be sullied, her heart lost to a man who will break it—and her daughter's after that, and her daughter's daughters. May a line of women suffer through the centuries everything that you, my love, have suffered for me. May this misfortune continue until the last drop of Laguna blood flows.'

"Olvido never returned to Castile. Some years later fishermen found the linguist's body on the beach, his face puffy from wine and his once dark eyes now inexplicably blue. Olvido's body was never found. Some say she was taken by her father, the sea, and rests in a coral grave. Others say she was devoured by the devil, paying body and soul for her condemnation of love."

Úrsula's empress manners slipped away as she listened to the story. Her eyes grew hazy and she forgot herself completely, and Santiago's gaze embraced a silent ghost that seemed to have awakened against his will. To Úrsula, who had twisted her hair into a long braid, everything tasted of him: her lips, the moon, his words as they echoed across the courtyard.

"That's how it all began. If you liked my story, I can tell you another tomorrow, and the day after that, and the day after that. I can tell you stories forever."

"You'll be my Scheherazade. But remember—when I no longer like them, I'll chop off your head."

"I'll take that chance."

"I must get to work. Good night."

Úrsula's flesh had begun to shred with inspiration as she watched him, listened to his story, plotlines flying through the inner patio on ribbons of skin.

"Can I watch you write until I'm tired enough to sleep?"

"You're asking permission now?"

Santiago blushed.

"You crawl into bed and I'll sing you a lullaby my grandmother taught me."

Úrsula watched him walk away from the window and lie on the bed. The muezzin's call to prayer softly filtered through the silence of the courtyard, reaching Santiago in a melancholy whisper. He closed his eyes. After two sleepless nights, he soon slipped into dreams.

That night, however, Úrsula Perla Montoya did not sleep. Any fatigue was erased from memory as she gave herself, body and soul, to the frenzy of the quill. She wrote her heart's desire before it reached her fingers, as her skin tattered to shreds with the pleasure of Santiago, even at a distance, as her emotions merged with her spirit, taking her to the greatest literary climax any man had ever given her, a climax that lasted for hours and hours.

She wrote well past dawn, exhausting three pots of violet ink, staining her fingers, her face, her chest with rosettes of passion. Only when the sun left the Madrid sky did she have the strength to stop. She walked into the kitchen and ate a piece of cake, determined to keep Santiago inside her. Then, even though it was Sunday, she phoned her editor to say she had finally begun the novel and would be done quite soon. "It'll be the best thing I've ever written," she assured him. She hung up euphoric, analyzing the glory of her future success, humming the muezzin's call, until, all of a sudden, as she lay in bed with one foot on the threshold of sleep, her stomach grew cloudy, felt empty, as if the cake had evaporated, leaving behind the unease of loss.

22

SANTIAGO LAGUNA DREAMED of a storm. His heart froze when he woke and saw a mass of gray clouds whirling in the Sunday sky. The cut on his finger had split, its purplish edges oozing pus like insect bile. He stuffed his hand under his pillow, but the pain continued. He curled up with the memory of the indecipherable lullaby Úrsula Perla Montoya had sung. A while later it felt as if the sky was growing even darker and thunder reverberated through him. He heard the patter of rain on the pavement, on the tiles, and on the flat zinc roofs. The patter grew into a drumbeat, until it erupted in an apocalyptic boom. Yet Santiago was more worried that his mouth smelled of whiskey, not morning breath, that cigarette smoke with a touch of beer and Irish coffee assaulted his nose while dozens of faces stared at him, feverish under the stage lights, waiting for something he could not quite understand. It was only when a glass coffee mug shattered following another crack of thunder and the bar was overrun by a mass of honeysuckle that he realized he was still caught in the nightmare that had plagued him all night. He struggled to awake. The sky was still gray but not a drop of water had fallen. Sunday morning still savored the coming squall.

Santiago lit a cigarette and lay back on the pillow waiting for certain urges to pass — the urge to hug Padre Rafael, to give him his medicine, to watch over his siestas and tell him stories with the aftertaste of consecrated wine in his mouth. He waited five minutes, ten, until he was able to placate his nostalgia, replace it with his overwhelming desire for Úrsula Perla Montoya. The whole room filled with her. The dagger of her neckline tortured him, the point drove him to delirium, and his cut finger burned at the thought of touching her for the very first time. He arched his back and held his breath. The agony of waiting was far more pleasurable than spilling himself all over the sheets. Once recovered, Santiago searched for her in the windows, but her white shutters were closed. Instead he slipped into a warm tub, rested his head on a towel, and began to read *Evening Passions on the Divan*.

The pages of the book he imagined written in violet ink transported him to a palace in ancient Persia, where a young maiden had been cursed by a genie for spurning his amorous advances. The maiden was turned into a diamond as punishment for her hard heart and imprisoned in a bedchamber, cared for by a slave who polished her, made her sparkle every morning for the wicked genie's delight. But under her veil and rings of gold, the slave hid the arts of a sorceress, and she took pity on the maiden. One day the slave brought in a divan, setting it under a window with bubbling fountains outside. Its damask silk held the power to counter any spell in the sunset's rays. And so, when the bedchamber succumbed to purple light, the sorceress slave set the diamond on the divan and the maiden regained her human form. A secret door was immediately then opened for her lover to come in, a desert man concealed up to his eyes, exhausted from navigating the labyrinth hallways, guided at times by the poetry of desire, at others by the rattle between his thighs.

At first they had to learn to love according to the architecture of magic, for as soon as any part of the maiden's body left the divan, it became diamond again, her lover suddenly delighting in the taste of stone. Disheveled by desperation, he would plead with his god to make it sunset again the next day. After weeks and months of ardor ending in the sparkle of a jewel, they became virtuosos of a calculated affair, cavorting fearlessly on the divan. But one night the sorceress slave spied on them from behind a folding screen and was surprised to see their amorous romps had ended, giving way to a melancholy that left them lying entwined on the divan.

Santiago finished his bath before the end of the book. As he toweled off, he imagined what he would do if Úrsula Perla Montoya lay on her divan at sunset and was transformed into a diamond. It wouldn't matter, he thought. I'm prepared to love her in whatever form she takes: alive, dead, or in dreams.

Santiago had agreed to meet Isidro for one o'clock Mass at the Cristo del Olivar cathedral. The guard was waiting for him at the front door, a serious look on his face.

"The sky is falling, my friend; it just doesn't know where to begin."

"That's what I'm afraid of."

Madrid lay oppressed under the leaden obesity of clouds. They lay siege to each of its streets, plunging a normal Sunday of tapas and Mass into a tortured wait. People sat in bars eating potatoes sautéed in spicy tomato sauce and pickled anchovies, staring out at the sky. "It hasn't let go. No, not yet," they commented with beer foam on their lips. "But it'll be a good one when it does."

A group of young people played guitars and sang at Mass. Santiago stood to light candles for his ancestors: one for the great-great grandmother he knew only through her oak-scented presence; another for his mother, named after a flower; one more for Manuela Laguna, without any childish remorse; one more for Olvido with a shaky hand; and the last for Padre Rafael, to bring him peace. He sat back down with Isidro, singing quietly in his hoarse cricket warble, a reminder of his curse. He received Communion nervously and prayed under Isidro's watchful eye. The guard listened intently for any prayers in the apocryphal gospel of Úrsula Perla Montoya.

The two went to a bar after church, where Santiago suddenly had a voracious appetite somehow related to the rain that was reluctant to fall. He was a thin young man with a French constitution and could not remember ever eating as much as he did that day. Isidro celebrated the boy's appetite with the first four dishes, believing it a sign of good physical and mental health, but began to worry when he grew full and Santiago continued to order grilled prawns, mushrooms and garlic, *tortilla española,* and other delicacies, washing them all down with cold beer.

"Maybe you've got one of those parasites where you eat and eat but never get full."

"If only the sky would clear, I wouldn't be so hungry — or just rain and get it all over with."

"What does the weather have to do with your stomach?" Isidro asked. "Maybe it's love devouring everything you put inside?"

"That, too."

Santiago kept eating until a rumble of thunder cracked the sky's grief and his stomach shut at the very same second.

"Let's go," he said to Isidro.

They paid the bill and stepped into the street, where everything was the same as before the thunder. Clouds squeezed tightly so not a drop of rain would fall, abandoning the city to this anxious portent once again.

And so it was as Isidro napped on his couch to the background noise of television documentaries that Santiago baked cinnamon cake and palmiers. At about five that afternoon, Úrsula Perla Montoya opened her shutters. The fresh breeze of morning had grown profligate. Overwhelmed, sparrows sought refuge in holes under the roof where they fainted, as doves spiraled beakfirst into fountains.

It was on this morbidly drowsy Sunday that Santiago Laguna first touched the skin of the woman he had been searching for for five years. It happened when he handed her the plate with his baked goods. Úrsula answered the door just out of the shower, wearing a knee-length bathrobe, her hair in a towel turban. At first they simply brushed hands when Úrsula took the plate, but Santiago prolonged it into a touch, an extended taste of flesh as, for a fleeting moment, he longed to die and be resurrected all at once.

"I'm going to drop it," Úrsula said, smiling at him.

Santiago let her go, following her down the dim hallway into the kitchen.

"This is the cinnamon cake I told you about last night. My grandmother taught me to make it."

Paragraphs for Ursula's new novel filled her head. She set the plate on the table. A bellyful of her neighbor would take her to her grave if she tried even one. She had eaten Santiago's lemon cake for breakfast, and the taste of him filled her mouth.

"Would you like coffee or maybe a beer?" she asked.

"No, thank you."

"Then how about you tell me another story, or more about you and your family?"

"I'll tell you whatever you like, even if it displeases you and you chop off my head."

"Let me change, then. It wouldn't be polite to condemn you to death in my bathrobe."

"You're just fine with that towel on your head."

An overwhelming heat stirred their emotions. Úrsula's bathrobe, her arms, her knees, grew impossibly heavy. She wanted Santiago to wait in the living room while she put on a dress, but he asked her to show him where she worked.

"You already know what my study looks like."

"It's not the same as being there."

It was smaller than it appeared through the window. Two corn plants stood in the corners Santiago could not see from his apartment. As soon as he walked into the room, they began to burst with new shoots. The only furniture was the desk, the chair, the divan, and a bookcase piled with scrolls among the books.

"What are those?"

Úrsula chose one, unrolling it with an adoration that brought her back to childhood.

"They're my grandmother's poems. She always wrote on parchment with the quill I inherited. She said she had an old soul and, despite the times, it was the only way she felt inspired."

Long, pointed calligraphy ran across the parchment.

"What language is this?"

"Persian. My grandmother was born in Iran, in Shiraz, the city of poets. She raised me."

"Is she still alive?"

"No, and neither are my parents. They were actors who spent all their time traveling. They died in a plane crash some years ago."

"I'm an orphan, too."

Úrsula put her hand on his cheek. She rolled up the parchment as Santiago's heart palpitated.

"Can I ask what happened?"

"Of course. I said I'd tell you anything. My mother threw herself out a window when I was just a baby. She was lovesick — the risk of being born into a cursed family. My father died of kidney disease a few years ago."

"I'm sorry. You're so young."

"I'm twenty-one."

Úrsula unrolled the parchment to distract herself.

"Do you speak Persian?"

"Yes, my grandmother taught me."

"Will you translate the poem for me?"

"Certainly. This one tells the story of a genie who refused to take pity on a young man's eyes."

Úrsula Perla Montoya began to recite verses in Persian, surrendering herself to the absurdity of the poetry. Though he could not understand the words, every hexameter stirred feelings, immersing him in effervescent, late-afternoon heat and the joy of being alive. When Úrsula finished, she let the scroll roll up and began to recite the poem again in Spanish, from memory, as her fingers twirled and untwirled locks of Santiago's hair. He could not wait for the end and, profaning those hexameters, kissed her on the lips. The scar on his wrist erupted in a wound of irises. The parchment fell from Úrsula's hands, and the towel from her head. The two lost themselves in a sleepless afternoon. A torrent of water rushed up and down through the pipes, disturbing their neighbors' siesta. Spots of mildew peeled from the walls. Úrsula undressed. Santiago lifted her by the waist onto the desk, her novel sailing through the air. They made love on the chair, against the bookshelf where scrolls exhaled golden desert sand and spells from centuries beyond mortal time. They wound up on the divan, crushing the peacock feather fan, Úrsula under the spell of this extraordinary creature Santiago Laguna, satiated but not full of her lover's taste.

At nine o'clock that night the Madrid sky was still being tormented by the threat of a coming storm. Santiago said goodbye to Úrsula and kissed her collarbone.

"I have to go. I have a show in the café at ten."

"Come by when you're done. I'll be waiting."

A blockade of clouds stopped the night sky from arriving, sketching the moon like a ghostly blot. Although Santiago had showered and put on clean clothes, everything about him still smelled of Úrsula, so he did not sense the rain amid the cars and traffic lights, amid the streetlights and centuries-old houses. The first drops fell just as he reached the café. Only then did he recall the insatiable premonition from his dreams, and his bones seized up in fear of the patter of rain, its watery monotone, brilliant lightning, and riotous thunder.

The crowd was bigger than usual for a Sunday night, with customers ordering expensive cocktails and bottles of imported beer. The tables were mostly full. Nacha Pop was playing on the stereo, lights were low, flames fluttering in glass candleholders. Ceiling fans sliced through the heat above.

"You're late," the bartender said, serving Santiago the glass of whiskey he always drank before performing. "Just so you know, the boss is here tonight, so I won't be going down to your favorite basement. You should also know I wouldn't go down there anyhow because you haven't been to see me all day, and yesterday you were an ass."

"I'm with someone now, and she's very important to me." Santiago drank his whiskey in two gulps.

"You're all a bunch of pricks," the bartender replied, throwing a cloth into the sink. "And the better you are, the bigger the prick."

The stage lights blinked, and Santiago walked over. The owner introduced him when the music ended, saying no one told a better story about the sea than this young man, even if he was from the frosty mountains and forests of Castile. Applause rang out. A spotlight hovered over him.

"They say that many years ago a phantom ship sailed the northern seas, terrorizing sailors and captains alike. A cold fog as thick as the manes of the dead blanketed water and sky so that nothing was clear, not even whether it was day or night." Santiago had to stop.

The sky over Madrid had opened up, just like in his dream, and rain pelted the café windows, steaming asphalt and roofs in an agonizing release. The spectators sat mesmerized by the power of the storm.

"Few dared head out on such seas," Santiago continued, "but those who did and made it back alive"—thunder crashed—"told that from out of the fog came the monstrous silhouette of a galleon fitted with mermaid cannons. The foam parted reverently and a vast silence reigned. They all knew what would happen next and covered their ears in vain, hoping to escape the terrible threat—the red bell that hung from the mainmast, as brilliant as fire." His voice cracked. He had just noticed the woman with a white scarf over her hair sitting on a barstool. He had not seen her come in and could have sworn she was not there when he arrived. Wherever she came from, her back was now turned to the stage, like the day before.

A surge of thunder roared and lightning lit up the sky; the café windows shook.

"The bell was rung by a shadow as the name of one sailor was pronounced. No matter how that poor man cried and begged, the captain was forced to hand him over to the specter unless he wanted to suffer the same fate. For that phantom ship, once it filled its hold with victims, would set sail for hell. One day . . . or night . . . a young man arrived . . . with horseshoes on the soles of his boots . . . like a mule . . ." Santiago was forced to stop as honeysuckle choked his throat.

The murmur of patrons filled the bar.

"Tattooed on his tongue . . . was a list of his exploits and glories . . . He assured the people he could free them from the threat . . . of the phantom ship . . . in exchange for three barrels of gold . . . 'All you have to do . . . is take . . . the red bell,' he said. 'The next time it rings . . . with the name . . . of some poor sod, I'll go in his place . . . and take it.'" He was deathly pale. "And so he did. He took the bell no problem, but . . . became a fabulous . . . galleon . . ."

Santiago could not go on. A heavy silence extended out over the tables. The woman on the barstool turned, looked at Santiago with identical eyes burdened by a tomb of tears, and he was swallowed by the past. The woman stood, uncovered her hair, walked, alive, toward the stage, and told the end of the story.

"His neck stretched until it was as long as the mainmast, with the red bell hanging there. They say the fog disappeared and the man-boat sailed into the horizon, his tongue now a flag flapping in the breeze. A hundred years passed before they saw him again, on stormy nights, when the sound of his approach is like mule hoofs on the earth, and sailors tremble in fear. They know he will have to make the bell ring and steal their souls."

Applause erupted as if this was all part of the show, but Santiago stood still under the artificial light, his face the very image of terror.

23

"Don't cry."

The storm had ended. Clouds dissipated, giving way to the outlines of constellations, but the city remained overwhelmed by the smell of rain. Tree beds overflowed, and water streamed down streets like the tears on Santiago's cheeks.

"Hold me."

Olvido held Santiago to her. Scarlet Manor germinated in his gut, choking him in a mass of memories. He returned to happy times in the kitchen, to its sweet, smoky smell, to kisses among wistful squash, nipples heaving with jams and doughs, floury games; he returned to days of painting, honeysuckle, and poems as they baked in the sun; he returned to readings of Saint John of the Cross, rose poisonings so they would be left in peace; he returned to bathtime tickles, nights lit up by the fire, and the taste of stories.

"Forgive me."

They held each other even tighter, and Santiago returned to the smell of drenched hills, the betrayal of sheep, cold clothes, and icy bones.

"I never should have left like that." Olvido looked him in the eye.

The few cars coming down the street splattered water and mud. Santiago leaned against a doorway and was thankful for the breeze that helped him breathe. The heavy ambience of the café had been suffocating.

"Why did you leave me?"

"After what happened, I thought Padre Rafael could take better care of you. He loved you like a son. I made him promise he'd bring you to live with him at the church, not leave you alone at Scarlet Manor, at the mercy of the lawyer's son or anyone else."

"Padre Rafael knew you were alive?"

"That day, early that morning, as you slept like a child, I set the stable on fire and ran to the church. I woke Padre Rafael and told him everything in confession. He thought my plan was crazy, and he was right. He asked me to reconsider. 'We'll find another way,' he insisted, but I was so desperate I would have done anything to free you from what we'd done. 'The stable's already on fire,' I told him. 'Promise me, Padre. There's no time. Go and save him!'" Flames ignited Olvido's gaze. "He was worried about his illness, worried he might die soon and leave you alone. 'I've prepared for that, too,' I assured him. I gave him your father's address in Paris, so he could write when death was near. I also gave him a letter I had written to Pierre, begging him to take you in, telling him I forgave him."

"You forgave him? What was there to forgive? Did my father treat you or my mother badly?"

The crease in Olvido Laguna's forehead sank into her skin.

"I couldn't do you any more harm. I had to set you free. My desire to protect you would only wind up ruining your life."

"My mother killed herself because her cursed blood made my father not love her anymore."

Olvido surrendered to her pain, her white hair and eyes sunken in by rivers of tears.

"Because Pierre Lesac loved me, Santiago. Me. Your mother found out and it was more than she could bear."

Santiago set off down Calle del Prado. Olvido followed. He stopped a few steps farther on, put one foot up on an old pink façade, and shoved his hands into his hair.

"Did you love him?"

"No. I've always loved your grandfather. Pierre's youth reminded me of Esteban, but that was all. I never encouraged him. Still, I had to learn to live with the guilt of your mother's death. My only relief came through devotion to you, to raising you, my determination to let nothing tear us apart, let nothing hurt you."

"Why have you come back?" Santiago was crying.

"I couldn't bear to think you might feel guilty about my death. I had condemned you to live with the same pain I suffered on losing your mother."

"It took you five years to tell me the truth."

"Once I had time to reflect, I didn't know how to go back. I spoke to Padre Rafael on the phone, and we corresponded. He assured me you were fine—sad, but you were back at school, you lacked for nothing with your inheritance, even though I wasn't sure. For years I didn't know which would hurt you more: learning I was alive when you seemed to be getting over my death or letting the ghost of guilt soar over your head. Then Padre Rafael died. The new priest told me. I asked if the boy who lived with Padre Rafael was in France, and he said you were doing your military service. I lost track of you and thought I'd go mad . . ."

"So, how did you find me?"

"It was one of those things that only happen in a city. Someone at the restaurant I cook at suggested I hire a private detective, and I did. When he told me you were in Madrid, so close, and that you were a storyteller, I thought: Of course." Olvido looked at Santiago, spellbound. "You are so handsome and so grown-up . . ."

"What made you want to come back into my life?" Santiago lit a cigarette.

"Santiago, I'm going home, to Scarlet Manor. I need to go back to the cemetery, touch the earth on your grandfather's grave, hold it in my hands, caress it. I need to breathe the mountain air once more, the pines, the oak grove, watch the beech trees turn gold in autumn. I need to hear the stags mating, inhale the smell of gunpowder. I need to go back to my kitchen, our kitchen, our garden, and smell the yard, watch the hydrangea, morning glories, honeysuckle, and daisies grow. I need to smell it all, feel it all one more time. And I needed you, too. I needed to hold you, look you in the eyes, beg forgiveness and be forgiven, go knowing you're happy, that you feel no guilt. Love sometimes goes astray when you love too much, but it's always love and it can get back on track again. I have always loved you." Olvido held his face in her hands. "You're my boy, my grandchild, my little one, and I am your grandmother." She took a deep breath, her cheeks on fire. "I'll be at Scarlet Manor whenever you want to visit."

"What choice do I have?" Santiago took a long pull on his cigarette. "After all, we're cursed."

Olvido smiled sadly.

"Have you ever hated me, in all these years? Have you ever hated me with all your might?"

"I've only ever known how to love you." The smoke from Santiago's cigarette dissolved into the night.

"You are the most extraordinary of all the Lagunas, the only male, the only one to be accepted by the townspeople, loved even. Because of you they began to smile at me after church; because of you they invited me to tea; because of you I had the opportunity to show the town my world, my recipes, and sometimes I even felt understood. You are, without a doubt, an exceptional Laguna. You've never known hate for another Laguna; you've never known revenge. During these long years away from Scarlet Manor, I came to understand that our true curse was this: to hate one another, to never forget. We spent our lives seeking revenge. Your great-grandmother was right: you are the chosen one. The hate and curse of the Lagunas will end with me."

Santiago ground the cigarette butt under his foot.

"Are you sick?"

"Let's walk awhile." Olvido took him by the arm. "I love strolling up and down El Prado at this time of night, particularly on a Sunday. The light is soft, the sidewalks freshly washed, the trees seem huge, there are almost no cars, and you feel different, as if your sorrow will simply disappear as you walk past these grand buildings. It's when I feel this great city speaks, just like the hills, but this is the only time of day you can hear it."

"You're going to die, aren't you, Abuela? That's why you want to go back to Scarlet Manor, and it's why you came to see me."

"Let's not talk about death. I'm just beginning to live again." Olvido pulled him close. "I'm alive again."

They walked Paseo del Prado from Plaza de Neptuno up to Plaza de Cibeles, from there down to Calle de Atocha and back to Plaza de Neptuno. Olvido told Santiago she had spent these last years in Madrid cooking at various restaurants. She lived in a rooming house on Calle Echegaray but would leave for Scarlet Manor in a few days. Santiago did not tell her about his suicide attempt using Saint Pantolomina of the Flowers' miraculous finger, and when his grandmother noticed the scar, he lied so as not to hurt her anymore, blaming it on an accident when cleaning his rifle bayonet in the army. He described the first time he saw the sea in Valencia. He assured her that, standing before that creature so like a stroke of calligraphy on the horizon and that shattered in waves on the beach, he thought only of her. He proposed they go see it before she went home, but the only sea Olvido wanted at this point in her life was the one in the picture that hung above her bed and the one she had inhaled since childhood in her mother's stories.

Santiago told Olvido about Isidro, about the Atlético matches they went to, shouting between mouthfuls of *tortilla española,* about their walks through the botanical gardens, showering the dahlias with stories. All of a sudden, he was surprised to hear himself talking about Úrsula, describing her torrent of chestnut hair and Persian eyes, how she held the quill that breathed life into her love stories; Úrsula reading her grandmother's poems written on parchment; Úrsula reciting them in Spanish; Úrsula leaning against the window, in the moonlight, listening to him; Úrsula singing lullabies as incomprehensible as they were spellbinding; Úrsula fanning herself with peacock feathers on the divan.

It was nearly three in the morning by the time Santiago walked his grandmother to her room and returned home. He pulled his collection of religious cards out of the secret pocket in his kit bag and held them to his chest. He prayed as tears fell, as a tortured grimace gave way to a smile. He put all the cards away but for one, Saint Pantolomina of the Flowers, which he put in his shirt pocket. He walked over to his bedroom window only to find Úrsula as he had seen her that first time, wearing her turquoise robe, writing.

"Is it too late for visitors?" he asked.

"I didn't think you'd be so long. I'm working." She put a cigarette in the long holder and took a deep puff.

"I never told you where I first saw you, before I moved in here."

"Must have been in a newspaper or literary insert, maybe on the cover of my book. Nothing out of the ordinary." Úrsula took another puff.

"It was somewhere else, but you know, if you don't like my story, you can always chop off my head."

"I hope you're not risking your life for nothing," she said, standing to open the door for him.

When they met in her entryway, all they could do was kiss. Úrsula led him to her bedroom, where the walls were covered with photos of deserts, ancient ruins, and salt flats. On top of a dresser was a black and white portrait of a woman caught wearing a pearl necklace. Naked, Úrsula and Santiago lay down. Santiago whispered that he had seen her first in his dreams and looked for her ever since. Úrsula could not tell if this was the truth or simply a ploy to further inflame the desire that consumed them both.

Once they had regained their composure, Úrsula stood to find a cigarette and saw the Saint Pantolomina of the Flowers card that had fallen from her lover's shirt pocket and lay among his rumpled clothing on the floor.

"Who's this?" she asked, showing it to Santiago.

"The patron saint of my hometown, with her miraculous finger."

Santiago held Úrsula's head on his lap and spoke for the first time of his home, coiled up among frost and hills, his home that smelled of mushrooms in fall as stags cracked heads, of deep, blue snow that sharpened mountain peaks, of springtime bursting into flower and summers beaming with cicada songs. He spoke to her of Scarlet Manor and the only Laguna woman still alive, his grandmother Olvido.

24

SCARLET MANOR WAS immersed in a battle of spirits. The gravel road through the pine forest had been paved and now appeared to be split by a charred scar. The welcome sign had lost the splendor of gold letters that brightened its brothel days and the reign of Manuela Laguna. Through the iron bars, the sight of the wild, parched yard was blinding, a mass of sterile branches and thickets tangled by ruthless winds and yellow heat. The honeysuckle was nothing but a memory; the chestnut tree, in whose shade Padre Imperio had sat, a skeletal frame; the garden, invaded by beetles and flying ants, a vegetable cemetery. Every hydrangea and every exquisite morning glory hummed a desolate hymn. The only things to survive the neglect were the daisies along the drive, pushing up like periscopes through endless spikes of dry leaves, and a sprig of eucalyptus in the middle of the rose garden. The rarified air of what had been and now was gone created a thick, transparent veil of sadness. And in the midst of it all, the stable like a mountain of ash in an act of contrition.

It was inside the house, however, where the biggest battle was being fought. The oak smell had slipped out from Clara Laguna's room and taken over the second floor, descending toward the entryway, hoping to occupy the first floor as well. But it had been overtaken by the soft stench of chicken blood and mentholated roses, branches crawling from the labyrinth to Manuela Laguna's room, climbing up the wall, breaking the window and sneaking into the parlor. The spiritual struggle for dominion over the manor house was horrifying: oaks clashed with chickens and roses in the entryway, a battleground where the rattle of cannon shot made the insides of the living hum like a swarm of bees.

"Everyone in their place!" Olvido Laguna ordered, clapping her hands when she arrived. "I'm in charge here now, and I want to die in peace."

Santiago, who had decided to come for a week to help his resurrected grandmother, felt the war suck the life from his body.

Olvido moved back into her bedroom, where everything was in its place: the silver metal bed, the desk for childhood lessons, the picture of the sea, the easy chair, the bricked-up window. Santiago occupied the room that had been his since he was a boy, the one his father, Pierre Lesac, had used during the time of the great storm.

The first few days were a frenzy of deep cleaning, beating the spirits back with rags, splashes of bleach, and detergent. The oaks retreated to Clara Laguna's room, the chickens and roses to Manuela's next to the kitchen. The window was repaired and the roses pruned, forced back to their labyrinth. But the conflict went on for several more nights when the living rested, roses knocking against windows, whirls of garters flying down stairs while brittle bones tried to climb them, attacking with chicken necks.

"How many times do I have to tell you that everyone has a place in this house and I decide where that is?" Olvido whispered so as not to wake her grandson. "You ruined my life; I will not let you ruin my death!"

Slowly but surely, the struggle was reduced to small odiferous skirmishes, primarily when Olvido was in the garden, which she resurrected much as she did herself.

When the old women in black, fanning fresh air in their chairs, first saw her walk by on Santiago's arm, they recognized the most beautiful woman in the world under that white hair and wrinkles, and retreated into their houses. Some crossed themselves at having witnessed a miracle, others at having seen Beelzebub himself stroll by.

Olvido's trip to the general store, which modernity had turned into a convenience store, caused such a commotion it paralyzed the August sunset, leaving it suspended in a purple puff of fright. Olvido Laguna eggplants and squash were still for sale, and nearby shoppers who knew who she was backed away, as if the vegetables themselves were ghostly, too.

"Don't be afraid," Olvido said with a smile. "Just think of it as an early resurrection."

This comment, repeated and exaggerated for days in the town square, narrow streets, living rooms, and kitchens, was eventually sown in hallowed ground. The new priest — a vain young man, his hair slicked back with gel — was forced to address it at church on Sunday when Olvido came with her grandson.

"Brothers and sisters, those of us here today are and have always been alive; anything else is just a tall tale told by mortals." He coughed, his neck scrawny like a baby bird's.

Santiago squirmed in the last pew, tortured by memories of Padre Rafael, the magic dais, and Saint Pantolomina's finger.

From that Sunday on, tongues wagged about where Olvido had been these last years and why she had faked her death. Olvido refuted not one rumor; on the contrary, she liked to encourage them all. Some said the sight of the fire led to amnesia, causing her to flee into the hills, where she survived by eating roots and live animals by the light of the moon, until her hair turned white and her memory returned one night when she was nearly devoured by wolves. The women in town preferred the story that Olvido had pretended to die in order to leave town, run away, and travel the world with a grandee from Logroño, wealthy but old, with a penchant for the descendants of famous prostitutes.

The lawyer's son, who managed the Laguna fortune for Santiago and had filed the papers for Olvido to be considered dead, called her into his office to legalize her return to life.

"Don't bother," she assured him. "It's not worth it. By the time the papers are ready, they'll only tell another lie. Leave things be. They'll soon sort themselves out."

Just as she had with her return home, Olvido Laguna held nothing back when it came time to revive the garden. She pulled mummified squash and tomatoes out by the roots, annihilated beetles and ants with a pink fog of insecticide that crystallized the insects, then fertilized the earth, pampered it, planted it, and sat each afternoon awaiting the breeze from its growth. Meanwhile, Santiago cleared the rest of the yard. He swept away the autumn floods, dismembered skeletons with a lawn mower, pulled out weeds; and when every trace of desolation had been erased from the yard, fertility flourished in the heat of a living Laguna. The hydrangea and morning glories leafed out, the honeysuckle turned green, the chestnut tree burst with white buds, and the rose garden was a multi-hued resurgence of eternal spring.

It was then time to decide what to do with the mountain of ash that had once been the stable. Santiago had noticed his grandmother cry every time she looked at it. He extended his stay one more week, even though he thought of Úrsula every hour of every day and was anxious to hold her in his arms. Shovelful after shovelful, as the August heat burned his back, he carried the ash in a wheelbarrow, pushing it outside the gate and helping to load it onto a truck that took it away.

In the weeks that passed as they dealt with resurrections and a spiritual truce, exhaustion barely allowed Olvido and Santiago to savor memories of resentment and forbidden love. More than once they tried to renew their evening storytelling before the fire, but by the first swell they were fast asleep, snoring until morning. Nor did they speak of Olvido's illness. However, on the day Santiago was finally to return to Madrid, her symptoms came crashing down, though she tried to hide them.

"I'm staying," Santiago said, dropping his suitcase in the entryway.
"But she's waiting for you," Olvido whispered with an ashen face.
"I'm in charge here now, and I say I'm going to look after you."

Santiago gave Olvido her medicine, dressed her, pressed cold cloths to her forehead when fever spiked and hallucinations brought her back to adolescence, where she walked through the pine grove with Esteban, he looking down at his shoes, then his nails, she chattering about the black horse while staring at his strong, sun-toasted hands. Santiago also cooked when his grandmother was too weak to get out of bed, and it was when he kissed the squash, caressed the red peppers, that his heart fumed with nostalgia. Sometimes he thought he could smell sheep belonging to the traitor Ezequiel Montes or would catch a glimpse of his figure, chiseled by the power of mountains, coming down the daisy-strewn drive. But Santiago knew this was impossible. They said it had been three winters now since the shepherd had taken his flock to Extremadura and was never heard from again. Either he had found a local woman in the meadows or he'd fallen into a ravine.

The one person Santiago missed was his companion in potions and love, the pharmacist's granddaughter. She was at university in the provincial capital, studying her family trade.

Just as he did with Padre Rafael, Santiago used stories and sedatives to distract Olvido from her pain. Whenever she dozed, he would sit on the porch and think of Úrsula, write her poems, read her novels. Once phone service had been reconnected, he would call her late at night. Often there was no answer, and he would imagine her working in the desert dust of parchment scrolls.

One morning, when he had been at Scarlet Manor for nearly six weeks, Santiago woke in tears and knew that would be the day. He carried his grandmother out to the honeysuckle clearing and, lying in the sun, wrote his last poems about the passion of nature while she read Saint John of the Cross. Then he took her into the kitchen — Olvido now a sparrow on the wings of death — where they made rabbit with onions, cinnamon cake, and palmiers, though her stomach refused to admit a single bite. They napped in chairs on the porch, comforted by the yard's fertile murmuring, and when the sun set, Santiago lit the fire and told stories for Olvido to finish. But the end did not come. Santiago held on to the hope that, for the first time, his dreams had been wrong.

"Why are you smiling?" his grandmother asked.

Santiago held her tight, and Olvido watched her life rush backward to that Sunday when he sucked at her empty breast in the pine grove inundated by the deluge.

Olvido went to bed early. Afraid it might happen near midnight, Santiago waited for his grandmother to fall asleep and sat in the easy chair Manuela Laguna once profaned to watch his grandmother breathe. He prayed to Saint Pantolomina of the Flowers, prayed to her iris-filled hair with the faith of the truly desperate. It was after twelve when he went back to his room, where he kept praying until overcome by exhaustion.

The next morning Olvido was miraculously better. She got out of bed with no pain, no fever, the color of the hills in her cheeks.

"You can go back to her now," she told her grandson as she prepared breakfast.

But Santiago waited another week in case she suffered a relapse. Despite his premonition, Olvido had been granted respite among the living, for her eyes had yet to witness one last wonder.

25

OCTOBER HAD BLANCHED the color from Úrsula Perla Montoya's face. Madrid was its usual frenzy of activity and *cafés con leche*. The day dawned to a blue sky dotted with chubby clouds. Santiago still smelled of the train when he reached the city, when he reached Úrsula's apartment and she opened the door, nausea in her cheeks, bathed in perspiration unusual for early fall. The moment Santiago saw her, transparent in a white nightgown, he realized he would have loved her even if she had never appeared in his dreams, even if she had not emerged from his wrist in a puff of smoke. He would have fallen in love with her anyway, the first time he saw her writing with a quill, fanning herself half-naked; smiling as she lunched on a sandwich, delighting in his stories, her face bathed in moonlight, reciting her grandmother's poems. And even if he could not have her, he thought as he held her by the waist, he would still love her in a state of platonic ecstasy for which there was no cure, not even in death.

"I missed you so much . . ." he said.

Úrsula pulled back and slapped his face. In accordance with his Christian upbringing, Santiago offered the other cheek as his skin burned red. Úrsula had ink spots on her lips, her neck, her hands, as if she had rolled in the quagmire of violet loss. Her fingers still hurt from her feverish scrawling that night and many other nights, when the tip of her pen hurtled forward out of a desire for his return. She had written like a wild woman, feeding on the inspiration he sowed in her belly, living for and because of it, scorched by the ice of remembering but not having him there, of waiting but not hearing him arrive. She had written hundreds of reckless pages, the best of her literary career as a romance novelist, and ripped them up at the first glimmer of dawn, lost in the madness of wanting to write them all over the next day, to feel him even more — if that were even possible. She had ripped them up in the fury of passion but also a fear of losing him, a fear of finishing the novel her editor was demanding, a fear that the void of being without it would drain her of him, banish her forever to the divan of forgotten novels and forgotten men, to continue a cycle of affairs that come and go, inspire and die. And yet, part of Úrsula wanted to go back to the peace of a routine that, until then, had provided her with precisely the right impetus. Too late, she thought, looking into Santiago's eyes, damning his beauty, his absurd youth, his infuriating voraciousness in love, the memory of which would not let her sleep. She damned the torment that was pleasure, the pleasure that was fear, the fear that sparked hate. Santiago kissed her on the mouth, pulling him to her, fierce, tearing sleep away with his hands, tearing her nightie, her conscience, as the Laguna child that swam inside her recognized the taste of its father.

Úrsula continued to write throughout her pregnancy, weaving a shroud of Penelope from words that unraveled in the morning as she watched Santiago sleep in her bed. She continued to write and rewrite when he began to draw woodland creatures on her growing belly, when he covered it in kisses, as happy as in his messianic years; she continued to write and rewrite after autumn days spent reading to him from her grandmother's dusty scrolls; she continued to write and rewrite after winter walks in luminous cold that hurried them home to their amorous romps; she continued to write and rewrite the snowy day when Santiago held her from behind and whispered "Marry me," as she laughingly reminded him of the story in her last novel.

"A love that's not free is miserable. Look what happened to the divan lovers: every move was calculated so no part of her body could leave its bounds, and that slavery was the end of them."

Úrsula continued to write and rewrite when Santiago countered with how the story ended.

"But remember, when they could not vanquish the genie's spell, the desert man wished only to suffer the same fate as his lover. Remember, that one evening the sorceress slave brought the genie to the bedchamber. When he found the maiden on the divan, in all her glorious nudity, he was so furious he cast another spell at the precise moment the desert man appeared, and he, too, became a diamond. And so they suffered their eternal condemnation together."

Úrsula continued to write and tear up her work while assuring her editor the novel would be ready in a few more months, as she worked away, promising not to rip up any more pages on afternoons when Santiago was at an Atlético match with Isidro or evenings when he was performing in a café.

But none of it was any use. At nearly eight months pregnant, Úrsula Perla Montoya continued to write and rip, even the spring afternoon when she fell asleep on the scrolls and dreamed of a gate with a funeral bow welcoming guests, a manor house painted scarlet red surrounded by an enormous yard and a woman who looked like Santiago waiting for her in a clay-tiled entryway. Úrsula watched a profusion of daisies, roses, and honeysuckle take root in her belly and woke with the taste of acorns in her mouth. She was so unsettled by this dream—which repeated whenever she napped, on nights interrupted by countless trips to relieve herself—that one radiant morning she said to Santiago, enveloped in the delirium of Persian eyes: "Take me to Scarlet Manor."

Úrsula continued to write and rip up pages when, moved by the wisdom of blessed Saint Pantolomina, Santiago granted her wish in order to placate fate. One late-March afternoon, with the baby turning somersaults the closer they came, Úrsula looked out the taxi window at the fountain with its three spouts, the church with its medieval tombs where her lover had lived, the pine grove split by an asphalt scar, and her dreams paved the way to reality: the gate, the bow, the house, the woman in the hall who swept Santiago into an embrace and kissed her affectionately on the forehead.

"Úrsula Perla Montoya, what a lovely name. Welcome to Scarlet Manor."

"Thank you. Would you mind if I rest for a while? It was an exhausting trip."

"Let me show you to the biggest bed in the house. It's where you belong now," Olvido said, taking her by the arm.

Ever since Santiago phoned to say they were coming, Olvido knew Úrsula had come to give birth to another Laguna child. And so it was. The moment Úrsula stepped into Clara Laguna's room, she recognized the aroma as the one in her mouth day in and day out. Olvido pulled back the heavy quilt and helped her climb into bed as Santiago watched from the door. It was then Úrsula's belly constricted, hurtling toward the agony of contractions. The child refused to wait. Ashen, Úrsula moaned and writhed on that mattress of revenge. She spread her legs and a torrent of water rushed out. Santiago, who had gone to her when the pain first started, asked Olvido: "What's happening?"

"Call the doctor. She's in labor. This is going to be one active, intelligent child! The baby knew precisely where to be born, and the minute it arrived, it gave in to the desire to greet this world. There wasn't even time to eat the lamb with raspberry sauce I made."

The blond doctor, who still lived in town, who still harbored secrets in his medical bag, secrets of a lemon and baking soda cure for jealousy, needle and thread for attempted suicide, arrived two hours later. Possessed by the power of desert storms, Úrsula Perla Montoya pushed with all her might, while Santiago held her hand and mopped her brow. With every push that brought the birth closer, Olvido grew weaker. She helped the doctor, passing his instruments, bringing warm water and clean cloths. But when the child's head appeared, Olvido's hands began to shake, fever returned to her cheeks, and pain crushed her bones once again. She excused herself as best she could, walked into the hallway and breathed deeply until she heard Santiago say: "Abuela! Abuela! The baby's here!"

The magic of a baby girl was born in the last light of sunset. Her eyes were open, as lucid and clairvoyant as her father's dreams, an amber color like wheat and autumn beech trees that filled the room with the rustle of Moorish pants. The doctor picked her up by the ankles and smacked her on the bum, but she was entirely unperturbed. The girl was distracted, inhaling a whiff of chicken blood that crept in through the door, and smiled when she heard a lament in the language of the spirits that another bastard Laguna girl had been born.

"Is the baby all right?" Santiago asked.

"Couldn't be better. She simply doesn't want to cry," the doctor replied in surprise.

He wrapped the baby in a towel and set her on her mother's chest. Still flushed from the effort, Úrsula looked at her with curiosity and realized those dreams were never hers but her daughter's, that the girl was finally where she wanted to be. Úrsula could write without sacrificing another page, could write a novel that just might be as eternal as springtime at Scarlet Manor.

Santiago leaned in and kissed each of them softly on the lips.

"A beautiful Laguna girl," he said, staring into his grandmother's eyes, "but she won't suffer like us."

Olvido, who had filled the blue arabesque basin with water, took her great-granddaughter from Úrsula's arms and bathed her as the pain of doubt shot through her heart. This was all she had the energy to do. It was Santiago's time now. She handed him the baby and took refuge in her room.

Olvido did not see the doctor out when he left after night fell. She lay on her bed to wait and fell asleep. At three o'clock that morning she was woken by a glorious melody as the church bells rang madly. She got up and went to the window; night air slipped in through the hole left to ventilate misfortune. As the melody grew more intense, Olvido smashed the chair against the bricked-up window. She hammered and hammered with one chair leg, splintering her nails, shredding the skin on her fingers. A blast from the pine forest tousled her hair, and the bells' voices grew into the crashing cymbals of love. Olvido went to Clara Laguna's room in her nightdress, where Santiago, Úrsula, and the baby slept.

"Goodbye, Clara. Take good care of them. The baby inherited your eyes, but God willing, she did not inherit our curse."

Laughter shook the canopy.

Olvido walked down the hall and descended the stairs. Starlight slipped in under the door.

"Goodbye, Madre," she said in the clay-tiled entryway. "We can settle our score now." She sensed a puff of lavender escape the linen cupboard but paid no attention.

Olvido Laguna walked up the daisy-strewn drive, a bunch of virginal irises now among the hydrangea and morning glories, left the funeral bow behind, and set off down the road, following the joyous bells. The pine forest said goodbye as she went: owls hooted, beech and pine branches whistled, lichen crunched. She was soon in town. Barefoot, her feet had exchanged infirmity for the agility of a teenager. Besieged by fountain spouts in the town square, people hammered on the church door, angry about the rejoicing bells that startled them from sleep. Olvido walked by with her halo of resurrection. Not everyone recognized her — her hair had turned black, her face young, her figure tall and slim — but those who did would forget the sight only when buried in their graves.

Olvido climbed the hill to the cemetery. The gate was open a crack when she arrived. She pushed it with a trembling hand, and as emotional as a bride walking down the aisle, knowing all has been forgiven, she headed for the old part of the cemetery. Stars put orange blossoms in her hands as rows of cypress trees watched in shadow tuxedos and magpies with shiny plumage occupied places of honor on vaults and tombs. It was then she saw Esteban waiting for her at the foot of his grave, as smooth-skinned as the young man he never ceased to be, his hair short, his stormy eyes lit up. She said his name, and before she could say "I do" and kiss him, the smell of wood shavings and sawdust overwhelmed her with bliss.

The undertaker found her dead on her lover's grave the next morning, the body of a middle-aged woman with a smile on her lips not even the sobriety of the shroud could hide.

Acknowledgments

My thanks to Clara Obligado for all she taught me and her support as I wrote this novel. And to my editor, Alberto Marcos, for his help and encouragement the whole way through.

Thanks also to Belén Cerrada and Miguel Ángel Rincón, who took me hunting, saved me from computer chaos, and always cheered me on. Finally, to my fellow workshop writers for all the evenings of stories we shared.